COLD TRUTH

Lou Mason hung on the ladder bolted to the elevator shaft, expecting a quick rescue. The crash had been deafening and had to bring police and firefighters to the scene in minutes. When no one came, when no elevator doors were opened and no high beams shined on him, he began to understand the trouble he was in.

No one knew where he was or had reason to look for him. He was a one-armed man hanging on a ladder in a blacked-out elevator shaft, bruised and bloodied.

Mason had been on the Gina Davenport case for forty-eight hours. A little soon for people to start hating him enough to want to kill him. He replayed the Channel 6 News videotape of Gina's plunge from her eighth-story window in his mind, seeing her jackknife through the glass, pancaking onto the pavement.

The camera had caught a shadow flickering in the window frame, like someone standing close enough to look out the window without being seen. The killer? Mason wondered, craning his head upward, looking for another shadow in the darkness.

Also by Joel Goldman

MOTION TO KILL

THE LAST WITNESS

COLD TRUTH

JOEL GOLDMAN

PINNACLE BOOKS
Kensington Publishing Corp.
http://www.kensingtonbooks.com

PINNACLE BOOKS are published by

Kensington Publishing Corp.
850 Third Avenue
New York, NY 10022

All Kensington Titles, Imprints, and Distributed Lines are available at special quantity discounts for bulk purchases for sales promotions, premiums, fund-raising, and educational or institutional use. Special book excerpts or customized printings can also be created to fit specific needs. For details, write or phone the office of the Kensington special sales manager: Kensington Publishing Corp., 850 Third Avenue, New York, NY 10022, attn: Special Sales Department, Phone: 1-800-221-2647.

Pinnacle and the P logo Reg. U.S. Pat. & TM Off.

First Pinnacle Books Printing: February 2004

10 9 8 7 6 5 4 3 2 1

Printed in the United States of America

To my parents, Marsha and Jules Goldman,
who made all things possible.

CHAPTER 1

Locked into his camera and headgear, Ted Phillips, the Channel 6 cameraman, didn't hear the window shatter eight stories above or the woman scream as she jackknifed through the glass. Earl Luke Fisher and Sherri Thomas saw it happen.

Earl Luke, a homeless panhandler still prospecting for donations on a hot night in Kansas City's deserted downtown, was sitting cross-legged in front of the Cable Depot answering questions for Sherri Thomas, the Channel 6 reporter, filling her slot on the ten o'clock broadcast of a slow-news Labor Day. Sherri dumped Earl Luke for the falling woman, motioning Phillips, who swung his camera in a quick skyward arc, not stopping until he caught the woman in his lens, pinwheeling in a fatal tumble and pancaking onto the pavement, one side of her head flattened like a splintered melon.

"Hold the shot," Phillips said to himself, keeping the camera on the woman's body. "Take it back," he whispered to no one, satisfied that he'd preserved the moment of her death.

Phillips aimed his camera at the broken window, lighting the way with its built-in lamp, zooming in until he had a tight shot of the ragged outline left by the remaining glass. His eye caught a shadow flickering in the window frame, or so he thought. He blinked, uncertain of what he'd seen, but confident that the camera had a steadier eye than he did.

"Son of a bitch! Tell me you got that, Ted! Son-of-a-fucking bitch! If you got that, we're golden!"

Phillips put his camera down, wiping away flecks of blood that had hung in the air like ruby raindrops before chasing the dead woman to the ground. Earl Luke was gone.

"And live on the air," he reminded her.

Lou Mason rewound the tape of the dead woman's plunge, replaying it for the tenth time, forcing himself to focus on the TV screen sitting next to the dry-erase board in his law office. The tape ended with Sherri Thomas covering her mouth, realizing that her ecstatic outburst had been broadcast throughout Channel 6's two-state viewing area. He punched rewind on the remote control.

The tape whirred inside its metal cage as Mason pulled a bottle of water from the small refrigerator beneath the bay window that looked out on the street from his second-story digs above Blues on Broadway, a jazz joint in midtown Kansas City. The street hummed with people heading home, back in the groove after the long Labor Day weekend. Most people hadn't worked yesterday, but Sherri Thomas and her cameraman had put in a full day. Earl Luke Fisher never worked or never stopped, depending on your view of panhandling. Gina Davenport was in her office at ten P.M., catching up on something. Her killer worked overtime. It had been some holiday, Mason thought to himself.

He'd seen the broadcast live the night before, coming out of his kitchen chair like he'd been launched, almost tripping over his sleeping dog, Tuffy. He was too young to have seen Jack Ruby kill Lee Harvey Oswald, the first live broadcast of a murder in television history. The immediacy of real-time coverage of wars, natural disasters, and terrorist attacks might have turned death into the ultimate reality show, but that didn't match the intimacy of a single murder captured by homicidal serendipity. And Mason had no doubt the woman had been murdered. Suicides jumped out of open windows. Killers broke the glass.

The front-page story the next morning in the *Kansas City Star* made up in detail what it lacked in televised drama. The victim was Gina Davenport, a shrink known by her first name, Dr. Gina, with a nationally syndicated radio gig on radio station KWIN. Her office and the radio station were both on the eighth floor of the Cable Depot. The broken window was hers. Rachel Firestone wrote the story, so Mason knew she got it right. Davenport's show was the highest-rated in town and one of the biggest in national syndication.

Arthur Hackett, who owned the building and the station, waited until Tuesday afternoon to call Mason, inviting him to his office at the Cable Depot, a renovated building put up in the early 1900s to house cable cars. It was on 6th Street, where the grade from the Missouri

River up to 6th was so steep that people used to fall off the cars. Today, the building was practically at the edge of the bluff hanging over the interstate on the west side of downtown.

When the cable cars went out of business, the building was boarded up. When he was a kid, Mason and his friends dared each other to pry the plywood off one of its first-floor windows and crawl around its dark insides. Then, twenty years ago, Hackett bought the building, got it placed on the National Register of Historic Landmarks, and parlayed the tax breaks into a hot downtown address.

Mason had been to KWIN's offices a number of times to talk with Max Coyle, the afternoon sports talk host and a client. Mason had recently settled Max's case against a lawyer who played investment advisor, churning Max's five-hundred-thousand-dollar nest egg into a goose egg. He'd caught glimpses of Hackett on those visits, but never met him.

"It's about our daughter, Jordan," Hackett began, gesturing to an empty chair next to the one occupied by his wife Carol.

She gave Mason a thin smile, though he suspected that her last plastic surgeon had tacked it into place. Carol's hair was a harvest color sprayed tight, her spare body a tribute to watercress and yoga. She massaged her cuticles while Arthur, his mid-life bulk spreading beneath his chin and between his arms, stood in front of a double-wide window, the Missouri and Kansas Rivers shaking hands two miles away and hundreds of feet below.

Jordan was a patient of Dr. Gina's until somebody killed the doctor. A twenty-one-year-old head case, her father said. The cops interviewed Jordan, took her fingerprints, hair samples, and fiber samples from her clothes, her parents waiting to call Mason until the cops were through. The Hacketts told Mason they didn't want to treat her like a criminal, asking him to represent her if she was charged with Dr. Gina's murder.

Mason assured them that the cops were probably talking to all of Dr. Gina's patients, gathering evidence to eliminate suspects as much as to incriminate them. The Hacketts nodded their agreement, gaining greater confidence when Mason told them he knew the detective handling the case, Samantha Greer. He left out the fact that he and Samantha had been dancing between the sheets up until a few months ago, when she told him that she wasn't a car battery he could jump-start whenever he felt too lonely for another night alone.

"Where's Jordan now?" Mason asked her parents.

Arthur hesitated, clearing his throat, looking at his wife, who rose like her limbs were hydraulic and left the room. "She lives at a place called Sanctuary. It's a residential facility for teenagers and young adults with emotional problems."

"Centurion Johnson's program," Mason said.

Centurion had given up a promising career as a drug and thug entrepreneur for the not-for-profit world of social services. Harry Ryman had busted Centurion a few times, sending him to jail for a long stretch the last time. Soon as he got out, he was back in the game until Blues helped him find religion. Next stop, saving the young.

Harry was a cop until he retired less than a year ago. He and Mason's Aunt Claire had been a couple since Mason was a kid breaking into the Cable Depot, Claire raising him after the death of his parents when he was three years old. Blues was Wilson Bluestone, Jr., another ex-cop, occasional PI, and the only Shawnee Indian jazz pianist Mason had ever met. Blues was also Mason's full-time landlord and part-time bodyguard. Mason was certain that Centurion didn't list Harry or Blues as references.

Mason asked, "What's wrong with your daughter?"

Hackett shook his head, turning to face the rivers that joined at the flood plain below—Kansas City, Kansas, to the west; Kansas City, Missouri, to the east.

"Dr. Gina said Jordan had problems with anger management. Shrink-speak bullshit, if you ask me. Whatever you're supposed to call it, Jordan was too violent to live at home." Hackett asked, "Will you help us?" His back was still to Mason.

"Sure," Mason replied. "I'd like a copy of the videotape."

Hackett wrote him a check for a retainer, called the general manager at Channel 6 to arrange for Mason to pick up the tape that day, and gave Mason a copy of Dr. Gina's book, *The Way You Do the Things You Do. New York Times* best-seller, the cover proclaimed.

Mason pressed the play button on his VCR again, fast-forwarding the videotape to the moment when the cameraman retraced Dr. Gina's flight back to the window. He used the freeze-frame function to break down the segment frame by frame so he could study each image. The cameraman had told him he thought he'd seen a shadow, like someone standing close enough to look out the window without being seen. The killer? Mason wondered. Or a witness?

More than a year earlier, Mason had taken an un-

planned New Year's Eve plunge into the Missouri River
while defending Blues on a murder charge. Ever since,
when Mason took a murder case, he felt like he was diving into that dark water again, worrying that he was taking the dive just to see if he could make it back to the
surface, gulping for air, beating the odds, wishing he
had a reason to play it safe.

Mason took a deep breath and opened the dry-erase
board on the wall, beginning, as he always began, by
writing down what he knew and what he had to learn to
keep Jordan Hackett off of death row. He wrote Gina
Davenport's name, circled it, and labeled her "victim."

Moving from left to right, Mason drew a line and
wrote Jordan Hackett's name, giving her a casting list of
roles: "patient, witness, killer." In the upper right-hand
corner, he drew a circle around Centurion Johnson's
name and labeled it "trouble," then added a capital T.

Returning to Gina Davenport, he drew a vertical line
straight down, capping it with a horizontal bar, labeling
it "winners and losers," wondering who he would find
when he dove into the dark water.

CHAPTER 2

Murder makes for a lousy party, Mason thought to himself as he parked his TR-6 in front of Café Allegro, an upscale restaurant where swank was an appetizer.

Claire Mason, who never threw parties, was throwing one for Harry Ryman's sixtieth birthday. That she had chosen Café Allegro was an even greater surprise to Mason. His aunt was a lawyer who shunned the haunts of Kansas City's upper crust as if they might possess her with the life-sucking grip of the Pod People. Unless, of course, she was there to serve a summons on behalf of a beaten-down client she had decided shouldn't take it anymore. Nearly six feet tall, big-boned and broad-shouldered, she rattled the well-possessed into submission.

Claire had inspired Mason to become a lawyer with her own brash pursuit of justice. Her practice had been a straight line, often uphill, but always clear-eyed. She used the law as a battering ram to knock down the walls surrounding the powerful, giving meaning to the rights and privileges promised to her clients. Mason's own path had meandered through small and big firms until he'd landed on his own, using the law as a shield for his clients who were accused of crimes.

Mason tried without success to tuck the image of Gina Davenport's pavement performance into the file marked *Not Tonight.* The ambiguous shadow in the window kept yanking Dr. Gina's body back to the here and now. Tomorrow, he told the shadow. After meeting Jordan Hackett for the first time, after he sees whether she fits the shadow's description. Tonight's a party.

I'll tag along, the shadow said, settling comfortably on Mason's shoulder. Mason gave a crisp tug to the lapels of his linen blazer in a final futile effort to shake the shadow. Well, he conceded, at least he had a date.

Café Allegro had a golden, glittering ambience that said prepare to be pampered, but don't look at the prices. Mason surveyed the room, noting one table of dark-suited men with fierce posture, before finding his own party gathered at a table for ten on the opposite side of the room. He did a quick head count.

Claire and Harry sat next to one another, arms interlocked with wineglasses touching, lost for the moment in a private celebration of their long relationship. Harry was a barrel-built bulldog, with a squat neck, butcher's hands, and bristle-cut hair. Neither he nor Claire was handsome alone, but together they shined.

Harry had retired from the Kansas City police department after twenty-nine years, the last twenty as a homicide detective. He could have put in his thirty, but that would have meant spending his last year listening to the whispers that forgot a dirty cop but didn't forgive Harry for bringing him down.

Claire dabbed a napkin at the corner of Harry's eye, her own expression shifting from wistfully romantic to tight-mouthed concern. Harry took her hand, easing it to the table.

Rachel Firestone, her red hair flashing like a beacon, and her partner, Candace, were laughing at something Mickey Shanahan said while Mickey waved his hands in protest that it was all true. Mickey was a twenty-something PR wannabe who rented the office down the hall from Mason's, paying his rent by bartending for Blues until Mason hired him as his legal assistant. Tina Esposito, Mickey's girlfriend, gave him a playful shove, convicting him of his latest scam. Mason had told Mickey about Jordan Hackett, Mickey's eyes lighting up with the PR angles.

Blues leaned back in his chair, his muscled frame wrapped in black, catching Mason's eye with a quick nod and wry smile. "It's your world, man," Blues's look said. "I'm just living in it."

Blues's date, a long-legged model whose name Mason couldn't remember but whose body he couldn't forget, sat next to another woman Mason didn't recognize. She was shorter than the model, with chin-length auburn hair, lively eyes, and a smile that danced with the rhythm of the table. The last empty seat, between the woman and Claire, was for Mason. "Shadow," Mason said, "take a hike."

Claire rose in greeting as the others hailed Mason with mock applause at his late arrival. She grabbed him by the shoulders, propelling him toward his empty seat. Mason used the momentum to circle the table first, greeting his friends with a succession of handshakes and kisses, finishing with a hand outstretched to the one person at the table he'd yet to meet.

"My nephew," Claire announced. "Abby Lieberman," she added as if no further introduction was required.

"Hey," he said, taking Abby's hand, covering it with both of his as he sat down.

"Hey, you," Abby said, waiting for Lou to release her hand. Mason held on, studying her fine features, offering his smile in trade for her hand until Abby's grin widened. "Okay. I'll lend it to you until the salad is served," she said of her hand. "But that's my best offer unless you plan on feeding me."

Mason was unprepared for Abby's effect on him. Maybe it was the warmth in her hand after the withering chill of watching Dr. Gina die over and over on videotape. Maybe it was the hint of promise in the sassy way she played along, flirting without being coy, interested without taking him seriously. Whatever it was, Rachel ruptured the moment.

"Let her go or get a room, Lou," she said.

Mason loved the crinkles in Abby's cheeks as he let go of her hand and she joined in the laughter. Her laugh was full-bodied, unembarrassed. She was a woman, Mason decided, who enjoyed herself.

Forcing himself to turn away, he said, "Happy birthday, Harry. I could use the party."

"Tough day?" Harry asked. "You should try turning sixty."

"New case. Murder. An ugly one," Mason answered.

In most crowds, Mason knew his announcement would have brought gasps. In this group, it brought understanding. Harry and Blues, both ex-homicide cops, had their Ph.D.s in killers from the University of the Street. Claire had seen the fallout in the lives of too many of her clients for whom violence arrived more easily than the rising sun. Rachel Firestone reported it all for the *Kansas City Star.*

"Can you talk about it?" Blues asked.

Before Mason could shake his head and explain that it was too soon, Mickey blurted out the answer.

"Talk about it? Are you kidding? It's the Gina Davenport murder. We're representing a patient who . . ."

"Mickey!" Mason said, cutting him off.

"Sorry, Boss," Mickey said, subdued by Mason's blast. "I just figured we're family, that's all." Tina rubbed Mickey's back, soothing him.

Mason sighed, regretting Mickey's hurt feelings, especially since Mickey was right. They were family, at least all of Mason's family. And Mickey's too. He knew they would help him if the shadow in the window turned deadly. Claire would remind him of the glorious burden of representing the accused. Harry would pull strings to find out what the prosecutor wouldn't tell Mason. Blues would knock the heads of those in need of head-knocking. Rachel would keep everything off the record unless he told her otherwise. That's what families did, Mason told himself. So Mason would tell them—just not tonight. Not before he had a better sense of what he had gotten into.

"I've been hired by the parents, but they aren't really my clients. They're just paying the bills. I'm meeting the client tomorrow. Unless the cops make an arrest, it stays quiet."

"Sure thing," Mickey said.

Mason looked around the table. He couldn't have ruined the party more thoroughly if he'd mooned the waiter. It wasn't the subject of murder or his rebuke of Mickey that doused everyone's mood. It was Abby. The light drained from her eyes and she couldn't meet his, glancing away, bent slightly as if she'd taken a punch.

She gathered herself and fished through her purse for a pager Mason was certain had not gone off. "Claire," Abby said, "it was lovely of you to include me, but my answering service has paged me. Client emergency. I'm sorry. Happy birthday, Harry," she said.

Mason watched her until she disappeared.

"Never give the hand back, Lou," Rachel said. "You've got to keep something to hold onto."

"Sage advice," Blues said.

"Okay, people," Mason said. "I know you aren't the support group for the perpetually single and relationship impaired, but what the hell just happened?"

"I invited her to dinner to fill out the table. Besides, you need to meet someone new," Claire explained.

"I'm not talking about that," Mason said. "You've fixed me up with every Matzo Ball Queen since Moses parted the Red Sea, but I still don't know what happened. I'm off to the fastest start since Secretariat won the Triple Crown until Mickey mentions Gina Davenport's murder. Next thing I know, I'm sitting between my aunt and an empty chair."

Claire said, "If she wants you to know, she'll tell you."

Tuffy was sleeping on her pillow in the otherwise empty living room when he got home. The German shepherd-collie-mixed-breed anti-watch dog opened one eye, yawned, and rolled over.

Mason walked around the sparsely furnished first floor of the house Claire had given him and his ex-wife, Kate, as a wedding present. Empty rooms and a sleeping dog were all that remained of that relationship. His great-grandparents stared down at him from their framed photographs on the dining room wall, a room they shared with his rowing machine.

"Yes, Abby is a nice Jewish girl," Mason said to his un-smiling ancestors. "And, yes, I blew it again," he added with an indulgent note of self-pity. "Okay," he told them. "Maybe I didn't blow it. I'll call her and tell her that de-fending people accused of murder doesn't have to ruin a party."

Yet Mason didn't believe that Abby's reaction had been to his job. She had to be connected to the case in some way that made Dr. Gina's death and Mason's in-volvement too personal for her. His first guess was that Abby was also Dr. Gina's patient, perhaps even making her a suspect. Neither possibility fit with her incendiary impact on Mason, though either would explain Claire's insistence on keeping him in the dark. Maybe, he thought, Abby and Dr. Gina were close friends and she couldn't hold hands with someone who was defending her friend's accused killer. The only thing Mason was certain of was his need to find the quickest way over the top of the wall that had risen between him and Abby Lieberman.

Mason's phone rang, spawning the instant fantasy that the caller was Abby. He picked up the phone in the kitchen.

"Hello," he said, kicking off his shoes.

"It's Sherri Thomas, Channel 6 News."

Mason sat down and rubbed his tired feet. "What can I do for you, Sherri?"

"Sorry to bother you at home. I hope I'm not calling too late."

The clock on the stove read 9:45 P.M. Mason knew that Sherri wasn't sorry about the bother or the time. The ten o'clock news was coming up and she was on deadline, trying to resurrect her reputation as a serious journalist. Her unprofessional broadcast of Dr. Gina's death would have cost her job except for the spike in her station's ratings. She apologized on the air and promised to follow the murder of Gina Davenport wherever it led, underscoring her commitment to hard-hitting reporting from the streets of Kansas City.

Mason had watched Sherri's apology, certain that her only regret was being caught reveling in tragedy. He had no interest in giving her career a boost.

"Not a problem," Mason said. "I'm staying up to watch the news. The Daily Show doesn't start until ten."

"They told me you were a smart-ass," Sherri said.

"Really. Who are they? Or are your smart-ass sources confidential?"

"I'm running a story at ten that the police are investigating possible ties between the Hackett family and the murder of Dr. Gina Davenport. Care to comment?"

"Why would I have any comment?" Mason asked.

"Because my sources—and they are confidential, whether they're assholes or otherwise—say that you are representing the family."

Mason didn't give her credit for intrepid reporting. Arthur Hackett had called the general manager at Channel 6 to request a copy of the videotape for Mason. Mason had talked to Ted Phillips, the cameraman, when he picked up the tape. He was a well-known criminal defense attorney who snagged his share of high-profile murder cases. It wasn't tough to put together.

"If that's true, you know I don't have any comment.

If it weren't true, I'd just be making something up. So what do you really want?"

"I'm going to stay on this story like white on rice, Lou. Help me out and you'll get more good coverage than you know what to do with. Besides, you can't give all your stories to Rachel Firestone. There's no payoff with her."

Mason wasn't interested in the spotlight, though his clients too often dragged him into its glare. Rachel had covered Mason's involvement in the collapse of Sullivan & Christenson, his one-time law firm, and in the Dream Casino case. They became close friends, turning their relationship into fodder for local media gossip, especially since Rachel was gay. If their relationship compromised her reporting, she left the reporting to someone else. Mason didn't know how that would work out in the Davenport case, but he doubted that Rachel would bring Sherri Thomas in off the bench. Sherri's crass pitch for his business was a step removed from a street solicitation—a small step.

"Like white on rice?" Mason asked. "Who writes your material? Never mind. I don't discuss my clients or people who aren't my clients. Keep your payoff for somebody who needs it. I don't."

Sherri laughed. "You've got to try harder than that to shame me, Lou. I make the news. You can either be the lead or the punch line, but you can't ignore me."

"Sure I can," Mason told her. "That's what the remote control is for. See you in the funny pages."

CHAPTER 3

Sanctuary was secreted off the interstate, off the back roads, in an unincorporated patch of Jackson County in the general direction of St. Louis. The locals called their piece of the action Eastern Jack. Downtown Kansas City was also in Jackson County, but Eastern Jack was a different world. Defined more by the blue collars of Independence and Raytown than the white collars of downtown, Eastern Jack made no pretense of its lack of pretension.

The unincorporated areas outside these smaller cities harbored woods, meadows, and streams that shut out concrete and high-rises, giving nature its own reservation in the civilized world. The natural defenses against the urban onslaught underscored the safety of Sanctuary, touting isolation as security.

"East of the sun and west of the moon, two stars to the right and on till morning." Mason recited the poem from memory unable to name the poet or finish the verse, as he navigated his TR-6 along the convoluted route he'd downloaded from Sanctuary's web site. It was a top-down morning, the sun soothing, not yet hot. Morning fog painted deer tracks with vapor trails. Moist earth, wild grasses, and unseen animals perfumed the air with a musk scent.

Mason had spent his whole life in the city. He wasn't a Boy Scout and couldn't find moss on the north side of a tree. The drive reminded him of Kelly Holt's log cabin sanctuary in the Ozark woods. She was the last woman who'd made him feel the way Abby had. Kelly's sanctuary had proved anything but, and his relationship with her had died in its ashes. Mason hoped the past was not prologue.

He was surprised that it took less than forty-five minutes to reach Sanctuary from the urban comforts of his office. It was set on the ridge of a broad gentle rise, and Mason immediately understood why Centurion Johnson had chosen the location. The road he'd been on emerged from the woods into a freshly cut meadow of several acres that surrounded a large white three-story plantation-style house, complete with a widow's walk around the roof. The natural elevation gave the house an imposing setting, making it appear larger than it was while giving its occupants a commanding view of the countryside. Mason guessed that Centurion could see the downtown skyline twenty miles to the west from the widow's walk.

He parked his car in the wide circle drive, walking onto the veranda that wrapped around three sides of the house. A continuous message engraved on the railing in platinum paint read *The New Century Investment Fund Veranda*. A freshly painted red barn was emblazoned with the logo of the Commercial Bank Group. Next to it was a machine shed, according to the boldly painted billboard on one wall naming it the *USA Telecom Machine Shed*. The Mid-America Business Network had paid to have its name embossed on the tractor that was parked next to the shed.

The kaleidoscope of advertising reminded Mason of Centurion Johnson's successful fund-raising campaign for Sanctuary. Pronouncing himself a survivor of the streets, not a victim, Centurion sold Sanctuary with the fervor of a Sunday morning television evangelist. The land was donated, the buildings erected and furnished, and the doors opened to the miscast and maladjusted. Sanctuary provided refuge for young people fleeing abuse, both parental and substance, and a haven for the emotionally brittle. The permanent ads for the contributing sponsors were a constant reminder of the harsh reality of the real world. Follow the money.

Centurion told his sponsors that Sanctuary was no kick-back-meditate-blame-the-old-folks hideout for troubled kids. Not on his watch, he told them. It was a working farmstead. These kids work, clear the land, plant the crops, care for the livestock. Sure, he promised, they would get professional counseling. But they'd also get blisters and backaches from a hard day's work. Nothing like sweat and strain to clear your brain, he told one cheering audience of businessmen who responded by throwing money at him like it was confetti.

Sanctuary was the model for successful partnerships between the business and social service communities, a not-for-profit that made a return on its sponsors' investment by giving them a visible stake in its success. When Mason saw a Mercedes 500 SL parked in the open garage with a vanity plate that read *Centurion,* he recognized another harsh reality. If crime doesn't pay, good works surely do.

"You must be Lou Mason," a voice said from behind him.

"That I am," Mason said, turning around to a man dressed in denim and tie-dye, his graying hair pulled back in a short ponytail held in place by a leather strap. His round face was sun-lined, open, and friendly. His body was soft, and shaking his hand felt like squeezing a small feather pillow.

"I'm Terry Nix. We spoke yesterday."

Sanctuary did not allow visitors without an appointment cleared in advance by the Executive Director. That was Nix. The policy prevented disruption of the work and therapy schedule, according to the web site. Mason had jumped through the hoops to meet Jordan Hackett, but he didn't like someone else controlling access to his client.

"Mr. Nix," Mason said, "I never know when I'm going to need to see Jordan. I assume you'll waive your appointment policy under these circumstances."

"Call me Terry," Nix said, giving Mason a pat on the back. "We're in the problem-solving business here. I think we can handle that one. Let's go inside."

Nix ushered Mason through the Phillips Pharmaceutical front hall, where a young woman, heavily pregnant, asked Mason to sign in and clip a guest badge to his shirt. They continued past the Kilbridge Foundation family room, down the S&J Railroad stairs, to the Hammond Industries Executive Director's Office. A secretary, also young and pregnant, sat at a desk outside the office, struggling with a word processing manual.

Nix's name was on the door too, though on an easily replaced magnetic strip. Nix sat on the edge of his desk, Mason standing, looking over Nix's shoulder at the framed diploma awarding Nix a master's degree in social work and family counseling from St. Louis University.

Plaques and certificates from grateful donors professing their admiration for Sanctuary's noble work flanked Nix's diploma. The one on the end caught Mason's eye. The certificate read *For Outstanding Service.* The donor was Emily's Fund, a name unfamiliar to Mason until he saw the signature at the bottom—Gina Davenport.

Mason gave up believing in coincidences when he gave up believing in the tooth fairy. He decided to save this one for later. "Where's Jordan?" Mason asked.

Nix looked at his watch. "She's digging postholes for a new stretch of fence. She should be back in about ten minutes."

The Hacketts had shown Mason a recent picture of their daughter. She had long, straight, light brown hair and an angular, unremarkable face. She looked past the camera like she wasn't listening when the photographer told her to say cheese. Her lips were closed in a flat seam. The camera overlooked the anger that forced her from her parents' home, giving no sense that she was a woman who could dig postholes.

Nix asked, "Why does Jordan need a lawyer?"

"Terry," Mason answered, "you know that's confidential."

"Hey, man. I'm her counselor. I need to know these things to do my job."

"Then you ask her. If she wants you to know, she'll tell you," he said, echoing Claire's admonition about Abby. "I thought Gina Davenport was Jordan's therapist."

"All of our residents are assigned an on-site counselor. I'm Jordan's. Some of our residents also see a private therapist, but most can't afford it."

"Her parents say that she lives here because she's too violent to stay at home. Are they right?" Mason asked.

"Lou," Nix answered, "you know that's confidential."

Mason smiled. "And if I tell you that I need to know so I can represent her, I'll bet you'll tell me to ask her."

It was Nix's turn to smile. "Same drill, man."

Mason suspected that Nix was one of those touchy-feely types who made every roadblock, turndown, and obstacle feel like a damn shame he couldn't do anything about and wouldn't if he could. It was a soft-soap style of aggression that was too slippery to get a grip on.

"Are you and I going to get along on this, Terry?" Mason asked.

"Absolutely, man," Nix answered with a grin that said "not likely."

"Any reason we won't?"

"Depends on what you're after. We do a good job here. Messed-up kids get a safe place to work, live, and get better. Most of them can't handle more of the real world than a hard day's work. Lawyers jack up the karma. That's a bad thing, Lou. Nothing personal."

"Maybe I should talk to Centurion about the karma," Mason said.

"Talk to me, baby," Centurion Johnson said with a deep laugh from behind Mason. "I love karma."

Centurion stood just inside Nix's office, his shoulders blocking the frame, his head barely clearing the top of the door. His father was African-American, his mother East Asian, giving him a dark-skinned mix of racial features that defied easy characterization. Life on the street and time in the prison yard had given him a powerful, heavily muscled build that combined with his natural salesmanship to make him a force of nature.

Mason shook hands with Centurion, watching his own hand disappear in the process. Centurion's grip was solid and reassuring. His oversized grin was comforting. He looked like he was ready for the back nine, wearing bone-colored chinos and a washed-out pink polo shirt that strained against his chest and biceps. Mason tried to picture him selling dope and busting heads, but couldn't summon the image.

"Lou Mason," he said as Centurion released his grip on his hand.

"Centurion Johnson," the big man replied, drawing out his name like a ring announcer, making fun of himself. "If you was my lawyer back in the day, I might never have done time. But if I never done time, I might never have straightened myself out. I woulda kept on dealin' and stealin' till some stone-cold motherfucker capped me with a nine. Then old Terry here be out of a job 'cause nobody gonna hire his sorry ass. Terry, I tell him, this ain't Haight Ashbury. It's fuckin' Missouri, man. Get over it. But these kids relate to him, you know what I'm sayin'? And without Terry, these kids wouldn't have nobody to straighten them out. And this gig is all about them kids, man."

Listening to him, Mason understood Centurion's talent. He played to his audience, picking the stereotype he guessed was expected. He chose a mix of street jive, humor, and humility to make Mason feel like one of his homeys. Mason bet Centurion did a killer Colin Powell for the Chamber of Commerce and a knockout Shug Knight for the brothers. Mason had represented enough street punks and boardroom con artists to withstand Centurion's charm.

"If they clean their plates and take out the trash, do

you let them drive the Mercedes on Saturday night?" Mason asked.

Centurion laughed again, an easy chuckle. "You know somethin', Mason? I didn't want that car 'cause I was afraid people like you might get the wrong idea about me. But the dealer, see, he sponsored the garage and said to me, CJ—he's one of those white boys calls everybody by their initials—I can't put the Mercedes logo on the outside of the garage and let you put a Ford Escort inside the garage. How's that going to look? Well, we needed a garage and that was that."

"No sacrifice too great," Mason said.

Centurion kept his smile. "Mason, why are you busting my chops on such a beautiful morning? My man Terry is doing his job. I'm doing my job. We're taking care of these kids. You're wantin' us to cut you some slack with Jordan Hackett. Didn't your momma tell you about getting more bees with honey than vinegar?"

"Sorry," he said to both of them. "You've got a great place here."

"That we do," Centurion said. "And we keep it great 'cause we stay focused and disciplined. Ain't that right, Terry?"

"Focused and disciplined," Terry repeated.

"So everybody makes an appointment in advance to see a resident. Ain't that right, Terry?" Centurion asked.

"Everybody," Terry answered.

"Everybody but you, Mason," Centurion said. " 'Cause you got the balls to bust my chops and the good sense to stop before I lose my sense of humor. Terry, you make sure Mason here gets what he needs. And Mason, you be careful. That Jordan is a handful."

* * *

Nix told Mason to wait for Jordan outside the machine shed. While he stood in the shade, a pickup truck carrying a load of teenagers in the cab and the truck bed skidded to a stop next to the barn. The kids scrambled out, wiping dust and sweat from their faces, and headed for the house. He could hear them joking and poking one another with the ease of summer camp friendships.

A few minutes later, Jordan drove up on a four-wheel ATV pulling a small flatbed trailer loaded with tools. She killed the engine and looked up at him.

"You Lou Mason?"

"That's me."

"My parents hired you, right?"

"Right."

She stepped off the ATV and began unloading the tools, putting them away in the shed without further comment. Mason watched her work, impressed with her economy and intensity. She was of average height, slender but strong enough to sling a shovel, pick, sledgehammer, and posthole digger over her shoulder one at a time like they were Wiffle-ball bats. Finished, she stood in front of him, hands on hips, narrow chin jutting out like a dare, breath a beat above steady. Her face and neck glistened with sweat.

"I didn't kill her, okay," she said.

"Okay," Mason answered.

He guessed that she'd been working since sunup and, judging from the layer of grime she wore, it had been hard, physical work. Still, she hadn't swung the sledgehammer enough times to pound out the rage he saw in her. It was in the knotted muscles of her shoulders and neck. It was in the impatient tapping of her gloved fingers against her hips. It was in the sharp crease of her eyes as she sized him up.

"We done here?" she asked him.

"Just a few more things."

"What?"

"Your parents are paying me, but you're my client. Do you want me to represent you?"

"Do I need a lawyer?"

"The cops took your fingerprints and they took samples from your clothes and hair. Maybe they're doing that with all of Dr. Gina's patients. But if they find your fingerprints, your hair, or your fibers on the broken window or the body and you don't have a good explanation or an alibi for the night of the murder, you need a lawyer."

Jordan yanked off her work gloves and stuffed them in her belt. "Fine. I need a lawyer. What else?"

"Are you always this much fun?"

She cocked her head, split a small grin, and dialed back her force field a notch. "Yeah," she said. "I'm a barrel of laughs."

"Where were you Monday night around ten o'clock?"

"Here. In my room. Lights-out is at ten."

"Does Terry do a bed check?"

"Whenever he gets a chance," she answered.

Mason filed away her double entendre for future reference. "When was the last time you saw Gina Davenport?"

Jordan straightened, her elbows stiff against her sides. "My last appointment was Friday, before the holiday. You can check her appointment book."

"The cops will do that for me. How did you get to her office?"

"Terry usually took me. Once in a while, Centurion would do it."

"What about your family?"

"What about them?"

"They ever take you?"

Jordan folded her arms in front of her. "Look, let's not talk about my family unless it's about where they were at ten o'clock on Monday night."

Mason couldn't tell if she was just venting or was serious. "Why should I ask your parents if they have an alibi?"

"Forget it," she said. "My brother and my parents have alibis for everything."

"I didn't know you had a brother."

"Oh, yes. Brother Trent, the fair-haired son. He's the real master of the alibi. Be sure to ask him."

A stream of kids poured out the front door of the house hurrying to their next projects, slapping hands and touching fists with one another like a football team taking the field. Two girls, one black, one Hispanic, walked past them into the machine shed, giving Jordan a cautious "Hey, girl" while pretending not to notice Mason. They emerged with a chain saw and heavy-duty shears. Jordan looked past Mason to the veranda, nodding her head, Mason following her gaze, Centurion and Terry Nix responding with friendly waves, Jordan putting on her work gloves.

"Time to get back to work?" he asked her.

"Yeah."

"You have a car?"

"Not here," she said, shaking her head. "We're supposed to stay focused and disciplined. Terry says we don't need a car to do that."

"Focused and disciplined," Mason said. "Sounds familiar. What if I wanted to take you back to my office to work on your case, maybe pick up a pizza and beer on the way."

Jordan lowered her head, as if Centurion and Terry could read her lips at a distance. "We can't be focused and disciplined all the time, can we?"

"Centurion and Terry can, but we can't," Mason answered. "I'll pick you up tomorrow afternoon around five. One last thing."

"What's that?"

"No more talking to the cops without me. Got it?"

"Got it."

CHAPTER 4

Mason kept his first meeting with Jordan brief, just to get a sense of her until they could spend serious time talking at his office. She said enough to worry him, claiming that she had an alibi but admitting she needed a lawyer. Telling him when she'd had her last appointment with Dr. Gina, but not when she had last seen her therapist. Implying that Terry wasn't the good shepherd after all. Tossing darts at her parents and brother.

Mason knew better than to expect a client to tell him everything. He even knew better than to expect a client to tell him the truth. He was satisfied when a client gave him something to work with. Jordan had done that, but he would need a lot more if she was charged with Davenport's murder.

Mason believed in first impressions, even if they were mixed, muddled, and messy. That's how Claire had described life to him since he was a kid. She was an unsentimental realist with a compassionate streak, a hell-raiser and stickler for the rule of law, proving her point.

Jordan fit the mold. She was tough, strong, and mad at the world, yet still just wanted to have fun. Sanctuary reined her in with its focused discipline. She was free to go but was stuck working in the fields, dependent on others to take her anywhere. Though she was strong enough to throw someone through a window, he didn't know if she was tough enough or mad enough.

Mason put the top up on the TR-6 for the drive back to town, taking a pass on neck burn. His cell phone rang as he climbed the ramp onto I-70. The TR-6 was the perfect car as far as Mason was concerned. Its perfection lay in the heart-stopping jolt it gave him the first time he saw one. Never a car guy, he was possessed nonetheless, happily overlooking shortcomings like the wind-tunnel noise level. He shouted hello into the hands-free microphone.

"Hey, Boss," Mickey shouted back. "You coming in today?"

"Later. I'm stopping at the Cable Depot first. I want to talk with the Hacketts and have a look at Dr. Gina's office. What's up?"

"We got the check in the Coyle case. Do you want me to call Mad Max and have him come in and endorse it?"

Max Coyle was a former professional football player turned professional wrestler until one too many head-locks forced him into a career in sports broadcasting. He wrestled under the name of Mad Max, a moniker he kept behind the microphone. Along the way, he held on to enough money to make a difference, putting it in the hands of David Evans, a lawyer and investment advisor who performed reverse alchemy, turning gold into garbage. Mason had taken the case, convincing the advisor to pay Max back, plus enough to cover Mason's fee.

Max's settlement check was made out to him and Mason, requiring both to endorse it. Mason would deposit the check in his account and write another check to Max after deducting his fee. It was a simple way of making certain the client and the lawyer both got paid.

"Don't bother. I'll swing by the office, pick up the check, find him at the radio station, and have him sign it."

"You get all the good ideas," Mickey said.

"It's all about focused discipline," Mason told him.

The Cable Depot, known by locals just as the Depot, was far from being Kansas City's tallest building, but its location on a bluff on the northwestern edge of downtown elevated it above much of its brick and mortar competition. It was eight stories of Kansas City history, rich enough in gothic architectural detail to be placed on the National Register of Historical Landmarks. That designation, and the tax breaks it carried, made it a good investment for Arthur and Carol Hackett when they bought it twenty years ago. Once renovated, it became an anchor in the redevelopment of the West Side and a favorite of those who lived in Quality Hill a few blocks south.

KWIN's studios and offices were on the eighth floor, space shared with only one other tenant, Gina Davenport, Ph.D. A mix of professionals and a deli on the first floor populated the rest of the building. Mason studied the building directory, surprised at finding one name on the list. David Evans's office was on the fourth floor. Mason pulled Evans's settlement check from his pocket. The address was a post office box, not the Cable Depot.

When Mason filed Max's lawsuit against Evans a year earlier, Evans's office had been on the twentieth floor of a high-rent high-rise on the Country Club Plaza. Though Evans was a lawyer, his malpractice insurance didn't cover Max Coyle's claim since Max sued Evans for cheating him out of his money, not for being a lousy lawyer. Evans came out of his own pocket for $650,000 or borrowed the money from someone else's pocket. Mason figured that hit knocked Evans from the twentieth floor on 47th Street to the fourth floor on 6th Street. Life is hard, Mason said to himself.

Arthur and Carol Hackett were waiting in Arthur's office as Mason walked in.

"What did she say?" Arthur asked, settling in behind his desk.

"Did you ask her if she did it?" Carol asked, their questions stumbling over one another.

"She said she was innocent," Mason said, answering both of their questions.

Arthur motioned Mason to take the chair across from Carol as he shuffled a stack of papers.

"She's our daughter," Carol said with more regret than grief.

"I understand," Mason said, not certain whether he did.

The Hacketts were well educated, well dressed, and buoyant with good fortune, none of which insulated them from the turmoil rocking their family. Mason had learned that many rich people assumed that their success inoculated their kids from bad judgment and bad genes, while poor people more often were resigned to trouble when it found their kids, having spent their whole lives waiting for it. Rich clients expected him to fix everything. Poor ones prayed for a lucky break. Mason knew that bucks and breaks weren't evenly distributed, though a parent's suffering was. Except the Hacketts were more annoyed than anguished.

"Is she going to be arrested?" Arthur asked. He took off his half-glasses, leaned back in his chair, the man in charge.

"I don't know. I'll talk to the detective running the investigation and find out what's going on."

"What else did she say?" Carol asked.

"Mrs. Hackett," Mason began. "This gets a little complicated. You and your husband are paying my fees, but your daughter is my client. Everything she tells me is privileged. If I tell you, even though you are her mother, she could lose that privilege."

"Carol," Arthur interrupted, "let Mason do his job. Jordan didn't kill Gina Davenport, so that's the end of it."

"It may not be that easy," Mason said. "Her fingerprints will be found in Dr. Gina's office. That makes sense since she was a patient. The same goes for her hair and clothing fibers. We could have a problem if any are found on the broken window or the body."

"If they are, they are," Carol said, concentrating on her manicure.

Arthur said, "Our son, Trent, manages the building for us. He told me that Gina had called in a repair request for that window last Friday. Apparently one of her patients went a little crazy and threw something against the window and cracked it. Since it was a holiday weekend, Trent figured he could wait until this week to fix it."

"Did Gina say who the patient was?"

Arthur shook his head. "Said it was privileged, just like you. It didn't matter anyway. The window still needed to be replaced. I told Trent he shouldn't have waited. He feels terrible. Plus, my insurance company says Gina's husband will probably sue us."

"Who's her husband?" Mason asked.

"Robert Davenport. He teaches painting at the Kansas City Art Institute."

"They have any children?"

Carol said, "They had a daughter, but she died a couple of years ago."

"What happened?" Mason asked.

"It was a real tragedy," Arthur said. "The girl jumped out of a window and killed herself. I give Gina credit, though. A lot of mothers would have tried to keep it quiet, but she went public, talking about it on the air. I guess it was her way of grieving. The really crazy thing is that's when Gina's show took off. Her daughter kills herself and Gina goes into national syndication. Now Gina dies in almost the same way."

Mason caught his breath calculating the odds. "What was her daughter's name?"

Carol whispered, "Emily."

Mason hesitated at his next question, betting another long shot on the answer. "Where did it happen?"

"Sanctuary," Carol said as she left her chair and her husband's office.

"Carol bottles everything up inside," Arthur explained. "It's not that she doesn't care. She does, but sometimes she comes across, well, I don't know."

"Like she'd rather be anyplace else?" Mason asked.

"Like that," Arthur agreed. "We both feel guilty that

Jordan can't live at home and we're not thrilled that she's at Sanctuary after what happened to Emily Davenport."

"Why not find someplace else for Jordan to live?"

"You ever try to make a twenty-one-year-old girl do anything she didn't want to do?"

"I can't even get my dog to bark," Mason answered. "When was the last time you saw Jordan before Monday night?"

Arthur paused, checking his mental calendar. "Last Friday, she stopped in before her appointment with Gina. I only saw her for a minute."

"Do you know how she got here?"

"Someone gave her a ride, I guess. I didn't ask. Is that important?"

Mason shrugged. "Probably not."

"Where were you and your wife Monday night?" Mason asked the question as if it was no more important that asking for the time, hoping Arthur would be as casual in his response.

"Home," he said, taking no offense at the question.

"How about Trent? Where was he?"

"That I don't know," Arthur said. "He had dinner with us at the Club. Carol and I were home by eight. I don't know where Trent went."

"Do Trent and Jordan get along?"

Arthur shook his head back and forth. "Trent is five years older. The age difference was a problem. They both thought the other was more trouble than they were worth. You'd think brothers and sisters would get along better."

Mason switched gears. "How does Gina's death affect your station?"

"It's a killer," Arthur said, unaware of his poor analogy. "Her show generated a third of our revenue. You don't replace that with a delayed broadcast of Rush Limbaugh. Fortunately, we have insurance on all of our air personalities. I hope that gets us by until we find another superstar."

"I'd like to get a look at Gina's office," Mason said.

"The police just took down the crime-scene tape this morning. Talk to Trent. His office is on the first floor. He'll give you a key."

Mason found Max Coyle in the station's break room polishing off a LaMar's doughnut. Max gave new meaning to being huge. Centurion Johnson was a big man, but Max was part man, part mastodon. He was six-eight, and Mason guessed he weighed at least 375 pounds. Mason saw Max wrestle once on a cable broadcast. He moved well for a big man, especially when he bounced his opponents off the rope before pile-driving them into the canvas.

He was sitting with a woman smoking a cigarette directly beneath the *Smoke Free Environment* sign on the wall. She had a thin face and figure that worked to give her a harsh attractiveness. She reminded Mason of something bright and sharp that would cut you if you grabbed it the wrong way.

"Hey, Lou," Max said. "Mickey called and told me you got the check. Lemme see it." Max wiped his hands on his pants and clapped them together with Christmas morning excitement. Mason handed him the check. "Ain't that sweet," Max said. "Gimme your pen so I can endorse it."

The woman stubbed out her cigarette and said, "I'm Paula Sutton and you're Lou Mason. Max is short on manners."

"Max is easily distracted by doughnuts and money," Mason said.

"I hear the Hacketts hired you to represent Jordan."

Mason ignored her comment. "You do the morning show, don't you?"

"Are you a long-time listener and first-time caller?"

"Neither. I saw your name on the program guide in the lobby."

"I do kind of an edgy, current events, call-in-and-blast-everybody kind of show. Give me a try. You may like me. Although the only thing my callers want to talk about at the moment is Gina Davenport doing a header from eight flights up."

"Probably spawn a whole new culture of conspiracy," Mason said. "I gather the two of you weren't close?"

"Couldn't stand the bitch," Paula said. "She was a phony that ducked under her morality bar like she was doing the limbo. Don't get me wrong. I didn't want her dead. I just wanted her ratings book." She checked the wall clock. "Three o'clock. I've got to tape some promos. Nice to meet you and don't forget to tune in."

"Paula's not so bad," Max said after she left. "Her ratings suck and she may get canceled. That's enough to put anyone on the rag."

"How are your ratings?"

"Primo, man. Number one in my time-slot, number two at the station."

"Gina was number one?" Mason asked.

"Not even a contest."

"Get this," Mason said. "David Evans is your neighbor. He's got an office on the fourth floor. Be nice when you see him in the elevator."

"Already saw the little prick."

"How did he end up down here? I would have thought he would want to stay away from you."

"I'm sure he does now, especially since his other KWIN client is gone."

"What other KWIN client?"

"Gina Davenport."

"Get out!" Mason said. "Evans was managing Gina's money too?"

"More than that. He was her lawyer and he managed her money. Made my account look like chump change."

"How did you know?"

"The asshole told me. It was part of his sales pitch. Gina must have put him on to me. He said he was managing the charitable foundation Gina set up after her daughter killed herself."

"Emily's Fund?" Mason asked.

"Right. That's it. Something like twenty million bucks."

"Where did she get that kind of money?"

"Don't ask me, Lou. Ask him."

"Good idea."

CHAPTER 5

Mason made it to the lobby when his cell phone rang.

"Hi, Lou. It's Abby Lieberman."

Mason caught her long bomb in stride, scooted into the end zone untouched, and dropped the ball on the ground like it was a routine play. "What's going on?" he asked, as if he'd expected her to call all along, though he hurried outside to make certain the cell-phone gods didn't drop her call.

"Listen, I'm really sorry about last night. I behaved very poorly. I hope I didn't ruin Harry's party."

"Not a chance. Besides, you can't apologize when a client has an emergency. It's good to be needed."

"You're too nice, especially since I didn't have a client emergency. I made that up. That's why I'm apologizing and that's why I want to buy you dinner tonight if you're free. I want to tell you the real reason I left."

Mason had a fleeting image that he'd run his touchdown into his own team's end zone. That would fit with everything else he'd learned today. Gina Davenport and her daughter both go through windows to their deaths. Dr. Gina's charitable foundation supports Sanctuary, the not-so-safe haven where Gina's daughter killed herself. Centurion Johnson and Terry Nix give creeps a bad name. David Evans, whom Mason just clipped for more than half a million dollars, not only represents Gina Davenport, but manages twenty million of her dollars. Mason's newest client, who may be charged with murdering Gina Davenport and who is one brick short of a load, goads him into suspecting her parents or brother killed Gina.

So he shouldn't have been surprised when a woman whom he met for five minutes—not long enough to know but long enough to love—asked him out to dinner. Not so she can propose to him, but so she can explain why the mention of Gina Davenport's murder sent her running for cover. Mason accepted her invitation, certain he would end up with food poisoning for dessert.

"Sure. That would be great. Where and when?"

"Metropolis Grill in Westport. Seven-thirty. See you then."

Trent Hackett handed Mason a key before Mason had a chance to introduce himself. They were in Trent's office, a sparsely furnished windowless room tucked behind the elevators, illuminated by fluorescent tubes in an open ceiling panel.

"Arthur called. Said to give you a key to Davenport's office," Trent said. "That's a passkey. The cops took all the extra keys to Gina's office."

"Not that it matters, but how do you know I'm the guy who's supposed to get the key?"

Trent looked up from his computer, his complexion a pale wash of monitor blue and fluorescence, his small frame made smaller by the low chair he was sitting on. "You're you," he told Mason, swinging the monitor around.

The screen was filled with a photograph of Mason taken when he'd been trapped in a burning building. He was grasping steel security bars covering a window that kept the bad guys out and the good guys flame-broiled. A bystander took the picture and the *Kansas City Star* ran it.

"Too bad you don't have the color version," Mason said. "I look good with red in my cheeks."

Trent tapped a few keys and Mason watched his image transformed from black and white to color. The metamorphosis continued as digitized flames rose in the background, melting his face and unveiling a banner that read *Welcome to Hell.*

"I'm thinking of doing a whole line of electronic greeting cards if real estate doesn't work out. What do you think?" Trent asked.

"I think you're lucky your mother loves you and your father signs your paycheck. I also think I'd like to know where you were Monday night when Gina Davenport took her trip to the other side."

Trent spun the monitor back, punched the escape button on his keyboard, and stood up. He was scrawny, made more so by his buzz cut, elongated neck, and thin face. Though he pushed his spine up and his round shoulders back, he was still the geek who never got the girl.

"That's the problem with you lawyers. No sense of humor."

"Try me. Say something funny," Mason said.

"Okay. My sister's a lying, paranoid slut."

"Not funny," Mason said.

"Not funny," Trent agreed, "but true."

"Doesn't matter and doesn't answer my question," Mason said. "Where were you Monday night when Gina Davenport was murdered?"

"I told the cops. I don't have to tell you," Trent said. "And don't lose the key. It'll cost you twenty-five bucks."

"Shame you didn't get Dr. Gina's window fixed," Mason said.

"Why? That's what insurance is for."

"Wrong. That's what the penitentiary is for. See you at the family reunion."

Mason chided himself for getting into a smack-talking match with Trent Hackett. Trent was a slacker with no place to go except home, where Mason bet he spent Monday night alone watching pay-per-view porn until his wrists got tired. Pimping Mason was Trent's way of flexing, and Mason knew better than to flex back.

Trent's charm was enough to make Mason wonder whether Trent took advantage of the cracked window in Gina Davenport's office to throw her through it. Though Mason had no idea why Trent might have killed Dr. Gina, or for that matter, why the police thought Jordan killed her. Suspicion, he realized, often lurks outside reason.

Mason took the day's only good news to the bank and deposited David Evans's check. He called the office, and Mickey told him that no clients were threatening to sue him for malpractice.

"Prosperity at home and peace abroad. I'm running for another term," Mason told Mickey. "See you tomorrow."

Instead, Mason ran five laps around Loose Park, the city's premier green space two blocks from his house, dodging moms, strollers, and lovers. He took Tuffy with him, leaving her on a long leash secured to a tree. Tuffy sniffed at the squirrels and rolled on her back so kids could rub her belly, grateful that she didn't have to run along with Mason. A couple of hours later, showered, shaved, and clad in casual cool, he left for dinner with Abby.

Westport first made its name as a trading post, then as a Civil War battleground, before being reborn as Kansas City's trend-barometer. From head shops in the sixties, it spawned bars in the eighties, before settling into baby-boomer hip in the nineties. Like boomers who thought they looked younger than everyone else their age, Westport was certain it looked better than the rest of the city.

Metropolis took hip and hung it on the walls, seasoning the food and mixing the drinks in a laid-back, eclectic blend of fanciful colors and offbeat flavors. Abby was waiting for him at a table in the window alcove at the front of the restaurant. Mason entered from the back, standing in the hallway next to the kitchen, watching her as she watched the street, giving his heart a reality check.

Mason saw a thoughtful, graceful woman with a dancer's elegance, comfortable with herself. He saw all this in her easy, ordinary gestures—sipping from her wineglass, leaning back in her chair, ignoring a stray bang that dangled over her eyes. He also saw an edginess she couldn't

suppress when the front door of the restaurant opened,
a burst of voices bringing her upright as she searched the
incoming customers for him, her smooth brow creased
with anticipation, then slack with disappointment when
he wasn't there.

All of her—her ease, her elegance, her edginess—
captivated him. He knew that he was reading too much
into the moment, as he had the first moment he'd seen
her, but he didn't care. That was how she affected him.

Mason wove between tables, smiling when she looked
his way, having caught him in the corner of her eye as
he approached. She offered her hand and he took it
hostage again with both of his, wondering if doing so
would become a ritual, tying them together like a secret. He held it long enough to feel her strength, resisting for an instant when she took it back.

"Hey," she said.

"Hey, you," he answered.

"Picking up where we left off?" she asked, a small
smile answering her question.

"Why give up such a good start?" Mason asked.

"You are confident, aren't you?"

"You think we can talk in questions all night?"

"Do we get a prize if we do?"

"You won't stop first, will you?"

"You'll get the wrong idea—that I give up too easily—won't you?"

"I don't think you ever give up," he said.

She cocked her head, widening her smile. "Thank
you."

"You're welcome."

"Stop it!" she said, not meaning it.

"Certainly."

"You're obnoxious," she said, still not meaning it.

"Unavoidably," he said.

"And unmanageable," she added.

"But domesticated, and done. Are you hungry?"

She took a deep breath. "No. I thought I was. I thought I could do this over a nice dinner and a good bottle of wine, but I can't."

"Do what?" Mason asked as his own appetite slipped away.

"You don't know me at all, Lou," she began. "I own my own business—Fresh Air. I'm a public relations consultant. I polish corporate images, manage bad news."

Mason shrugged. "That's nothing to be ashamed of," he joked. "That's Mickey Shanahan's died-and-gone-to-heaven dream. I'm surprised he hasn't already proposed."

Abby clenched her jaw. "Claire warned me you would be like this."

"Like what?" Mason said, palms up in protest.

"She said you would fall in love with me at first sight and dazzle me with one-liners."

"It's on my business card," he said.

Abby withheld her smile. "I saw Sherri Thomas's report on Channel Six last night. She said the police suspect a woman named Jordan Hackett killed Gina Davenport and that you're representing her."

Mason softened his tone. "Abby—"

She interrupted. "Lou, please don't talk to me about privilege and confidentiality. I've spent my life living with secrets."

Mason had also watched Thomas's broadcast, despite his promise to ignore it. He paused and nodded. "Okay. I am representing her and she may be a suspect. What's that got to do with you?"

Abby drew another deep breath, gripping the table with both hands. "Jordan Hackett may be my daughter."

Mason had prepared himself for every possible permutation of Abby's involvement in Gina Davenport's murder—patient, suspect, friend of the victim—but not this one. Abby's squared shoulders rolled inward, her well-toned arms quivered, her eyes pooled. Mason didn't know if it was true, but he felt Abby's torment that it might be.

Neither Jordan nor her parents had said that she was adopted. He wouldn't have cared because it wouldn't have mattered. He would learn the root of Jordan's emotional problems if she was charged with murder. Adoption was an unlikely source. Adopted kids look for their birth parents. They don't kill their therapists.

"Is that why you called Claire?"

Abby nodded, the moment of confession passed, and she rallied. "I didn't know about Jordan at first, just Gina Davenport."

"I don't get the connection," Mason said.

"I got a telephone call last Friday from a woman who didn't identify herself. She said if I wanted to find my daughter to call a number." Abby reached into her purse for a yellow Post-it note and handed it to Mason. "816-555-2319," she recited.

Mason asked, "Whose number is it?"

"Gina Davenport's."

"You spoke with her?"

"She identified herself when I called. I'm the same way. I always answer the phone with 'It's Abby.' She said, 'Dr. Davenport.' I told her who I was and how I had gotten her number. She went ballistic, said she didn't know anything about my daughter and that if I called again she would sue me for harassment."

Mason said, "You've left out one pretty important piece of the story."

"I know. The part about having a daughter. I was seventeen and stupid. I thought it was love at first sight. I gave my baby girl up for adoption."

"Had you tried to find her before last Friday?"

Abby wiped her hands and eyes with a napkin. "No. Being an unwed mother was my first experience with public relations. I grew up here. My parents were mortified when I got pregnant and sent me to live with an uncle in St. Louis until I had the baby. They told everyone I was enrolled in a school for gifted children. I came home after graduation."

"Did your parents get over it?"

"They moved away. We don't talk much. Their story became my story. I went to school, went to work, pretended it didn't happen. I refused to read stories about women who searched for the children they gave up. It wasn't about me. Then I got that phone call and I couldn't pretend anymore."

"So you called."

"When I'm helping a business manage a crisis, I focus on proportional response. Gina Davenport's response was way out of proportion, which made me think she was lying."

"What did you do next?"

"Nothing. I didn't know what to do. Claire and I worked together on a fund-raiser last year. I called her after Gina was murdered. If there was a connection between Gina and my daughter and someone murdered Gina, my daughter could be in danger too. I asked Claire to help me find my daughter and she invited me to dinner."

"She was fixing us up. I'm surprised she didn't do it before."

"She tried. I was with someone," Abby said.

"Timing is everything. Why do you think Jordan may be your daughter?"

Abby looked at her hands for an answer, then straight at Mason. "In my business, I go with my gut. I size up people and problems for a living. I couldn't attribute the anonymous phone call I got to a bad joke. The woman who called me knew I had given up my daughter for adoption. She wanted me to think that Gina Davenport knew where my daughter was and she wanted me to call Gina. Gina's reaction didn't make sense to me unless she did know something. Then Gina was killed and a girl the same age as my daughter was named a suspect. It's all I have to work with."

"Have you told the police?"

Abby bit her lower lip. "Yes. The detective was very polite, but I think I just made her more suspicious of Jordan."

"The phone call and Davenport's murder were certainly a jolt, but I still don't understand why my involvement upset you so much."

Abby blushed, her eyes pooling again. "You said you were defending someone who might be charged with Gina Davenport's murder. My feelings about my daughter were so close to the surface after all these years, I guess I overreacted the same way Gina overreacted to my phone call."

"Is that all?"

"No," she answered, dipping her head before looking at him again. "Love at first sight hasn't been kind to me."

Mason reached across the table, wrapping his hand around hers. "Why don't we start with dinner and see how that goes before we worry about dessert."

CHAPTER 6

Mason stood outside the Cable Depot at eleven P.M., forty-nine hours after Gina Davenport's murder. The eighth-floor window was boarded up, facing south above 6th Street, the building flanked by Jefferson on the west and Washington on the east—dead presidents immortalized in side streets. The bloody stains and chalk outline marking the spot where Gina died were still faintly visible under the lights along 6th.

Mason had watched Sherri Thomas's continuing coverage of the murder on the ten o'clock news. While Mason and Abby were having dinner, her cameraman had filmed a Depot janitor as he scrubbed the pavement. Sherri caught Arthur Hackett in an ambush interview, asking him if his daughter had confessed to the murder. Arthur took the bait, shoving both Sherri and the cameraman.

"Great," Mason said to the television. "I can represent the daughter on a murder charge and the father on assault and battery."

His dinner with Abby had not been the romantic water-shed he'd hoped for even though their attraction for one another was more than passing, each sensing something in the other that was missing in their lives. That **was** plain in the way they touched, their hands molding together like a matched set.

Abby's involvement with Gina Davenport and Jordan held them back, sending each of them home alone. Abby knew of nothing that tied her to them beyond the phone call she had received. Mason realized he'd have to uncover the connection regardless of the consequences, setting aside his personal feelings for his client's life.

They didn't talk of any of this over dinner. It was there as they danced around intimacy, reaching out and retreating while they stumbled over the superficial details of their daily lives. Abby didn't have to ask him to find out whether Jordan was her daughter. She just put it on the table. Mason almost asked the waiter to box it up so he could take it home and chew on it tomorrow, knowing that he would do what he could.

The cops needed a motive for Jordan to kill Dr. Gina. Mason supposed that Jordan's rage could be tied to her adoption and that she could have somehow blamed her therapist for keeping her from her birth mother. Mason would be happy if that lame theory was the high point of the prosecutor's case. Yet someone had gone to a lot of trouble to connect Abby and Gina Davenport. Abby wouldn't have guessed that Jordan was the next link in the chain until Gina was murdered.

Mason and Abby promised to see each other again—soon, they both added in the same breath. Mason knew it would have to wait until he had a better handle on this case. He had to know whether his client's relation-

ship with Abby—if there was one—would help Jordan
or put her on death row.

Mason didn't wait to find out. That's why he was standing outside the Cable Depot at eleven o'clock, flipping
the passkey in his hand like a coin.

"Heads I win, tails I win," Mason said, betting against
the odds.

The revolving door at the front entrance and the single door to his right were both locked. Mason found
the dead bolt at the base of the single door, the bolt giving way with a sharp metallic snap when he tried the
passkey, no security guard asking him to state his business.

The lobby was small, made smaller by dim after-hours
lighting, a rectangular passage with the building directory on one side, two elevators on the other, a narrow
corridor leading behind them to Trent's office. The floor
was marble, the high ceiling painted with a snapshot of
Kansas City in its frontier days.

Stepping off the elevator on the eighth floor, he
could see into KWIN's office through glass double doors.
The reception area was dark, but lights were on in the
hallway leading back to the studio. KWIN broadcast
around the clock, the late-night hours filled with syndicated programs, the station operating on autopilot.
The doors were locked. Mason resisted the temptation
to use his passkey just to look around.

Pieces of crime-scene tape clung to the frame around
the door to Dr. Gina's office. The name plate—*Gina
Davenport, Ph.D.*—was more than understated, leaving
out her celebrity life and sensational death.

Mason stepped inside, closed the door, and turned on the small but powerful mag light he kept in his car for poking around after dark. He found the light switch and slipped the flashlight back into his pants pocket, surveying the office, getting a feel for the dead woman—who she was, how she lived, and why she died.

Mason had worked in two law firms before he started his own. The first was a small personal-injury firm and the second was a big corporate firm. In both, his office had reflected more of the firm than of him. Now his office was like a second skin. There was no receptionist, file room, mail room, or library. Everything was in one room, nothing separating him from the business he did. During a trial, he spent more time there than at home. Rugby gear tossed over a chair, jazz CDs piled on top of the refrigerator, shoes stuffed under the sofa were all clues to his life that couldn't be separated from his practice.

Dr. Gina's office struck him the same way. There was no room for a receptionist. No place for someone sitting behind a counter shuffling insurance forms beneath a sign requiring payment at the time service was rendered. The room wasn't large, but it was comfortable. A pair of small sofas framed around a low table with a chair formed a circle where Mason assumed Gina met with her patients. Plants on the floor, abstract posters in soothing colors on the walls, and candles on the table made it an inviting place to sit down and talk.

A small desk sat in a corner, abandoned, papers strewn across it. Mason wondered whether Gina shared his aversion to a clean desk or whether the cops had sorted through everything, leaving the mess behind for someone else to clean up.

Mason glanced through the papers, finding nothing more interesting than a few bills and offers for low-interest-rate credit cards. Dr. Gina's phone sat on the edge of the desk, the phone number printed in bold type on the faceplate of the receiver. The number was 816-555-4684—not even close to the number Abby had given him. He didn't find any other phones in the office. Maybe, he thought, Abby had called Dr. Gina's cell phone.

Mason skimmed through the bills again, not surprised that he didn't find a cell-phone bill. He realized the cops would have taken it to check the list of calls made and received for any leads. He did find a notice from the cell-phone company offering Gina five thousand frequent-flier miles if she renewed her service contract for two years. The letter referenced her cell-phone number. It too was different. That left Gina's home phone number. Mason found a phone book in a desk drawer and tossed it back when the only listing he found for Gina was for her office. Directory assistance confirmed that her home number was unlisted.

The rest of her desk drawers were empty, as were the filing cabinets behind the desk marked *Patient Records, Billings, Insurance,* and *Correspondence.* He found a separate file cabinet with two drawers—one labeled *KWIN* and the other marked *Emily's Fund*—in a closet. They too were empty. The police had emptied the office of anything tied to Dr. Gina's practice.

There were two windows. Plywood had been nailed to the fatal one, preventing Mason from examining any part of it. The other window was on the same wall, raised two feet off the floor and set back a foot. Mason stood against it, his six-foot frame matching the window's height. He pressed his body against the glass, the single sheet pressing back against him, vibrating slightly, warning him not to rely too heavily on its support.

Still, throwing someone through a window raised off the floor and set back from the wall was not a slam dunk. Mason guessed that the crack in the window had to have been just right and the impact of Gina's body even more precise to carry her to her death. All of which meant that the homicide might not have been intentional. It may have been reckless, careless, or accidental—three qualifiers that could mean the difference between jail time and no time.

The one thing Mason didn't expect to find was an elevator in the center of the wall to the left of the door, flanked by bookshelves heavy with psychology texts. He pressed the call button and listened as the elevator ascended from a lower floor, humming louder as it came closer. It stopped with an unsteady clang, the floor still wobbling when the door opened.

Mason stepped inside and the door closed. It was an old elevator with raised buttons for each floor, the lobby, and the basement. The elevator floor was carpeted, the walls and ceiling paneled in dark wood and lit by recessed lights around the perimeter of the ceiling. A video camera was mounted in one corner, the first sign of security Mason had seen anywhere in the Depot. He took comfort in the sign that said the certificate of elevator inspection was on file in the building manager's office until he remembered that Trent Hackett was the building manager.

He pressed the *open* button and the door, to his relief, opened. He allowed it to close again, this time pressing the button for the seventh floor. The button didn't light up and the elevator didn't move. He tried each button in succession, getting no response until he pushed the button marked *B*, which he assumed was for the basement.

The elevator gears began their deep hum as the car slowly descended, Mason concluding that the elevator had been programmed to run exclusively between the basement and Dr. Gina's office. He didn't know what was in the basement, but guessed there was underground parking, making the elevator a special perk for KWIN's top star.

Seconds later, the elevator jerked to a stop and the lights went out. Disoriented, Mason swore he felt the car sway in an imaginary breeze. He flicked on his flashlight, running the beam along the control panel until he found the alarm button. He pushed it three times with no result. There was no emergency phone and he'd left his cell phone in the car. He yelled for help, with no response, and banged on the wall for added effect until the car dropped a foot like an airplane hitting an air pocket, taking Mason down on one knee.

Mason braced himself against the wall, trying to steady the elevator and his nerves. He didn't know anything about elevators, but he knew enough to know that an elevator playing freeze tag in the dark was a bad thing.

Aiming his flashlight against the ceiling, Mason found the escape hatch used to reach the roof of the car. Certain only that he didn't want to be inside the elevator if it plunged to the bottom of the shaft, he boosted himself onto the waist-high rail around the interior of the car and popped the hatch open with his forearm.

The hatch, an eighteen-inch square in the corner where he was perched, gave him the room and the angle to pull himself through the opening. Flashlight clamped between his teeth, he stuck his head and arms through the hatch, grabbing hold of the housing for the wire-rope cables to pull himself up on the roof of the car.

His flashlight wasn't strong enough to penetrate much of the pitch-black shaft, and he couldn't tell where he was until he saw an elevator door marked 6 several feet below him. A service ladder was bolted into the wall of the shaft alongside the doors, a good five feet from where he stood. Peering over the edge of the elevator, he nearly lost his balance as the car lurched again.

Mason retreated to the center of the car, standing on top of the housing, his left arm wrapped around the greasy steel ropes, the flashlight aimed at the wall, his breathing echoing against the shaft. He measured the distance to the service ladder again, debating whether to try for the ladder or take his chances with the elevator.

The debate ended when the elevator plunged like an amusement park nightmare, Mason stumbling off the housing, throwing himself at the service ladder, slamming his face and chest against the cold metal while he fought for a handhold, sliding down a half dozen rungs before stopping his fall, his left arm dangling at his side, suddenly numb.

He'd dropped his flashlight onto the roof of the elevator, its pinpoint light vanishing in the instant before the car crashed into the pit at the bottom of the shaft, launching a plume of dust, choking and blinding him more than the darkness of the elevator shaft. He felt a warm, sticky flow down his left arm, touching it with his right hand, knowing it was blood, not knowing whether his skin had been ripped by the cable or pierced by his collision with the ladder. Either way, his arm wouldn't do what he told it to do.

Leaning hard against the ladder for support, Mason loosened his belt, pulled it out of three loops on his left side, and rethreaded it over his forearm, cinching his arm against his side before rebuckling his belt. He couldn't tell if he was making his injury worse since he had no feeling in his arm. At least it didn't hurt, he thought.

Mason hung on the ladder, expecting a quick rescue. The crash had been deafening and had to bring police and firefighters to the scene in minutes, he was convinced. When no one came, when no elevator doors were opened and no high beams shined on him, he began to understand the trouble he was in.

There were no security guards. The only office that might have been occupied at that time of night was the radio station. Anyone working there was probably in a soundproof studio wearing headphones that shut out the rest of the world. It reminded Mason of the existential puzzle—if a tree falls in the forest and no one hears it, does it make any noise?

No one knew where he was or had reason to look for him. He was a one-armed man hanging on a ladder in a blacked-out elevator shaft, bruised and bloodied from a self-inflicted beating.

The only thing he knew for certain was that there were elevator doors above and below him. If the ladder was used to service the doors, there had to be a way to open them from inside the shaft. Mason ignored the fact that the serviceman would be equipped with tools, two arms to use them, and light to see what the hell he was doing.

He closed his eyes, not to shut out the darkness, but

to concentrate on what he had seen in the brief moment he had shined his flashlight on the elevator door for the sixth floor. He pictured a bar extending across the door that he hoped would open it when the bar was pulled or pushed in the right direction.

Mason didn't like his options. He could climb up the ladder to the seventh floor and try the bar with his right arm. He didn't know if he had the strength to move it, and even if he could, he had no way to keep his balance at the same time. He could climb down to the sixth-floor door, using his right leg to work the bar while holding on with his good arm.

Or he could climb down the ladder all the way to the bottom of the shaft. He looked down, even though he couldn't see, his head swimming from shock, blood loss, and darkness. That option was last on his list, and certain to land him in a heap on top of the wrecked elevator with one wrong step.

Mason chose the sixth floor, lowering his feet, descending one at a time, one rung at a time. After each step, he swung his right leg out, feeling for the elevator door. It took three steps before his shoe found the smooth surface of the door and two more before it found the bar.

He edged his shoe along the bar, pressing down as he went, frustrated when the door didn't yield, near exhaustion from the effort. He couldn't reach far enough. Pulling his leg back to the ladder, Mason held on and gathered his strength. He realized he had to flip his position on the ladder, putting his back to the wall, holding on with his right hand while using his left leg to force the door open. The maneuver would double his reach if he didn't fall.

Taking a deep breath, Mason swung his body around, keeping only his right hand and foot on the ladder as his left leg slapped against the elevator door and jammed down hard against the bar. The first movement of the bar almost caused Mason to lose his grip on the ladder, he was so unprepared for it. Steadying himself, he renewed the pressure on the bar until the door began to slide open away from him. A dim light leaked into the shaft from the other side of the door.

Mason panicked, realizing that he would quickly lose his hold on the bar and the door would slide shut again. He had no time to think. He gave the bar a final shove, swung his body back onto the ladder, and slid down three more rungs until he was even with the bottom of the open door. Once again, he whirled away from the ladder, letting go and landing halfway in the opening, his head glancing off something harder than his skull. The door slid back, stopping against his legs.

Mason crawled the rest of the way in from the shaft, grabbing onto metal shelves, pulling himself to his feet. He was in a closet lit only by light oozing in from the hall. There was no handle on the inside of the locked door. He thumped his good hand against the door without conviction, slid to the floor, and passed out amid the smell of cleaning supplies.

CHAPTER 7

A burst of hard raps against the closet door roused Mason. He shook the cobwebs from his brain, concentrating on the deep, muffled voice giving orders from the other side. "Police! Open up! Anybody in there?"

"Can't," Mason whispered, unable to pump more volume into his reply. He was lying on his side facing the closet door, wedged in a fetal position, his bloody left arm draped over his middle, having slipped out of his belt when he spun off the ladder.

"Police! Open up!" the cop repeated.

Mason kicked the door in reply.

"Get a grip, Kenny," a woman said. "Whoever is in there can't talk and can't get out. Call the paramedics. We've got blood leaking out from under the door. And get the building manager up here with the goddamn key to this closet. We find a body in there, I'm changing the name of this place to the House of Usher."

Recognizing the woman's voice, Mason tried to laugh,

but hacked instead, discovering a ragged pain in his side. Samantha Greer had a black-and-blue sense of humor Mason couldn't resist. She'd crack up when he rolled out of the closet.

Mason's body was regaining consciousness in waves, each one cresting with fresh complaints. Though his arm was still numb and his ribs raw, his head throbbed like a psychotic sub-woofer, filling his ears with static. Disconnected sounds filtered through the white noise. Running footsteps. Snapping voices. He wondered if he'd made up or dreamt Samantha's voice until he heard her again.

"Ease it open, Kenny. Let's meet the neighbors."

Mason scrunched his eyes as light flooded the closet. Opening them, all he could see were shoes, ankles, and shins.

"Lou!" Samantha said. "When did you start playing extreme hide-and-seek?"

Before Mason could answer, two paramedics ran their hands over his body checking for obvious injuries. They soon straightened him out, eased him onto a spine board, and lifted him onto a gurney.

"Sam," he said as she smiled down at him, stroking the side of his face.

"Don't talk," she said. "You're shaken but not stirred. I'll see you at the hospital."

"I want my goddamn key back! Ask him about the key," Trent Hackett said.

Samantha looked up, Mason rolling his head to the other side of the gurney, Trent Hackett standing behind the paramedics as they packed up, pushing his way past them, Kenny holding him back.

"I think it can wait, Mr. Hackett," she told him.

"My father made me give him a key to Gina Davenport's office. I didn't have any since you guys took them all," he said to Samantha. "So I had to give him a passkey. It's twenty-five bucks if he lost it."

"Lou, were you in Gina Davenport's office tonight?" Samantha asked him, no longer willing to wait until he got to the hospital.

"Yeah," he said. "Should have taken the stairs."

"What were you doing there?"

"I've got a client you're interested in."

"Jordan Hackett?" Samantha asked.

"She's the one," Mason answered.

"We think so too," Samantha said. "She confessed to the murder of Gina Davenport an hour ago."

"Should have taken the stairs," Mason said, closing his eyes.

Samantha was standing at the end of Mason's hospital bed when he woke the next morning. He had always liked the way she looked when they woke up together. Blond hair fanned across her pillow, green eyes grinning as she teased him about snoring. He liked watching her walk naked to the bathroom, her slender body catching rays of sunlight peeking through the shades. At first, they were more friends than lovers, the sex more needy than heartfelt. Then Samantha wanted the whole package, Mason pulling back when he couldn't give it to her, the friendship somehow surviving.

"Have you been here all night?" he asked her.

"Are you nuts? That's what nurses are for. How do you feel?"

Mason rubbed his stubbled face with both hands,

aware for the first time that his left arm was back in service. "I'd have to feel better to die, but at least I've got my health." He slipped his left arm out of the hospital gown and examined the bandage that was wrapped around his biceps.

"You sliced it deeply enough to bleed a bucket, but not enough to cut it off, according to the doctor. When you jumped off the elevator, you must have hit a nerve in your shoulder. Football players call it a stinger. It goes away and you're fine."

"How do you know about the elevator?" he asked.

"You mumbled enough on the way to the hospital that I could figure out some of what happened."

"You rode with me in the ambulance?"

"Don't get excited. I was just taking advantage of your condition to find out what happened before you decided not to tell me." She said it with a smile that covered her concern, though Mason knew she was telling the truth, just not the whole truth. "Here," she said, handing him a mirror, "take a look."

Mason groaned at the black eye he would carry around for the next week. "I guess that's from hitting my head when I jumped into the closet."

"Don't forget the bruised ribs. You had quite a ride. Fill me in on the details you left out while you were delirious."

"How did you find me?" Mason asked after telling her what had happened.

"When the elevator crashed, it ripped through a water line. We got a call from the utility company, searched the building, and found your blood leaking from under the door to the utility closet on the sixth floor. One of the cops called me because of the Davenport case. Smart guy. Wants to be a detective."

"Tell him I said thanks. What happened with the elevator?" he asked.

"It's almost as old as the building. They call it a drum elevator because the steel rope that pulls it up and down the shaft wraps around a drum in the basement where the controls are. It's not too complicated. There's a power switch that turns it on and off and an emergency release that turns it into an express. We called in an elevator expert to figure out why the system failed."

"Let me know, will you," Mason said. "How did you get Jordan Hackett to confess? Didn't she tell you I was representing her?"

"We're open twenty-fours a day. She came in, told the desk sergeant she killed Dr. Gina, and asked who she needed to talk to. I read her the *Miranda* spiel in front of two witnesses and she wrote it down."

"Wrote what down?"

"Dr. Gina and Jordan's father were having some tough contract negotiations. Gina wanted out so she could sign a better deal with a national radio syndication outfit from New York. Her father said no way. Gina said either she walks or Jordan finds a new shrink. Arthur Hackett called her bluff and Gina fired Jordan."

Mason sat up and swung his legs over the edge of the hospital bed. "Let me guess. Gina gave Jordan the bad news on Friday. Jordan freaks, throws something at the window, cracks it, and comes back Monday night to fire Dr. Gina."

"Bingo," Samantha said. "Watch your gown, big boy. There's a cool breeze blowing."

"Don't get excited," he said. "I'm not that glad to see you. I've just got to pee. Her story doesn't hold up. Why come back Monday night? She had the weekend to cool off. She wouldn't have known that Davenport was in her office. She was stuck out in the country with no car and she didn't have a key to get into the building."

Mason eased off the bed, wobbling enough that Samantha took his arm. "You okay, cowboy?"

"Peachy. Find my pants. I'm going home," he said as he staggered into the bathroom, his hospital gown flapping behind him.

"Nice butt," Samantha said as he closed the bathroom door. She handed him his pants when he came out. "Jordan says she called Dr. Gina and arranged to meet her that night. She borrowed a car and Gina let her in the building. They argued about Gina dropping her as a patient. Jordan ended the argument the old-fashioned way."

"I don't buy it," Mason said, pulling on his pants, his back to Samantha, who was staring out the window. Though they used to be lovers and could still tease each other, their days of watching each other get dressed were over.

"Why not? Not all your clients are innocent."

Mason winced as he put on his shirt, the pain in his ribs still fresh. "I talked to Jordan yesterday. We made an appointment for today. I told her not to talk to the cops again without me. Something happened and I'm going to find out what it was. How about giving me a lift back to my car."

"Not necessary. I called Harry a little while ago. Blues and Mickey picked up your car. Harry is waiting outside. He'll take you home. I've got other cases to solve. This one is over."

* * *

Harry drove an eight-year-old Suburban. He didn't need the space. He just liked driving a car that was as broad-shouldered as he was. Mason grunted at the effort of hoisting himself into the front passenger seat, but waved off Harry's offer of a boost.

"Damn," Mason said. "I feel like I've been kicked by a horse with all four feet."

Harry said, "Don't go to bed. You'll just freeze up and we'll have to chisel the spasms out of your muscles." He pulled a tissue from a box on the floor and wiped his eyes, then squinted at the stoplight that had just turned green. He waited until the driver behind him honked twice.

"I'm going," Harry muttered, wiping his eyes again.

"Your eyes okay?" Mason asked.

"They're fine," Harry answered. "Just these damn allergies."

Harry was not normally talkative, except about old cases he'd handled. Some baseball pitchers could recite every pitch they ever threw in a game, adding location, speed, and spin to the name of the opposing batter, the balls and strikes, and who won the battle. Harry was like that with cases he'd investigated, especially murder cases. Outside of that, he wasn't much for small talk. Mason often wondered what Harry and his Aunt Claire talked about. She must have tapped into Harry's other dimension. Mason envied them. They had been together as long as he could remember. Though they'd never married, they were as tightly bound as any couple he'd ever known.

Mason was certain that Samantha had briefed Harry as a professional courtesy, even though Harry was retired. Mason expected Harry to cross-examine him on the way home, but Harry didn't say a word. Mason appreciated the quiet ride. He would eventually use Harry as a sounding board to test different murder scenarios. At the moment, he was still digesting what Samantha had told him and wasn't ready to talk. Still, he wondered about Harry's allergies, especially since he couldn't remember the last time Harry had even sneezed.

Harry pulled in the driveway behind Mason's TR-6. Blues and Mickey had dropped it off but not waited around. As Mason got out of the car, Harry turned to him.

"One other thing," Harry said, as if they'd been talking the whole time.

"What's that?"

"Sam told me they checked that elevator the night Davenport was killed. There was nothing wrong with it. The certificate of inspection had been renewed a month ago."

Mason leaned against the open door, one foot on the ground, the other on the running board. "You think I should sue the elevator inspector?" Harry just looked at him. "No," Mason answered for him. "You think someone sabotaged the elevator because they knew I was in it? Did Samantha tell you that?"

"Something to think about," Harry said. "Remember what I told you. Don't go to bed."

Mason thought about Harry's advice as he stood under a hot shower. If his adventure in the elevator had been a murder attempt, Harry's warning about not going to bed was good advice. He'd better stay awake.

And he'd better take Trent Hackett more seriously.

Trent was the building manager, so he had access to the elevator control room and, probably, enough knowledge to make it happen. He gave Mason the key to Davenport's office and could count on Mason taking a ride. Since the elevator didn't stop on any other floors, Trent knew that no one else would be at risk. If Mason stayed off the elevator, Trent could fix it before anyone discovered what he'd done. Plus, Trent scored high on the freak-o-meter.

It was then that Mason remembered the video camera on the elevator. If he had escaped a murder attempt, the killer had to have known he was on the elevator. He called Samantha.

"What about the camera on the elevator?" he asked, skipping hello. "Where's the video?"

"Gone," she answered. "The monitor and the VCR is in the control room. There was no tape. Watch your back, Lou."

If Trent had tried to kill Mason, there was a good chance Jordan was innocent or Trent was guilty of something else that he was afraid Mason would uncover. The Hacketts were starting to look like a nuclear family in the midst of a runaway meltdown.

CHAPTER 8

Mason liked privacy. He liked shutting out the rest of the world when he prepared for trial or wrestled with the devil. All of which meant he hated jails and the claustrophobic cubicles reserved for prisoners to meet with their lawyers. Mason took the jailers at their word that his conversations with his clients were not recorded, but in a crowded corner of his heart he made room for distrust of cops, jailers, and prosecutors. It was enough to keep his jailhouse office hours short and meetings with his clients shorter.

He worried about innocent clients who were guilty of nothing except bad luck. He worried about clients who were innocent of the charge that landed them in jail, but were guilty of other offenses. He worried about clients who were guilty as charged. For each of these clients, he had cards to play, deals to make. Mason knew what to do with them. But a client who confessed to a crime Mason believed in his gut she hadn't committed was the client he worried about the most.

Jordan Hackett had spent the night in jail, long enough to drain her reservoir of anger and refill it with the sullen realization that she would spend the rest of her life wearing government-issued clothes and eating with a spoon she had to turn in after every meal. Her brown hair was grimy and she was wearing a dirt tattoo around her neck. She must have come straight from digging fence posts to surrender, Mason decided. He knew that took a lot of nerve, but not as much as taking her first prison shower. They'd let her stink for a few days, but force her to wash before her first court appearance.

They sat across from one another at a metal table scarred with initials and bolted to the floor. Jordan looked past Mason to the small window in the door, big enough for the eyes and nose of the deputy sheriff on the other side. She looked at her feet, clad in paper slippers, her heels sticking out past the outer edge of one-size-fits-all. She stuck her hands in her armpits, covering them with the billowing sleeves of her orange jumpsuit. She looked everywhere but at Mason, who watched and waited.

"What?" she said at last. "Is this the silent treatment from my lawyer? I don't have to go to jail for that. I can get it at home."

Mason said, "Why did you do it?"

Jordan tightened her grip on herself. "It's all in my confession. I thought you would have read it." She finally looked at him. "What happened to your eye?"

"I ran into a door," he said. "I'm not talking about the murder. I'm talking about the confession. Why did you do it without talking to me?"

"I didn't mean to hurt your feelings," she answered, tucking her chin to her chest, giving a cigarette butt on the floor her undivided attention.

"Cut the crap, Jordan. We made a deal yesterday. You don't talk to the cops without me. What happened?"

She stood, paced, sat back down. Assumed the position again. "After you left, I had my session with Terry. I told him what was going on. He told me I had to clear the decks if I was going to deal with my issues. Confessing was the way to do that, the way to get everything straight in my mind."

"Did he tell you what a great psychotherapy program they have in prison?"

She grabbed the edges of the table, whitening her knuckles before taking a breath and relaxing her grip. "Centurion says it was involuntary manslaughter at the worst. He says I may even get off with careless homicide and that I'll get probation."

"Did Centurion tell you that there's no such crime as careless homicide? Did he tell you that waiting three days after you had your argument with Gina Davenport to kill her is a textbook example of premeditation and a short course in first-degree murder? Did he tell you that you could get life without parole or death by lethal injection, depending on what the jury had for breakfast? Did he tell you that you should talk to a real lawyer, not some jailhouse lawyer like him, before you throw your life away?"

Jordan's cheeks hollowed with instant aging, her eyes bleeding tears. "Centurion said you would talk me out of it so you could drag the case out and plea-bargain after you collected your fee from my parents. He said this was better. He said it would come out the same and be over a lot faster."

"Jordan, yesterday you were digging postholes and making plans to sneak off with me for pizza and beer.

You were full of enough piss and vinegar to sterilize a swamp. You told me you were innocent, then you confessed. What gives?"

She wiped her nose with her sleeve. "Why are you so mad at me? What difference does it make to you?"

It was Mason's turn to stand. "Call me crazy, Jordan, but it pisses me off when a dope-dealing scam artist like Centurion Johnson and a snake-oil Dr. Feel Good like Terry Nix manipulate a screwed-up kid into confessing to a murder she didn't commit."

"Centurion isn't a dope dealer—at least, not anymore," she said. "And Terry helps me a lot. Besides, I did it."

"Why? Because Dr. Gina told you to get another therapist? Terry Nix was treating you too. You said he was helping you. Was he doing such a bad job that you had to kill Gina? Or was killing Gina part of Terry's clear-the-decks therapy?"

"You don't understand anything!"

Mason planted both hands on the table and leaned over her. "You're right. Help me understand."

Jordan pushed her chair back. "It's all in my confession. Dr. Gina used me to bargain with my father on her contract. My father used me. He said he was just calling Gina's bluff—like I was a poker chip in their fucking card game!" She bent over, her head in her lap, sobbing on folded arms. "Everyone uses me. It has to end."

She trembled, Mason placing a hand on her shoulder, Jordan jerking away like his touch was electrified, Mason letting her cry.

"What's your brother Trent have to do with all of this?" Mason asked when she lifted her head.

"Nothing," she said.

Mason picked up the legal pad he'd brought with him. He hadn't made any notes. "I'm not like the others," he said. "I'm not your brother or your parents. I'm not Centurion and I'm not Terry. I only want one thing from you."

"What?"

"The truth. Call me when you're ready."

Mason already had one conversation with Arthur Hackett that morning. Hackett had called as Mason was leaving for the county jail. Mason didn't need the phone. He could have opened his window and heard Hackett yelling from the Cable Depot. Mason let Arthur rant and promised a report after his meeting with Jordan.

Mason was more than a little jumpy as he rode the elevator to KWIN's offices, certain that his reaction was normal, doubting that Dr. Gina or her brethren had much experience with people who jumped off the roofs of elevators and lived to be spooked by the next ride. He thought about taking the stairs, telling himself that he could use the exercise, but he opted for the get-back-on-the-horse approach, not realizing he'd been holding his breath until he stepped out onto the eighth floor. Fresh crime-scene tape blocked the entrance to Dr. Gina's office, confirming Samantha's suspicion that Mason's elevator ride had not been an accident.

Arthur and Carol Hackett didn't have to say a word. Her bloodshot eyes and bloodless lips, his fiery eyes and puckered mouth, fixed in fury, condemned Mason as he crossed their threshold. They let him in and unloaded, questioning him at the same time, each oblivious to what the other was saying.

"How could you do this?" Carol asked.

"Mason, I'm not paying you to send my daughter to jail for the rest of her life! What in the hell am I paying you for?" added Arthur.

Mason suspected they'd spent their entire lives talking without listening to one another. He was certain they'd never heard much that Jordan had to say and probably tuned out Trent in self-defense.

"One at a time," Mason told them. "First, I didn't do anything to Jordan. She did it to herself, though she had help from your friends at Sanctuary. Second, you were paying me to keep your daughter out of jail, only now you're paying me to get her out. We're on the same side here, so let's focus on that for now."

Carol Hackett stalked out of the room, repeating the problem-solving approach she took at their last meeting. Arthur didn't bother apologizing for her this time. Mason was learning the family music. It was a classical piece composed of blame conducted with fingers pointed at everyone else.

Mason asked, "Was Gina Davenport trying to get out of her contract with you?"

"What if she was? What's that got to do with any of this?" Arthur asked.

"It's the story line in Jordan's confession, that's all," Mason said. "Dr. Gina threatened to cut off Jordan's treatment if you didn't let her out of her contract. You didn't think the good doctor was that bad, but she was. Last Friday, Gina told Jordan good-bye and why. Jordan didn't take it well and threw a brass paperweight at the window, leaving a nice long crack. After spending the weekend thinking it over—what the prosecutor calls premeditating—she called Dr. Gina and arranged to meet her Monday night so she could throw Gina out the window."

Arthur Hackett stood behind his desk chair, shielding himself from Mason's explanation. He folded his arms over the back of the chair, pulling it toward him, backing up until he slumped against the credenza along the wall.

"My God," he whispered, the enormity of Mason's description beginning to take hold. "I didn't think she would do it."

"Do what?" Mason asked.

"Both of them. Everything," Arthur said. "Gina had lost her own daughter. The poor girl killed herself. I never dreamt she would abandon Jordan over money. That's what it was all about—just money."

"And your daughter?"

Arthur shook his head. "Jordan has a temper," he said. "That's a little like saying a volcano makes smoke. But I always believed she could control herself if she wanted to."

Mason asked, "Is Jordan adopted?"

Arthur Hackett came out of his slump, raising his eyebrows. "Why do you ask?"

"There may be another angle to this. Was she adopted?"

Arthur pushed his desk chair away and stared out the window for a moment. "Yes. Trent's birth was very difficult. Carol couldn't have more children afterward. She didn't want another baby, but I did. We were living in St. Louis at the time. I was selling advertising for radio, just getting started in this business. Some young girl got herself pregnant and we adopted her baby." He shook his head, "We didn't know anything about the mother," he added as if that was a curse.

"You didn't like that?" Mason asked.

Hackett squared his shoulders. He was shorter than Mason, but broader, more full than fit, but powerful enough to throw Gina Davenport through the window.

"I like to know what I'm getting, that's all," Hackett said. "When Jordan started having so many problems, all I could think about was the mother—was she like that?"

"Did you ever try to find Jordan's birth mother?"

"No. We asked Gina if we should look for the mother in case she had a history of psychological problems. Gina said it wouldn't matter, that we had to deal with Jordan, not her mother."

"Do you have Gina's home phone number?"

"Of course, but don't expect much help from Robert—that's her husband."

"Why not?" Mason asked, though he was more interested in whether the number matched the one Abby had called.

"He's a painter, teaches at the Kansas City Art Institute."

"That's okay with me," Mason said. "I never got past paint-by-numbers."

"He's a drug addict," Arthur said. "Cocaine. Gina couldn't do anything with him. He was in and out of treatment centers all over the country. Cocaine is an expensive way to kill yourself." Arthur wrote the number on a slip of paper and handed it to Mason. "It's unlisted, but I guess that doesn't matter so much anymore."

Mason looked at the number. It didn't match Abby's. He was zero for three. "Do you recognize this phone number?" Mason asked Arthur as he wrote the number Abby had given him on the same paper.

"Where did you get this number?" Arthur asked, a tremor rippling through him.

"That's confidential for the moment. Whose number is it?"

"It's Jordan's cell-phone number. What's going on here, Mason? I'm paying you and I want to know."

Mason said, "I don't know. When I find out, I'll tell you if I can."

"You'll by God tell me period!" Hackett told him, pounding his desk with a fury, making Mason wonder whether Jordan's temper was the product of nature or nurture.

"Arthur," Mason said. "You're paying my fees, but you're not my client. I'll tell you what I can. Get used to it."

The ride back down the elevator was easier. Mason didn't hold his breath and turn blue, though he did breathe easier when he spun through the revolving door onto the sidewalk and into the midday sun of a perfect fall day. The Cable Depot had a heavy feel. He didn't know whether it was Gina's death or his near-death. Or whether it was the Hackett family imprint or the lingering ghosts of earlier tenants. The building had a way of laying cold hands on him and he was glad to be outside.

Mason knew that technically speaking, it was still summer, but he operated on a separate calendar he had devised in elementary school. It started the seasons on the first days of September, December, March, and June. It was a lot simpler than remembering the equinox and appealed to his optimistic off-balance logic.

Always too impatient for summer, he decided it should start on June 1. He was back in school by September 1, and that meant it was fall. December was too cold not to be winter. Best of all, his spring started on March 1 when everyone else was suffering through three more weeks of winter. His system was a child's invention that worked in an adult world. It was fall in Mason's world, the heat unseasonable.

There was a small park across the street with a pair of benches beneath a modest oak tree, broad enough for shade, open enough to mix in the sun. David Evans sat on one of the benches, watching Mason as he stood on the sidewalk, taking in the day. He caught Mason's eye with a wave, inviting Mason to join him.

Mason found Evans hard not to like. Evans, like Centurion Johnson, had the gift of schmooze. It was how they made people trust them. When they were caught, they used good humor and glad hands to lessen the blow. Evans had fought Mason hard in Max Coyle's case, representing himself and paying up only at the last moment. Throughout, he had never raised his voice at Mason or taken offense at Mason's harsh allegations. It was as if Evans wanted Mason to like him in spite of the fact that he had ripped off Mason's client.

Evans was in his mid-fifties, aging well, spending enough time in the gym and enough time touching up the gray to fool younger women and trusting investors, though not Mother Nature. He had more charm than good looks, but enough of both to slide by more on form than substance. He was a slick package.

"Lou," he said when Mason crossed the street. "It looks like we'll be on the same side this time. I prefer that since I can't afford fighting you again."

"That gives me great comfort, David, but how is it that we're on the same side?"

"I watch the news, Lou. Your client confessed to killing my client. Your job is to get her off. I can help you."

Mason looked down at Evans, whose return smile made Mason regret his next question. "How?"

"I know who did it."

CHAPTER 9

"Call a priest. I don't take confessions," Mason said.

"Lou, give me some credit. If I did it, I wouldn't confess to you until I hired you. I wouldn't want you telling the wrong people. Besides, you've already got a client and I don't need a lawyer."

"Okay," Mason said. "Solve the case for me."

"Sit down first," Evans said, patting the bench. "Enjoy the day."

Mason hesitated but sat. He suspected that Evans was playing him, but was interested in what he had to say.

"Excellent," Evans said. "Arthur Hackett did it."

Mason got up. "That's your best shot? The father did it and he's going to let his daughter take the fall?"

"Easy, easy," Evans said. "Just listen to me. I was negotiating with Arthur Hackett to get Gina out of her contract. She had an offer from a national network and a chance to own a piece of her show."

"Old news," Mason said as he turned away.

"Christ, man!" Evans said. "If you were in this big of a hurry in Max Coyle's case, I never would have had to pay you a cent!"

Mason sat back down. "Get to the point."

"Gina only had another year to go on her contract. Then she was gone. A radio station isn't like a baseball team. You can't trade your star player to avoid losing her in free agency. There was only one way for Hackett to get any value out of her."

"Kill her?" Mason asked.

"And collect on the life insurance policy he took out on her six months ago. Five million dollars is better than nothing."

Mason bit the inside of his lip to keep his mouth shut. He felt like a fish in Evans's barrel, unable to resist the bait.

Evans continued, pointing his finger at Mason like a rod, reeling him in. "You don't have to believe me, Lou. Ask Arthur. He took policies out on all the top talent, which at his station meant Gina and Max Coyle. Not that Max should be worried. He's too big for Arthur to throw him out the window."

"That doesn't explain why he would let his daughter go to jail."

"That's why he hired you. I'm certain Arthur didn't expect his daughter to confess."

"Have you told the police your theory?" Mason asked.

"Of course. I would rather Detective Greer interrogate me than you. She's much better looking."

"Why do you want to hang this on Arthur Hackett? Was Gina Davenport your last client?"

Evans laughed. "Nearly so, I'm afraid. You scared everyone else away. Gina was loyal. She understood that my problem with Max was bad timing in the stock market, not bad faith on my part."

"Six hundred and fifty thousand dollars is a lot to pay for something that wasn't your fault."

"Oh, don't tell me that, Lou. We both know cases get settled for all kinds of reasons. I didn't have insurance and I couldn't take the risk of a big punitive-damage verdict. You took advantage of my vulnerability. Don't gloat, especially when I'm trying to help you."

Mason had a sudden insight. "Gina gave you the money for the settlement, didn't she?"

"As I said, she was a loyal client and friend. She loaned me the money. We trusted each other."

"Enough that she let you manage the money in Emily's Fund. Twenty million dollars is a lot of trust. Where did Emily's Fund get that kind of money?"

Evans answered, enjoying the moment. "I can't take all the credit, Lou. After all, you don't think I'm much of an investment expert, but I made the right picks in the market. The seed money came from the sale of Gina's books, her personal appearance fees, things like that. Gina was financially set when Emily died, and insisted the money go into the foundation."

"Did you tell Samantha Greer about the settlement money and your involvement in Emily's Fund?"

"I am not stupid, despite what you and Max might think. I told Detective Greer everything. I even gave her the records for Emily's Fund, and I'll give a set to you if that will make you happy. Gina Davenport was my friend and my client. What do you do when your friends and clients are murdered?"

Evans rose without waiting for Mason to answer, patting Mason on the shoulder, sauntering away, leaving

Mason riveted to the bench, uncertain whether he was ashamed of himself or overwhelmed by Evans's performance. Two birds swooped down to the sidewalk, snapping up crumbs, Mason wondering if he was another one of David Evans's pigeons.

A navy-blue Ford Crown Victoria pulled up to the curb in front of Mason's bench. The window on the passenger side descended into the door panel and the driver said, "Get in."

Mason smiled. "Yes, officer." He slid into the passenger seat. "Why do cops all drive Crown Vics?" he asked Samantha Greer. "They stick out like sore thumbs. How can you ever go undercover, especially with that thing sticking out of your armpit?"

Samantha was wearing a lightweight jacket that barely concealed her shoulder holster. When they first started going out, Mason teased her about the .45-caliber pistol she carried. She said the smaller guns that some detectives wore behind their backs didn't have the stopping power she wanted and were harder to get at. She wasn't a big woman and wanted the bad guys to know she packed a serious weapon.

"Unlike a TR-6, a Crown Vic can take a bullet and still do a hundred twenty miles an hour. You still look like hell. Are you feeling okay?"

"Not bad for a guy who sucker-punched himself. The worst part is that it doesn't make a good story. I sound like I was too stupid to live."

"No, it sounds like you're in it for the wrong reason."

"What's that supposed to mean?" Mason asked.

"You're like a cop that always wants to be the first one

through the door, not because he wants to bag the bad guys but because he wants the jolt of taking the chance that he won't make it through. That's a dangerous way to practice law, Lou. You're not that good."

Mason stared out the window, not answering because he didn't have an answer, afraid that Samantha was more right than wrong, not fully understanding why she was right. He'd stepped over a lot of lines in the past few years. Some of them small, like slipping into an office and snooping around. Some of them huge, like killing a man, even if it was in self-defense. Some of them hard to measure, like inviting violence into his life. He couldn't remember when that murky world became normal.

"Mickey calls it diving into the dark water," Mason said.

"Yeah? Well, do me a favor. Don't end up dead in the water. Let's get some pasta for lunch."

She drove east to Walnut, then north to the City Market, where they parked. Balzano's was an Italian diner where they were both regulars. The same family had owned it for three generations. Josephine, the matriarch, had taken it personally when Mason had told her that he and Samantha weren't getting married. She hugged both of them when they walked in, telling them that lunch was on the house if they were back together.

"Separate checks," Samantha told her, sending Josephine away, shaking her head in disappointment.

Mason asked Samantha, "What's up? Or were you just in the neighborhood?"

"Would you prefer that I was in the neighborhood or that I was checking up on you like I do all my old boyfriends?"

Josephine returned with plates of moscattioli and meat sauce, setting them down without a word.

"She's mad at us," Mason said. "My preference doesn't matter. You showed up right after David Evans left. Were you staking us out?" he asked with a grin.

"David Evans is a treat," she said. "He was in my office the morning after Gina Davenport was killed. It's nice that everyone has been so cooperative in this investigation. The killer confesses. The victim's lawyer rats out the killer's father. Very nice."

"Why didn't you look at Arthur Hackett for the murder?"

"We did. Evans's story is as good as any other, but it doesn't beat a confession that matches the physical evidence. We took elimination prints from Hackett, even though we expected to find his prints in Davenport's office. And we did."

"He's got motive and opportunity," Mason said.

Samantha said, "And a daughter whose fingerprints were found on the window frame, and whose hair and clothing fibers were found on the body and who conveniently confessed."

Mason hadn't seen the police reports and forensic analysis yet. Normally, he wouldn't get copies until just before the preliminary hearing. Samantha was cutting him some slack, and not just for old times' sake. She was doing it so he would know what a strong case the prosecutor had.

"But the confession isn't reliable. She's been under treatment—" Mason said.

"Lou," Samantha interrupted. "Save it. I'm not your audience. Besides, we've got a witness that places her at the scene."

Mason stopped sprinkling Parmesan cheese on his pasta. "Who?"

"Remember the homeless guy in the Channel 6 videotape? Earl Luke Fisher. The bench you were sitting on is his master bedroom. He ID'd Jordan. Says that he saw her park a Mercedes a couple of blocks away and let herself in the front door."

"That contradicts Jordan's confession. She says that Gina let her in."

"It's not a perfect world, Lou."

"What about Evans? Gina Davenport supposedly loaned him six hundred and fifty thousand dollars. Plus he was managing twenty million dollars in the foundation Gina set up in memory of her daughter."

"He signed a promissory note with a market rate of interest. The foundation's books are clean and so is Evans. He and Gina had been friends since they lived in St. Louis twenty years ago. He may have even been in love with her for all I know."

"Maybe they were in love," Mason said. "Maybe they were having an affair and Gina's husband found out. I hear he has a drug problem. Don't you think he could have gotten high and killed her?" Mason regretted the desperate tone of his questions, but he was running out of options.

"Robert Davenport is a recovering drug addict, I'll give you that. Someone called in an anonymous tip that Dr. Gina was dealing drugs out of her office. I talked to the narcotics detectives. They thought it was bullshit except for the husband, who's been busted a couple of times, but nothing stuck. They didn't have time to check it out before she was killed. We did find a stash of cocaine in her office."

"When did the call come in?"

"Saturday morning before Gina was killed."

"So maybe she was dealing drugs or at least supplying her husband. Maybe that had something to do with her death."

"Maybe. But not likely. Look, no case happens in a vacuum. People lead messy lives that crisscross in strange ways. That doesn't make them murderers. It just makes them screwed up. Your client confessed because she's guilty. That's not why I was parked outside the Cable Depot watching you make nice with David Evans."

"The elevator," Mason said.

Samantha nodded. "Our expert tells us that there was nothing wrong with the elevator. Somebody hit the switches that disconnected the power and released the emergency brake. What have you done that would make someone want to kill you?"

"Today?" he asked. Samantha didn't laugh. "Okay," he said. "Other than today, I don't know. I've been in this case for forty-eight hours. That's a little soon for people to start hating me enough to want to kill me."

"Keep joking," she told him, "and you'll shorten the time it takes."

"If I was the intended victim, the killer would have had to know that I was on the elevator, have access to the controls, and know how to cause the accident. That should narrow the field."

"There was a security camera on the elevator. Anyone watching the monitor would have known you were there," Samantha said.

"And the videotape is missing," Mason said.

"Gone," Samantha said, spooning the last of her pasta.

"Have you talked with Trent Hackett? He gave me the passkey. He's the building manager and he's a freak. We didn't get off on the right foot."

"He had access, but he says he was at the movies and he has a ticket stub to prove it."

Mason asked, "Anybody vouch for him?"

"He was alone."

"If that's supposed to make me feel better, it doesn't."

"It's not. It's supposed to keep you out of the dark water."

"So which case are you investigating? Gina Davenport's murder or the attempt to kill me?"

Samantha twirled the last strands of pasta around her spoon. "The Davenport case is the prosecuting attorney's problem now. I'm working the elevator."

Mason watched as she finished her pasta. Her appetite was fine. His was gone. Harry always talked about the importance of keeping his personal life separate from his cases. He wasn't always able to do it. Samantha had been trained the same way. Saying that she was working the elevator rather than trying to find out who wanted to kill him was her way of drawing the line. She wiped a fleck of sauce that had splattered onto the butt of her gun. Mason was glad it was a big gun.

CHAPTER 10

Mason popped a Modern Jazz Quartet CD into his office stereo and opened the cabinet doors covering his dry-erase board. Listening to Milt Jackson work the xylophone keys helped clear his mind. He was a classic jazz fan uninterested in digitized, techno-driven sound. Basie, Peterson, Coltrane, and Monk were better company.

He wrote Arthur Hackett's name beneath the *Winners and Losers* column, putting *$5 million* next to Arthur's name, and drew a line connecting the money to the winners' side of the ledger. Next, he added David Evans's name to the losers' column.

Trent Hackett belonged in the losers' column on general principles, but that column was for people who lost something valuable as a result of Dr. Gina's death. It wasn't for people who were just losers. Instead he added a column titled *Connections?* and put Trent's name at the top. He drew lines from Trent's name to Jordan's and Arthur's, adding one to Gina's labeled *broken win-dow.*

Robert Davenport's name was next. He wrote *drugs* across the line connecting the widower to his mate, adding another line with a question mark at the end leading to Centurion Johnson, the only past or present drug dealer on the board. Mason didn't know where Robert Davenport got his drugs. He doubted it was from his wife. Which meant that someone other than Gina had put the drugs in her office. The best reason to do that was to discredit Gina. The only person on the board who would benefit from that was Arthur Hackett. Arthur could have blackmailed Gina into staying, trumping her play of the Jordan card.

Mason drew a line between Arthur Hackett's and Robert Davenport's names, wondering if Robert provided the drugs to Arthur. Even if Mason was right about that, it didn't explain where the drugs came from. Mason drew a line connecting Arthur Hackett and Centurion Johnson, trying that conspiracy theory on for size.

Mason was guessing at most of these conclusions and stretching for others. It was like that at the beginning of a case. He had to consider every possibility because he didn't know enough to exclude any of them.

When he finished, he stepped back to gain a better perspective. Without realizing it, he had connected every name on the board to at least two other names and connected all of them to Gina Davenport. If that was progress, he was in trouble.

Claire Mason opened the door to his office, interrupting his graffiti analysis of the case. She was wearing one of the severe, dark suits she wore year-round, regardless of weather. It wasn't that she was severe or dark. She was the opposite. She was large, and larger than life, but oblivious to fashion, preferring clothes that were functional and durable.

"Except for that shiner, you don't look too bad to me," she said, taking a seat on Mason's sofa and motioning him to join her.

"Don't ask me to take my clothes off. I look like the Kansas City Chiefs used me for a tackling dummy."

"From what I hear, you've got the dummy part down right."

"You can join the chorus singing that tune," Mason told her.

Claire studied the dry-erase board. "I'm glad Abby Lieberman's name isn't on there. I was afraid she was somehow involved when she told me about calling Gina Davenport."

"Abby told me about the call," Mason said. "The phone number was for Jordan Hackett's cell phone."

"Why did Gina Davenport answer the phone?" Claire asked.

"Either she had Jordan's phone or the phone had been programmed to forward calls to Gina's number. I'll ask Jordan."

"That sounds like a lot of trouble. Why not just give Gina's phone number to Abby?"

"Because that wouldn't have linked Gina, Abby, and Jordan together."

Claire said, "It still doesn't make sense. Neither Abby nor Gina knew that Abby was calling Jordan's cell-phone number. How do any of them make the connection?"

Mason shook his head. "Got me." He returned to the board, adding Abby's name with lines drawn to Gina Davenport and Jordan Hackett. "Jordan was adopted.

Someone wants Abby to believe that Jordan is her daughter and that Gina Davenport knew that. Don't ask me why." Mason added lines connecting Abby to Arthur Hackett.

"What a mess," Claire said. "When is Jordan's arraignment?"

"Tomorrow morning, nine o'clock."

"You want my advice, Lou? Take the rest of the day off," his aunt said. "You're too tired to see clearly."

Mason shuddered with weariness. He hadn't slept much in two days. That was no way to prepare for an arraignment. "Okay," he said. "I'm going home. Speaking of seeing clearly—what's wrong with Harry's eyes?"

Claire stood, brushing her suit and pursing her lips. "Have you asked him?"

"Yeah. He said it was allergies and the man doesn't know how to sneeze. The other night at the restaurant, you were wiping his eyes. He was wiping them when he drove me home from the hospital. Plus, he was squinting like Mr. Magoo at the traffic lights and road signs."

Mason knew his aunt wasn't capable of deception. She would rely on privilege and confidences to withhold information, but she wasn't afraid to give bad news. She gave it and took it straight on, like everything else in life.

"Come on, Claire," Mason said. "It's you, me, and Harry. No secrets."

Claire nodded. "You're right. Harry has macular degeneration. It's an irreversible disease with no cure that destroys the central vision. He won't go blind, but his visible world will shrink in bits and pieces until he can't drive, read, or see my face across the kitchen table. So far, he's having trouble with small print and distances."

Mason exhaled like a punctured tire. "Jesus Christ," he said.

"Not available. Harry already asked," Claire said. "The doctors use lasers to slow things down and they've got some other new procedures that might help. The disease kind of limps along, then eventually speeds up. Harry doesn't like to talk about it, so don't go overboard the next time you see him. Good luck tomorrow."

Mason was turning off the light in his office when the phone rang.

"Can you come see me?" Jordan Hackett asked.

"Sure," Mason said. "It's four o'clock. I'll be there in twenty minutes."

The drive to the county jail was quick, but like a power nap, the top-down ride gave Mason a boost. He finger-tapped a light beat on the steering wheel, dividing his thoughts between Jordan and Harry. He hoped she would tell him something he could use, while hoping that he would be able to do the same for Harry.

Jordan had showered but not slept. The dirt was gone, but the circles under her eyes were as dark as his black eye. Her cheeks had flattened, and her body folded in-ward from the shoulders, like she was trying to disap-pear into herself.

"I want to get out of here," she said.

They were in the same room as before, the light dull, the paint bleak. A perfect match for Jordan's jailhouse patina.

"We'll see the judge tomorrow morning at your ar-raignment. I'll ask him to release you on bail."

"Will he let me go?"

"Maybe. It's a high-profile case, so there's always po-
litical pressure for the prosecutor to oppose bail. Your
history of violence and your confession may make it
tough."

"What if," she began in a small voice, "I didn't do it?"

Mason scooted his chair back, the uneven legs scratching the vinyl floor. He walked around the tiny room, stopping at the corner farthest from the door, feeding his
latent paranoia that someone was listening. "That would
make you a liar but not a murderer. Which are you?"

Jordan watched Mason circle and followed him into
the corner, standing close, her hand on his arm. In another setting, the gesture would have been sexual. Here,
it was need.

"A liar. I didn't do it."

Mason kept his voice low, more to pull her in than to
keep from being overheard. He tested her with the pre-
liminaries. "Were you there that night?"

"Yes."

"Were you there when Gina was killed?"

"Yes."

"The videotape shows a shadow in the window immediately after the murder. Was that you?"

"Yes."

Jordan's answers came easily, without nervous tics in
the corners of her eyes and mouth to betray her. Her
breathing was calm and steady, her grip on his arm assured, not panic-tight. Mason believed her.

"Did you see it happen?"

She let go of his arm, covering her chest with both of
hers, and turned away. "No," she said, her back to him.

Mason spun her around, his hands on her shoulders.
"Did you see it happen?" he repeated.

She grabbed his wrists, pinching pressure points that shot bolts of pain the length of his arms. He winced and let go. She cast his arms away like empty husks. "I told you," she said. "I didn't see it happen."

Mason crossed his arms, rubbing both biceps, trying to regain the upper hand with a woman who said she needed him in one instant and dismissed him like he was a nuisance in the next.

"What did you see?"

"Nothing except for the broken window. Then I saw Gina's body on the ground and those TV people pointing the camera at me. I was afraid what would happen if anyone saw me there, so I left the way I came, on the elevator."

"A witness saw you enter the building on the ground floor. The elevator only runs from the basement to Dr. Gina's office. Why did you go up that way?"

"My father gave me a key to the building a long time ago. I didn't have a key to Gina's office, but I wouldn't need one if I used the elevator."

"Weren't you meeting Gina? Wouldn't she have let you in?"

"I didn't know she was going to be there."

"Then what were you doing there?" Jordan sat down again, thumping her balled fist on the metal table. Mason sat across from her and covered her fist with his hands. "I need to know," he said.

Jordan gnawed at her lower lip and pulled her fist away. Mason clamped his hands around hers, yanking her toward him. She was meaner but he was stronger. "I need to know," he said again.

"You're hurting me."

"I'm sorry," he said, feeling small but uncertain of any other way to break through to her. "Tell me."

She glared at him until he released her, leaving her rubbing her wrist, Mason feeling like a bully, his arms still tingling. They were finding a common language that he wasn't anxious to learn.

"Gina didn't take notes during a session. She always said that she didn't want to have anything she might have to turn over to the insurance companies. Sometimes I gave her stuff I wrote and she kept it. After she said she wouldn't treat me any more, I wanted it back. I knew where she kept it and I took it and got out of there."

"What did you write about, Jordan?"

She squirmed in her chair, glancing around, looking for a way out, finding none, dipping her head, letting her hair cover her face, tugging on it like a mask. She hid beneath her hair, her breathing growing ragged, finally throwing her head back, slapping both palms against the table. The metal sang, bringing the guard to the window in the door. Mason waved him off.

"Mr. Mason," she said through clenched teeth. "It took eight years of therapy with Gina Davenport before I could tell her. I don't know you. I didn't even hire you and you want me to tell you."

"You're wrong, Jordan," he said. "It's you who wants to tell me."

She clutched her neck with one hand as it reddened with blood creeping up to her chin. She ran her other hand through her hair. Her eyes grew large and wet. "Okay, okay, okay," she said, talking herself down from the emotional ledge she was standing on. "When I was thirteen, my brother raped me. My parents didn't believe me when I told them. I put it all in my diary. The day it happened and every day after, when my parents called me a liar and my brother called me a slut when they weren't around. I told Gina everything a couple of weeks ago and gave her the diary."

Mason felt the walls close in around them, the air too thick with Jordan's shame for them to breathe. He understood with crippling clarity the source of her rage. He wanted to comfort her, but he didn't know how. All he knew was that there wasn't enough room on his dry-erase board for these new lines.

"Did your parents know that you told Gina?"

"We had a session with my parents. They said the same thing they always said. That I made it up. They even said there must have been something wrong with my birth mother and I inherited it."

"What did Dr. Gina say?"

"She said that she believed me and that she was obligated to report cases of child abuse to the police. My father threatened to sue her. My mother stormed out of the room, like she always does, like it was my fault."

"Did your father bring it up again after that session?"

"Last weekend. We had a real screamer. I was mad because Gina wouldn't see me anymore. That's when he told me about Gina's contract and that she wouldn't keep treating me unless he let her out of her contract. Then he started hollering at me about the rape story, saying that Gina was going to report Trent to the police if he didn't let her go."

"Did Trent know that Gina had threatened to turn him in to the cops?"

"I don't talk to the little worm," Jordan said. "You'll have to ask my parents."

"Why after all of that did you confess to killing Dr. Gina?"

"Terry Nix caught me when I came back to Sanctuary.

I'd broken curfew. I was pretty shook up and I told him what had happened. I showed him my diary. Terry said my brother probably killed Gina, just like you said. Terry said my real problem was that my parents didn't save me from my brother. If I confessed, they'd have to choose between me and Trent. He said they'd choose me this time."

Mason clasped his hands behind his neck, stretching his back and neck muscles. He didn't know whether Jordan was still telling the truth, but as long as she believed it, his representation of her had just gotten more complicated.

"Your father is paying my fees, but I can't take any more money from him. He covered up the rape. Trent may have killed Gina to keep the rape story from coming out and your father could be covering up for him again."

Jordan wiped her eyes. "I can't afford to pay you. I don't have any money of my own."

"Don't worry, the court will appoint me to represent you. My hourly rate goes down but the friendly service stays the same," he said with a smile.

"You believe me?"

Mason clasped her shoulders. "I believe you." At the moment, he knew it was more important that she believe him than that he believe her. "I need to know something else. It may not be important. Did you program your cell phone to forward your calls to Gina Davenport?"

She furrowed her brow. "Why would I do that?"

"I couldn't begin to guess," he answered. "Where's your phone?"

"I lost it. I had it with me when I left Sanctuary last Friday. I must have put it down somewhere because I didn't have it when I got back Friday afternoon."

"Where were you last Friday?"

"Terry Nix brought me in for my appointment with Gina. That's when she told me she wouldn't treat me anymore, but she wouldn't say why. She said I should talk to my father. I stopped at the radio station to talk to him, but he wouldn't tell me anything. Then Terry took me home. I don't understand what this is about."

Mason asked, "Have you ever tried to find your birth mother?"

Jordan shook her head. "My parents always blamed my problems on my birth mother. I used to hear my dad tell my mom that they didn't get the pick of the litter with me. I never thought about looking for my birth mother. I was afraid my parents might be right."

"What if they were wrong?" Mason asked.

"I was afraid of that too," she said.

CHAPTER 11

Courtrooms have personalities, Mason thought as he made his way to the counsel table in front of Associate Circuit Court Judge Joe Pistone's bench. Pistone's courtroom reminded him of a hundred-year-old saloon, where the floor had absorbed lifetimes of blood, booze, and spit, sagging from perpetual fatigue, resigned to the next spilled fluid. Judge Pistone was well matched to his courtroom, having sentenced himself to a life term in associate circuit court, first as a lawyer, then as a judge. Mason bet he was gray-haired and shoulder-hunched at birth, holding his mother in contempt the first time she burped him.

Mason felt as worn as the floorboards in the saloon. His body creaked like it had been trampled on. His eye looked like a doorstop. He ignored Sherri Thomas and her cameraman, who had set up shop in the hallway outside the courtroom. He smiled with unfelt good nature at the jabs from other lawyers who asked if he'd gotten the license number of the truck that hit him, or if the other guy looked worse than Mason.

He was hopeful that Jordan's arraignment would be brief and routine. He would waive formal reading of the charge, enter a plea of not guilty, and ask for bail. The prosecutor would demand bail in six figures, at which point he knew hope would go out the window like Gina Davenport if Arthur Hackett made good on his threat of the night before.

Mason had called Hackett after his jailhouse meeting with Jordan. He had to talk with Hackett about Jordan's rape story, and tell Hackett that he couldn't let him pay his fees any longer. Mason also wanted to see if Hackett would choose between his children again, defending his son, condemning his daughter.

Their meeting had been brief, more of a monologue delivered by Mason to a stone-faced audience of one. Hackett had absorbed Mason's report without comment, save one question.

"Do you believe her?" he asked Mason.

"It doesn't matter what I believe. She believes it. I've got to investigate it. That means your son is a possible suspect. I can't take any more of your money."

"You don't have to," Hackett said. "You're fired."

Mason had been too tired to remind Hackett that Jordan was his client, not him. An uneasy night's sleep hadn't soothed the kinks out of Mason's body or mind as he waited for the deputies to bring in his client and introduce her to Judge Pistone.

Rachel Firestone stood in the far corner of the courtroom. She had passed on covering Jordan's case, as he thought she would. Her impish smile framed by her molten red hair boosted his spirits from across the room.

Abby Lieberman joined her, giving Mason a slight, waist-high wave that he grabbed like a lifeline, before she huddled with Rachel like co-conspirators.

Mason was trying to figure out what they were up to when someone bumped into the back of his chair, apologized, and slid into the seat next to his.

"Sorry, Lou," said Brandon Potter.

Potter was a grizzled criminal defense lawyer who ruled the courtroom in his youth, drank his way through mid-life, and was plea-bargaining his way to retirement.

"Goddamn Pistone," Potter muttered. "I can't wait for that bastard to die. I swear his favorite words are 'bail denied.' "

Before Mason could commiserate with Potter, a trio of sheriff's deputies ushered a platoon of prisoners into the courtroom, shackles rasping against their ankles, slapping against the chairs in the jury box where they were seated, Jordan on the end of the front row, back ramrod-straight, jaw clamped. Rage made for good posture, Mason thought as he watched her.

Jordan searched the courtroom, finding her parents in the second-to-the-last row on the opposite side from Rachel and Abby. Centurion Johnson and Terry Nix were seated behind Arthur and Carol Hackett. Jordan nodded in their direction, Mason wondering which of them Jordan was glad to see.

Judge Pistone processed the first three cases, keeping his head down, as he always did, not looking at the lawyers or the defendants as he set bail and scheduled trials.

"State v. Hackett," the judge announced. "State your appearances."

"The State appears by Alan Walker, assistant prosecuting attorney."

Mason hadn't dealt with Walker previously, but knew he was a good lawyer since Patrick Ortiz had hired him. Since being elected prosecuting attorney, Ortiz had upgraded his staff with career prosecutors. Unlike his predecessor, who was more politician than prosecutor, Ortiz was all prosecutor, all the time. He required the same from the lawyers who worked for him. Mason wouldn't get any breaks.

Mason rose to announce his appearance, surprised that Brandon Potter rose alongside him. He was more surprised when Potter joined him in telling Judge Pistone they were representing Jordan Hackett, their duet bringing the judge's head up.

"You gentlemen rehearse that before you came down here?" he asked, frowning with disappointment when no one in the audience laughed. Judge Pistone could kill a punch line just by letting the words collect in his mouth.

"Your Honor—" Mason began.

"He is no longer representing Miss Hackett," Potter said, interrupting Mason. "The family retained me last night after Mr. Mason quit the case. I wasn't able to reach Mr. Mason to inform him of the change in counsel."

"Gee, Brandon," Mason said. "You were sitting right next to me while we were waiting for this case to be called. You couldn't have been any closer to me if you were doing a lap dance."

The spectators laughed and Judge Pistone gaveled them into silence, reminding Mason that he had broken one of the cardinal rules of the courtroom—never be funnier than the judge.

"Okay, Counselors," Judge Pistone said. "Who's it going to be?"

Mason beat Potter out of the blocks. "Your Honor, the defendant's father has been paying my fees on behalf of his daughter. Yesterday, I told him that I couldn't accept any further payments from him, but I didn't quit the case. Jordan Hackett is my client, not her father. My client is indigent and I ask the Court to appoint me as her counsel."

"If I may, Your Honor," Potter began.

"You may not, Mr. Potter," Judge Pistone replied. "Miss Hackett, which of these two lawyers do you want to defend you?"

Jordan looked at her parents. Carol Hackett hid behind dark glasses, concealing her response. Arthur Hackett burned his unspoken demand with a steel-eyed glare. Behind them, Centurion Johnson opened his beaming smile for business, holding up one hand, the thumb and forefinger in the shape of an *L*.

"I want Mr. Mason," she said. "But I don't have any money and I don't have a job."

"Very well, Miss Hackett," Judge Pistone said, banging his gavel like an auctioneer. "Mr. Mason it is, for fifty dollars an hour, courtesy of the taxpayers."

Brandon Potter shrugged off the defeat, mentally dividing his fee by the cost of a fifth of gin, and left the courtroom. Mason waited for Potter to exit, punctuating his victory.

"We'll waive reading of the charges, Your Honor, and enter a plea of not guilty. We request a reasonable bail. The defendant is a lifelong resident, not a flight risk or a danger to others. She surrendered voluntarily. She needs psychological counseling she can't get in jail."

Judge Pistone asked, "What's your position, Mr. Walker."

"The defendant confessed to killing Gina Davenport. She is charged with first-degree murder with aggravating circumstances. If convicted, she'll be sentenced to life without parole or death by lethal injection. She shouldn't get bail at all. If she does, the State insists on a million dollars."

"Mr. Walker," Judge Pistone said. "I'm the only one who insists on anything in this courtroom. Everybody else asks. Bail is set at three hundred thousand dollars. Mr. Mason, can your client post bail?"

Mason looked first at Jordan, then her father. Arthur Hackett rose from his pew, took his wife by the arm, and left the courtroom. "I don't know," he said.

"Excuse me, Your Honor," Rachel Firestone said. "May I have a word with Mr. Mason?"

"Don't tell me the *Kansas City Star* is going into the bail bond business, Ms. Firestone."

"No, sir. We're sticking to newspapers," Rachel said as she approached the rail that divided the lawyers from the spectators, leaned over, and whispered to Mason.

"The bail is taken care of. Get Jordan out of here," Rachel said.

"Mind telling me who her fairy godmother is?" Mason asked.

"More like mother than fairy godmother," she answered, hiking her thumb at Abby and handing Abby's business card to Mason.

Mason took a deep breath. "I wouldn't put my money on that quite yet."

"It's not your money, Counselor."

Abby stared at Jordan, biting her lip and holding her elbows in her palms. Nothing complicates a family reunion like murder, Mason thought. "We can post the bond," he told the judge.

"Very well. Given the defendant's history of psychological problems, I'll require that she be supervised as a condition of her bail. Who will be responsible for her?" Judge Pistone asked.

"I'll take her," Centurion Johnson said, rising slowly so everyone had time to turn around. "She was living at Sanctuary when she asked me if she should turn herself in. I told her that the courts and police would do the right thing and I was right. You let me take her back to Sanctuary, Judge, and I'll make sure she stays put until you're ready for her to come back. And believe me, Judge, I know how to find the courthouse."

Judge Pistone rapped his gavel again, silencing the crowd, who were thrilled with the show they'd seen.

"The Court is very familiar with both you and Sanctuary, Mr. Johnson. Any objections, Mr. Mason?"

Mason looked at Jordan, whose grin was all the answer he needed. "None. I do want to make one thing clear on the record, however. Jordan Hackett is innocent. She recants her confession."

"Save it for the preliminary hearing, Mr. Mason, which I'm setting for two weeks from today." Judge Pistone said, his head down. "Next case."

Mason caught up to Abby and Rachel on the sidewalk outside the courthouse. Centurion Johnson was holding a press conference inside, keeping the reporters from chasing Mason.

"Nice closing, Lou," Rachel said. "Jordan Hackett is innocent. She recants her confession. Very good. I'd lead with it if I was writing the story."

Mason said, "Thanks. Tell your editor anyway. Make sure he spells recants correctly." He took Abby by the arm, "We need to talk," he said, leading her away.

"Hey," Rachel yelled.

"Alone," Mason said over his shoulder.

They stopped at the corner of 12th and Oak. A city bus wheezed to a stop and a dozen people climbed out, stepping around and between them, leaving them to decipher each other's body language. Mason's hands on his hips said he was serious. Abby's cocked head, chin in her hand, one finger over her lips, said she was amused that he was so serious. Their eyes never left one another, signaling more than either would say on the street.

"Abby, that was a very generous and dumb thing to do."

"Because she might not be my daughter?"

"Because she's a head case charged with murder living with a con man who was a dope dealer in his last job."

"You said she was innocent. Who's the con man now?"

"That's different. A trial starts before the jury ever sits down in the box. You're asking for trouble. What if she's not your daughter? What if she is your daughter and she's a murderer?"

"Then she needs me."

"She doesn't even know you. You show up out of the blue and say let's catch up after twenty-one years, what do you think is going to happen? Jordan is filled with more anger at her parents and the world than you can imagine. You think she's going to throw a welcome-home party for you? Wrong. You'll be her next lightning rod. As far as Jordan's concerned, you're the woman who abandoned her and left her to be raised by wolves.

She'll be so pissed at you, she'll jump bail just to screw you out of the three hundred grand."

Abby's face began to tremble, her finger sliding off her lips as her mouth crumbled. "I did abandon my daughter. Every day since they took her away from me, I told myself that it was the right thing to do, but it was a lie. Giving my daughter up was a horrible thing to do. If Jordan's my daughter, I won't abandon her again."

Mason ran his fingers through his hair, tilted his head skyward, more to relieve the tension in his neck than to find a sign from above, though he wouldn't have turned down the sign.

"We'll get a DNA test. It only takes about ten days to get the results. Then you'll know."

Abby shook her head. "No. Not yet. You're right about the timing. Just tell Jordan that a friend posted the bond."

"It may not be that simple," Mason said. "You told the cops about your call to Gina Davenport. The phone number was for Jordan's cell phone. If the cops don't know that yet, they'll figure it out eventually. Someone was trying to connect you, Gina, and Jordan. I don't know who and I don't know why. But I do know one thing. The courtroom is the wrong place for Jordan to find out that you are her mother."

CHAPTER 12

Family ties come with more knots than any sailor ever tied, Mason thought as he drove south from the courthouse toward the Kansas City Art Institute. Even his truncated family entwined him with love, duty, debt, and regret, among other assets and liabilities. He hadn't shown any talent for family building during his marriage to Kate, and couldn't imagine trying to salvage a mother-and-child reunion from the lost and found, as Abby was determined to do.

He'd asked Rachel once how she felt about missing out on creating her own nuclear family.

"Only seven percent of households still fit the two-parent Mom-stays-at-home-with-the-kids-while-Dad works profile. Everyone else is blending and separating. I figure the straight world is missing out on my world, not the other way around," she told him.

Robert Davenport was the only member of anyone's family who'd skipped the arraignment. Mason wanted to know why and he wanted to know how cocaine ended up in Gina Davenport's office since that was her husband's drug of choice. The trail that tied this case together, Mason suspected, was sprinkled with white powder.

Mason found Robert in his studio, a high-ceilinged, bare-walled box of a room, pungent with paint thinner and littered with easels and canvases. He walked in as Robert was putting the finishing touches on a nude model—without brushes or paint. The model, a young girl with broad hips, Earth Mother breasts, and hair down to the middle of her back, stood on a low platform, holding Robert to her nipple as he grappled with her bottom, his back to Mason. The girl giggled at Mason and clutched Robert's head tightly to her.

"Which one of you gets extra credit for that?" Mason asked.

Robert shoved the girl away from him and she stumbled off the pedestal, still giggling as she landed bottoms-up on a beanbag.

"Who the hell are you?" Robert demanded.

He was all elbows and joints, his bony arms sticking out of his paint-splattered T-shirt like sticks on an all-day sucker. He needed rocks in his pockets to keep anchored in a stiff breeze. A three-day growth of his salt-and-pepper beard rounded out his cocaine-diet glow.

"Lucky for you, Professor, I'm not on the tenure committee," Mason said. "Tell teacher's pet school's out."

The girl got to her feet, gathering her clothes, putting them on a piece at a time, wandering about the studio like she was on a treasure hunt, her giggles subsiding as she covered more of her body. After donning her sandals, bra, and dress, she reached behind a stack of blank canvases and retrieved her panties.

"Ta-dah!" she said, then, "What the hell," as she stuffed them back where she found them. "Later," she promised, leaving with a last laugh.

"Get out," Robert told Mason, wiping his face on his sleeve, pretending to organize his paintings.

"Come on, Professor," Mason said. "Next time you want to bang the model, lock the door."

"Fuck you," Robert said. "Get out or I'll call campus security."

"No, you won't, because I'll tell them that you and your model were playing let's-mold-the-clay. Besides, when they search for evidence, they might find your dope tucked behind your girlfriend's panties."

"Who are you and what do you want?"

"My name is Lou Mason. I represent Jordan Hackett. She's been charged with killing your wife. You do remember your wife, don't you? Dr. Gina Davenport? Had her own radio show until someone threw her out the window?"

Robert retrieved the model's panties, holding them over a metal trash can, lighting them with a butane lighter, dropping the flaming fabric into the can. "The police told me your client killed my wife. What do you want from me?"

"You don't seem too upset that someone murdered your wife, Professor. Is that because you're too coked up or are you just not the emotional type?"

"Excuse me for not sharing my grief with you, but it's none of your fucking business. Besides, my marriage was over a long time ago."

"Why? Dr. Gina was too busy solving everyone else's problems, she didn't have time for yours?"

Robert sat down on a stool, his feet tapping a nervous beat on the concrete floor. "No. She was too busy solving everyone else's problems and didn't have time for our daughter's. So Emily solved her problems by killing herself."

Mason took the head shot but counterpunched, knowing that Robert expected him to fold out of pity. "So you took the hard road, blaming her and stuffing your nose with a few extra lines of cocaine."

"I took the road I knew. I'm not bragging about it, but I'm honest about it. Unlike my late wife."

"Meaning what?" Mason asked.

"Meaning Gina sold the public a bill of goods with a phony-baloney do-the-right-thing morality. She only cared about her show. When Emily got to be too much, Gina dumped her at Sanctuary. When Emily killed herself, Gina turned it into a radio show, not because she wanted to share our grief with her listeners, but because it was a fucking ratings sweeps month. She rode my daughter's death all the way to a national syndication deal."

"What made you hate her more—that she was more successful than you or that she cashed in on your daughter's suicide?"

Robert bounced off his stool. "Look, Mason. I'm a decent artist, not a great one. I make a living doing what I want to do. I screw around with co-eds because it's easy. But I'm not applying for sainthood, and I didn't build my career on my daughter's grave."

"Who supplies your cocaine?" Mason asked.

Robert made a squealing sound that Mason guessed passed for laughter. "Sure. Let me write down the name and address. Would you like a letter of introduction too?"

"The cops found cocaine in your wife's office after she was killed. Did you put it there?"

Robert fished a cigarette from the pocket of his T-shirt, using the butane lighter, drawing hard, shaking his head as he released the smoke. "Wasn't me. I wouldn't have wasted it on Gina."

"How much money will you inherit from your wife?"

Robert flicked the cigarette onto the floor, grinding it with his heel. "I don't know. She had her money and I had mine. Except she always had more."

"Do you have an alibi for the night your wife was killed?" Mason asked.

"You see this body, Mason," he said, turning sideways and flexing his emaciated biceps. "I can hardly throw out the trash. How am I going to throw my wife out the window? Besides, I do have an alibi. Her name is Belinda. You met her when you forgot to knock. Sorry I skipped the formal introduction."

"Did Gina mind that you screwed around?"

"No more than I minded her screwing around. Satisfied?"

"Disgusted," Mason said. "Who was Gina seeing?"

Robert shoved his hands in his pants pockets, studying the cigarette butt before he kicked it across the floor. "I don't know," he said. "But she'd been real bitchy lately. I think whoever the guy was, he dumped her."

"Is David Evans handling Gina's estate for you?" Mason asked.

"He may be handling the estate, but he sure as hell isn't representing me."

Mason asked, "Why not?"

"You're a lawyer, Mason. Would you want to be represented by the same guy who served you with divorce papers last week?"

"No, Robert," Mason said. "I don't think I would. If I was a cocaine addict whose wife was murdered and my favorite drug was found in her office and she was divorcing me and my alibi was the co-ed I was banging in my art studio—I'd like to be represented by a good criminal defense lawyer."

"Don't need one of those, Mason. I'm innocent and your client confessed."

"My client is out on bail and she's recanted her confession. You might want to reconsider."

The Art Institute is east of Main, just north of the Country Club Plaza, a shopping, drinking, and eating district that was prime Friday afternoon grazing territory for upwardly mobile beautiful people. Mason's office was farther north and west on Broadway, back toward the grittier side of the city.

He wasn't in the mood for either destination. Still beat up from his elevator escapade, and beaten down by the pathetic Hackett and Davenport clans, he had no interest in single bars or solo practice at the moment. The top was down on his TR-6, but his spirits were lower.

He sat in his car in the Art Institute parking lot, thinking about taking a drive wherever the TR-6 felt like going. Reaching into his jacket pocket for his keys, he found Abby Lieberman's business card. It was lilac-colored with the name of her company, Fresh Air, engraved in silver and black. The mix was feminine and tough at the same time. Abby understood public relations.

Mason hoped she understood human relations as well. He and Abby had connected—that was clear to both of them. Yet instead of doing something about it, he was ducking it, using Jordan's case as a reason to step back.

The reason wasn't an altogether bad one. Then again, he told himself as he dialed her number, it wasn't an altogether good one either.

"It's Abby," her answering machine said, "leave a message." Mason was tempted to hang up and dial again just to hear her voice invite him to leave a message a second time.

"Abby, it's Lou Mason. I was too hard on you today. You did a good thing and I hope it turns out well. Listen, if you're not doing anything for dinner, give me a call."

He left his cell phone number and called his office to check for messages. When he finished, his phone beeped, signaling that he'd missed a call. He listened to the message. It was Abby.

"Hi, Lou! Sorry I missed your call. My place at seven-thirty. Bring the wine," she said, and ended with her address.

Mason gunned the engine. His top was down and his chin was up. The only downside was the wine. Mason's alcohol repertoire was limited to beer. The only thing he knew about wine was the colors—red, white, and the other one that was kind of in between red and white. He called Blues.

"I need a good bottle of wine for tonight. You have anything in the Blues on Broadway wine cellar?"

"Since when is the closet in my office a wine cellar?"

"I can't tell my date I got the wine out of your closet, can I?"

"You can't even tell her what color it is. How are you going to tell her where you got it?"

"I'll be there in five minutes. Pick a good one and give me one of those things to get the cork out."

* * *

Abby lived in a loft in the Crossroads District in the shadow of Union Station. Ten years ago, the neighborhood was dominated by run-down warehouses and cheap dives. Now it was a mix of lofts and businesses, art galleries and restaurants. The area was still rough around the edges, with a strip joint and residential hotels one step removed from flophouses hanging on to the old days.

Abby's loft was on the top floor of a four-story building. She had taped a message to the front door, telling him to come in and take the stairs to the roof. The loft was a vast open space surrounded by sandblasted brick walls, the high ceiling supported by brick columns. Black and white photographs and sculptures made of woven fabric hung on the walls, softening the brick's coarse mortar. Simple furniture heavy with pillows rested on throw rugs like an oasis on the hardwood floors. Music drifted along air currents stirred by broad-limbed ceiling fans. He listened for a moment to be certain. It was Oscar Peterson on the piano. God is good, Mason thought.

A wrought-iron spiral staircase near the center of one wall led to a platform and an open door to the roof. Outside, Abby was leaning against a waist-high limestone rail at the building's edge, watching the early evening foot traffic below. She was wearing jeans, her white denim shirt untucked, sleeves half rolled up.

"Hey," Mason said.

Abby turned, stretching her arms out along the low wall, shimmering in the trailing light left as the sun sank behind her, a burnt orange pearl slipping into an indigo sea.

"Hey, you," she said.

"Nice roof."

"It's just something to keep over my head. Nothing special," Abby said.

Mason grinned. "We're being very cool, aren't we?"

"The coolest."

"I brought wine," he said.

"What color?" she asked.

"The one in between red and white," he said joining her at the rail, holding the bottle up to catch the last rays of sun. "I'm no expert, but I think it's called pink."

"Pink is a very good color," she said.

He handed her the bottle, keeping both their hands around its neck, taking her other hand in his, drawing her close. "I thought I'd try both hands this time."

"Don't let go," she said, and kissed him.

"Not a chance," he said, wrapping his arm around her, taking his turn to kiss her.

Abby slipped her hand behind his neck, pulling him to her, both lowering the bottle of wine until it dangled from their joined hands, inches from the ground, releasing it, laughing when it landed upright.

"Who knew they sold that stuff in plastic bottles," Mason said.

"Only at the really good convenience stores," she said, Mason stroking her cheek, brushing her hair back, smiling like he had a secret.

"What?" she asked.

"Nothing," Mason said. "I was just thinking that magic and miracles aren't often found on rooftops."

"You said it was a nice roof."

"That I did," he said, kissing her again, feeling her warmth and the soft comfort of her body against his.

"It's gone," she said as the sun disappeared. "Think we should eat dinner?"

"I'd hate to disappoint the cook."

"I'd hate to disappoint the rotisserie chicken I bought at Costco. I promised the butcher I'd give it a good home," she said.

"We could give the chicken a reprieve," he said, gathering her in his arms again, his cell phone ringing, Mason ignoring it until Abby plucked it off the clip on his belt.

"The client is job one," she said, handing him the phone and kissing the tip of his nose.

"Mason!" Centurion Johnson said. "That bitch of yours done cleaned out her room, split, and stole my goddamn Mercedes!"

CHAPTER 13

"I'm going with you," Abby told Mason.

"Bad idea. I don't even know where I'm going."

"Of course you do. You're going to find Jordan and I'm going with you."

Mason picked up the bottle of wine. "It would be better if you chilled this until I came back."

"I'll let it turn to vinegar first. Don't patronize me, Lou. If it will make you feel any better, I don't want to lose three hundred thousand dollars on a hunch and a prayer that Jordan may be my daughter."

Mason did a double take. "I wouldn't have pegged you for a mercenary."

"I'm not. I'm giving you a reason I'm going with you that you can justify without giving me a bunch of crap about being an emotional female who will get in the way."

"You're good at this public relations stuff," he said.

"I'm the best. Let's get going."

Mason called Jordan's parents, counting it as his first break when Carol Hackett answered. If Arthur knew that his daughter was missing, he'd call the cops and Jordan would be back in jail. Mason wasn't certain she didn't belong there. He wasn't certain of anything, including her innocence. That's why he had to find her. Carol Hackett hadn't heard from Jordan. Mason didn't tell Carol that Jordan had disappeared, and Carol didn't ask the reason for his call. Sometimes, Mason realized, denial came in handy.

Mason and Abby sat in Mason's TR-6 at the curb in front of Abby's building, Mason realizing how little he knew about his client, who her friends were, where she liked to hang out, anything that would help him find her.

Abby said, "Any chance Jordan just took Centurion's Mercedes for a joy ride or that she went shopping with a girlfriend?"

"Centurion said she cleaned out her room. Didn't even leave a toothbrush. Doesn't sound like she was planning on coming back."

"If she's running away, that Mercedes is going to be easy to find," Abby said. "Did Centurion report the car as stolen?"

"Not yet," Mason said. "My guess is that Centurion doesn't want the cops crawling all over it. A car like that with an owner like Centurion may have a few secrets of its own."

"So where do we go? I don't think she's going to drive by and wave while we sit here," Abby said.

"The last time she skipped out, she went to Gina Davenport's office looking for a diary she'd given to Gina. Maybe she went back to get something else."

The Cable Depot was five minutes from Abby's loft. Mason took his time, circling the streets within several blocks of the Depot.

"Looking for a good parking space?" Abby asked.

"We're looking for Centurion's Mercedes. It has a vanity plate with his name on it. Last time, Jordan parked somewhere around here."

"We've taken the tour three times," Abby said a short while later. "The car isn't here."

Mason edged the nose of the TR-6 down an alley behind a row of apartment buildings two blocks south of the Cable Depot. The Mercedes was wedged between two buildings, blocking a side alley. Mason climbed out of his car, peered through the tinted windows, jiggled the locked doors and trunk, and called Mickey Shanahan.

"I lost the keys to my Mercedes," Mason told Mickey.

"Boss, you don't own a Mercedes."

"If I did and I lost the keys, could you unlock it for me?"

"Piece of cake. Where's this Mercedes you don't own and can't find the keys for?"

Mason told him. "Bring Blues. Tell him there may be some dirty laundry in the car. Take it somewhere we can get a closer look at it."

Abby said, "Tell me you aren't stealing that car."

"I'm not stealing that car," Mason said. "According to Centurion, it's already been stolen. I'm just helping him get it back."

Abby laughed, leaving out the humor. "If Centurion buys that story, I'm hiring you to do my PR."

Earl Luke Fisher was camped out on the park bench across the street from the Cable Depot, a grocery cart

crammed with stuffed black trash bags screening him
from the street. Though Mason had watched the Channel
6 videotape enough times that he could pick Fisher out
of a hobo convention, he asked to be polite.

"You Earl Luke Fisher?" Mason asked.

Earl Luke was stretched out on the bench, using a
filthy bedroll as a pillow, the green neck of a bottle
sticking out of a brown bag nestled under one arm like
the favorite stuffed animal a child took to bed. Mason
and Abby caught their breath; Earl Luke reeked like
warm garbage on a hot day. If begging didn't work out,
he could rent himself out as a breeding ground for blue-
bottle flies.

"Mebbe," Earl Luke muttered.

"I saw you on TV," Mason said.

Earl Luke sat up, rubbing his red-rimmed eyes, ignoring Mason. "Pretty lady," he said to Abby, giving her
a jack-o'-lantern smile showcasing his few remaining
teeth. "I was on TV, you know."

"I've got a videotape of it. Any time you want to
watch it, you give me a call," Mason told him, handing
him a business card. "How long have you been here
tonight?"

Earl Luke wiped his face with his hands, trying to
focus on something so unimportant to him as the time.
He pulled the bottle of wine from the paper bag, measuring how much remained with his fingers.

"A while," he said. "Since before dark. This is my
spot," he added, making it clear that was explanation
enough.

"Did you see a woman go into that building? A young
woman with brown hair, probably wearing jeans and a
T-shirt."

Earl Luke took a long pull on his bottle and flashed his horror-show gums at Abby.

"It's very important, Mr. Fisher," Abby said. "I'd really appreciate any help you can give me."

Earl Luke lit up with a glow he wouldn't find in the wine bottle. "Yes, ma'am," he told her. "I seen that girl a while ago."

"Has she come back out?" Abby asked.

"Don't know," Earl Luke said. "My eyes ain't what they used to be. The VA, they used to gimme glasses, but I quit going over there. They was always talking to me 'bout getting into some goddamn program or 'nother. Shit, I say to those goddamn bureaucrats! I ain't never comin' back to your goddamn hospital, I tole 'em, and by God, I ain't been back neither."

"Thank you, Earl Luke," Abby told him, Mason crossing the street. "You've been a great help."

Mason had kept the key Trent Hackett had given him. "I thought you were going to take Earl Luke home," he said to Abby as he unlocked the front door to the Cable Depot.

Abby said, "There's no room at the inn. I'm already booked."

"Will you hold the reservation for a late arrival?"

"Well . . ." she said with a sly smile, drawing out her answer. "Unless I get a better offer." Mason stared at Abby, wide-eyed and hopeful. "It's okay, Lou. You don't have to win all the banter battles," she told him.

"I surrender," he said.

"Careful," she answered. "You haven't heard my terms."

Gina Davenport's office was empty, the latest round of crime-scene tape gone. KWIN's offices were unlocked.

"Let's have a look," Mason said.

Abby followed him through the vacant lobby, down the hall to Arthur Hackett's office, nearly colliding with Max Coyle, carrying a tall Starbuck's cup in one hand and a sheaf of papers in the other.

"Lou!" Coyle said, "What are you doing here?"

"Looking for Jordan. Have you seen her?"

"Nope. I was just wrapping up some promos."

"Anyone else here?" Mason asked him.

"Just me. The nighttime programming is all syndicated and runs on automation. Isn't Jordan supposed to be out at the joint in the country for the whacked-out kids, what's it called?"

"Sanctuary," Mason said.

"Right. So if she's supposed to be there, why are you looking for her in here?"

"I need the exercise, Max. Do me a favor, forget I asked."

Max nodded. "No problem, Lou. You gonna introduce me?" he asked, beaming down on Abby, Abby beaming back up.

"I'm Abby Lieberman," she said. "I saw you when you won the heavyweight belt."

"You know him?" Mason asked.

"You were more fun as a wrestler than you were as a football player. I like your show."

"Watch out, Lou. She likes wrestlers," Max told him. "I'm outta here."

Mason and Abby finished a quick tour of KWIN, checking Gina's office again in case Jordan had slipped past them.

"The Hacketts' son, Trent, is the building manager," Mason said. "Let's see if he's working late. Maybe he's seen Jordan."

Light showed along the bottom of the door to Trent's office. They stood outside the door listening to grinding rap music blaring inside. There was no reply when Mason knocked on the door.

"Trent, open up! It's Lou Mason," he said, knocking harder.

Abby reached in front of Mason, turning the doorknob. "See how easy this is," she said as she pushed the door open and screamed.

Trent Hackett was slumped over his desk, his head punched halfway through his computer monitor, blood pooling on the desk from his slashed throat, running down his dangling arm, dripping onto the floor.

Samantha Greer told Mason and Abby to wait outside while detectives and forensics swarmed over the scene. One uniformed cop stretched yellow crime-scene tape across the revolving door while another cop set up barricades blocking traffic on 6th Street. Sirens summoned people living on Quality Hill a few blocks south, the crowd gathering in Earl Luke's park across the street.

Half an hour after the cops arrived, Arthur Hackett shoved his way through the crowd and demanded to be let inside. Mason had listened when Samantha called him, asking him to come down, but not telling him about his son, preferring to tell him in person. She wanted to spare him the intolerable ride downtown and gauge firsthand his reaction to his son's murder.

"That's my building!" Hackett said when a cop tried to turn him away. The officer relented when Hackett produced identification.

Mason was glad that Hackett had not noticed him. There would be plenty of time for that confrontation. Hackett would demand answers Mason couldn't give even if he knew what they were. He had already had a similar conversation with Samantha.

"Lou, what were you and Ms. Lieberman doing here?"

Mason caught the undertone of Samantha's question, calling him by his first name, a soft concession to past intimacy, calling Abby by her last name, a stiff reminder that their relationship hadn't ended as easily as they pretended.

"I stopped by to return the key Trent gave me the other day. You remember he said it would cost me twenty-five dollars if I didn't."

Samantha nodded. "I'll disregard the bullshit for now, Lou. You get your story straight and we'll talk tomorrow. Any reason I should ask your client where she spent her evening?"

"None that I can think of," Mason said. Except, he thought, that Trent Hackett raped Jordan eight years ago, spawning a simmering rage that she may have vented by killing her therapist and her brother. "Don't forget she is my client and accidentally show up at Sanctuary to talk with her when I'm not around."

"That would be against the rules, Counselor. Same as obstructing justice. Wait outside."

Mason was good at doing what he was told when he had no choice, especially when he was buying time. He crossed the street to the park looking for Earl Luke. He wanted to question him further before the cops got to him. Earl Luke was holding forth in front of a small group, including David Evans. Evans handed Earl Luke a five-dollar bill, peeling away, bumping into Mason.

"Trolling for another piece of business?" he asked Mason.

"Nope. Just enjoying the crisp night air. What brings you downtown to a murder scene on a Friday night? No movies left at Blockbuster?"

Evans smiled. "Okay, I was out of line. Sorry. I live on Quality Hill. I was sitting on my deck and heard the sirens so I thought I'd take a look. People here look out for one another. We're a neighborhood watch area."

"Yeah," Mason said. "With a bum for a night watchman."

"You mean Earl Luke? He's harmless, except for a smell that will bleach your teeth. I give him a few bucks now and then. I know he spends it on booze, but it makes me feel better."

"Kind of like your work for Emily's Fund, huh?" Mason couldn't rinse the hostility out of his question, and Evans made him regret it.

"You don't give up, do you, Mason? You're like a dog that keeps gnawing a bone even after sucking out all the marrow. Private foundations like Emily's Fund file annual reports with the IRS called Form 990. The form covers all income, expenses, and disbursements. You can download the forms for Emily's Fund from the Internet. Knock yourself out, but leave me alone."

Abby took Mason's hand, leading him away. "You don't make friends easily," she teased him.

"David Evans is a lawyer who also claims to be a money manager. A hot market makes guys like him look smart and lets them suck in unsophisticated clients. Your hero, Max Coyle, was one of them. Evans put Max into high-risk stuff, promising it was guaranteed, and churned the account until Max went bust. I sued Evans and he settled a couple of weeks ago. I don't think I'm on his Christmas list."

Samantha Greer cut through the crowd, stopping in front of Mason and Abby. Mason started to release Abby's hand, but she pulled his fingers back into her palm. Samantha cleared her throat, making certain they knew she was pretending not to notice or care.

"Where's your client, Lou? I need to talk to her."

"Why?"

"For starters, her brother has been murdered."

"I'd rather tell her about that," he said.

"You can have the honors. I want to know where she's been since she left the courthouse today."

"I'll talk to her and let you know."

Samantha pointed her balled fist and forefinger at Lou. "Don't do this, Lou. Your client has already confessed to one murder."

"A confession she made under pressure and which she has recanted. That doesn't make her a suspect in this murder."

"Maybe not, but her father does," Samantha said.

Mason knew what was coming, but he had to make Samantha say it. "How's that?"

Samantha said, "I think we both know, Lou. Jordan claims Trent raped her when she was thirteen. She's been carrying that around with her for eight years, until tonight. I'll give you until tomorrow morning to bring her in for questioning. If she's not in my office at eight A.M., I'll find her. Don't make me do that."

CHAPTER 14

Blues drove Centurion's Mercedes to George's Body Shop near 35th and Troost. George's mortgage included favors owed to Blues ever since Blues helped him restructure his business debt with lenders that didn't charge broken legs as late fees.

Troost Avenue had squandered the cachet of being an avenue of burned-out storefronts and payday loan drive-throughs. Further south, Troost skirted the edges of two colleges and an internationally renowned research institute, testaments to the hope that daily squared off against urban decay. But in the core, Troost divided the city between the East Side and everything else.

East Side was one of the city's most convenient euphemisms. It was shorthand for high crime and low property values. It was a comfortable way of saying ghetto. It even implied, in its geographic neutrality, a sort of blamelessness for the rest of the city that had too long ignored it. Of course, people would say with knowing nods when another innocent died in a drive-by shooting, or a crack house was shut down only to be replaced by another down the block—that's what happens on the East Side. Since they were convinced that there was nothing they could do about it, they didn't.

George's Body Shop was a single-story dusty red brick garage with a parking lot ringed in chain link and razor wire. George worked alone, except for a rotweiller, also named George, that patrolled the grounds.

When Mason and Abby arrived, the two-legged George was reassembling the door panels on the Mercedes. The four-legged George was practicing his hall-of-fame snarl, Blues clicking his tongue at the dog, calming the animal, while Mickey surveyed the garage for high ground in case the dog hadn't been fed.

"What did you find?" Mason asked Blues.

"Found the keys under the visor, for starters. The front passenger door had a nine-millimeter automatic hidden behind a spring-loaded panel. Same setup in the glove box. Driver's side had Centurion's stash. A little coke and some crystal meth. Back doors rigged the same way, except they were empty. I'd say Centurion was still a homeboy at heart."

"Did you put everything back?" Mason asked.

"Just like we found it," Blues said.

"Was there anything that looked like it might have belonged to Jordan? Clothes, cosmetics—anything?"

Mickey answered. "Not a thing, Boss. I thought this was Centurion's ride."

"It is," Mason said. "Centurion told me that Jordan stole the car and took off with everything she owned. If she stopped at the Cable Depot to kill her brother, I doubt she carried her worldly possessions on her back."

"What do you want to do with the car?" Blues asked.

"That's easy," Mason said. "Give it back to its rightful owner. Maybe we'll even get a reward."

"How do you want to do that?" Blues asked.

"I'll drive the Mercedes. You and Mickey follow us."

"Us?" Blues asked, keeping his reaction on an even keel regardless of what he was thinking, his one-word question leaving no doubt that he thought Mason was out of his mind.

Mason said, "Don't bother. She's got better answers than either of us have questions."

"Hey, George," Blues said to the body shop owner. "Lou's taking your dog for a ride."

"Don't let him stick his head out the window. Gets dirt in his eyes," George said.

"You expect me to put that psychopathic animal in the backseat of the Mercedes?" Mason said. "You're nuts."

"That dog was a canine cop," Blues said. "He got a little out of hand and George took him in. Calmed him down. Made him a good pet. People don't know the dog get the wrong idea. Figure the dog is gonna rip their throat out they so much as say *Here, boy*. That's what you want Centurion thinking when you drive up to his house with his car full of guns and drugs. Only thing you want on his mind is to get that fucking dog out of his car and off of his property and you and Abby along with it."

"That's swell," Mason said. "How do I keep the dog from biting my hand off before we get there?"

"Simple," Blues said. "Don't pet him. You'll need a ride home. That's why Mickey and I will be behind you. If Centurion gets feisty and the dog's asleep, we'll know it."

"How will you know if we need help?" Abby asked, speaking up for the first time since they arrived.

"We'll use cell phones," Blues said. "Call me when you get there and keep the phone on."

"I was hoping for a secret decoder ring, but that will do," Abby said. "Here, boy, c'mon, George," she added with a sharp whistle, crouching to meet the dog head-on as he trotted over to her. The dog sniffed Abby as she rubbed him behind the ears and under the chin. "You're a good boy," she told the dog. "Don't forget to eat the bad guys, okay? Let's go for a ride."

Nighttime in the city is never completely dark. There's always light from somebody or something. Everything from porch lights to searchlights casts a glow that obscures the stars.

Nighttime in the country is swallow-you-whole dark. No trace of anything ahead or behind, everything invisible until stumbled upon. Add a wall of trees flanking a narrow, winding, unlit gravel road and the night becomes a turnpike into the belly of the beast.

Mason swallowed, feeling the claustrophobic grip of the darkness even as the Mercedes's headlights shot in front of them, picking out the curves ahead. The headlights on Blues's SUV danced behind him, glancing off Mason's rearview mirror in blinding flashes. The dog sat on his haunches, his nose pressed against the glass, sharing a guttural growl with the unseen.

"Is it much farther?" Abby asked.

"Another mile, maybe, on this road and we should run right into Sanctuary."

"How do you know Centurion will be there?"

"I don't, but I'm betting he wants to be surrounded by a lot of friends and witnesses until this car turns up." Mason called Blues. "We're almost there," he said, then slipped the cell phone into a clip on his belt.

"Wouldn't it be simpler to call and make certain he's home?"

"Simpler, yes. Better, no. I want him surprised, grateful, and a little worried. That's the best combination for getting information from someone who wouldn't tell the truth unless he could leverage it."

"If Centurion is such a bad guy, how did he manage to raise all the money for Sanctuary?"

"He's very good at what he does and he figured out that it's easy to hide in plain sight when you let people see what they want to see."

"The Emperor may not be happy if you tell him he's not wearing any clothes."

"I'm not going to tell him," Mason said, slowing down for another twist in the road. "There it is," he said as the headlights illuminated the *Welcome Home to Sanctuary* sign and its glittering list of corporate sponsors.

The crunch of gravel was replaced by the quiet of concrete as Mason drove up the long driveway to the main house. A series of motion-sensitive lights popped on, leading him to the front circle drive. Centurion Johnson, silhouetted by an arc of lamps, was waiting on the veranda, larger in shadow than in life.

"Wait here," Mason told Abby as he killed the engine and stepped out of the car. Blues was stopped a hundred yards back, his high beams spotlighting Mason's stage.

"Damn, Mason!" Centurion said. "Not only are you a nut-busting lawyer, but you're a fucking repo man too!"

Mason tossed Centurion the keys. "I got lucky, that's all."

"Where'd that bitch leave it?" Centurion asked.

"Over on Quality Hill. It was unlocked and the key was in it. I thought I'd save you the trip into town to pick it up."

"You find anything in it?" Centurion asked, keeping his distance from the car.

Mason shook his head. "Not a thing. Jordan must have dropped her stuff off somewhere. You have any idea where she might have gone?"

Centurion's grin matched the sliver of moon hanging in the sky. "No fucking clue, man. I mean that," he said, bouncing down the stairs past Mason, opening the driver's door where the dog was now sitting, its ears flat and lips curled.

Centurion jumped back, slamming the door. "Shit! What the fuck is that? Get that fucking dog outta my car!"

Mason opened the door again. "Oh, that dog? That's just George. Abby, bring George over here to meet Centurion."

Abby got out, followed by the dog, Centurion retreating another step, the dog lowering its head, keeping its eyes fixed on Centurion, its growl idling like a rough engine. Abby put her hand on the dog's head and it relaxed, sitting at her side.

Mason said, "Centurion, I've got to find Jordan tonight. Who did she hang with? Where did she like to go? I need some help."

"I figured you want to know, so I asked Terry Nix. He said she used to have a boyfriend that played in a band, the Deadly Deed. They had a regular gig on Friday nights at a bar called Meltdown on 39th Street. Terry checked. They're playing tonight. That's the best I got."

Mason believed him. Mason had solved Centurion's biggest problem by returning his car. Centurion had promised Judge Pistone he would be responsible for Jordan, and he couldn't afford the loss of credibility if she disappeared. That would be bad for the corporate sponsor business. If Mason could solve that problem for him as easily as he found the Mercedes, they would both sleep better.

"Thanks. We'll check it out."

"Who's your ride?" Centurion asked, motioning to the SUV.

"Friend of mine," Mason said.

"Shit!" Centurion answered. "I'll bet it's that Indian brother of yours, Blues. Damn, Mason. What you think I am, you bring that big, ugly thug and that big, ugly dog out here in the middle of the night? The only nice person you brought is this fine-looking woman you ain't even introduced me to yet."

"And I'm not going to introduce you, Centurion. She's a dog lover, not a corporate sponsor. I need to know something else. The cops found cocaine in Gina Davenport's office after she was killed. Her husband buys in bulk. There may be a connection. I'd like to find out where the husband gets his."

"Can't help you with that, Mason. My dopin' days is behind me. I got no part of that shit no more, and that's the truth."

Abby took her hand off the dog's head. George stood, flared, and growled.

Centurion said, "Cut that shit out, girl." He pulled a gun from beneath his shirt and pointed it at the dog. "I don't like dogs, but I do like pretty women, so I won't kill your dog." He turned to Mason, tapping his gun in the air for emphasis, ignoring the sound of Blues revving his engine as he crept up the driveway. "You find that bitch, Mason. We both need her. But you stay out of my business, hear?"

Mason put his hand over the muzzle of Centurion's gun. "I don't like guns, but I do like dogs, so I won't let George kill you. I'll find my client, but you stay out of my case. Hear?"

Blues pulled up, stepping out of the SUV, the engine still running. Centurion laughed. "You are one nut-busting motherfucker, Mason. I give you that. You shoulda done time. Coulda busted nuts with cons in the yard like a fuckin' lifer. Man, you are something else," he added, turning his back and walking up the stairs, adding over his shoulder, "Bring that bitch back here now. Don't forget."

Mason and Abby climbed into the backseat of the SUV, the dog lying between them, Blues completing the circle in the drive, aiming for the darkness.

"You believe him?" Blues asked.

"About Jordan, yeah. Not about the drugs. He won't be happy if he figures out we searched his car. Will he be able to tell George took it apart?"

"Could be. George didn't leave any marks, but Centurion might have some way to tell if those panels have been opened."

"What will he do if he figures out you found his guns and drugs?" Abby asked. She was holding her middle with one arm, the other wrapped around the dog's neck. Both arms were trembling, vibrating the rest of her. The dog nuzzled her lap. She smiled at Mason, letting go long enough to wipe her eyes. He reached across the dog, taking her hand.

"God, Lou," she said. "The guns, the drugs, the playground macho bullshit. I thought you were a nice Jewish boy, a lawyer like my mother always wanted me to bring home."

"He is," Blue said from the front seat, watching them in the rearview mirror. "He just keeps bad company—until now."

"Thank you, Blues. But what will Centurion do?" Abby asked.

Mason answered. "Depends on what I do. If I leave it alone, he'll leave me alone."

"Will you leave it alone?" Abby asked.

Mason didn't answer.

CHAPTER 15

The Meltdown was a bar on the western edge of the 39th Street strip, covering a corner at the intersection with State Line Road, the street separating Missouri and Kansas. The University of Kansas Medical Center was on the other side of State Line, ensuring a steady flow of sleep-deprived medical students across its threshold. The neo-docs in their white jackets and stethoscopes mingled with the street traffic the bar attracted with its reputation for showcasing local hard-rock bands.

Mason and Abby stood inside the door to the bar, their eyes adjusting to the weak light and heavy smoke. It was close to midnight and people were jammed hip-to-pelvis across the crowded floor, jostling to the music.

"Herd dancing," Mason said. "My favorite."

"Be thankful the herd is not in mating season," Abby shouted over the lead guitarist, who was having an affair with his distortion pedal, slamming the crowd with punishing chords as he wailed into the mike.

They pushed into the crowd, weaving and twisting between people as they got closer to the stage. Jordan was sharing a table with two other girls next to a stack of speakers, ignoring each other and the music. Mason guessed each was a girlfriend of one of the boys in the band. They'd heard the music too many times to pay attention anymore.

Jordan looked up as Mason broke through a wall of people, bolting from her table, knocking her chair over, darting around the speakers. Mason would have yelled for her to stop, but realized she couldn't hear him and wouldn't stop if she had.

He vaulted Jordan's chair, trusting Abby to keep up. The bar was small and the stage made it smaller, leaving a narrow passage behind leading to a back door that was still closing when Mason reached it. He banged into the door, skidding to a stop in the alley behind the bar where Blues was waiting, his arms wrapped around Jordan. The more she thrashed, the tighter Blues held her until she wore herself out.

"Okay," she wheezed. "Okay. Let me go."

Mason nodded and Blues opened his arms. "We need to talk," Mason told her.

"I'm not going back to Sanctuary," Jordan said. "You can't make me."

"You didn't complain in court today when Centurion offered to take you back there. What happened?" Mason asked.

"I changed my mind."

"People out on bail on a murder charge don't get to change their minds," Mason told her. "And they don't get to steal cars either."

"I didn't steal anything."

"How did you get back to town?" Mason asked.

"I borrowed Centurion's car. I was going to call him tomorrow and tell him where I left it."

Mason said to Abby and Blues, "Pull the car around. We'll catch up to you."

"Aren't you afraid I'll run away again?" Jordan asked.

"Right now, I'm your best and only friend. You want to run, run. Next time, I'll let the cops find you and you'll get a real public defender buried under a stack of hopeless hard cases who needs directions to the courthouse."

Jordan scuffed the pavement with the toe of her shoe. "I'm not going back," she said again.

"Tell me why."

"Everything I tell you is confidential, isn't it? That's why you made the others leave."

"That's right."

The alley was as poorly lighted as the bar, the only illumination coming from a black-light bug zapper and a bare yellow bulb mounted above the bar's back door. The light favored neither of them, bringing out the purple and yellow stains of Mason's fading black eye and the washed-out, hollow cheeks that flattened Jordan's face.

"I saw something I shouldn't have seen," she said.

"What?"

"Cocaine. A lot of cocaine."

"Where?"

"In Centurion's apartment. He's got the third floor of the house."

"What were you doing in his apartment?" Mason asked, not wanting to hear the answer.

"He said I owed him for getting me out of jail. I didn't know what to do. He said he wanted to take a shower first. I was looking for his car keys and I found the cocaine in a drawer, probably six bags. I grabbed the keys and split."

"How did you have time to pack all your clothes? Centurion said you took everything with you."

"I didn't have much. Everything fit in my backpack. Centurion had it brought to his apartment, like I was moving in with him."

"Does Centurion know you found the drugs?"

"I don't know. I wasn't going to wait around to find out. So I split."

"Why did you leave the Mercedes on Quality Hill?"

"No reason. I had to leave it somewhere. I called my ex-boyfriend—he's the drummer—and he picked me up."

"Aren't you leaving something out?" Mason asked her.

"Like what?" she asked, looking around but not at him.

"Like going into the Cable Depot. Someone saw you."

"So what. My father owns the building and I've got a key. Is that a crime?"

"Jordan," Mason said. "Look at me. I know about Trent. The police want to talk to you. Tell me what happened."

Blues pulled his SUV up to the mouth of the alley and Abby got out, walking slowly toward them. Mason stepped closer to Jordan, his hand on her chin, guiding her eyes to his. "Tell me," he said.

Jordan held Mason's wrist, keeping his hand on her face to collect the pieces as she crumbled. Her lips quivered, then parted. Her eyes pooled, then overflowed, as she began to shake. Mason pulled her head to his shoulder, his arms around her, as she dissolved.

"He raped me," she said, sobbing. "He raped me and

they let him and they said I was a liar and a whore and I'm not and they let him."

The tremors reached her legs and Mason couldn't hold her up. He eased them both to the ground, cradling her. "Tell me," Mason said again, softly, like a prayer.

Jordan buried her face against Mason's neck, clinging to him, her tears running down his collar. "He was dead. There was blood everywhere." She lifted her head. "It wasn't me, but I wasn't sorry. Do you understand me? I wasn't sorry."

Abby crouched down alongside them, stroking Jordan's back as Mason held her. No one spoke until Jordan's breathing settled and she sat up on her own, the three of them in a ring on the floor of the alley.

"We can't take her back to Sanctuary," Mason said.

"You can stay with me," Abby told her.

"Who are you?" Jordan asked, wiping her nose with her T-shirt.

"My name is Abby. I'm a friend."

"This is a bad idea for a whole lot of reasons," Mason told Abby two hours later.

Jordan was asleep on Abby's sofa. Mason and Abby were back on the roof. She had furnished it with a queen-sized inflated air mattress. They were lying on their backs, arms intertwined.

"You said she couldn't go back to Sanctuary," Abby said.

"That's not what I meant, and you know it. You're setting yourself up for a terrible disappointment. If Jordan isn't your daughter, you'll feel like you've lost her all over again. If she is your daughter, it's not going to be the glorious reunion you want. The girl is a mess, to say nothing of the likelihood that she's going to be charged with another murder."

"She said she didn't kill Gina and that she didn't kill Trent."

"Wrong. She said she did kill Gina but changed her mind on that one. So far, she's sticking to her story on Trent."

Abby propped herself on her elbow and thumped Mason on his chest. "You're her lawyer. You're supposed to believe her. If you don't, what chance does she have?"

Mason rolled on his side, facing her. "You're right. That's what I tell Mickey all the time. I'm not allowed to doubt."

"Good. I'm glad we settled that. I have something else to tell you. I found Jordan's driver's license while she was taking a shower."

"You mean you went through her purse?" Mason teased.

"Stop it. You stole a car. I can look in a purse. Jordan was born the same day as my baby."

Mason sat up, rocking them both on the air mattress. "What hospital were you at when you delivered?"

"Caulfield Medical Center in St. Louis."

"I don't suppose you had time to ask Jordan where she was born?"

"I was trying to get her to relax, open up a little," Abby said, not fighting the catch in her throat.

"Same hospital?" Mason asked.

Abby nodded, tears brimming and catching on her smile. Mason opened his arms and she filled them. They lay down, wrapped in each other and the impossibility of the moment.

"You said there was magic and miracles on my roof. I guess you were right," Abby said.

"And you said you were holding my reservation for late arrival. Then you gave my room away."

"Will you take an upgrade to the penthouse?" she asked as she unbuttoned her blouse. "Room service is included."

"Do I get frequent-guest points?" he asked as they fumbled with each other's clothes.

"Depends on how many times you come," she said.

Mason left before dawn. His clothes were damp with morning dew, but he didn't notice. His last image of Abby had been of her standing in her doorway. She was wearing her shirt and nothing else, making it very hard for him to leave. They had laughed at the circles embedded on their bodies by the air mattress, dressing with the ease of old lovers.

It was that ease, that immediate intimacy they had felt when he first took her hand that enthralled him. He was pushing forty, too old to be deceived by his hormones. Abby had invaded his heart. Whether it was magic or a miracle didn't matter. It was enough that it had happened.

The early morning air was moist with the promise of a warm day. His clothes dried out by the time he got home, courtesy of the top-down ride. Tuffy greeted him when he walked inside, sniffing and nudging, puzzled by the latent scents of rotweiller and woman Mason carried.

He left again at 7:30 to pick up Jordan, focusing more on the day ahead than the night just past. He had cautioned Abby about the unlikely odds of Jordan being her daughter and the mixed blessing it could prove to be if she were. Centurion, though, was the greater danger for Abby and Jordan.

Centurion might forget Jordan's sexual snub, knowing that he could replace her easily enough. Should she complain of his crude effort, he would deny it, relying on his greater credibility and her admitted unreliability as a defense. If he suspected that Jordan found the cocaine, he wouldn't forget that. Even if he cleaned house well enough that a drug-sniffing dog would hyperventilate before finding anything, Centurion couldn't tolerate the allegation or the scrutiny. That meant Jordan was in danger, as was anyone protecting her, including Abby.

Mason decided not to raise this problem with Abby or Jordan until after he talked with Samantha Greer and Centurion. Both demanded that he bring Jordan to them. He would do it for Samantha but not Centurion. Centurion wouldn't believe any explanation Mason would give him except the truth, and that was the last thing Mason would tell him.

CHAPTER 16

Samantha Greer didn't look like a homicide cop pulling a Saturday morning shift. Her hair, normally an afterthought, had a fresh wave. Her makeup, usually understated, was upgraded with eye shadow and pink lipstick. She toyed with the third button on her blouse, undecided whether to keep it buttoned. Mason wondered if she had a date or wanted one.

Their relationship had been casual but satisfying for Mason. He'd never pretended to be operating on anything other than friendship and need. When Samantha let him know that she wanted and needed something more, he'd backed off, taking refuge in his own shortcomings as an excuse to let their affair die of neglect. He'd been relieved when she stopped calling. They had stepped gingerly back to being professional friends and he didn't want to reverse course, especially after last night.

Mason had left Jordan in an interrogation room with

strict instructions that she was not to be questioned outside his presence. He made the speech for the benefit of the officer keeping her company and for Jordan, whose last protective veneer of anger had been stripped away by her brother's murder. She was tentative and jittery, making him reluctant to leave her alone until she forced a smile, said she understood and would be fine.

Sitting next to Samantha's desk in the homicide bullpen, Mason hoped she would leave the third button alone. The last thing he wanted was for her to watch his eyes wander. In spite of everything, he knew they would, even though the rest of him would stay put.

"Okay, Lou," she began. "Are you going to let me question your client?"

"No. You told me to bring her in and I did. Now we're ready to go." He didn't get up, knowing that Samantha wouldn't let him off that easy.

"We found her prints in Trent's office."

"Are you going to arrest everyone else whose prints you found? They were brother and sister. Their parents owned the building. There were lots of reasons she could have been in Trent's office."

"Of course there are. I'm sure Jordan could give me a few if you let her talk to me," Samantha said, her fingers absently straying to her third button, easing it out of the hole.

"Tempting, but not tempting enough," Mason said. "It's hard to stop after getting started."

Samantha thumbed her button back in place, turning the pages of the report on Trent Hackett's murder with a pencil eraser. "The coroner says he was hit over the head with everyone's favorite weapon—the blunt instrument—and knocked unconscious. Then the killer slammed his head into the computer monitor, lacerating his jugular vein. He bled out."

"I haven't seen a murder yet that was pretty," Mason said.

"Two vicious murders in the same building in the same week—not to mention the rather clumsy attempt to kill you—is a little out of the ordinary. Particularly when your client is tied to both victims."

"On that logic, she should be a suspect in the elevator case," Mason said, not willing to christen that investigation with his own name.

Samantha said, "She would be if she hadn't been busy confessing to killing Gina Davenport at the same time you were auditioning for *Fear Factor.*"

Mason shrugged, pretending nonchalance at the casual discussion of his attempted murder. "Most unhappy clients just fire me. It's a lot less trouble than killing me. What have you got on the elevator?"

"A dead suspect. Trent Hackett and his father were the only people with access to the control room and Carol Hackett alibis her husband. I'm closing the book on the elevator. Don't piss off anyone else."

"At least I can quit taking the stairs," Mason said.

"Why would Trent have tried to kill you?" Samantha asked.

"Jordan told me about the rape. Maybe Trent knew I would come after him. Maybe that explains Gina Davenport's murder too."

"Maybe, but it doesn't explain Trent's," Samantha said.

"So the circle remains unbroken," Mason said. "I know you've got more reasons that I should let you talk to Jordan. I'm not going to let you, but lay them out anyway. I had a long night and would like to take the rest of the day off."

"That's not the way it works. The gate swings both ways. You let me talk with Jordan, and I'll tell you what I know."

Mason said, "I don't need to know what you know unless you charge her, and you would have done that when we walked in if you had enough for the prosecuting attorney. I'll do this much. I'll give you good reasons to look at a few other people before you come down on Jordan."

"Such as?"

"Such as Arthur Hackett. Jordan told Gina Davenport that Trent had raped her. That's a crime, not a story. Gina was trying to get out of her contract with Hackett. That's why she cut off Jordan's treatment. Arthur wouldn't let her go, so Gina upped the ante. She threatened to turn Trent in for raping Jordan. Arthur knew Gina was gone when her contract expired even if he didn't release her. He had a five-million-dollar insurance policy on her and a son to protect. That's better than nothing."

"It's not good enough. Why would he kill his son?"

"Who knows? You met the kid. Would you have wanted your daughter to bring him home? Maybe Arthur blamed Trent for the whole mess."

"Is that all you've got—a father who kills his daughter's therapist to cash in and kills his son to tie up the loose ends?"

Mason stood. "That's more than a jury will need to acquit Jordan, but you might want to try this one too. You found cocaine in Gina's office the night she was killed. Her husband Robert is a coke-head who likes to bang his student models. Centurion Johnson is still in the trade, in spite of his refurbished not-for-profit-save-the-kids-and-the-world bullshit. He raised Jordan's Sanctuary rent to include sex. She wasn't interested and split. Before she did, she found a drawer full of cocaine in Centurion's bedroom. If I had all the resources of the police department at my disposal, I'd find out if Centurion was supplying Robert and if he was, how and why that cocaine ended up in Gina's office."

Samantha put on a pair of glasses and jotted down notes as Mason spoke. "You know that knocks out Jordan's alibi for Trent's murder. She splits and her brother is found dead. Where's Jordan staying now?"

"Last night she stayed with Abby Lieberman."

"Your new . . ."

"Yeah, Sam," Mason said, soft-pedaling his response. "My new."

"Ms. Lieberman told me about the phone call she got about her long-lost daughter," Samantha said, consulting her notes. "She thinks Jordan may be her daughter. Is it a good idea to put the two of them together if Centurion figures out why Jordan skipped out?"

"No. It's a bad idea. That's why I'm moving her."

"I can offer her protective custody," Samantha said.

"Thanks. Maybe later, but I'll make my own arrangements for now."

"Blues is good," Samantha said. "But Centurion had a reputation as a very bad man before he went corporate. Blues may not be enough."

"There's Harry too," Mason said. "And me. Can I go now?"

"Sure. One last thing, Lou," she said. "Good luck with your new."

"Thanks, Sam," Mason said.

* * *

Mason had been inside police headquarters long enough for clouds to roll in. He put the top up on the TR-6 just as the rain began. It was a steady cleansing rain, comforting as a warm shower, dancing on the rag-top like a fountain spray.

"We'll stop at Abby's to pick up your gear," he told Jordan. "I want you to stay with someone else until things settle down a bit."

"Why can't I stay there?"

"Centurion isn't going to be happy when I tell him you aren't coming back to Sanctuary. He may pout and get over it. He may not. I want you someplace where you're hard to find being kept company by people Centurion doesn't want to find."

"Are you saying Centurion would hurt me?" Jordan asked. "Why would he do that?"

"Depends on what he thinks you saw. Centurion is smart. He's conned the Kansas City business community into giving him a ton of dough to run Sanctuary. It's beginning to look like that was just seed money to set up his new drug deal. He's not going to risk all that on whether you saw something you shouldn't have seen."

"I won't tell anyone. I promise," Jordan said, fear creeping in where anger had been.

"I'll tell him if he asks, but Centurion can't afford to believe that."

"Why are you going to talk to him?"

"He expects me to bring you back. If I don't talk to him, he'll assume the worst. If I do, he might buy what I tell him."

"What will you tell him?" Jordan asked.

"Can't wait to find out," Mason said.

* * *

Abby protested when Mason told her he was moving Jordan out of her loft. "She needs stability. I can give that to her," Abby said.

"She needs security more than stability until I know where things stand with Centurion. Then she needs an acquittal. After that, you can give her anything you want."

They were back on Abby's roof, the only place they could have a private conversation with someone else in the loft. Jordan was packing. The rain had tapered off, but was picking up again carried by a sharp, wet wind. The air mattress was deflated, crumpled in a corner, taking on water in its creases.

"Jordan needs me now, Lou. Don't take her away from me," Abby said, her arms folded across her body, offering faint resistance to the weather and Mason. "Why are you doing this?"

"Murder doesn't end anything except the victim's life," he told her. "It threatens anyone within six degrees of separation of the killer and the victim. People do crazy things because they're guilty or because they think the cops think they're guilty or because they're guilty of something the cops haven't even thought of. Centurion could fit into any or all of those categories. I can't take any chances with Jordan or you."

"Me?" Abby asked. "You came here to take Jordan away from me and justify it by scaring me? I can't believe it!" The rain came harder, matching Abby's fury, stinging both of them.

"Centurion knows you are connected to me and to Jordan. He won't care how or why. If he can use you to get what he wants, he will."

"That's ridiculous!" Abby said. "I've read about your

other cases in the newspaper. Rachel Firestone told me all about you," she said, riding a wave of indignation. "You look for trouble. Like climbing on top of that elevator like you're some kind of an action hero. Well, I won't be a part of that!"

Abby ran inside, pounding down the spiral staircase. Mason stood in the rain, Abby's last words soaking him to the bone, before he followed her. Abby was at the door with Jordan, fussing with Jordan's hair. Mason joined them.

"Ready?" he asked Jordan.

"Yeah. What's up with you guys on the roof in the rain?" They didn't answer. Mason jammed his hands in his pockets. Abby wiped the water from her face. "You guys ought to be married," Jordan said. "You remind me of my parents."

CHAPTER 17

Mason took Jordan to Daphne's B&B, a bed-and-breakfast near the Nelson Atkins Museum of Art owned by Daphne Bacchelder. Daphne had been a school secretary at an exclusive private school for wealthy kids, and those not so wealthy who could make a three-point basket, until she timed the crash in tech stocks perfectly, riding the bull market to an early retirement. Bored with retirement, she bought the B&B. She hired Mason after an audit of the school revealed that money had been embezzled. The headmaster accused Daphne, who was mortified at the charge. Mason proved that the headmaster had been the embezzler and tried to frame Daphne. Daphne promised Mason the use of a suite for the rest of his life as a bonus for saving her good name.

Mason and Samantha had been frequent guests, spending their last night together there, ending the weekend with uneasy good-byes. He had hoped to return with Abby, not Jordan. As Harry and Blues walked around the three-room suite on the third floor of the B&B, checking windows and doors, Mason explained to Daphne that no one was to know they were there. Daphne gave him a conspiratorial wink, telling him that her bad fortune was his good luck. Business was down and they were the only guests. She refused when Mason tried to pay for the suite, telling him that it was she who still owed him.

Centurion took the news that Jordan was not coming back without obvious disappointment. "That's cool, Mason," he said when Mason called him.

"I'll tell the judge and the prosecutor on Monday," Mason said. "They won't care as long as I promise she'll show up at her preliminary hearing."

"Where's Jordan stayin' at?" Centurion asked. "Terry Nix says she's got a therapy session scheduled he don't want her missin'. Says he'll make a house call if she don't want to come back here. That's the kind of dedication we got for these kids, Mason. You know what I'm sayin'?"

"Yeah," Mason said. "It's really heartwarming. I'll pass the message on and Jordan will call him if she feels the need."

"Tell you what, Mason," Centurion said. "I'm hungry. Why don't you and me meet somewhere for lunch?"

Mason took Centurion's question for an invitation he shouldn't refuse. "Sure. How about the Sidewalk Café on the Plaza?"

"Mason, look out the window, man. It's raining. What's the matter with you?"

"Don't worry, Centurion. You won't melt. I'll see you there in an hour."

* * *

The Sidewalk Café was on 47th Street in the heart of the Plaza. There were inside and outdoor sections, the outside covered with a heavy-duty plastic awning that was supposed to keep customers dry. The outdoor section was deserted. Even with the awning, rain blew across the tables. The hostess, inside and dry, ignored Mason as he sat at a wet table, his windbreaker zippered to his chin.

Mason wasn't hungry and didn't care about the rain. He preferred being out in the open with Centurion Johnson than in a dark booth of a quiet bar where a dead man could be mistaken for someone sleeping off a drunk.

Centurion's Mercedes glided to a stop at the curb in front of the café. The passenger window retreated, Centurion shaking his head at Mason, who couldn't see past Centurion to the driver. Centurion motioned Mason to join him, Mason leaning back in his chair, stretching his legs, picking up a menu that had been left on the table before the rain began.

"Shit," Centurion said, shoving the car door open and slamming it shut. He kicked Mason's feet away from an empty chair and sat down. "You are starting to annoy me, Mason."

"Hey, you invited me to lunch. What are you going to have?" he asked, sliding the menu to Centurion.

"I lost my appetite," Centurion answered, flinging the menu to the ground. "That bitch of yours took something that belongs to me."

Mason sat up. "Let's get something straight. Her name is Jordan. A bitch is a female dog. While you're probably more familiar with them as sexual partners, don't confuse them with my client."

Centurion dimmed his glare and turned up his high-wattage smile. "I guess I was all wrong about you, Mason. You just ain't gonna back down, is you?"

"Nope. Not until you treat me like one of your corporate donors and talk like a high school graduate. Thug-speak is lost on me."

"Fine. Let me put it this way," Centurion said. "Your client left Sanctuary in a hurry. In her haste, she took something that belongs to me, not her. I'm certain it was an innocent mistake. I'd appreciate your assistance in returning it to me."

"Much better, CJ. What would this item be?"

"You talk to her. I'm certain you can convince her to tell you. You can also assure her that if she returns this item to me today, there will be no questions asked and I'll consider the matter closed."

"That's very generous of you. If she doesn't have this item or is unable to return it to you by your deadline, what should I tell her?"

Centurion's happy grin morphed into a snarl. "You tell that bitch she better stay away from windows."

"That's a little over the top, don't you think? You're in the running for humanitarian of the year at the same time as you're threatening to throw my client out a window. If she does take a fall, I tell the cops about our little chat, which I might have to do anyway since you're threatening to kill her the same way Gina Davenport was killed. What little item did Jordan take from you?"

Centurion took a deep breath, a full wind-up before throwing his next pitch. "There are a lot of windows in this town, Mason."

"Great. I get a threat too. What? Are you running a special?"

Centurion opened his jacket, letting Mason see the butt of his gun. "Mason, what do I have to do to convince you that I'm serious as a motherfuckin' heart attack? That bitch," he said, but Mason raised his hand, stopping him. "Your client," he continued as Mason nodded, "made a bad decision. I'm willing to give her and you a free pass, but she's got to put it right."

"Look, Centurion. You're not going to shoot me in the middle of the Country Club Plaza in front of a restaurant full of witnesses. You've got a problem. Maybe I can help. I've got a problem, maybe you can help me."

Centurion laughed, this time with genuine amusement. "Damn, Mason. You just been playing me this whole time. You want to make a deal, we'll make a deal. What do you want?"

"I'll tell you what I don't want. I don't want to jack up your deal with Sanctuary. If you can soothe the guilty consciences of the power elite by selling them shares in Sanctuary, more power to you. If you do those kids some good, even more power to you. If there's something extra on the side for you, well, my friend, this is America—the land of opportunity. I only want one thing—to get my client acquitted. And I need your help to do that."

"I ain't confessin', if that's what you got in mind," Centurion said.

"I wouldn't expect that, especially if you were guilty. I need to know more about Gina Davenport. The foundation she set up in memory of her daughter was a big contributor to Sanctuary. How did you hook up with her in the first place? What's the story on her daughter's suicide? How does her husband and his coke habit fit in? Who supplies him? I don't care if you're in or out of the business, Centurion. Just give me something to work with and I'll get you back whatever Jordan took."

"You're asking a lot, Mason."

"A lot is at stake for Jordan. I get the impression a lot is at stake for you too."

The wind picked up, slapping them with pellets of rain. Centurion turned his collar up. "Come on," he said to Mason. "We'll go for a ride." Mason kept his seat. "I said, let's go for a fuckin' ride. I'm not going to kill you. Leastways, not today."

Mason followed Centurion to the Mercedes, sliding into the backseat after him. The driver was a young black man Mason didn't recognize. Centurion tapped him on the shoulder, and the driver pulled away from the curb heading east on 47th Street.

"Gina Davenport was one of the first people I signed up. She really dug the concept, especially the part about the kids working on the farm. She volunteered her time doing counseling. When Emily got all fucked up, she put her out there."

"What was Emily's problem?"

"Shit, man. I don't know nothing about psychology except what I learned on the street and in the joint. These kids—they all got too much of everything or not enough of anything. After that, it's all a bunch of social-worker bullshit, if you ask me. That Terry Nix can rattle off more diagnostic bullshit than you can imagine, and insurance will reimburse for every last one of them."

"Emily killed herself. That can't be good for business."

"Emily got high and thought she could fly. That's what happened with Emily. She was blowin' coke and shooting up when she got to Sanctuary. She sneaked some shit in and we didn't catch it."

"Was anyone with her when she died?"

"Yeah. Now that you mention it. Your client was," Centurion said. "Damn. I'd forgotten all about that. Your client was Emily's roommate. Ain't that a bitch."

"Yeah," Mason said. "A real bitch. Take me back to my car. I'll get you what you want."

CHAPTER 18

Mason took a quick inventory when he got back in his car. He still had his watch, wallet, fingers, toes, and eyeteeth. Centurion had tried to take him for every-thing he had, and Mason was pleased he didn't leave anything behind. He was scamming Centurion at the same time. The trick was to sort through the lies and figure out which ones contained clues—intentional or accidental—and which ones were just lies.

Centurion continued denying that he was involved with drugs even though Mason knew he was lying. In a trial, Mason always assumed the opposition would find out the bad facts and tell them to the jury. That was the only way he could prepare for disaster. He applied the same rule now, concluding that Centurion knew what he himself knew.

Which led to Mason's lie that he wouldn't cause trou-ble for Centurion. That was a lie Centurion could never afford to believe. Mason was glad he'd moved Jordan.

Centurion wouldn't wait long before doing whatever he could to protect himself from Mason.

That reality exposed Centurion's next lie—that he wouldn't kill Mason. A promise limited to that day. Mason believed him. Centurion wouldn't kill Mason today. Tomorrow was another story.

Centurion would wait until he knew whether Mason's promise to return whatever Jordan had taken from him was a lie. If Mason delivered, Centurion would take him out to make certain he didn't talk out of school. If he didn't deliver, Centurion would have one more reason to do the same thing. Mason wouldn't decide how to play that card until he knew what Jordan had and why it was so important to Centurion. He doubted that Jordan had stolen drugs from Centurion. Unless it was a huge quantity, it wasn't worth Centurion's trouble to get it back, especially with Mason's help. That would ensure Centurion's exposure as a drug dealer.

Mason gave Centurion credit for perhaps telling the biggest lie, implying that Jordan was somehow involved in Emily's death. The beauty of that lie was not just in the similarity between the deaths of mother and daughter. The real power of it lay in the desire to believe it. That Jordan could have thrown Gina Davenport out the window to her death was infinitely more believable if she had done the same thing to Gina's daughter, Emily. Though more horrible, it was easier to accept, making a perverse sort of sense.

The lie carried a more subtle threat. Even if Centurion decided not to kill Mason, he could sign Jordan's death warrant by whispering to the police that they should reopen the investigation into Emily Davenport's suicide. No doubt, Centurion would help the cops find their way to Jordan. A triple-murderer was assured of a reservation on death row.

That, Mason realized, was the real message Centurion delivered in the car. He knew that Mason wouldn't toady to him out of fear for his own safety. Mason's track record was proof of that. Threatening to tie Jordan to Emily's death was a brilliant stroke aimed at Mason's soft underbelly—his client.

Mason could defend Jordan against the charge that she had killed Dr. Gina. The hill got steeper with Trent's murder, but the slope went vertical with Emily's. No one, Mason included, could expect to win an acquittal on three murder charges tied so closely together.

Mason reordered his thoughts, listing two questions at the top. What was Jordan Hackett's relationship with Emily Davenport? And what did Jordan take from Centurion Johnson?

Harry, Mickey, and Blues were sitting around the dining room table at Daphne's when Mason returned. The rain had dwindled to a mist Mason shook from his coat and stamped from his shoes onto the Oriental rug in the entry hall. Mickey and Blues were studying a rough sketch Mickey had made of the exterior of the Victorian B&B. Harry was gazing out the window. Mason wanted to ask him about his eyesight, but waited for a private moment.

Daphne carried a tray of steaming mugs into the dining room, setting them onto the table. She was glowing with more than the warmth billowing from the cups.

"Lou," she said. "This is all very exciting." Daphne was petite, almost pocket-sized, vain enough to color the gray from her hair and dress for success on a Saturday afternoon. Mason guessed she was as old as Claire and Harry, though she resisted the visible hallmarks of her years with greater success. "Plus, Harry is going to fix the lock on the back door, aren't you, dear?"

Harry blended a smile with a wince as he picked up his mug. He was devoted to Claire and embarrassed at Daphne's attention. "Yes, ma'am," he said, taking a sip.

"We're each taking eight-hour shifts," Blues said. "Mickey is on till midnight, then me, then Harry. How long will this go on?"

Mason shrugged. "I don't know. Centurion Johnson says Jordan took something that belongs to him. He wants it back in a serious way. If I can take care of that, we might be able to step down to Def-Con Three."

"Did he say what it was?" Blues asked.

"Nope. He just sent me on a scavenger hunt," Mason said. "Daphne, do you have a computer hooked up to the Internet?"

"It's in my study," she said. "I don't normally let guests use it because I don't want people going to those awful web sites. Someone did that once and I got nothing but e-mails about barnyard sex for a month."

"Mickey," Mason said. "Go on-line, but leave Old McDonald alone. Private foundations have to file an annual report. I want the annual reports called Form 990 for Sanctuary for each year since it was formed. If you find anything interesting, see where it takes you. Where's Jordan?"

"She's in her room, dear," Daphne said.

Jordan's bedroom continued the Victorian theme with vanilla chintz curtains, a four-poster, canopied bed, and overstuffed furniture covered in muted floral fabric. It was a grandmother's room guaranteed to chafe a restless twenty-one-year-old.

"This place sucks and Daphne sucks," Jordan said. "I want to go back to Abby's loft." She was slouched in a wing-backed chair, her feet up on the bed, leafing through a magazine.

"Abby would like that," Mason said.

Jordan perked up. "She would? Really? Why can't we then?"

"We can as soon as we take care of some business. We might even be able to go back tonight."

"Great. Let's do it. This place is for people who've been dead thirty years and don't know it."

Mason sat down on the edge of the bed, slid his hand under Jordan's shoes, and dropped her feet to the floor. "I need a couple of things from you."

Jordan nodded, still slouched in the chair. "What do you want? I don't have any money and I saw how you and Abby look at each other, so I know you don't want to sleep with me," she said with the first sign of humor since he'd met her.

"Tell me about Emily Davenport."

Jordan shuddered at the mention of Emily's name. Her body convulsed so quickly—eyes snapping, veins popping, muscles tensing—that Mason thought she might have a seizure. She shook her shoulders and arms like an athlete loosening up, got up from her chair, and rubbed her arms with her hands to warm up from the sudden chill Mason had given her.

Breathing deeply, she said, "That's a name I haven't heard in a while."

"Centurion says you two were roommates at Sanctuary."

Jordan's color drained. "You talked to Centurion?"

"Yeah. We met for lunch on the Plaza and went for a ride in his Mercedes. He's not such a bad guy once you get to know him."

"He's a pig!"

"True, but for a pig, he's not bad once you get to know him."

"Do you joke about everything?" Jordan asked.

"Sometimes it helps keep the conversation moving until people are ready to talk about the tough stuff."

"Like Emily?"

Mason said, "Like Emily. Centurion said Emily got high and thought she could fly right out the window. Is that the way it happened?"

Jordan's chin found her chest. "If that's what Centurion said."

"What do you say?" Mason asked.

Jordan did a slow turn, running her hands over the chintz curtains, crumpling them, releasing them, and then smoothing the wrinkles from the fabric. She pulled the blackout shade down, gave it a yank, and held on as it rolled back up. She leaned her palms against the window, pressing her fingertips hard against the glass, making both Mason and the window quiver.

Mason said, "Talk to me, Jordan."

"We were best friends," she whispered, the words slipping out so softly Mason stepped closer to catch them.

"Was Centurion telling the truth?" he asked.

He looked over her shoulder, out the window into the rain that had returned, pinging against the window. An oak tree soared past the window, its branches scraping the house. Jordan craned her neck, searching for the treetop or a way out. The wood frame smelled of the dampness harbored in its pores.

"Emily was high. That part's true. She was also eight months pregnant. She wanted an abortion, but Terry Nix talked her out of it until it was too late. I don't know if that's why she jumped or if she was just too fucked up to know what she was doing."

"Did you try to stop her?"

Jordan gripped the window frame with both hands, rattling it, stopping when it didn't give way. She looked again for the crown of the oak tree.

"It was late summer, like today, only it was a beautiful night," she began. "That's why we had the window open. It was bigger than this one. You could sit in the opening, practically stretching your legs out. Emily was leaning her back against the frame with her feet against the other side." Jordan smiled at the memory, Mason seeing her reflection in the glass. "It was like she was inside a picture frame. I told her she looked like a painting. She said, yeah, call me a portrait of an unwed mother. Then she started singing this weird song, like a twisted nursery rhyme. *Hush, little baby, we're gonna die. Momma and baby, we can't fly.* I told her to cut it out, that it wasn't funny. Terry came in our room. She got this cold look, like she was going to do it. I tried to grab her. Terry said I shoved her, but I didn't. I know I didn't. I couldn't have," she said, balling her fists against the pane.

"I believe you," he said, sensing that it was she who lacked faith, not him. "I'm sorry," he added, regretting that was all he had to offer.

"Me too." Jordan ran her hands through her hair, turned, and dipped past Mason, circling to the other side of the bed. "Well, thanks for that trip down memory lane. You said there were two things you wanted to talk about."

Mason was glad to change the subject. "Centurion said you took something that belongs to him when you left Sanctuary. He wants it back."

"Can we get out of here if I give it back to him? Can I go back to Abby's?"

"I hope so."

Jordan opened the closet door and picked up her backpack. She unzipped a compartment on the front, pulled out a slender leather-bound ledger, and handed it to Mason. The pages were filled with a series of initials separated by slashes, followed by dates and dollar amounts ranging from $10,000 to $100,000 and either the letter *P* or *B* in parentheses.

"What is it?" Mason asked.

"Nothing. It doesn't matter. Give it back to him."

"It can't be nothing," Mason said. "Centurion all but threatened to kill me and you to get this little book back."

Jordan tapped into a wellspring of venom Mason thought had run dry. "I said it's nothing! Give it back to the fucking pig and tell him I'll rip his fucking heart out if he comes near me!"

Mason thought about the lies he'd told and heard that day, adding Jordan's outburst to the list. The ledger was something—maybe gold, maybe poison, maybe both— but it was the opposite of nothing. That was Jordan's lie. That she would rip out Centurion's heart if she had the chance was nothing but the truth.

Mason left Jordan in the bedroom. He used the all-in-one fax, copier, printer, and scanner in Daphne's study to make a copy of the pages in the book. Then he called

Centurion, arranging to meet him in another very public place. Mason thought his choice was perfect for returning a book. Besides, he doubted whether Centurion had ever been in the public library.

CHAPTER 19

Mickey was in the study, seated at Daphne's computer, scrolling through a web site and muttering under his breath, as Mason confirmed his meeting with Centurion Johnson. Maroon velvet wallpaper shrank the study, already cramped by a rolltop desk, its cubbyholes stuffed with incoming and outgoing mail.

"Is that a good idea, Boss?" Mickey asked.

"Is what a good idea?"

"You going out in the rain to meet Centurion?"

"I'm meeting him at the public library. That's the safest place I know unless you take a sex education book back into the stacks."

"Bad idea to go alone."

"Who said anything about going alone. I'll call Blues."

"He's tending bar tonight since the regular bartender called in sick. Normally, I'd fill in, but I'm babysitting Jordan."

"That's why he calls the place Blues on Broadway. The customers expect to see him. I'll call Harry."

"Not home. Claire picked him up a few minutes ago. They're flying to Chicago for dinner."

"Get real, Mickey. Nobody flies to Chicago for dinner, especially Harry and Claire."

"She said it's for Harry's birthday, the celebration that never ends. She's acting like he won't see another one. Their flight is at six and their reservations are at nine. They're coming back in the morning."

Mason knew his aunt better than he knew anyone alive. She had raised him on a regimen of duty disciplined by frugality. She was a serious woman with serious values moderated by a serious humor that rarely indulged in flights of fancy, let alone flights to Chicago for dinner. Mason gave Mickey credit for his unintentional insight. Claire wasn't worried that Harry wouldn't live to see his next birthday. She was worried that he wouldn't *see* by his next birthday, and she was determined that he would see as much as he could for as long as he could. He envied her devotion to Harry as he rubbed the ache left by Abby's last angry words.

Mason agreed with Mickey that it was a bad idea to meet Centurion alone, even at the public library, but he was out of backups and it was a worse idea to back out now. Centurion would assume that Mason was setting him up, and that was the worst idea Centurion could get.

"We'll use our cell phones again. I'll call you when I get to the library and you listen in. If Centurion doesn't use his library card to check out this book," Mason said, palming the ledger, "call the cops."

"Swell, but still stupid," Mickey said, studying the computer screen. "Check this out. I found a web site that has all the Form 990s for private foundations. Here's the one for Sanctuary."

Mason pulled up a chair next to Mickey, crowding him for a view of the screen. The form looked like every other tax return Mason had ever seen, an indecipherable grid of add, subtract, multiply, and divide adopted by Congress as the Accountant's Full Employment Act.

"David Evans told me that this form lists all the donations and expenses for the foundation. Find that part."

Mickey scrolled through the pages, stopping at the list of donors. "It lists the names of donors making contributions in excess of five thousand dollars. Let's take a spin," Mickey said as he rolled the cursor down the list, stopping at Emily's Fund.

"One hundred thousand dollars," Mason said. "That's a lot of cheddar for Dr. Gina to give to a place that didn't stop her daughter from committing suicide. See if there's anything interesting on the expense side."

"It lists compensation for the highest-salaried people," Mickey said, clicking the mouse to find those entries. "Nice work if you can get it," he added. "Centurion is knocking down three hundred and fifty K, and Brother Terry Nix is alive and well at one hundred and seventy-five."

"Don't forget the free room and board," Mason added with a sour laugh. "Who sits on the board of directors?"

Mickey pulled that page up on the screen. "It's a Who's Who of the big-bucks crowd," he said. "Plus a few more familiar names, Gina Davenport, David Evans, and Arthur Hackett. Hackett chairs the investment committee. Evans got nice fees as the outside investment advisor and lawyer for Sanctuary. Guess how much?"

"One hundred thousand dollars," Mason said.

"You got it, Boss. Dr. Gina brought the money in the front door and David Evans took it out the back door."

"The world is round," Mason said, looking at his watch. "I've got to get going." He handed Mickey the copy he'd made of Centurion's ledger book. "See if you can figure this out. It may be a list of contributors. Compare the initials to the names on the donor list."

Mickey asked, "If it's a list of donors, why would Centurion make such a big deal out of it? Those people are already on the Form 990."

"I don't know," Mason said. "Maybe they were contributing to a different cause."

"Centurion is going to ask you if you made a copy of his ledger. What are you going to tell him?"

"A lie."

Mason wished he was back at his office, diagramming the day's developments on his dry-erase board instead of trying to connect the dots as he drove to the library. The storm front that had parked over Kansas City all day had dropped more coins in the meter and settled in for the night, painting the town with a heavy black brush. The rain was steady now, in no hurry to move on.

The main branch of the public library was downtown, a block from the triangle formed by City Hall, the County Courthouse, and Police Headquarters. Though open until nine o'clock, it couldn't compete with the bars nearby or the multiplexes in the suburbs, and was empty except for a skeletal staff manning the checkout and information desks.

Mason chose a round table in the center of the first floor near the information desk. A circle of other tables ringed the one he had chosen. Study cubicles equipped with computer terminals abutted these tables. Beyond them, more tables and chairs were arrayed for newspaper and periodical fans. The walls rose twenty feet, giving the room a cavernous feel. More than the size of the space, Mason liked that there was no place for anyone to hide.

The woman working at the information desk looked like she hadn't left her post in years, her hair and skin the same color as the binding of the book she was reading. Mason had called Mickey from the parking lot. Settling in at his table with a polite nod to the librarian, he checked the cell phone clipped to his belt, reassured by its flashing green light that his phone-a-friend lifeline was hanging on. The cell phone, he wagered, had a stronger signal than did the librarian.

At eight forty-five, Terry Nix walked into the library wearing a rain poncho and a wide-brimmed canvas jungle hat cinched under his chin. Nix spotted Mason and joined him at his table, smiling the wide, crooked smile of the overly laid-back.

"Mason," he said with practiced surprise. "I didn't think I'd run into you here."

"You mean you left Paradise on a rainy Saturday night to come to the library to check out *Chicken Soup for the Social Worker* and just happened to catch me on my night out alone?"

"Life is full of the unexpected, Lou. It's a mysterious tapestry of interwoven threads—"

"Dipped in bullshit, Terry," Mason interrupted. "Are you naked under that poncho, or just using it to cover the tape recorder Centurion stapled to your testicles to record our innocent conversation?" Mason said loudly enough to rouse the librarian at the information desk.

She dropped her book, knocking over a bottle of

water perched in her lap. Sporting a watermark that spread across the front of her faded jeans, she hustled from her chair to the bathroom, glaring at Mason as she passed. "We close in ten minutes," she said.

"You have a gift for chasing people away, Lou," Nix said. "I'll keep you guessing about what's under my poncho. I'm looking for a special book to pick up. Have you seen it?"

Mason reached inside his windbreaker, removing the ledger from the inside pocket. "This one is pretty boring," he said, waving the small book at Nix, "but you're welcome to give it a try. I couldn't get into it."

Nix shoved his hat off the back of his head, wiping his lips with his tongue and extending his hand to Mason palm-up to receive the ledger. Mason tapped the ledger against the edge of the table and wrapped his fingers around it, bending the spine. Nix winced, his tongue poking from the corner of his mouth, as if Mason was squeezing his throat.

"It's not for everyone," Nix managed. "That's why I need to know if you made any copies."

"Of this?" Mason asked, opening the ledger and spreading the covers to expose two pages of entries. "Why would I want copies of this? I don't even know what the hell it is."

Mason didn't expect an answer. He just wanted Nix to tell Centurion that he was an idiot who didn't understand the significance of what he had.

"It's a list of donors," Nix volunteered. "We need it for tax purposes so we can send everyone a tax deduction form."

Mason studied the pages, his lips pursed in mock concentration. "Makes sense. I'll buy it," he said, dropping the ledger on the table.

Terry Nix shot his hand across the table, coming down on Mason's hand that beat him to the ledger. "You have some issues you should deal with, Lou," Nix said. "Taunting and teasing are power games symptomatic of sexual dysfunction, you know that. I can recommend someone very good for you to see."

"What's it mean when a man wearing a poncho in the library tries to hold hands with another man?"

"Take it easy, Lou," Nix said, withdrawing his hand and easing back in his chair. "It means I was impatient, and I'm sorry. I can see you have something on your mind. Let's talk about it."

"For starters, why did you tell Jordan to confess to a crime she didn't commit?"

"I don't expect you to understand the intricacies of psychotherapy, Mason. Jordan was in a lot of pain. She needed to know if her parents would validate her existence by coming to her defense."

"You mean by pinning Gina's murder on Trent, making the parents choose one child over the other?"

"It's the oldest story in the Bible, beginning with Jacob and Esau," Nix said.

"You forgot that Jacob framed Esau, though he didn't try to get away with murder. If you used the same kind of therapy with Emily Davenport, I'm not surprised she killed herself."

Nix loosened the knot on his chin strap and pulled his hat off, setting it on the table. "Actually, I do take responsibility for Emily's death, though it's stretching the facts to call it suicide. She was pregnant, like a lot of girls we see. She wanted an abortion. I talked her out of it."

"You've got the sixties, touchy-feely, left-wing schtick down pat, Terry. I didn't figure you as pro-life."

"It's not about politics for me. It's about the person. Some girls can handle an abortion. Some can't. I didn't think Emily could. I thought she'd be better off having the baby and giving it up."

"She killed herself rather than have the baby?"

Nix shook his head. "She was doing crack. I told her the baby would be born an addict. I don't know what she was thinking. I walked in on her and Jordan."

"Jordan says she tried to save her but you accused her of shoving Emily out the window."

"I know what I saw. Centurion and I talked it over. Under the circumstances, we decided to let it go because of Jordan's condition at the time."

"What was her condition?" Mason asked.

"Don't you talk to your clients, Lou? She was pregnant too. Telling the police that Jordan killed Emily wouldn't have helped anyone, especially Jordan's baby."

Mason's hand covering the ledger went slack as he absorbed what Nix had said. Children having babies was no longer news. Those babies growing up to be children having babies made for too circular a world. From Abby to Jordan to Jordan's baby, he thought, at last willing to acknowledge the possibility that Abby was both mother and grandmother. He didn't resist when Terry Nix picked up the ledger and walked away.

CHAPTER 20

Mason sat for another moment after Nix left, ignoring the librarian's officious paper shuffling as she counted down the final minutes of the library's day. He wasn't surprised that Centurion sent Nix to retrieve the ledger, rather than put himself at risk. It didn't matter to Mason whether Nix recorded their meeting from the cover of his poncho since Mickey had been listening. Mason snapped the cell phone out of the cradle on his belt.

"Could you hear all that?" he asked.

"It was pin-drop quality," Mickey said. "Daphne had a tape recorder. I put the mike next to the phone. The recording has a hiss soundtrack, but it can probably be enhanced."

"Good job. Where's Jordan?"

"Upstairs. Daphne checks on her every fifteen minutes. She's driving Jordan crazy. You think Nix was bullshitting you about Emily and Jordan?" Mickey asked.

"Centurion, Nix, and Jordan tell pretty much the

same story about Emily Davenport, except for the small detail about whether Emily jumped or Jordan pushed her. The part about Jordan having a baby should be easy enough to verify. On Monday, check the city's birth certificate records."

"Why not ask Jordan? Don't you think she'd remember?"

"I think she would have told me when I asked her about Emily, but she didn't. She's got a reason for not telling me, so I'd rather find out on my own until she's ready to talk about it. I'm beat. I'm going to get some dinner and go home. See you tomorrow."

The rain had stopped and the clouds had parted for the debut of a new moon when Mason walked out of the library, proving his aunt's adage that if you didn't like the weather in Kansas City, wait fifteen minutes and it would change. A warm breeze dried the air, carrying the smell of a barbecue joint a couple of blocks away that was renowned for its burnt ends, and answering Mason's question of what he would have for dinner.

Mason had parked his car on 12th Street in front of the library. He put the top down and circled back west to the barbecue restaurant on the corner of 13th and Grand, picked up an order of burnt ends, and headed south on Grand, already tasting the beer waiting in his refrigerator that would chase the barbecue. He popped a Coltrane CD into the player he'd had installed in the dash, letting the mellow sound take him home.

Traffic was light, in keeping with downtown's dead-on-Saturday-night reputation. Mason stopped for a red light at 17th Street, wishing he'd left the top up when a two-tone Chevy Caprice, one dent shy of the demolition derby hall of fame, stopped alongside him in the outside lane, bleeding bone-jarring rap from its open windows, overpowering Coltrane.

The driver looked to Mason to be no more than twenty, in spite of a patchy beard that failed to cover his patchy skin. His left arm hung over the open window, a tattoo of a snake wrapped around a naked woman writhing with the car's vibrations against his pale skin. The driver's passenger, a black man wearing a do-rag and a cold stare, drew hard on a joint, its sweet, pungent odor leaking out of the car. He burned the joint down to his knuckle and passed the butt to the driver.

The light changed, Mason popping the clutch, jumping out to put distance between him and the Caprice. The Caprice kept pace, escorting Mason to the next light at 18th Street, then roaring ahead, cutting in front of Mason just before they reached the intersection.

Mason slammed on his brakes, leaning on his horn, not stopping before the front bumper of the TR-6 kissed the rear of the Caprice. The passenger jumped out, sprinting to Mason's car. He leapt into the seat next to Mason, pointing a gun at Mason's belly.

It was a smoothly executed car-jacking, over in seconds and witnessed by no one. Mason was smart enough not to resist. "You want the car?" Mason asked, keeping his hands on the wheel. "You can have the car. Just leave me the burnt ends."

"Don't want this pussy piece of shit," the gunman said. "Want your sorry ass." He jabbed Mason in the ribs with the barrel of his gun. "Now shut the fuck up and follow my man."

The light turned green and the Caprice pulled away,

its music suddenly muted, drawing no attention as they turned east on 18th. The gunman rode with his back against the passenger door, both hands gripping his pistol, staying out of Mason's reach. Mason doubted that he was the victim of a random street crime, certain now that Centurion Johnson had played him like a chump from the beginning.

Centurion had worked Mason with a velvet glove, stroking him and threatening him until Mason brought him the ledger, using Terry Nix as a cover. Mason imagined Centurion watching from a safe distance, laughing as Mason put his ragtop—and his guard—down. Mason would have to wait for a rematch with Centurion. In the meantime, he tried the gunman.

"You meet a lot of nice people in your line of work?" Mason asked.

The gunman motioned with his pistol to the road ahead, silently telling Mason to watch where he was going. Mason knew where they were going—into the East Side where Centurion and his Ebony and Ivory carjacking team would have the home-court advantage. Mason swerved to avoid a pothole that the Caprice rode over without fanfare. The gunman rolled with the car's pitch, casting an anxious look at the street, then pressing the barrel of his gun under Mason's armpit.

"Easy, slick," Mason said. "The car has a low ground clearance. I hit a pothole like that one and we'll have to tow the car out of it. I'm not going to turn stupid and give you an excuse to use that thing, so relax and tell me where we're meeting Centurion."

"I tole you before," the gunman said. "Shut the fuck up and drive. That's all you gotta do. You do that, and I won't shoot your ass."

The Caprice turned north a couple of miles east of downtown, following a maze of side streets and alleys until the only thing Mason was certain of was that he wasn't in Kansas anymore. The neighborhood had its own measure of darkness, devoid of streetlights and porch lights, illuminated only by passing headlights. The few houses Mason could make out had barred or boarded doors, overgrown yards, and no candles in the windows.

The Caprice pulled to a curb in the middle of a blacked-out street, Mason easing to a stop behind him, his passenger sitting up, tightening the grip on his gun. The driver of the Caprice walked toward Mason, a gun in one hand, his other hand behind his back, hiding something worse than the gun.

Mason tallied his odds. His passenger was too far away to jump without getting a bullet for his trouble. The driver was three steps away, close enough for a fatal shot. Mason squeezed the steering wheel, screaming inside at the futility of dying without trying, smelling his own sweat.

The passenger lunged at Mason as his partner reached the TR-6, jamming the barrel of his gun under Mason's chin. "Hold real still," he said, blowing dope breath in Mason's mouth. The driver stuck his gun in his belt, showing Mason the black bag he'd been hiding behind his back, shaking the bag open, pulling it over Mason's head, clotting his vision.

The bag reeked of a medicinal scent. Mason gasped and gagged, the rough fabric against his face. His sweat turned cold as a suffocating panic swept over him. He tore at the bag, trying to rip it from his face, the dark water taking him.

* * *

Consciousness came in painful pieces. Voices floated overhead, out of reach. Mason wanted to move, but couldn't, his head too heavy, his body too weak. Someone was playing a drum, he thought, until he recognized the internal percussion throbbing between his ears. Movement came to his arms and legs, whether by his own effort or others he couldn't tell, still struggling to open his eyes. Blinking at last in the dim light of a squalid room, knocked back by the stench of foul, dead air, he found the floor with his hands, then a wall behind him, then a hazy face in front of him.

"You not dead," the face said.

"Too early to tell," Mason said. "Where am I?"

The face came into focus. It belonged to a boy sitting cross-legged on the floor, his round black face faintly familiar. "My room," the boy said.

"Are you dead?" Mason asked.

"Not yet," the boy said.

"Then I guess I'm not dead yet either."

Mason looked around, getting his bearings. The room was small, barely big enough for the mattress on the floor, a dresser missing its top drawer in one corner, a pile of dirty clothes in another, a poster of Shaq and Kobe on one wall, crumbling Sheetrock and exposed wiring on another. Black plastic trash bags were tacked around a window, shutting out the light that crept around the edges, catching dust mites.

"You got a name?" Mason asked the boy.

"Donnell," the boy answered.

"You got a bathroom, Donnell?"

The boy smiled. "You're funny," he said, offering Mason his hand, helping Mason to his feet. "Come on."

The bathroom was in a hall outside Donnell's bedroom. There was a mirror above the sink with fluorescent lights on each side, the left side burnt out, the right side flickering like a gray candle. Donnell stood in the doorway, gazing up at Mason with unblinking eyes as if he'd made a grand discovery, finding a white man dead on the floor in his bedroom, miraculously resurrected.

"Give me a minute," Mason told the boy, closing the door. He wasn't surprised when the toilet didn't flush or when the water ran from the sink faucet with a rusty hue. It was enough to be alive, even if he didn't know why. It was enough to be in Donnell's house, even if he didn't know where it was. And it was oddly comforting that the boy was familiar to him, even if he couldn't place him. He opened the bathroom door, pleased that Donnell was waiting for him.

"Donnell, are there any other grown-ups here?" Donnell nodded. "Where are they?" Donnell pointed down the stairs at the end of the narrow hall. "How many?" Donnell shrugged. "You forget how to talk?" Donnell shook his head, giggling. The door to another bedroom opened and a stick-thin black woman called to the boy.

"Donnell, what you doin'? Get outta this hall!"

She grabbed the boy by the collar and dragged him back to his room, closing the door behind him. She leaned against the door, one hand on the knob, exhausted by the effort. A thin black dress, shapeless against her bony frame, hung on her like a sheet on a clothesline. Her eyes were dull, but Mason caught something in her look, the same familiarity he'd seen in the boy.

"Varonda? Is that you?" Mason asked.

"I didn't think you'd remember me," she said. "Be better if you forgot."

"It hasn't been that long," Mason said. "What, nine, ten months? You were charged with possession with the intent to sell. I got you into a diversion program. Donnell was in court with you. That's why I recognized him."

"He's a good boy, but he don't mind me like he should."

"It's hard for a kid to stay in a dark room. Why does he have to stay in there?"

"Only safe place in a crack house like this," she said, looking over Mason's shoulder.

Mason heard footsteps on the stairs as she spoke. He turned in time to see the passenger from the Caprice standing at the top of the stairs, his gun pointed at him again.

"Thought you was never wakin' up," the man said.

"Was I supposed to?" Mason asked.

"Don't matter to me," the man said. "Varonda, you know him?"

"He was my lawyer. Got me into that diversion program."

The man laughed. "You done got diverted all right, girl. Straight back to the fuckin' street sellin' your ass for a rock."

Mason remembered Varonda. She carried twenty more pounds and a glimmer of hope when he negotiated the diversion deal. She was on the edge then, having spent time on the street, but not too much time to get off. Since then, she'd gone back, hustling for crack, wasting her body until there was little left to hold or hustle.

"Fuck you, Tyrone," she said, joining Donnell in his room, shutting out the rest of the world as she slammed the door.

"So, Tyrone, what do you say you and me go out to the ballpark and catch the Royals," Mason said.

"Only thing you gonna catch is this," Tyrone said, waving his gun at Mason.

"If you were going to shoot me, you would have done that last night," Mason said. "Tell Centurion I want to talk to him. We'll work something out."

"Don't know no Centurion," Tyrone said.

"Fine. You don't know him. I do. Give me a phone and I'll call him."

"Don't got no phone and you ain't callin' nobody. Get your ass on downstairs," he said, motioning Mason to go first.

The driver of the Caprice waited at the bottom of the stairs, leading Mason like a slow-moving target with a shotgun wedged under his arm, aiming Mason toward a straight-backed chair in the middle of the front room. A couch littered with remnants of fast food was shoved against the wall opposite a wide picture window covered with a slender sheet of plywood. A whiskey-colored, short-haired mutt, its ribs riding hard against its skin, burrowed its nose into the cushions, digging for a meal.

Tyrone grabbed a roll of duct tape and a length of rope from the couch, the dog snapping at him.

"Tyrone," the driver said, "quit playin' with that dog. We don't got all day."

"Easy, Richie," Tyrone said to the driver. "I ain't playin' with your dog. That bitch is a killer."

"Just smack that dog, it bites you. That's the way I trained it," Richie said, pointing the shotgun at the dog. Mason took advantage, wheeling, grabbing the shotgun. Richie rammed the barrel into Mason's gut, breaking Mason's hold. "Settle down, man!" Richie said. "You're gonna get all this you can handle soon enough," he added, prodding Mason with the shotgun, backing him into the chair. Tyrone clamped Mason by the shoulder, planting him on the seat. At least, Mason thought, he knew their names.

"Tyrone, Richie," Mason said as Tyrone looped the rope around his ankles and the legs of the chair, binding his upper arms at his sides with duct tape, his hands free but helpless. "Give me a clue here. You want something. You need something. Tell me what it is and we'll work it out."

They didn't answer. Tyrone disappeared while Richie kept the shotgun a dismembering distance from Mason's chest.

"Fellas, be reasonable," Mason said, fighting to keep his voice a notch below pleading. They had to want something, and he was ready to give it to them if they would only tell him what it was. It was hard to bargain with people who acted like they didn't hear you. "Tell Centurion that I don't care what he's doing at Sanctuary. It's none of my business."

Tyrone came back carrying a can of sterno, a bag of white powder, a syringe, and a lighter. He tapped out a measure of powder into a small cup made of tinfoil, added a liquid from a plastic tube in his shirt pocket, and stirred the mixture with his finger. Setting the tinfoil on a three-legged stand, he lit the sterno, slipping the flame beneath the tin foil.

"Hey, guys. Get real," Mason said, seeing his future in the barrel of the syringe, not the barrel of the shotgun.

Tyrone peeled off another strip of duct tape, grabbed Mason's left wrist, taping it to the side of the chair, flicking the large vein in the center of Mason's arm, rubbing the surrounding skin and raising the vein to the surface like a swollen blue ribbon. Tyrone dipped the syringe in the tinfoil, and drew the plunger back, filling the barrel, squirting a drop onto the floor to be certain the needle was ready.

Mason lunged, bucking the chair into Tyrone. "Goddammit! Give me a chance! It's the ledger! I made a copy. I'll get it for you."

It was all Mason could think of, but they ignored him, going about the business of killing him without threat or explanation. Tyrone tore off another piece of masking tape, trying to press it against Mason's mouth as Mason spat at him, whiplashing his head to avoid Tyrone's grasp.

The dog bounded off the sofa, nipping at Tyrone. Tyrone cursed and swiped at the dog as Mason bucked one more time, knocking the chair over. The dog was straddling Mason, Richie grabbing it by the scruff of the neck, escalating the game from dog play to dogfight as the mutt bit Richie's hand, drawing blood and fury. Tyrone was laughing, a giddy screech.

Richie clubbed the dog with the butt of the shotgun. The dog yelped, springing at Richie's trigger hand, the shotgun errupting, catching Tyrone in the gut, blowing him onto the couch, dropping the loaded syringe next to Mason. Richie howled as the dog kept ripping his hand. When he dropped the shotgun, Mason scooted to pick it up, cradling it in the crook of his arm, aiming at Richie.

"Get out or I'll kill you!" Mason shouted. Richie finally broke the dog's grip, clutching his ruined hand to his belly. "Run while you can!" Mason said.

"Varonda!" Mason yelled. "It's okay. It's over. Help me! Varonda!"

Varonda crept down the stairs, Donnell on her hip, hugging her waist. She tiptoed past the whimpering dog, spitting on Tyrone's body.

Donnell sat down next to Mason. "You not dead yet," he said.

CHAPTER 21

"The practice of law is not about the pursuit of justice," a professor of Mason's once told him. "The practice of law is about the economic resolution of disputes. Justice is too elusive for mere mortals."

Mason thought about his law professor's cynical admonition as he stood next to the open back end of an ambulance. A paramedic wiped blood and brains off him while two others carried Tyrone's body out of the house. Centurion's resolution of his dispute with Mason had run into another harsh reality of the marketplace. Good help is hard to find.

Donnell was in a squad car, crying for his mother, who sat in another car, handcuffed and trembling. Mason couldn't tell if she was shaking because of the shooting or because she needed a rock. He knew it would be a long time before Donnell saw his mother again, longer still before he understood why.

Samantha Greer came toward him from the house,

stripping latex gloves from her hands. Two detectives offered her a preliminary report on the neighbors, and she dismissed them with a not-now wave, bearing down on Mason, who checked the inside of the ambulance for cover.

She gave the thumb to the paramedic and pointed her forefinger at Mason like a switchblade. "Not one smart-ass remark, not one excuse, not one goddamn lie, or I'll tie you back up in that chair myself, so help me God, Lou!"

"That doesn't leave me much room, does it?" Mason said.

"Do not push me, Lou. I mean it!" she said. "I've got a dead body, a strung-out hooker, and a little boy using blood for finger paints. What in the hell are you mixed up in?"

"What day is it?"

A red tide rose in Samantha's face and she raised a hand, more to stop herself than him.

"I'm not kidding," Mason said. "I don't know what day it is for sure."

"It's Sunday, my day off, except when my ex-boyfriend gets a front-row seat at a homicide. How could you not know what day it is?"

"I was on my way home last night when I was carjacked. The dead guy's name is Tyrone. He and his partner, a white guy named Richie, grabbed me at 18th and Grand. They were driving a beat-up Caprice. Tyrone jumped in my car and made me follow the Caprice. They put a bag over my head that was laced with some kind of drug, and I was out until today. When I came around, they strapped me to the chair and were about to needle me to death. The dog saved my life."

Samantha shook her head, hands on her hips. "Right. I suppose the dog's mother was Lassie."

"I don't think this dog had a mother," Mason said. "Richie hit the dog with the butt of the shotgun and the dog attacked him. The shotgun went off and Tyrone took the hit. The dog was on Richie and when he dropped the shotgun, I was able to get it and Richie took off."

"You were tied to a chair lying on your back!"

"I'm a very good scooter when someone is trying to kill me," Mason said.

"And I'm supposed to believe they picked you at random as part of a new urban sport?"

"I don't know why they picked me. They didn't take my money. They didn't ask me for anything. They just did it."

"Well, since they wouldn't tell you what they wanted, what did you tell them? You must have offered them something. No one, especially you, sits politely waiting to be called on while the bad boys are getting ready to kill you. You begged or bargained. What did you think they wanted?"

Mason realized Samantha was right. They had interrogated him with silence, letting his fear of dying do the talking. "Best guess, they were working for Centurion Johnson. Jordan Hackett took something from Centurion. I gave it back, but I kept a copy. I told them I would give them the copy. Apparently, that wasn't good enough for Centurion."

"Did you see Centurion Johnson during your escapade?"

"No."

"Did they mention his name?"

"Actually, the only one who ever talked to me said he didn't know Centurion."

"Why would they deny it if they were going to kill you? Isn't that when they tell you everything so you don't die of curiosity?"

"Bad manners, I guess," Mason said.

"What did Jordan take?"

"A ledger book containing names, initials, dates, and amounts of money. I couldn't figure out what it meant."

"Did Centurion tell you that's what she took from him?"

Mason hit his first speed bump. "No, but that's what he wanted."

"Who told you that?"

"Terry Nix, the social worker at Sanctuary. I set the meeting up with Centurion for the downtown library. Nix showed up and I gave him the ledger. I was on my way home when they grabbed me."

"Did Nix mention Centurion's name?"

"No."

"What did he say was in the ledger?"

"The names of donors to Sanctuary," Mason answered, feeling the stupid stick whack him in the back of the head.

"Let me get this straight, Lou. You gave Terry Nix a ledger of donors that Centurion Johnson didn't ask for, then you get car-jacked by two freaks that won't tell you why they are going to kill you and deny knowing Centurion Johnson. Then, when one of the freaks get dead, you want me to go arrest Centurion Johnson. Is that about it?"

"Not good enough, huh?"

"Duh!" she said, looking him over from head to toe,

satisfying herself that he was still in one piece. "Throw away your clothes. Blood never comes out."

"That's it? End of investigation?" Mason asked.

"No, Lou. End of interrogation, beginning of investigation. You said you made a copy of the ledger. That's why they snatched you. I want the copy."

"Well, yeah," Mason said, feeling a lot less clever. "But I offered to give it to them and they weren't interested."

Samantha said, "If you're right about Centurion and the ledger, they were interested. Once you told them you had a copy, it was okay to kill you. Now Centurion will go after the copy and anyone else who has seen it. Care to give me a list?"

"Mickey Shanahan has the only copy. I'll drop it off this afternoon."

"You don't have a car, remember. I'll take you. Just tell me where."

"Daphne's B&B," he told her.

Samantha pursed her lips and nodded. "Perfect," she said. "Just perfect."

Mason's body clock had kicked into a twilight time zone the moment Richie dropped the black bag over his head. Waiting for Samantha to finish buttoning up the murder scene, he tried to reset his clock beginning with the last time he'd eaten. At first, he thought that had been lunch the day before until he remembered that lunch had been a "soup sandwich" in the rain with Centurion. When he couldn't remember the meal or the menu, his stomach growled, telling him to skip the details and feed it now. When Samantha finally pointed him toward her car, he was a little wobbly. Dried blood and day-old sweat gave him a slaughterhouse aura.

"You really should consider corporate law," Samantha told him as she lowered all the windows in her car and turned the air-conditioning on high. "It's easier on your wardrobe."

"Lower class of clientele," Mason answered. "I'm starved. Drive through the first fast-food you find."

"Why not. A dose of quarter-pounder breath will make you irresistible," Samantha said.

Samantha watched Mason devour a burger, fries, another burger, and a drink large enough for a diving board, as they sat in her Crown Victoria.

"If my car turns up, tell them to take it to George's Body Shop at 35th and Troost," Mason said between bites.

"We don't deliver," Samantha told him. "You're welcome to tour the city lot during normal office hours."

Mason wiped his mouth with his sleeve, adding another stain. "I pay my taxes," he said. "What kind of service is that?"

"Pay more taxes, you get better service," she said. "Why are you trying so hard not to tell me about what happened? I'm on your side."

"I told you what happened. You told me I was a moron. That doesn't encourage class participation. Besides, you've already decided that my client is guilty. The only evidence you're interested in is the evidence against her, and there's damn little of that."

"There was enough evidence to arrest her. There is enough evidence to bind her over for trial, and if I do my job, there will be enough evidence to convict her. That doesn't mean you have to run around playing knight-errant tempting the fates—and me—with your life. I don't like finding you on the floor in a pool of blood every time I open the door to an elevator or crack house."

"It's not about you and me, Sam. We're both doing our jobs," Mason said. "That's all."

"No, Lou," she said, holding the steering wheel like it was a life preserver. "It is about us even if there isn't any us anymore. I don't want to find your body behind one of those doors. Don't make that part of my job."

Samantha reminded Mason of the difficulty he'd had letting go of his ex-wife, Kate. Mason didn't stop loving Kate because she stopped loving him. If anything, it made him love her more and want her more. It was a long time before he could think about her without feeling the hole in his heart. Self-pity filled the hole for a while, giving way to a dull emptiness, not healing until he met Abby. Mason hadn't understood the depth of Samantha's feelings for him when he let their relationship wither. After Kate, it was easier than a straight-ahead breakup, but it was cowardly, and he wasn't proud of himself.

"I'll do my best," he said.

"So, how's your new?" she asked him.

"Her name is Abby," Mason answered. "She's fine."

"That's nice," Samantha said, shifting the Crown Vic out of neutral.

It was mid-afternoon when Mason walked into Daphne's, followed by Samantha. Mickey, Claire, Harry, Blues, and Rachel Firestone were sitting at the dining room table, each poring over pages of the ledger. Daphne was circling the table, pouring lemonade.

"Oh, Dear Lord!" Daphne said when she saw Mason, blood-soaked and ragged. The pitcher slipped from her hand, shattering when it hit the hardwood floor.

Rachel bolted from her chair, grabbing Mason by the shoulders. "You're all right?" she asked.

Mickey slapped the table with an I-told-you-so thump. Blues and Harry permitted themselves small grins, while Claire waited quietly, her eyes filling. Mason walked to her side, putting his hand on her shoulder as he leaned over and kissed her on the cheek, whispering in her ear.

"I'm fine," he assured his aunt, squeezing the hand she placed over his.

Mickey and Rachel retrieved paper towels from the kitchen and began soaking up the lemonade. Daphne covered her mouth, regaining her composure.

"Samantha," she said. "Welcome back. I'm so pleased to see you again, especially with Lou," she added.

"It's good to see you again too, Daphne," Samantha said. "But this is a business call. I'm just dropping Lou off and picking up some papers. This looks like what I came for," she said, gathering the pages of the ledger from the table. "Is this it?" she asked Mason.

"That's it."

Looking at the people around the table, she said, "Looks like my list just got a little longer."

Mason didn't answer. Abby and Jordan were standing in the entry hall at the bottom of the stairs. Jordan backed away from Samantha, edging behind Blues. Abby took Mason's face in her hands.

"I'm sorry," Abby said, and kissed him softly, not caring about the crowd.

Daphne flushed and said, "Oh, my, I didn't realize," and took refuge in the kitchen.

Samantha cleared her throat, drawing Mason's attention. "I guess I better add another name," she said to him, and left.

"What list is she talking about?" Abby asked after Samantha drove away.

"I don't think it's her Christmas list," Blues answered. "Where the hell have you been and whose blood are you wearing?" he asked Mason.

Mason described the car-jacking and the dogfight. "Detective Greer thinks that if Centurion was willing to kill me because I kept a copy of the ledger, anyone who knows about it could be at risk."

"Since when did Sam become Detective Greer?" Mickey asked.

Rachel answered, "Since Daphne welcomed her and Lou home and Abby kissed and made up with Lou."

"Oh, my," Daphne said again. "I'll make some more lemonade."

"By the way," Mason said, aiming his cross-examination at Mickey. "What are Abby, Claire, and Rachel doing here?"

"Hey," Abby snapped. "Don't blame Mickey. Blame yourself for getting car-jacked and shot at instead of answering your phone. I got worried when I couldn't find you or Jordan, so I called Rachel and Claire. They guessed you would bring Jordan here. Apparently, you're something of a regular," she added with a sharp edge.

"Abby's right," Claire said. "You disappeared without a trace after you told Mickey you were going home and going to bed."

"This is a helluva story," Rachel said.

"Well, you can't write it yet," Mason told her. "Not without painting a bull's-eye on everyone's backs."

"Samantha is a good cop," Harry said. "Let her handle it."

"That would make sense except for one thing," Mason said. "Sam has a different agenda. She thinks Jordan killed Gina Davenport and Trent Hackett. She may look at Centurion for the car-jacking, but she won't try to tie them together and consider someone else in the murders unless I can convince her it's all connected. The ledger is the only link and we don't know what it means. Terry Nix said it was a list of donors, but that's public information and this ledger is in code."

"Question is," Blues said, "what did they donate?"

"Or buy," Harry suggested. "Centurion was one of the biggest drug dealers in the region until we took him down. He would have gone away for the rest of his natural life if he hadn't rolled over on the people he was buying from. I'd say that he's still dealing and that ledger is a list of his preferred customers."

Mason said, "I admit that's the logical choice. But why risk the sweet deal he's got with Sanctuary to sell dope? He's paying himself a salary of three hundred and fifty thousand bucks, driving a Mercedes, and living large in the country."

"Then if he's not selling drugs, what is he selling?" Abby asked.

"Babies," Jordan said from the corner of the dining room.

They had ignored Jordan, almost forgetting that she was there. She captured their attention with a single word that none of them had considered.

"What are you saying?" Abby asked her.

"It's a list of illegal adoptions. Centurion sells babies."

"How do you know that?" Mason asked.

Jordan looked at them, hugging herself as she abandoned her corner. "Because he sold my baby girl. I want her back and I'll do anything I have to do to find her. That's why I took the ledger. Centurion is the one who should be worried, not us."

"Mickey," Mason said. "Did you make an extra copy of that ledger?"

"You know I did, Boss."

"Pass it out," Mason told him.

CHAPTER 22

Mason chased Jordan's ghosts and demons as he prepared for her preliminary hearing. He didn't trust Centurion to let matters lie, and convinced Jordan to remain at Daphne's. Mickey, Harry, and Blues continued their rotation. Abby found excuses to drop by, but didn't ask Jordan for a DNA sample, settling instead for Jordan's face-splitting smile each time Abby walked in the room. At Samantha Greer's direction, a patrol car cruised the neighborhood every couple of hours. It was, she told Mason, the best she could do.

Mason found Centurion's ledger easy to understand and hard to decipher. He assumed that the initials shown on each entry were those of the adoptive parents; that the date shown was the date of the adoption; and that the amount listed was the purchase price for the baby. Either the letter *P* or *B* followed each entry, citations he couldn't interpret.

Abby broke that code at Mason's house Monday evening where she and Mason were observing the one-week anniversary of Gina Davenport's murder. Tuffy was stretched out between them as they sat on the living room floor, rotating her head from one lap to the other, displaying a politician's loyalty to whoever did the better job of scratching behind her ears.

Abby sat up, plunking Tuffy's head on the floor. "*P* is for pink and *B* is for blue. Girls are pink and boys are blue," she announced. Tuffy stuck out her tongue, cuffed Abby on the thigh with her paw, and abandoned her for Mason. "I wish we could identify the adoptive parents," she said.

"That might help Jordan find her daughter, but it won't help me defend her," Mason said. "Maybe I've run down this blind alley long enough. I've got to get back to the murder, the physical evidence—anything to poke holes in the prosecutor's case."

"The entries in the ledger go back over twenty years," Abby said as if she hadn't heard him. "That's a long time." She handed Mason the ledger, pointing to the earliest entries.

"You're right," Mason said. "Plus some of these entries were made while Centurion was a guest of the State. I don't get that, but it still doesn't help me."

Abby nestled into Mason's shoulder, forcing Tuffy to share his lap with her. "What if," Abby said, hesitating to finish her question.

"What if what?" Mason asked. Abby's scent had become imprinted on him, as had the fine line from her chin to her neck and the way she absently brushed her hair behind her ear. She fit against him and he against her like pottery shards dug up and reunited, belonging, not clinging. "What?" he asked again, running his hand down her arm.

"What if the dates in the ledger aren't the dates of

the adoptions. What if they are the dates the babies were born."

"So what?"

"So," she said, taking his hand, kissing the tip of his finger, and guiding it to an entry on the first page. "That's the date my baby and Jordan were born. Plus, it's a *P*—pink for girl."

Mason draped his arm across Abby, holding her. "You're trying too hard," he whispered.

"Maybe not hard enough," she said. "Call Jordan. Ask her when her baby was born."

"Okay," Mason said, sighing as he got up. He retrieved the cordless phone from the kitchen and came back to the living room as he spoke with Jordan. Abby was pacing. Tuffy was watching. He thanked Jordan and checked the date in the ledger. "It's a match, including the letter *P*," he said. "But that doesn't mean your baby, or Jordan, or her baby are in this book. Your baby and Jordan were born in St. Louis. Centurion does business in Kansas City. He doesn't have a St. Louis branch."

"Then why does he have a ledger with both those dates in it? And who dragged me into this mess in the first place?" A small ceiling spotlight meant for a painting long since removed splashed her face, casting her shadow against the empty wall where she stood. "Why would somebody do that?"

Mason went to her, blocking the light, dwarfing the shadow. "I don't know," he said. "But I'm beginning to think we better find out."

The next afternoon, Mason attended Trent Hackett's funeral, forcing his unwelcome condolences on Arthur and Carol Hackett. As he waited his turn in the throng that surrounded the family before the service, Mason overheard one woman remark to another how poised Carol Hackett was in the face of such an unspeakable tragedy that would only get worse if the rumors of the daughter's guilt proved true.

The Hacketts chose cremation, reminding Mason of Trent's hellfire greeting card. He hadn't figured Trent for a prophet, though he doubted Trent had seen his own future in the flames.

He sat with Jordan and Abby, one row behind the family section. Parents and daughter did not speak, though Jordan looked at them with such longing and despair that Mason thought she would vaporize if they touched. Arthur Hackett, his hard arrogance splintered, sheltered his wife with his burly arm, not able to make room for Jordan in his grief.

Jordan sat between Mason and Abby, her head bowed, her long hair obscuring her face from the unrelenting stares of mourning voyeurs, her tears falling onto her lap and disappearing into the dark fabric of her dress. When the minister began his eulogy, she grasped Abby's hand, interlocking their fingers, anchoring her to the pew. The minister spoke of family love, community sorrow, and God's forgiveness, none of which, Mason knew, would bind the Hacketts' wounds. Instead, he was reminded of his Aunt Claire's more earthbound philosophy—take care with the people you love because some things can't be fixed.

Samantha Greer watched from the rear of the church, waiting until afterward to talk to Mason as Abby ushered Jordan through the crowd.

"Centurion's lawyer invited me to Sanctuary," she told

him as they stood outside. Mourners swept past them, anxious to escape the unspeakable grief of parents burying a murdered child.

"For dinner or just dessert?" Mason asked.

"Appetizers, plus a tour of the house," she said.

"Hoping you won't seek a search warrant," Mason said. "When are you going?"

"I went this morning. The lawyer answered all my questions. Centurion shined his smile on me and gave the tour."

"Waste of time?"

"Not for them. If I get a warrant to search or arrest, they'll say they have nothing to hide and are cooperating fully, using my visit as proof. Centurion knows we're watching him, so he'll be on his best behavior for a while. That takes some heat off of you."

"Any sign of my car? The rented Camry I'm driving is bad for my self-image."

"I'll let you know when your car hits the top of my give-a-shit list," Samantha said.

"That's not a charitable attitude," he said, enjoying the comfortable give-and-take that had first drawn them together. "What did you find out about my friends from the crack house?"

"I don't think they'll be missed since no one has claimed Tyrone's body and no one has filed a missing person's report on Richie. They had loose connections to Centurion from his days in the drug trade, but we haven't found evidence of any current contacts."

She wouldn't tell him anything else about her investigation, except to promise that she'd tell him what he needed to know when he needed to know it. Mason knew that wouldn't be until after Jordan's preliminary hearing.

"Your client is guilty," Samantha told him when Mason pressed her for more information. "Centurion's business—whether it's troubled kids, illegal drugs, or Babies-R-Us—has nothing to do with Gina Davenport's murder."

"You don't know that," Mason said, though he was less certain than she. He considered telling her about the entries in the baby ledger, but decided to wait until he had something more concrete to trade.

Samantha switched from ex-girlfriend to cop. "The investigation is ongoing and that's all you're getting out of me, so give it a rest. Besides, Jordan is about to become one of your best repeat clients. Tomorrow, we're charging her with killing her brother. The funeral is the only reason we waited. Bring her in by nine A.M. and tell her to bring a toothbrush. Judge Pistone will revoke her bail before you can say *Your Honor.*"

"You can't be serious," Mason said, never doubting that she was.

"You know me better. Earl Luke Fisher puts her in the building for both Trent's and Gina's murders. Her fingerprints are all over her brother's office, including the computer monitor. She's got a motive, and the similarities to the Davenport murder make it an easy call."

"What similarities?"

"She threw one victim out the window and another through the computer screen. They're both windows, just different kinds."

Mason couldn't give it a rest, but he couldn't prove the connection between Centurion's drug and baby business and the murders. Worse, he had no evidence that would convince Judge Pistone not to bind Jordan over for trial on the charge that she murdered Gina Davenport.

He considered calling Terry Nix to testify at the preliminary hearing that he had convinced Jordan to make a false confession. That, he realized, would force Nix to also testify that Jordan claimed Trent had raped her, setting up the motive for Trent's murder. Even if Nix's testimony caused Judge Pistone to doubt Jordan's confession, it would blow a hole in his defense of Jordan in the murder of her brother. Mason was caught in a vicious cross-rough and couldn't see his way out.

Abby escorted Jordan to Harry's car. He pulled out behind Mickey, Blues following, completing the three-car caravan. Mason watched them go before asking Abby to come to Daphne's that evening, wondering how to tell Jordan to pack her bag.

He told Jordan the only way he could—straight. She reacted the only way she knew—violently. They were alone in the den at Daphne's, a room crowded with overstuffed furniture, soft light, and thick carpet. Jordan hurled a Tiffany lamp, snapping the cord from the wall, slamming it into the fireplace mantel.

"I didn't kill the little bastard," she said, her breath heaving through clenched teeth. "I goddamn wish I did, but I'm not going to jail for something I didn't do!" Blues rushed into the room, trailed by Abby, who slipped past him before he sealed the doorway with his body. Mason held Abby back.

Jordan had confessed to killing Gina with near serenity compared to her attack on the lamp. Mason preferred spontaneous, volcanic denials to studied confessions, though he knew that neither guaranteed honesty. It was the contrast that struck him most, though he didn't have time to sort out its meaning as Jordan cast about for another missile.

"I can't make it sound like something it isn't," Mason told her, encouraged for the moment that her hands were balled in fists instead of wrapped around another antique. "The judge is going to revoke your bail. You're in a bad spot, but you're just going to have to gut it out. Gina's case will go to trial first. If we win, the judge may let you out on bail."

Jordan's eyes opened wide as Mason's words registered. She was going to jail and she might never get out. Her face contorted into an anguished mask, a guttural wail erupting from her belly. She lowered her head and charged Blues, who was blocking her escape. He let her hit him dead on, grunting at the impact, bear-hugging her as he let her pummel his chest until she collapsed, Abby swarming her, searching for the place that hurt most.

Mason tried to find a common genetic thread that tied Abby to Jordan as she stroked Jordan's face and hair, calming her. They didn't look like mother and daughter, each a mirror reflecting the other's past or future. A child could favor either parent or neither, Mason knew from his own experience when well-meaning people told his aunt how he looked like her, though they only shared a faint resemblance. Abby hadn't described her child's father, except as the worst mistake of her life.

Abby was both soft and strong. Jordan had a prickly, hard veneer shot through with hairline fractures. Abby was beautiful, graced with a lively sensuality. Jordan was too ill at ease with herself to summon passion. He knew that their differences didn't exclude the possibility they were mother and daughter, though they underscored

how unlikely it was that that link would be found in
their blood.

Still, he had witnessed how Jordan and Abby reacted
to each other with visceral, intuitive affection. Abby accepted her, welcomed her, and Jordan responded, loosening a bit, clamoring to be like Abby, a woman possessed
of her life, not possessed by it. Now, Abby held her in a
mother's unconditional embrace, a bond strong enough
for the moment.

Wednesday dawned with a cold, biting rain spit from
cement clouds, too harsh for the last September days of
summer, but a perfect backdrop for surrender. Samantha
let Mason bring Jordan in through the police garage,
away from the cameras that waited in response to a leak
from "a source close to the investigation," as Channel
6's Sherri Thomas reported. Samantha cursed the leak,
promising Mason she would plug it if she could find it,
both of them knowing that leaks and cockroaches were
permanent residents of government offices.

Mason didn't object to the quick arraignment, preferring to keep Jordan's courtroom appearances to a
minimum and hoping the full press corps might not yet
have gotten the word. Judge Pistone made short work
of the arraignment, revoking Jordan's bail and ordering a preliminary hearing two weeks after the preliminary hearing on the Davenport murder charge, now
only ten days away.

Microphones surrounded Mason when he stepped
into the hall outside the courtroom. Sherri Thomas
wielded hers like a machete, slicing through the competition, squaring off in front of Mason.

"Mr. Mason," she said. "Now that your client is off the streets, is the killing over? What's next?"

Mason knew she wasn't interested in his answer. The story she wanted was in her question. "Justice," he told her, brushing aside the rest of the pack.

CHAPTER 23

Mason loved old westerns. *The Magnificent Seven,* a movie about seven hired gunslingers who saved a poor Mexican village from a band of outlaws, was one of his favorites. The youngest gunman, barely out of his teens, was infatuated with the romantic heroism of the veterans. Two of the older gunmen indoctrinated him in the perks of their profession, one saying that they had no enemies, the other adding they had no enemies still alive, the last boast a bluff to cloak his lost nerve.

Mason felt like the aging gunslinger, his promise of justice blowing away like dust-bowl dirt as he sat in the courtroom waiting for Judge Pistone to gavel to life the first of Jordan's preliminary hearings. He hadn't lost his nerve, only his way. Jordan's case—now cases—had punched and pulled him in too many different directions. He forced himself to focus on the proof, a mantra he repeated under his breath.

Jordan sat beside him, wearing a charcoal-gray skirt and white blouse Abby had bought her. Modest, not severe, Abby, ever the PR expert, had told her, reminding Jordan to look at the witnesses and the judge. Jordan looked over her shoulder, casting an anxious look at Abby, who nodded encouragement from the first row of spectators. A courtroom deputy evicted a reporter from a spot on the end of the row at the center aisle, making way for Jordan's mother as the bailiff instructed everyone to rise.

Carol Hackett was wrapped in a black suit with a Prozac lining, her face so flat and her eyes so dull, Mason wasn't certain she knew where she was. He checked the courtroom for Arthur Hackett, not finding him among the crowd. That was a bad sign for reasons other than family relations. Witnesses were not allowed in the courtroom until they testified so that they were not influenced by what they heard from other witnesses. Arthur Hackett was going to testify against his daughter.

Patrick Ortiz had taken over for his assistant prosecutor, not because he was grandstanding for votes, but because he loved a meaty case. With his average build, rumpled suits, and elbows-on-the-counter-it's-just-you-and-me-talking style, Ortiz was the lawyer as Everyman, inviting his opponents' underestimation. By the end of a trial, jurors wanted to buy him a beer and defense attorneys wanted to spike it.

The purpose of the preliminary hearing was not to establish Jordan's guilt or innocence. It was to establish that there was sufficient proof to require Jordan to stand trial for the murder of Gina Davenport. Ortiz didn't have to prove she did it. He only had to convince the judge that he was likely to prove that at trial.

Stripped of its sensational trappings, Ortiz had a simple case. He had a victim—Gina Davenport. He had a defendant with a motive for murder—Jordan Hackett, who was furious that Dr. Gina refused to continue treating her because of a contract dispute with her father. He had an unimpeachable witness to testify about Jordan's motive—her father, whose pain on testifying would confirm his truthfulness. He had a witness who placed Jordan at the scene—Earl Luke Fisher. He had physical evidence that showed the defendant had laid hands on the victim—Jordan's hair and clothing fibers. Best of all, he had a confession. And—in a world where everything was caught on tape, from drivers running red lights to terrorists flying passenger planes into office buildings—Patrick Ortiz had Gina Davenport's murder on video.

Ortiz explained all of that to Judge Pistone, who, as usual, kept his head down as if it hung on a broken hinge until Ortiz mentioned the videotape. The judge raised an eyebrow, pulling the rest of his face up along with it.

"You intend to introduce the videotape?" the Judge asked Ortiz.

"Yes, sir, I do," Ortiz answered.

"For what purpose?"

Mason caught the annoyance in Judge Pistone's question, knowing the answer. Ortiz wanted to show the videotape not just because it was evidence of the crime, but because—for a trial lawyer—it was cool. It was cooler than any piece of evidence the prosecutor could have, short of footage showing Jordan pitching Dr. Gina through the glass.

"It's evidence of the crime," Ortiz answered.

"Does it show who did it?" the judge asked.

"No."

"You're not worried that I won't believe that Dr. Davenport is dead, are you, Mr. Ortiz?"

Mason bit his cheek to keep from laughing. Displaying gruesome photographs of the victim was the first tactic every prosecutor learned. Every defense lawyer objected to that evidence because its only purpose was to inflame the jury. Everyone knew the victim was dead. That's why they were in the courtroom. Mason had never seen a judge refuse to allow this kind of evidence, especially on the judge's own initiative without an objection from the defense lawyer. Judge Pistone was known for his roughshod treatment of criminal defendants, making his questions all the more surprising. Mason sat back, knowing better than to open his mouth.

"Even so, Your Honor, this sort of evidence is routinely admitted—"

"For a jury. I'm not the jury. I know she's dead. You want to put on some evidence that the defendant did it, I'm all ears. Save the show for the jury. Now get on with it."

Ortiz got the judge's message and swallowed his irritation. Earl Luke Fisher was the first witness. Earl Luke kept his story straight, testifying that Jordan had let herself in the front door of the Cable Depot just before ten o'clock the night of the murder. He rejected Mason's suggestion on cross-examination that Gina Davenport had let Jordan in as Jordan claimed in her confession. Mason highlighted the inconsistency in the hope of raising doubt in the judge's mind when Ortiz offered the confession into evidence.

Arthur Hackett's entrance into the courtroom elicited

a swoon of sympathy from the gallery. His face was ashen, his eyes bleak. He walked with the tired gait of someone as exhausted by the prospect of sleep as of waking, unable to find peace in either state. The destruction of his family had leveled him. He stopped at the end of the first row of spectators, placing his hand on his wife's shoulder for a moment—to rest, to reassure, to gather the strength to damn his daughter.

"Do you love your daughter?" Patrick Ortiz began.

Arthur, hunched forward in the witness chair after taking his oath, straightened with surprise at the question. "Yes, of course," he said, looking at his wife. Jordan had been sketching abstract images on a legal pad, but stopped at her father's answer.

"Did you love your son?"

"I do," Arthur said, his voice heavy, unable to accept the prosecutor's past tense.

"Mr. Hackett," Ortiz continued, "I cannot imagine what you and your wife are experiencing in this courtroom today. You both have my profound sympathy. I wish there were some other way to do this, but there isn't. I have to ask you some very difficult questions and your answers may result in Judge Pistone ordering your daughter to stand trial for the murder of Gina Davenport. Understanding all you have been through, are you able to answer my questions?"

Arthur examined his hands, rolled his shoulders forward as if bracing for a blow. "Yes," he said with such dread certainty that Mason knew his testimony would be heard as gospel.

Ortiz led Arthur through his contract negotiations with Gina Davenport, her threat to cut off Jordan's treatment, her threat to report Trent Hackett's alleged rape of Jordan to the police, and Jordan's incendiary reaction when Arthur told her of Gina's threats. He gently probed Jordan's history of emotional problems and violent behavior that had led the Hacketts to bar Jordan from living at home.

Ortiz's direct examination lasted barely an hour, and cast the Hacketts as parents overwhelmed by a tortured child who was victimized by an unscrupulous therapist. Mason knew he had to strip Arthur Hackett of the credibility he carried as another victim of the crime.

"You loved your daughter and you love your son, is that right, Mr. Hackett?" Mason began, intentionally reversing the tenses from the prosecutor's questions.

"That's right," Hackett answered, not quick enough to catch the difference.

"You loved your daughter when you first adopted her?"

"Of course."

"But that changed when she started having emotional problems, didn't it? It changed when you began telling your wife that you had bought damaged goods when you adopted Jordan. Isn't that true?"

Hackett reddened, stunned at Mason's attack. "No, it isn't."

"When Jordan was thirteen and told you that her brother had raped her, did you believe her?"

"No."

"Why not?"

"Trent would never have done such a thing."

"Did you take your daughter to a doctor to be examined for evidence of rape?"

Hackett shook his head. "There was no reason. It wasn't true."

"Why do you think Jordan made such an accusation against her brother?"

"I don't know. They didn't get along. She was always very dramatic. She's been . . . difficult," he added, searching for the word.

"So your daughter is a disturbed liar who makes up dramatic stories about crimes. Is that what you are telling the court?"

Ortiz interrupted, "Objection. Mr. Mason is badgering the witness. Why, I don't know, but it's still badgering."

"I get the point, Mr. Mason. Move on," Judge Pistone said.

"You didn't think Gina Davenport would make good on her threat to stop treating Jordan, did you?"

"No, I didn't. Her own daughter had killed herself. She was a therapist, for God's sake. I couldn't imagine she would do that."

"But you took the chance with your daughter's mental health to save a few bucks for your radio station and you were wrong," Mason said. "Did you tell your son that Dr. Davenport also threatened to turn him in to the police for raping your daughter?" Arthur hesitated, looking to the judge, the prosecutor, and his wife for a way out. "Answer the question, Mr. Hackett," Mason said.

Arthur took a breath and said, "Yes."

"Was that before or after Gina Davenport reported that one of the windows in her office was cracked and needed to be replaced?"

"After," Hackett said in a whisper.

"And your son, who managed the Cable Depot for you, didn't bother to fix the window, did he?"

"That's not true. He said it could wait."

"You took out a life insurance policy on Gina Davenport a few months ago. Have you submitted a claim?"

Arthur slumped back in the witness chair like a fighter on the ropes. "Yes," he answered in a voice so low Judge Pistone ordered him to speak up and repeat his answer. "Yes, I turned in a claim," Arthur said.

"You understand that you can't collect on that policy if you killed Gina Davenport, don't you?"

"I didn't kill her, Mr. Mason," Hackett answered.

"How much will you collect if your daughter is convicted of killing Gina Davenport?" Arthur Hackett didn't answer, and Mason let his silence hang like the accusation it was. "Tell us how much, Mr. Hackett. It's my last question," Mason said.

"Five million dollars," Arthur said.

As Arthur Hackett stepped down from the witness stand, he met his daughter's trembling gaze. His testimony was a spear thrown at her heart. He had confirmed what she had always believed—that he had chosen his natural-born son and his hard-earned money over his adopted daughter. Carol Hackett rose as he passed through the gate separating the lawyers and judge from the spectators. They made their way down the aisle, weaving slightly as they leaned on one another before disappearing into the hall.

Judge Pistone declared a recess, departing without any indication whether Mason's questions had undermined the judge's confidence in the prosecution's case. Jordan laid her head on the counsel table, clasping her hands behind her neck, swatting away Mason's hand.

*   *   *

Samantha Greer testified about the homicide investigation, including the physical evidence recovered from the murder scene, concluding with Jordan's surprise visit to police headquarters to confess. Ortiz kept his questions short and Samantha's answers followed suit, giving her testimony precision and credibility.

"Do innocent people confess to crimes, Detective Greer?" Mason asked her, rising from his seat. It was the first time he'd cross-examined Samantha. During their time together, his cases and hers had not intersected, as if the love gods were giving them a demilitarized zone for their relationship.

"Sometimes, Mr. Mason," she said, allowing a hint of a smile to escape the corner of her mouth, sensing the charade they were playing. "It happens."

Mason stood at one side of the lectern the lawyers used for questioning, leaning his elbow on the edge. "You've been doing this a long time, Detective. Why do innocent people confess to crimes they didn't commit?"

"There can be many reasons," she answered. "Some people want attention, some are mentally handicapped."

"Some people are coerced into confessing, true?" Mason asked.

"Not by me, Counselor."

"Of course not. I didn't mean to imply that you would, but someone in a position of trust or authority could coerce an innocent person to confess. That's happened, hasn't it?"

"I suppose it has," she admitted.

"Some people confess because they're scared or exhausted, or they black out and think they might have committed the crime and not remembered. Isn't that right, Detective?" Mason asked, setting aside their past, pushing her to lay the foundation for his attack on Jordan's confession.

"I can't speculate about all the reasons, but none of those things happened here," Samantha said, taking off her gloves to jab back. "The defendant walked into police headquarters voluntarily, in complete control of her mental faculties, and announced her desire to confess. She was informed of her rights, declined to have an attorney present, and she confessed."

"What about children?" Mason asked, ignoring Samantha's devastating answer. "Why do kids confess to crimes they didn't commit?"

"I don't know," Samantha said, dismissing the question.

Mason picked up a manila file he had placed on the lectern. "Do you remember giving a lecture on confessions at the police academy last year?" Mason asked her. Harry had given a lecture on the same program before he retired, and gave Mason a copy of Samantha's paper. Mason had set Samantha up, and she had obliged by playing the role of the tough cop, too certain of the defendant's guilt to consider other possibilities. Normally, he relished these moments as much as Ortiz enjoyed his videotapes. This time was different.

"Yes," she answered, losing the glow from her performance.

"You wrote—and I quote—*Be careful with a child's confession. More than anything else, kids just want to go home. They'll admit to almost anything because they figure their parents will make it all go away.* Did I read that correctly, Detective?"

"You did."

"Isn't that what Jordan Hackett wanted, to go home? Did you consider the possibility that she confessed so her parents would take her back and make it all go away?"

"The defendant isn't a child. She's an adult."

"Who grew up with parents who called her damaged goods and a liar until they threw her out of the house. Since when does being an adult make that any easier to take?"

Samantha edged forward in the witness stand. "People like that commit murder all the time, Counselor. They become violent, like the defendant."

"Jordan Hackett isn't the only member of her family you suspected of committing a violent crime, is she, Detective?"

Samantha sighed, pursing her lips, realizing the trap she'd walked into. "No, she isn't."

"Who was the other person?"

"Trent Hackett," she said, forcing Mason to drag it out of her.

"What violent crime did you suspect he committed?"

"He tampered with the elevator in the Cable Depot, causing it to crash. He was the building manager and had access to the elevator controls."

"Who was Trent Hackett's intended victim?" Mason asked, boring in as Judge Pistone sat upright in the still courtroom.

Samantha said, "You were. We suspected that Trent was trying to prevent you from investigating the defendant's claim that he had raped her."

"Arthur and Carol Hackett didn't believe Jordan's claim against her brother and they're both alive. Gina Davenport believed it and she's dead. I believed it and

Trent Hackett tried to kill me. That's what you thought, isn't it, Detective Greer?"

"Yes," Samantha answered, glaring at Mason, forgetting their past.

"No further questions."

CHAPTER 24

Blues on Broadway was a throwback to piano bars and gin joints that flourished during Kansas City's jazz heyday, before night clubs and restaurants became mini-theme parks for corporations more concerned with demographics than getting down with the sound. A rectangular bar struck from mahogany stood in the middle of the floor. An ebony grand piano on a low riser with room to add a trio, plus black-leather-lined booths bathed in blue shadows tossed from pinpoint spots buried in the ceiling, said this was a place to kick back and listen.

It was early Saturday morning and the last paying customers had tumbled out the door. Mickey was tending bar for Mason and Harry, who were perched on stools listening to Blues pick riffs off the piano. The notes clung together, fell apart, and found each other again, like subatomic particles.

"Putting Dr. Gina's murder on Trent was the smart

play," Mickey said. "I mean Pistone was going to bind her over no matter what you did," he told Mason.

"Pistone did the only thing he could do—order Jordan to stand trial and let the jury decide. Blaming Trent was a chump's play," Mason said, "but it was the only one I had."

"I don't get why it was a chump's play," Mickey said. "It fits with the evidence and gives the jury a way out."

Harry tapped his empty bottle on the bar and Mickey replaced it with another cold one. "It's like this," Harry explained. "Blaming Trent for killing Gina gives Jordan another motive for killing Trent, not that she needed one. First her brother raped her, then he killed the one person who believed her story and was going to do something about it."

"Then all we have to do is figure out who killed Trent," Mickey said. "Why is everyone acting like the dog died?"

"Because," Blues said, running his knuckles across the keys, "I'm betting on one killer, not two. The murders are tied together by the killer's rage. Throwing Gina through the window and slam-dunking Trent into the computer monitor takes a whole lot of poison. So far, Jordan is the only one that fits that description."

"So, where do we start?" Mickey asked.

No one answered. Harry nursed his beer. Blues tapped out a string of chords, not finding the melody he wanted. Mason leafed through Dr. Gina's book, *The Way You Do the Things You Do,* stopping at the chapter about her daughter's suicide, reading the opening paragraph twice.

"Gina's daughter, Emily, was born in St. Louis," he said, looking up from the book.

"And I was born under a lucky star," Mickey said. "So what?"

"She was born in the same hospital as Jordan, only a week earlier. Gina says her hard labor was a sign of things to come," Mason said. "Take a look," he told Harry, sliding the open book in front of him.

"I take your word for it," Harry said, finishing his beer, Mason feeling stupid, forgetting about Harry's eyesight.

Mickey picked up the book. "I don't," he said, reading the chapter to himself.

Mason said, "Jordan and Emily were best friends. Both of them end up pregnant and living at Sanctuary. Emily killed herself before her baby was born. Jordan says Centurion sold her baby. Somebody hooks Abby up with Gina Davenport, implying that Gina knows what happened to the baby Abby gave up for adoption. The dates in Centurion's baby ledger match up with the birth dates of Abby's and Jordan's daughters."

Harry said, "What's the connection to the murders?"

"I don't know," Mason said. "But if we're looking for someone else to tie to both murders, we might as well start at the beginning and it looks like the beginning is at a hospital in St. Louis."

"Here's something else I don't get," Mickey said, putting the book down. "Dr. Gina writes about Emily committing suicide, but leaves out the part about Emily being pregnant. I wonder why she'd do that."

"I'll add it to my list of things that don't make sense about this case," Mason said. "In the meantime, we've got to take everyone back to when they were in diapers. Harry, can you get one of your buddies in the department to run a check on Robert Davenport? Find out if he's ever been busted for buying or dealing dope. Maybe he was hooked up with Centurion."

"I've still got a few favors coming," Harry said. "Might

even be easier on the weekend. Less chance Samantha might catch someone bird-dogging her case."

"Great," Mason said. "Mickey, take another look at those IRS reports for Sanctuary. Follow the money. We're missing something, let's find it."

"No problem. You want me to check out Emily's Fund at the same time?"

"Good call. Start fresh with everything and everybody," Mason told him. "Blues, take a look at Centurion. I want to know how he got into the baby business and if he's still in the drug business."

"Samantha's got him on good behavior for the time being. I start poking around, he may come after you again," Blues said.

"Then don't get caught poking around," Mason said, grinning at his friend.

"I'll tiptoe," Blues said. "What are you going to do?"

"I'm going to St. Louis."

Abby and Mason had rocketed through the official dates that marked the first stage of a new relationship, cruising into the what-are-we-doing-tonight stage that assumed they would be together that night and every night. They hadn't talked about it or negotiated terms, they'd just let it happen, each catching the other staring with bemused satisfaction, sharing a quick smile, a dip of the head, or a knowing wink.

He left her a message Saturday morning explaining why he wasn't available that night, that he was going for a run and would call her later. When he got back from Loose Park, she was waiting on his front step with an overnight bag, scratching Tuffy behind the ears.

"Don't tell me I'm not going, or that I'll be in the way, or that it will be too dangerous or too boring. I'm going," Abby said.

"Do I look lucky or stupid?" Mason asked her, wiping sweat from his face with his T-shirt.

"Stupid if you give me any trouble. Lucky if you pick a good hotel."

"How about the Ritz in Clayton?"

"Umm," she said, standing up. "It's good to be lucky, but lucky and loaded is most unusual." She rubbed her hand on his chest, balling his sweaty T-shirt in her fingers.

"You'll have to settle for lucky. I've got a coupon for a free weekend at a Marriott Courtyard. Continental breakfast included. Still interested?"

"Definitely" she said, kissing him. "I love Continental breakfasts. The oatmeal buffet is very romantic."

"I'll get you extra brown sugar. I've got one stop to make before we go," he said.

"I hope it's the shower."

"Okay, two stops. The second one is at Robert Davenport's studio and that's a solo appearance. He's tough enough to get anything out of without having to explain why you are there. I want him focused on me, not you."

"Are you patronizing me or flattering me?" she asked, twisting his T-shirt again with playful annoyance.

"You already ruled out stupid," Mason answered.

Mason found Robert in his studio, stretched out on a futon, nodding his head to a beat only he could hear. Mason watched him paint imaginary strokes with imaginary brushes, his eyelids fluttering. An empty needle lay on the floor next to the futon, explaining why Robert could hear music without sound, paint without brushes, and see with his eyes closed.

Mason squatted at Robert's side. "Hey, Robert. You got company, man."

Robert opened his eyes, squinting and grimacing as if Mason was a bad dream. "Go way," Robert mumbled. "No assholes today."

Mason grabbed him, pulling him up. Robert was all rubber arms and legs, like a doped-up, life-sized Gumby doll. Mason tried propping him up on a stool, but had to catch him before he fell over. Hoisting Robert again, Mason dumped him back on the futon, letting the high pass, using the time to look around the studio.

Robert had described himself as a decent artist. Mason thumbed through the canvasses stacked around the studio, finding nothing that stirred him, including the nudes. Robert painted the women without facial features, exaggerating their breasts and genitalia. Mason couldn't tell whether the paintings were unfinished or a reflection of Robert's inner psyche.

A corner of the studio was partitioned with a desk on the other side. Mason sat in the swivel desk chair, and began a methodical search of the drawers, finding nothing more interesting than class schedules. The bottom drawer was for files that hung on metal rails on the sides of the drawer, though Robert's files were laid flat, stacked one on top of another. When Mason lifted them out, he discovered why the files weren't hung from the sides. The drawer had a false bottom. Mason found a letter opener and pried the bottom panel out of the drawer.

The hidden space was Robert's combination medicine cabinet and safety deposit box, concealing a small bag of cocaine, three smaller bags of a darker powder Mason guessed to be heroin, and three syringes. Mason found a letter-size envelope underneath the drugs. He opened the envelope, pulling out four photographs that jolted him like one of Robert's needles.

The photographs were fish-eyed images of Gina Davenport and Max Coyle locked in naked embraces that gave new meaning to his client's nickname, Mad Max. The date of the photographs—August 15—was superimposed in the corner of each frame, confirming that Max was the boyfriend Gina had broken up with two weeks before she was killed. Mason guessed that Robert hid the camera in the ceiling above their bed as an insurance policy against the day Gina decided to dump him.

The first time Mason and Robert talked, Robert denied knowing whom Gina had been seeing. Mason wasn't surprised that Robert lied, though he did wonder what Robert intended to do with the photographs now that his wife was dead. He doubted that Robert had shown them to the police. If he had, the cops would have questioned Max and Max would have called Mason. Mason kept the photographs, but put the drugs back. Robert was curled on his side, his knees to his chest, moaning as the heroin slowly released him. Mason didn't say good-bye.

The pictures of Max and Gina reaffirmed Mason's confidence in the capacity of people to be stupid. It wasn't that people would lie, cheat, and steal. He depended on that to make a living. It was that some people would get up in the morning, make a list of the dumbest things they could do, and spend the rest of the day checking them off after completing each one. Max, Gina, and Robert were at the head of the class.

When the people were strangers, Mason found their behavior puzzling, amusing, and intriguing. When the people were his friends—as Max was—he found it sad. Max was also his client, which made his discovery of the photographs more complicated. He had represented Max only in Max's lawsuit against David Evans. Technically, there was nothing about that representation that required Mason to suppress evidence that would make Max a suspect in Gina's murder.

That was a lawyer's distinction Max would not appreciate. As far as Max was concerned, Mason was his lawyer, charged with keeping his secrets secret. He wouldn't understand when Mason told him the pictures made him a suspect in Gina's murder and that he'd better get another lawyer. Mason called Max on his cell phone, finding him playing in a charity golf tournament to raise money for kids with leukemia. He told Mason to meet him at the halfway house between the ninth and tenth holes.

Mason had played golf enough times to know that his talents lay elsewhere and to be grateful that his law practice wasn't cultivated on the links. His backswing was so twisted that it positioned his club for self-colonoscopy, producing shots that put everyone on the course in harm's way.

The tournament was being played at a course built to sell the million-dollar homes that surrounded it in what the developers called a lifestyle community. Calling it a mere subdivision devalued the experience. Putting a guardhouse at the entrance of the private street that led past homes to the golf course reminded the residents that the rich were different.

Max was waiting in his golf cart parked outside the halfway house, signing autographs and posing for pictures, beaming from beneath his wide-brimmed straw hat as each photo was snapped. Mason doubted Max would be as eager to see the photographs in the envelope tucked under his arm.

Paula Sutton, the acerbic host of KWIN's morning show, intercepted Mason with the beer cart she was driving before he reached Max.

"Hey, stranger," she said. "You missed the tee-off, but you can still get a cold beer."

"I'll pass," Mason said. "How'd you get stuck playing bartender instead of golf?"

"Highest and best use," she answered. "The station is a big sponsor of the tournament. The Hacketts are keeping a low profile after everything that's happened, but Arthur ordered the rest of us to show the flag. You don't strike me as a country-clubber. What are you doing here?"

"I'm going to audit Max's scorecard," Mason joked, knowing she would see him talking with Max. "Tell me something," he said, changing the subject. "When we talked at the radio station, you said that Gina Davenport ducked under her morality bar like she was doing the limbo. What did you mean? That dance may have gotten her killed."

Paula flashed a sly smile, giving Mason a fleeting image of her doing the limbo while the crowd chanted, "How low can you go?" She patted the empty passenger seat. "Climb aboard," she said.

Mason waved at Max as they passed him, mouthing

that he'd be right back. Paula stopped in a grove of apple trees on a hill overlooking the green at the end of a long fairway. She got out of the cart, plucked two apples, tossing one to Mason and taking a bite out of hers. A foursome was working its way toward them.

"A good-looking woman offers me an apple in the middle of a twenty-first-century Garden of Eden," Mason said. "Pretty tempting."

"You like forbidden fruit?" she asked, taking another bite and wiping the juice from her mouth with the back of her hand.

"As long as it doesn't come from a poisonous tree," he said. "Tell me about Gina."

Paula tossed the half-eaten apple on the ground. "All business," she said, disappointed at Mason's answer. "What a waste. Gina slept around, but I bet you figured that out already."

"How long had you known her?" Mason asked.

"Since she was on the air, five or six years, I guess."

"What did you know about her daughter, Emily?" Mason asked.

Paula blanched, caught off guard by Mason's question, relieved by the shouted orders for cold beer from the golfers who had reached the green. She delivered four cans to the golfers, regaining her composure when she returned to the cart.

"I better get you back to Max before he tries to add up his score by himself. Since you settled his case, he can't add anything less than six figures."

"Does that mean you'll tell me about Gina sleeping around, but not about her daughter?"

Paula took a breath. "There's not much to tell. I'd met Emily a few times. She was a head case. Gina had plenty of advice for everyone else. None of it worked with her own kid."

Paula pushed the cart's gas pedal to the floor, flying down the hill and taking a turn so sharply Mason had to hold on to keep from being thrown out. After wanting to take him for a ride, Paula couldn't wait to get him out of her cart. Mason wanted to know why and took a shot at one of the missing links in the case.

"Did you ever hear Gina mention a woman named Abby Lieberman?" he asked.

They were back at the halfway house where the driver of another golf cart appeared from around a tree, causing Paula to veer hard to her left as the cart skidded to a stop. "Shit!" she said as the beer cooler bounced off the back of the cart, spilling cans and bottles.

Max pulled up on his cart, laughing. "Christ, Paula. We're giving the stuff away, not throwing it away," he said, until he saw how Paula was trembling. "Hey, girl— are you okay?"

Paula waved off his concern. "Yeah, I'm great. I need a cigarette," she said, leaving Mason and Max to clean up her mess.

"What was that all about?" Max asked Mason.

"She's not a fan of the game, I guess," Mason answered. "We need to talk, Max."

"So talk, Lou."

Mason looked around, spying an empty gazebo near the halfway house. "Privately," Mason said, leading the way, waiting until they were out of earshot. The gazebo was barely big enough for the wooden table and four chairs underneath its pitched roof. Mason felt himself shrink in Max's shadow, sensing the intimidation opposing linemen or wrestlers must have felt the instant before Max earned his nickname.

"Sit down, Max," Mason said, hoping to contain him, but knowing better than to dance around the subject. "Were you and Gina Davenport screwing around?"

Max laughed, banging his ham-sized hand on the table. "Are you kidding me? Is that what you came out here to ask me? Why the hell would a classy, uptown woman like Gina take a tumble with me?"

"I don't know, Max. You tell me, because her husband says she broke off an affair with someone just before she was killed. The cops would want to talk with the boyfriend."

"Lou," he said, his face darkening, "you got something to say, say it."

Mason tapped the envelope on the table. "I'm not saying anything, Max. I'm asking."

Max bit his lower lip and tugged at his chin as he eyed the envelope. "You're my lawyer, right? Anything I tell you is confidential, right?"

Mason shook his head. "Not on this, Max. Jordan Hackett is my client. If you and Gina were having an affair, you need another lawyer. I'll be glad to give you a name."

Max nodded, his huge head looming over Mason like a boulder. "That envelope," Max said. "Pictures?"

Mason said, "Yeah."

Max nodded again, taking shallow breaths, then a deep one as his chest and neck expanded, popping his veins. He burst out of his chair, snarling, overturning the table with one hand like it was made of air, grabbing Mason by the collar with the other, and throwing him onto the grass like a bag of dirty laundry.

Mason landed on his back, stunned and breathless, opening his eyes to find Max towering over him, the envelope in his hands. "I may need another lawyer, Lou, but you're going to need a doctor. I'll be glad to give you a name."

CHAPTER 25

History, geography, and Interstate 70 connect Kansas City and St. Louis in a perpetual rivalry. Both claim, rightly, to have been jumping-off points for the country's westward expansion. Each sits on a border, orbiting the state like moons competing for the gravitational pull of the capital that, not accidentally, is located dead center in the middle of Missouri. St. Louis, its residents often sniff, is an Eastern city—*read sophisticated*—while Kansas City, they note from the view looking down their noses, is a Western city—*read not sophisticated*. Kansas-Citians, not above trash talk or cheap shots, still remind their St. Louis brethren of the 1985 World Series, and wonder aloud why a city's movers and shakers rank one another according to the high school they attended.

The highway is a 250-mile concrete tether connecting the cities, a four-hour-drive, long enough for Mason and Abby to exhaust the possible explanations for Paula Sutton's nervous reaction to Mason's questions about

Emily Davenport and her near accident when he asked about Abby.

"Are you certain you never ran across Paula before?" Mason asked for the tenth time.

"I'm certain," Abby answered with diminished patience. "I've never heard of the woman, never met the woman, never even listened to her damn show!"

"Okay, I'm convinced," Mason said. "But Paula knows enough about you that she wasn't happy to hear your name. Or Emily's, for that matter."

Abby said, "At least it's easy to understand Max's reaction to the pictures. Gina broke up with him. He doesn't take rejection well, especially when he finds out someone was watching over his shoulder. Plus, he's got a reputation for violence and he's so big, he could have sneezed at Gina and knocked her out that window. I don't blame him for not wanting the police to find out they were involved."

"He is that strong, I'll give you that," Mason said. "Only, I always thought that his Mad Max routine was just an act to psych himself up for football games and sell tickets to wrestling."

"Until today," Abby reminded him.

"Yeah," Mason said. "For someone his size, he's very quick. I never had a chance to get out of the way. He wouldn't be the first guy who killed the woman that dumped him, though I don't know why he'd go after Trent."

"Maybe you and Blues and Harry are wrong about there being one killer. Maybe the murders aren't connected."

Mason shook his head. "I wouldn't bet against Blues and Harry on something like this."

"Are they that good?"

"Yep. They're that good."

"Then maybe you should pay more attention to Trent. All your suspects start out with Gina and dead-end with Trent. Try looking at the case from the other direction."

"You're that good?" he asked her.

"Oh, yeah," she answered as Mason took the Highway 40 exit off I-70, entering St. Louis through the area called West County.

It was also Abby's idea that they talk to her uncle, Nathan Ruben. He might, she said, know who was involved in the adoption of her baby. They had to wait until Monday to see the hospital's records on Abby and Jordan, but could talk to her uncle on Sunday. Abby hadn't thought to ask her uncle at the time, and she hadn't seen or talked with him since her baby was born. Her parents never mentioned his name, as if doing so would remind them of the shame their daughter had visited on them. Abby had her own reasons for wanting to erase her uncle from her memory.

"He was an ugly drunk," she told Mason as they lay in bed that night. "He never hit me, or touched me, but he scared the crap out of me when he drank, which was most of the time. He was a little man and the booze made him mean. He'd threaten to get even with all the people who'd screwed him over."

"Why did he take you in?"

"It wasn't because he was my mother's brother. That's for sure. My parents paid him for my room and board. He needed the money."

"Didn't your parents know what he was like? Didn't you tell them?"

Abby propped herself up on one elbow. "They had to know, but they pretended they didn't. My pregnancy mortified them. That's all they could deal with and they didn't deal with it very well. I had to deal with the rest, and I didn't do such a bang-up job myself."

Mason stroked her bare shoulder, pushing the sheet to her waist. "You were only seventeen. Don't be so hard on yourself."

"If I hadn't gotten pregnant, if I hadn't given up my baby—"

"What?" Mason interrupted. "None of this ever would have happened? You don't know that. You don't even know if your baby has anything to do with any of this. There's only one thing that wouldn't have happened," he told her.

"What's that," she said, her mood downcast.

"Us," he said. "Come here."

Nathan Ruben lived in University City, an urban pocket of St. Louis where the houses were compact, built close together, with narrow lawns sticking out from front doors to curbs like green tongues.

Abby didn't remember her uncle's address, but there was only one Nathan Ruben listed in the phone book. She recognized the street and, when they stopped in front of it, the house. It was dark brick with a low-pitched roof that looked like a hat pulled low on the brow. The driveway was crumbling, ground to concrete pebbles and dust in some places, broken into uneven slabs in others. The patch of grass that passed for a front yard had burnt up in the August heat and not been resuscitated by September rain.

They sat in the car, Mason listening to Abby's quick, unsteady breath, not knowing what to say, waiting for her to open the car door. They hadn't called Nathan because Mason preferred to show up unannounced, catching the old man off guard, and because Abby wanted to put off as long as possible the moment when she heard her uncle's voice again. The sky was gray like rippled aluminum. The wind came in sharp bursts, stripping the trees of their weakest leaves.

Abby gathered her jacket around her. "Okay," she said. "Let's go."

Mason followed her to the front door. Abby pressed the doorbell once and turned, as if to run away like a child playing a joke. Mason put his hands on her shoulders, easing her back to the door. She rang the bell twice more, then, with uncovered anger, rapped her fist on the hard wood.

A voice filtered through from inside the house. "I'm coming, I'm coming! Who the hell is it anyway? I'm coming."

The door opened, filling the dark entry hall with daylight, causing the old man to squint and shield his eyes. He was as small as Abby had said, not much over five feet. His gray hair was thin, more loose strands than anything else. He was thin, made thinner by his loose-fitting clothes, unshaven face, and milky eyes. Nathan Ruben was a ruined man, past caring that he was. Mason saw nothing frightening about him, though Abby quivered in the doorway, remembering her uncle in a different way.

"Hello, Uncle Nathan. It's me. Abby."

"Abby?" he said, rolling his tongue from cheek to cheek, searching for the connection.

"Your niece. Linda's daughter," she explained, using her mother's name for the first time since Mason had met her.

Memory came to Nathan with a flicker of fear as he stepped back to close the door. Mason moved past Abby, pushing the door and Nathan inside. "Thanks," Mason said. "We'd love to come in."

"Hey, you!" Nathan said. "You can't bust in here! Who the hell are you anyway? I'm gonna call the cops, you don't get outta here!"

His eyes narrowed to black beads, hinting of the menace they once carried for a seventeen-year-old girl. Abby stood in the doorway, now framed by the light. Mason watched as she squared her shoulders, stamping out old fears like a smoldering campfire.

"Uncle Nathan, we just want to talk to you," she said. "Then we'll leave you alone."

"Talk? What about? I don't hear nothing from you in twenty years after all I done for you," he said.

Abby wanted to tell him how little he'd done, but resisted the impulse, knowing that she had to reassure him to learn anything. "Let's sit down," she said, leading the way into his living room.

Drawn curtains and stale air gave the house a tomb-like feel, as if Nathan had cut off the rest of the world while he drank himself to death. A half-empty quart bottle of scotch sat on an end table next to a sofa covered with old newspapers. A mangy tabby cat lay across the top of the sofa. Nathan gave the cat the back of his hand, sending it scurrying away. Abby sat next to her uncle on the sofa, Mason taking a chair opposite them.

"Uncle Nathan," Abby began again, "I'm trying to find my daughter, the one I gave up for adoption. This man is Lou Mason. He's a friend of mine and he's helping me."

"What's that got to do with me? I don't know nothing about that." The little man sat with his arms crossed, his eyes darting back and forth between Mason and the whiskey bottle.

Abby said, "You helped with the adoption. I only want to know who you dealt with, who made the arrangements. Please, Uncle Nathan. It's very important."

"I don't know nothing about any of that. I can't help you," he said.

"Mr. Ruben," Mason said. "You can talk to us or you can talk to the police. We know that your niece's baby was adopted illegally. We know that you were involved. Selling babies is a felony. You can spend the rest of your life living here with your cat and your booze or you can go to jail. Tell us what we want to know and we'll leave you alone."

Mason didn't know any of that, but he ran the bluff to shake up Nathan, convinced that Nathan was immune to Abby's softer approach. Nathan reached for the bottle of scotch, but Mason beat him to it.

"It's not time for your bottle yet, Nathan," Mason said.

"Gimme that!" Nathan said, coming off the sofa and reaching for the bottle.

Mason pressed his hand against Nathan's chest, pushing him back on the sofa. Nathan turned to Abby. "This is how you repay me? You bring this schmuck into my house to beat me up! I'm an old man and you let him beat me up!"

Abby was saucer-eyed, caught between Mason's unexpected harshness and her instinctive sympathy for her uncle in spite of their past. "Lou! Please! It's okay, Uncle Nathan. No one is going to beat you up and no one is going to call the police. Just help us. Please."

Mason stood over Nathan, invoking a silent threat. "Tell your friend to get outta my house or I'm not telling nobody nothing," Nathan said, casting a defiant glare at Mason.

Abby looked at Mason, her eyes pleading. "Fine," Mason said, putting the bottle down. "I'll be in the car."

Abby emerged half an hour later, her eyes red, her cheeks puffy. She slid into the car, closed the door, and turned on Mason.

"You were awful to him! How could you have been so awful?"

"Abby, he's an awful little man. He wasn't going to give us anything unless I shook him up. What did he tell you?"

Abby's eyes filled again. "He is an awful man. He sold my baby because he needed the money. He started crying when he finally told me, but that made it worse for me. He was crying for himself, not for me."

Mason took Abby in his arms. "Did he give you a name?"

Abby shook her head, sitting up and wiping her nose. "No. He said it was a man he met when he was going through the hospital's alcohol treatment program before I even came to St. Louis. The man was a social worker who approached Nathan when he saw the two of us check into the hospital. Nathan didn't remember his name, only that he dressed like a hippy. It's not much to go on, but that's all he remembers except for the money."

"How much?" Mason asked.

Abby clenched her jaw. "Five hundred dollars," she said, "for my baby."

CHAPTER 26

"Hospitals are where the future is fought over," Abby said. "A nurse on the maternity ward told me that when I was in labor. She said that maternity was the only place where they fought to live because that's where the babies were born. Everyone else was fighting not to die."

They were standing in the lobby of the Caulfield Medical Center studying the directory for the location of the medical records department that was scheduled to open at eight o'clock. The lobby was already crowded with doctors, staff, and visitors, who swirled past them, confident of their destinations. Like all hospitals, it smelled of disinfectant. Mason wrinkled his nose, preferring the lingering tang of smoke and beer that drifted into his office from Blues on Broadway.

"Room B-23," Mason read aloud. "That's in the basement."

They were fifteen minutes early. Abby had been awake since five, tossing restlessly, finally shaking Mason at six.

"I hope it's Jordan," she said. "I mean, I know it's a long shot and it would probably cause more problems than it solves, but I hope Jordan is my daughter."

Mason knew that nothing plays with you more than hope. The sliver of daylight left by the long odds of a dark prognosis. The guarantee of salvation that can't be cashed in this lifetime. The promise of love. Mason knew the truth about hope. That it was a tricky thing people stretched well past specifications, sticking its square peg into too many round holes, forcing it to fit until the peg splintered and the hole snapped shut. He knew that, but wouldn't say it, letting Abby hope a while longer.

The medical records department was across from the elevator. Instead of a door, there was a long white customer counter, furnished with a bell to ring for service and authorization forms for patients to sign permitting the hospital to release their records. The only thing the department was missing was someone to answer the bell, accept the authorization forms, and retrieve the records.

Mason often had to obtain a client's medical records, and used a standard authorization form that hospitals accepted. He'd had Jordan sign one authorizing the release of her records to him before they left Kansas City. Abby filled out one of the hospital's forms requesting her records, clutching it as she paced the empty hallway, the sound of her footsteps absorbed by the carpet, the persistent overhead paging of doctors interrupting their thoughts.

Mason leaned against the counter, watching her, wondering what it was like to reach back into the past and find a piece of yourself. His parents had been killed in a car wreck when he was three, bequeathing him memories that were now little more than vapor. Without the pictures Claire had kept in their house while he was growing up, he doubted he would have remembered what they looked like.

As if sensing his thoughts, Abby said, "You know, it's funny. I remember my labor. It was awful. I kept asking for more drugs. I remember delivery and feeling like my insides were falling out every time I pushed. I remember holding my baby for a few minutes after she was born, before the nurses took her away. But I don't remember her face. How do you forget something like that?"

Mason didn't answer because he didn't know, though he suspected that memory sometimes protected people from remembering. A clerk appeared at the medical records counter. Mason checked his watch. It was exactly eight o'clock. He motioned to Abby, who had slipped back in her memories, searching for a face.

"Can I help you?" the clerk asked.

He was a slender, middle-aged man with dull eyes who asked his question with an uncertain voice, suggesting that he didn't think so. He wore a photo ID badge around his neck identifying him as Gene. Mason had worse luck with bureaucrats, private and public, than he had with women and bad guys. He was convinced they had a secret web site where they posted his picture under the heading *Make Him Beg*. Mason decided to make Gene his friend, figuring Gene was the kind of guy who needed one.

"You bet, Gene," Mason said. "We need some medical records." Mason and Abby handed him their authorizations.

"ID?" Gene asked them.

"Absolutely," Mason said, "glad you asked. Can't be too careful, huh?"

Gene carefully studied their driver's licenses. "It's the rules," Gene said. "Patient Social Security numbers?" he asked. "That's how we search for the records," he explained, pointing to the computer terminal behind the counter.

"They're on the authorizations," Mason said, forcing his smile to stay on duty, deciding that Gene would probably ask his own mother for her ID and Social Security number.

Gene ignored Mason's goodwill, sitting down at the computer, his back to them. He disappeared a few moments later, returning with a thin file of papers he handed to Mason.

"That'll be twenty-five dollars," Gene said.

Mason looked at the records. The cover sheet was labeled "Baby Girl Doe." Beneath that was a stamp that read "Adoption," and next to the stamp, a handwritten note that said "Baby named Jordan Hackett per adoptive parents." Mason handed the records to Abby as he wrote a check.

"The birth mother's name is blacked out," Abby said, her voice cracking with the strain.

"The baby was adopted, so the natural mother's identity is sealed by state law," Gene said.

"But what about my records? Where are my records?" Abby demanded, gripping the edge of the counter as if she was about to vault over it.

"I'm sorry, ma'am," Gene said. "We don't have any records on you. Are you sure you've got the right hospital?"

Abby's grip gave way, Mason supporting her with his hand pressed against the small of her back. "You're kidding, right? This is some kind of a sick joke, right?" Abby asked. "I was a patient here twenty-one years ago. I gave birth here. They took my baby away from me in this hospital twenty-one years ago! You don't seriously think I would forget what hospital I was in, do you?"

Gene raised his palms in self-defense. "I'm not saying anything, lady. The computer doesn't have any records for you. As far as the hospital is concerned, you were never here. That's all I know."

Abby shuddered, fighting for self-control. "Check it again," she said. "It's a mistake. Check it again, please."

"I already did, ma'am. There's no mistake."

Mason put his hands on Abby's shoulders. She twisted away from him. "No!" she said. "There is a mistake. I was here! Let's go," she said to Mason.

"Where?"

"The maternity ward," she answered, practically running for the elevator.

Mason caught up to her as the elevator doors opened. She punched the button for the sixth floor without checking the directory. "It's there, I know it," she said.

"What's there?" Mason asked.

"They called it the Baby Book. All the mothers signed it when they checked in. They had at least ten volumes, hundreds of pages for all the babies born here. The nurses made a big deal of it."

Abby burst out of the elevator onto the sixth floor, Mason trailing her, not doubting her memory of the hospital's layout, hoping her memory of the Baby Book was as accurate. She pushed through the double doors marked *Maternity*, breathless, glancing around in near panic.

"They changed it," Abby said. "It used to be right over there." She pointed to a waiting area decorated in rainbow wallpaper and worn furniture, then marched to the nurse's station.

"Hi," she said to the nurse, catching her breath.

The nurse, a large gray-haired, black woman with a round, tender face, put down her charts. "What is it?" she asked evenly, accustomed to excited women.

"The Baby Books, where the mothers wrote their names when they checked in, what happened to them?"

"Oh, honey," the nurse said. "Just like everything else, it's all done by computer now."

"But what happened to the old books, the ones from twenty years ago?"

The nurse smiled. "Are you in one of those books?" Abby nodded. "Well, come on then," the nurse said. "I wouldn't let them throw those books away. I'm Evelyn," she said, taking Abby by the hand. "When were you here, child?"

Abby told her as Evelyn led them past the nursery where the newborn babies were on display, Mason following a few steps back, feeling like a stranger in a strange land, sensing again the depth of Abby's longing. They stopped at a linen closet filled with sheets and towels, except for three shelves that were lined with alternating pink and blue three-ring binders, each dated for the years they covered. Evelyn and Mason stood aside as Abby traced her finger along the binders, stopping at the one she was searching for, yanking it off the shelf.

Sitting cross-legged on the hallway floor, with Mason crouched next to her, Abby flipped through the pages, checking the date at the top of each page. Each page was divided into columns for the mother's signature, the date of admission, the date of the baby's birth, the sex, weight, and length of the baby, and the baby's name.

"Yes! There I am!" she said, jabbing the page with her finger.

Mason followed her finger across the line that began with Abby's signature, continued with the entries for the birth of a seven-pound baby girl, twenty-one inches long, and ended with a blank space for the baby's name.

"There's no name," Mason said, looking up at the nurse.

"Did you give your baby up for adoption?" Evelyn asked Abby. Abby, tears brimming, nodded. "That's why. Sometimes a birth mother didn't name her baby. It made it a little easier for some of the girls."

Abby stood, the binder sliding from her lap onto the floor, and walked back toward the nursery. Mason picked up the binder, found the pages for the two weeks before and after Abby's entries, and handed Evelyn the notebook. "Could you make copies of these pages for me?"

"Of course," Evelyn said.

Mason joined Abby at the nursery window, standing behind her, his hands on her shoulders. Abby pressed her hands against the glass, reaching for the babies more than waving at them. A nurse cradling one of the newborns in her arms smiled broadly and mouthed *which one* to Abby and Mason. Abby shook her head. Evelyn found them a few minutes later, handing Mason the copies. Mason thanked her, tugging gently at Abby's sleeve.

"It's time to go," he said.

Abby held onto Mason's arm, letting him lead her, blinking her eyes when they emerged from the hospital. The city was wrapped in a gauzy haze reflecting sunlight in a filtered glare, the day not sunny or cloudy, the uncomfortable ambiguity matching her confusion and disappointment.

Mason found a walkway that led around the hospital grounds, following it to a bench in a garden alongside a small fishpond. The flowers had been trimmed back for fall. Burnt orange leaves shed by the surrounding oaks floated on the surface of the pond, their tips upturned, like miniature junks. The air was crisp, a solidly autumn day.

Abby sat on the bench, her arms folded, rocking slightly. Mason studied Jordan's medical records and the pages from the Baby Books, letting Abby find her voice. The medical records were devoid of anything that identified Jordan's natural parents, reporting her birth and first days of life in neutral medical tones. The last page of the records was a copy of an order from the Family Court Division of the City of St. Louis Circuit Court granting Arthur and Carol Hackett custody of Jordan Hackett, the order noting that the unnamed natural parents had waived their parental rights.

Mason read every entry in the Baby Book. There were several others where the space for the baby's name had been left blank, a hole in the mother's history filled without the mother's knowledge by strangers.

"How could they have lost my records?" Abby asked at last.

"It's a big place. It's been a long time," Mason said, reciting the obvious excuses. "I'll tell you something else that's missing," he said.

"What?"

"Gina Davenport's signature in the Baby Book. The nurse gave me copies of the pages for the two weeks before and after you were there. Emily Davenport was born one week before your baby and Jordan were born. Either she didn't sign in, or she wasn't there."

"That's not possible," Abby said, sitting up and shaking off her funk. "Every mother signed the book. It was a ritual."

"Not Gina," Mason said.

Abby grabbed the pages from the Baby Book, studying each entry. Mason tried to tie the loose ends of Abby's missing medical records to Gina's missing Baby Book entry, but the knot kept unraveling. His cell phone rang, saving him from another attempt.

"Mason," he answered.

"Lou, it's Harry. Where are you?"

"Caulfield Medical Center in St. Louis. We talked to Abby's uncle. He sold Abby's baby, but claims he doesn't know who the buyer was. He's been marinated in booze so long, it's a miracle he remembers his name. We didn't do much better at the hospital. I hope you've come up with something."

"Your hunch about Robert Davenport was half right," Harry said.

"Which half?" Mason asked.

"The half about Davenport getting busted. It happened when he was living in St. Louis."

"Which half was wrong?"

"There's no connection to Centurion Johnson."

"I wouldn't have expected one in St. Louis. Centurion always stayed close to home," Mason said.

"There's still another half," Harry said. "Davenport was busted along with a few other guys. It was strictly small-time stuff, nickle-and-dime bags, but you'll be interested in who one of the other guys was."

"Harry, don't make me beg."

"Habit," Harry said. "It was Terry Nix."

"Do not shit me, Harry," Mason said, "or I'll tell Claire to put saltpeter in your warm milk."

"I shit you not," Harry said. "The charges were thrown out because of a problem with the search. I tracked down one of the arresting cops. Turns out we know some of the same guys. His name is Roy Bowen. He used to work narcotics, undercover. Now he's behind a desk. Said he'd be glad to talk to you."

"Where do we find him?" Mason asked.

"Where do you think?" Harry asked.

"Krispy Kreme?" Mason said.

"Very funny," Harry answered. "Turn yourself in at noon, downtown."

CHAPTER 27

"We've got three hours to kill before we meet Roy Bowen," Mason said, "and we're not spending it on this bench. Come on."

Abby said, "I'm not in the mood for sightseeing."

"And I'm not coming to your pity party," Mason told her. Abby's face fell, Mason cupping her chin in his hand. "I need your help," he told her. "I need you in the game, not on the bench feeling sorry for yourself."

Abby held his wrist, nodding her head. "Okay. What's next."

"Vital records," he said. "Another bureaucratic adventure. Emily's birth certificate will say where she was born. I want a copy. Might as well get one for Jordan while we're there."

An hour later, they were sitting in a Starbucks in downtown St. Louis, the birth certificates, medical records, and Baby Book entries spread in front of them, alongside a copy of the *St. Louis Post Dispatch*. Mason didn't like the taste of coffee, but he did like the smell. The double latte Abby ordered revived her.

"Emily's birth certificate confirms she was born at Caulfield and that Gina and Robert Davenport were her parents," Abby said.

"Gina just didn't sign the Baby Book, that's all," Mason said. "We can't check her medical records without an authorization or a subpoena, and the hospital would fight a subpoena."

"Why?" Abby asked. "She's dead. What do they care?"

"They don't, except they would want a judge to order them to turn over the records so that Robert Davenport doesn't sue them for invasion of privacy. If Davenport objected, the court wouldn't order the hospital to turn over the records unless I could establish some relevance to Jordan's case, which I can't do at the moment. That song and dance will take at least a month."

Abby leafed through Jordan's medical records again, smoothing the pages, stopping at the court order granting custody to the Hacketts. "What's this mean?" she said, pointing to the language in the order reciting that the natural parents had waived their parental rights.

"It means that the natural parents consented to the adoption. Otherwise, one of the parents could have shown up later and asked to have their baby back. I know what you're thinking," he said. "We could find the father, talk to him, but those records are sealed too."

Abby grinned for the first time that morning. "Don't be so certain you know what I'm thinking, mister. We don't need the court records. I know the father."

"Assuming Jordan is your daughter, you know where he is after twenty-one years?" Mason asked, basking in her smile.

Abby showed him the front page of the newspaper's sports section, pointing to the picture of a columnist whose byline and picture appeared beneath a column titled, "Kramer's World." Mason studied the photograph of Tony Kramer, resisting an unexpected twinge of jealousy. Kramer was bald on top, his full cheeks made heavier by a thick beard. Mason felt better.

"You followed his career after all these years?" Mason asked.

"Not really," she answered. "I knew he went to the University of Missouri for journalism. I heard from some friends that he ended up in St. Louis with the *Post Dispatch.*" Abby turned the paper toward her. "In high school, his hair was on his head, not his face. He was cute and I was easy. Turned out to be a bad combination. Let's call him."

"Bad idea. Most guys don't like starting the week with a phone call from the girl they knocked up in high school. You won't get anything out of him."

"What do you suggest?"

"A personal visit. Really shake him up."

Roy Bowen was having a bowl of fresh fruit and raw vegetables for lunch. "I'm on a fruit-and-vegetable diet," he explained, patting his belly. "My wife tells me I've got done-fell syndrome. She says my stomach done fell and I can't see my feet anymore. My wife, she's a panic," he said with no trace of humor.

Bowen's desk job was deputy chief of police. His office was on the top floor of police headquarters, two doors down from the chief. The walls were lined with commendations and photographs with dignitaries. His desk was thick with paper. The Arch dominated the landscape beyond the windows behind his desk, reducing the Mississippi River to an afterthought.

"Harry Ryman said you used to work narcotics," Mason said.

"That was back when I thought it was fun to get shot at," Bowen said. "My wife didn't mind that so much, or the pierced ears. She drew the line at tattoos, so I went into management," he said with the forced laugh of a joke told too often.

"What can you tell us about Robert Davenport and Terry Nix?"

Bowen picked up a file from his desk. "I had somebody dig this out after I talked to Harry," Bowen said. "One of the perks of this job is that you can actually make somebody do something if it's about a two-bit bust twenty years ago. Davenport and Nix were small-time dealers. One of the cops screwed up the warrant and the case got thrown out. End of story," he said.

"You run into either one of them again?"

"Nope," Bowen answered. "We kept tabs on them for a little while. The bust cost Nix his job and he left town. I don't know what happened to Davenport."

"Where did Nix work?" Mason asked.

"That was the part that made me remember him when Harry called," Bowen said. "Nix was a substance-abuse counselor working at Caulfield Medical Center. The guy was supposed to be treating people and he was selling them dope. Can you believe it?"

"Yeah," Mason said. "I can. If you have a picture of Nix from when he was arrested, I could use a copy."

"No problem. Making copies is one of my secretary's specialties. There's one other thing you might be interested in based on what Harry told me about your case," Bowen said.

"What's that?"

"We heard rumors at the time that Nix had another sideline brokering illegal adoptions. Some of the girls he counseled were pregnant, and he offered them cash or drugs if they sold their babies. Nix left town before we could prove anything. You snag this guy or need some help, let me know," Bowen said, writing his home phone number on a business card and handing it to Mason.

"Count on it," Mason said.

A security guard stopped Mason and Abby in the lobby of the *Post Dispatch* building, making them sign in, produce identification, and wait while he called Tony Kramer.

"So much for shaking him up. I understand the need for security, but do we look like terrorists?" Abby asked, resuming the jittery pacing she'd done at the hospital.

"When your old boyfriend finds out you're waiting in the lobby, he might prefer someone with a bomb. He's probably got a wife, three kids, and a dog, none of whom know they have a relative about to climb out of the woodpile. And when he sees you bouncing off the walls, he'll figure you're here to ask for child support."

"I can't help it," she said, tapping her fingers on crossed arms. "First my uncle, then the hospital, now Tony. That's a lot of baggage to unpack."

"Abby? Abby Lieberman?" Tony Kramer said from behind them. Abby and Mason turned around. "I took the stairs," Kramer said, pointing to the door at his back.

Abby brushed her hair back, smoothed her blouse, and smiled weakly. "Hello, Tony. Long time."

Kramer exhaled, hiking his trousers around his spreading middle, tugging at his beard. "Just a couple of lifetimes," he said, waiting for Abby to fill the void, neither of them knowing what to say.

Mason broke the awkward silence. "I'm Lou Mason, a friend of Abby's. Is there someplace here where we can talk privately."

"Are you kidding?" Kramer asked. "At a newspaper? What's this about, Abby?"

"It's not what you think, Tony. It's about . . ."

Tony raised his hand. "Let's go for a walk."

The newspaper's offices were downtown on Tucker Boulevard. Tony led them down Tucker, turning left on Cole. Mason gave Abby and Tony room, letting Abby break the ice as he trailed behind them, Tony looking over his shoulder at Mason as she spoke, Mason waving back at him, trying to picture them as teenagers, shutting the image down when it heated up.

They stopped in Carr Square Park. Tony was breathing heavily after the short walk, glancing around for witnesses as Mason caught up with them. "I want nothing to do with this, Mason," he said so quietly the birds couldn't hear. "You understand that. I've got a very nice life here. Abby and I made a mistake. We were kids and kids make mistakes. Giving that baby up for adoption was best for everyone."

"I do understand that, Tony. I don't want to bring either you or Abby into this case, but my client is on trial for her life. That trumps everything."

"All I know is that a guy showed up at my dorm. I was a freshman in college for Christ's sake," Tony said. "He told me if I signed the waiver, I wouldn't have to pay child support. So I signed it."

Mason showed him the picture of Terry Nix. "Was this the guy?"

"You want me to remember a guy I saw one time over twenty years ago?" Tony asked. "I don't remember what I looked like twenty years ago. I'm sorry," he said to Abby. "That's the best I can do. I'm on deadline. I've got to get back to the paper."

Mason and Abby stopped at her uncle's house before leaving town to show him Terry Nix's picture. He wouldn't let them in, shaking his head at the photograph before slamming the door closed. Mason dropped Abby off shortly after eight o'clock that night, understanding when she didn't invite him in. She shouldered her bag, her lips tight, her face drained from a short trip that had taken her too far into her past.

Tuffy jumped Mason when he got home, forgiving him for leaving her to be fed by a neighbor while he was gone. Mason had brought Jordan's file home from the office. He spread it out on his kitchen table, searching it for missing pieces while he drank a beer for dinner.

Mason had read every word on every page too many times to count. He didn't expect the words to change, but he knew that their importance could as he learned more about his case. The trick was to figure out what had changed. He finished his beer and started another, picking up Gina Davenport's autopsy report.

He forced himself to pay attention to each of the pathologist's findings, including the weight and color of each internal organ, the splintering of Gina's skull, and the pulverizing impact on her brain when she hit the pavement. He read the description of Gina's reproductive system twice, the second time out loud, to make certain he understood what he was reading.

Mason called his Aunt Claire. "Female anatomy is not my strong point," he told her.

"I'm so sorry," Claire said. "I thought by now you were more experienced."

"I'm good with the surface structures," he assured her. "Help me out with the internal stuff."

"You are such a sophisticated man," his aunt said. "How can I help?"

"If a woman's fallopian tubes are blocked, she can't get pregnant, right?"

"Good guess," Claire said. "Next question."

"A congenital abnormality is one from birth. That means that a woman who was born with her fallopian tubes blocked could never get pregnant. Still right?"

Claire sharpened her tone. "Get to the point."

"I just read Gina Davenport's autopsy report for the tenth time. She had a congenital abnormality that caused blockage of her fallopian tubes. She couldn't get pregnant, but the city of St. Louis issued a birth certificate for her daughter, Emily, showing Gina as the mother."

"Gina couldn't have given birth," Claire said.

"Exactly. Plus, Emily's birth certificate says that she was born at Caulfield Medical Center in St. Louis. That makes Gina the only mother in the history of the hospital that didn't sign the maternity ward Baby Book," Mason said, explaining what they had learned at the hospital.

"You said that the hospital has no record that Abby was ever a patient there," Claire repeated. "Didn't you?"

"That's what they say, even though Abby's signature is in the Baby Book."

"Why would Gina Davenport falsify the birth of a baby? Why not adopt?" Claire asked.

"Because no court was going to allow a couple to adopt a baby when the father was a drug addict," Mason explained. "Gina Davenport bought a baby and claimed it as her own because that's the only way she could get one. She and her husband probably left St. Louis at the same time so that no one would become suspicious."

Claire followed the implications of Mason's theory. "You're suggesting that Gina Davenport bought Abby's baby along with a phony birth certificate and that she managed to get rid of Abby's medical records in the process. You know what that means if you're right?"

"Yes," Mason said. "It means that Abby's daughter is dead."

CHAPTER 28

Mason's theory was so disastrous for Abby that he couldn't tell her unless he was certain. Even then, he didn't know how he would do it. He shoved that prospect to the side and focused on the implications for his defense of Jordan.

He was now convinced that the phone call Abby received about finding her daughter had set in motion the chain of events that ended with the murders of Gina Davenport and Trent Hackett. That was the only way to tie the available evidence together.

Terry Nix was the only person Mason could think of that knew the Davenports had purchased their child, though he also knew that at least one other person had to be involved. While he believed that Terry Nix stole Abby's medical records to cover up the illegal adoption, Mason doubted that Nix also forged Emily's birth certificate. That required help from someone working in the city's Vital Records department. Mason found Roy Bowen's business card and called him at home.

"You don't waste time, do you?" Bowen told him.

"I don't have time to waste," Mason said, explaining what he was looking for.

"I'll see what I can do," Bowen told him. "They may not keep records that far back. This may take a while."

Mason gave Tuffy fresh water and promised to take her on a long walk in the morning. Tuffy sniffed the water and wandered off, not impressed, ignoring Mason's pat on the back as he left again. How, Mason wondered, could he ever manage a long-term relationship with a woman if his dog could make him feel guilty for ignoring her?

Mason didn't find Robert Davenport at home, so he headed for his studio. It was almost ten o'clock when he parked a block away after finding the street barricaded by police officers. Satellite trucks from local TV stations lined the curb. Mason ducked his head when he saw Sherri Thomas and her Channel 6 cameraman. He was in no mood to make the late evening news.

"What's going on?" Mason asked one of the cops.

"Guy OD'd," the cop answered.

Mason knew the answer to his next question but asked it anyway. "Robert Davenport?"

The cop looked past him. "No names released yet."

"Is Samantha Greer in charge of the investigation?"

"Yeah," the cop answered, paying more attention. "Who are you?"

"Lou Mason. Do me a favor, call Detective Greer. Tell her I'd like to talk to her."

The cop spoke into the radio clipped to his shirt, waving Mason through. Mason found Samantha waiting for him next to a sculpture planted on the lawn outside the studio. The sculpture was an irregular cone of bronze affixed nose-down to a polished black granite base. The police had set up bright lights around the studio to assist in the search for physical evidence. The beams collided with the sculpture, making it glow like an errant space probe just returned to earth.

"At least you can't blame this one on my client," Mason told her.

"It's hard for one person to kill everybody," she said.

Mason said, "One of the cops directing traffic said Davenport OD'd."

"Looks like it. What brings you here?" Samantha asked.

"Loose ends," Mason answered. "I'm getting ready for the preliminary hearing in the Trent Hackett murder. I had some questions for Robert."

"You accused Trent Hackett of killing Gina Davenport. Are you going to accuse Robert Davenport of killing Trent to avenge his wife's death?"

Mason shrugged. "It's a theory," he said, not wanting to thank Samantha for thinking of a red herring he'd overlooked.

"Don't bother," she told him. "Davenport was giving a lecture that night. He's got a hundred alibis. Tell your client to plead guilty and get this mess over with."

"She's not guilty, Sam," Mason said.

Samantha grimaced, grinding her heel in the grass. "It's me you're talking to Lou, not some fresh cop out of the academy, not some reporter who wants to make you the lead in her story. I'm a damn good cop. We both know the evidence against your client is enough to send her away forever. If you don't have something better by now than the smoke you've been blowing, call Ortiz and make a deal."

They were both right, Mason realized. He believed Jordan was innocent even though there was enough evidence to convict her. Samantha was also right that Mason's defense had so far been little more than a bluff. Mason saw no point in telling Samantha his newest theory, knowing that she would rightly dismiss it as the ravings of a lawyer whose latest scapegoat conveniently died of a drug overdose.

Mason got up early enough on Tuesday morning to take Tuffy on a grand tour of Loose Park, leaving her panting on her living room pillow, her bushy tail thumping against the floor in gratitude. Mason even thought the dog winked at him when he promised to be home in time to give her dinner.

The Cable Depot was his first stop. Jordan had told him that she had gone to Dr. Gina's office the Friday before Gina was murdered and that she had discovered her cell phone was missing after her therapy session with Gina. Arthur Hackett had told him that Gina had stopped at KWIN after her session with Jordan, making the radio station the likely place to start looking for Jordan's cell phone.

Mason still had the passkey Trent Hackett gave him, but he knew he couldn't simply walk into KWIN, flash his American Bar Association membership card, and start rifling through desk drawers. He'd have to make peace, or at least reach a truce, with Arthur Hackett.

Hackett was seated behind his desk gazing out the window to the north, his back to the door, watching private planes land at the downtown airport, when a secretary brought Mason into his office. He slowly swiveled his chair around to face Mason as the secretary closed the door, leaving them alone, shocking Mason with his deteriorated appearance. His face was gray, skin hanging loose from his cheeks, his eyes flat as if nothing he saw was worth the view. He'd lost enough weight that his clothes sagged, covering him like hand-me-downs. Hackett raised a limp hand from his lap, gesturing Mason to have a seat.

"Thank you for seeing me," Mason said. "I know this is a difficult time for you and your wife."

"Do you?" Arthur asked. "How would you know such a thing, Mr. Mason? Have you buried one of your children? Have you condemned another?" Each question was cut with a dull knife, the sharp edge worn from the many times he'd asked them of himself, trying to fathom how such horror fell to him.

"No, sir," Mason answered, caught in the quicksand of Hackett's grief. "I won't presume to know what you're going through, though I am sorry you have to go through it."

Arthur drew a deep breath. "That's more honesty than I'm accustomed to. My home is crawling with people trying to make my wife and me feel better. I'm in no mind to work, but at least I can be left alone here."

"Then why did you see me?" Mason asked.

"There's no understanding something like this, Mason. There's no way of reconciling to it. Carol and I weren't perfect parents. Hell, we weren't even good parents. Trent was our failure. Jordan was a mystery, bad genes, bad parents. Who knows? They were ours to take care of and we failed them. I was hoping that you found something that would make sense out all of this, maybe let my wife and me off the hook a little bit."

"I'm trying, Arthur," Mason said, steeling himself to Arthur's excruciating confession, knowing he couldn't give the absolution Arthur needed. "I was wondering if Jordan's cell phone ever turned up. Someone used it to make a call that could be important."

Arthur shook his head. "You asked me about that once before. I took a look around and didn't find it, though it should have been easy enough to find. Jordan bought a hot pink faceplate for the phone. It practically glowed in the dark."

"Did the bills come to you?" Mason asked. "I'd like to see the last one." Arthur pursed his lips, drumming his fingers on his desk.

"I can subpoena it from the cellular company, but that's a lot of trouble if you've got the bill," Mason said. He waited to ask Hackett why he was holding back.

"You don't have to do that," Hackett said. "It's too late to be embarrassed for Jordan anyway. I got the bill the other day," he said, removing it from a folder on his desk and handing it to Mason. "It was over a thousand dollars, most of it to one of those psychic hotlines. Why she bothered with that rubbish, I don't know. I canceled the account."

Mason studied the bill. He found the entry for the call made to Abby's phone and her return call to Jordan's phone. The other calls were made to the psychic hotline. "Did you ask the cell phone company if they could find out who placed the calls?"

"They said there was no way to know unless the calls were recorded. Does any of that help you?"

"I don't know," Mason said. "I heard that Max Coyle was involved with Gina. Do you know anything about that?"

"There are no secrets in a place like this, Mason. They were both grownups. A lot of people screw around if they get the chance. I heard that you and Max discussed his relationship with Gina at the golf tournament," he added with a pleased grunt.

"What about Paula Sutton?" Mason asked, ignoring Hackett's jab. "Who was she screwing around with?"

"Ask her. She'll tell you. She isn't the shy type."

"I thought there were no secrets in a place like this," Mason said.

"There aren't. I just don't have time for all of them. Is that all?"

"One last question. Have you heard anyone at the station ever mention someone named Abby Lieberman?"

"No," Arthur said without hesitation. "Should I have?"

"I hope not."

On his way out, Mason walked past the broadcast studio where Paula Sutton was doing her morning show. He stopped and watched through the glass wall dividing the studio from the interior corridor, listening to the broadcast piped over the intercom. Paula listened while her caller denounced public education as a government thought-control plot. She noticed Mason as her caller finished his tirade, answering Mason's pantomimed request that she call him with dead air, her caller hanging up in frustration as the program engineer cut to a commercial.

Max Coyle lumbered down the hallway, dipping his shoulder and knocking Mason to his knees as he passed, not saying a word. When Mason got up, Paula had slipped out of the studio through another door. He made it to the street without being steamrolled again, certain that Max wouldn't be doing any testimonials on his behalf.

Mickey was waiting for him when he got to the office, shooting Nerf Balls at the basketball goal above the door. Mason caught the ball as he crossed the threshold.

"Goaltending," Mickey said.

"My goal," Mason answered. "I can tend it whenever I want. Are we still in business?"

"You bet. I've figured out the great thing about the practice of law. When times are good, people can afford to fight. When times are bad, people can't afford not to fight. And criminals don't pay any attention to the economy. You'll never go out of business."

"I love this country," Mason said. "How's the not-for-profit world compare?"

"I don't know why they call it not-for-profit," Mickey answered. "As far as I can tell, everyone is making a killing."

"What did you find out about Sanctuary?"

"Nothing new. Centurion and Terry Nix are living large, but they're smart enough to do it up front. It's all in the reports. Emily's Fund is another story."

"Tell me the story," Mason said, opening his dry-erase board, hoping the crisscrossed lines would lead him to an answer instead of another dead end.

"Emily's Fund reported making donations to about a dozen other charities. All of them had to file the same annual report listing their contributions. The only one that matches up is Sanctuary. The others reported getting about half of what Emily's Fund says it gave them."

"What's the total difference between the two amounts?"

"More than two million bucks over the last couple of years," Mickey said. "Emily's Fund has a fiscal year that ends June 30, and that's when it makes a lot of its contributions. Almost a million of the discrepancy was from contributions made on June 30."

"Wouldn't somebody notice the discrepancy?" Mason asked.

"Doubtful," Mickey answered. "From what I found out, these charities rarely get audited by anybody, especially if the charity's directors are the same people playing with the dough. Plus, anyone looking at the report for one charity probably wouldn't cross-check it against the reports of another charity, especially if the first charity's books balanced."

"Gina Davenport and David Evans were the only directors of Emily's Fund, right?" Mason asked.

"Kind of convenient," Mickey answered.

"Did Gina Davenport sign the reports?"

"In front of a notary," Mickey said, "swearing they were accurate."

Mason picked up Gina's book, her picture staring back at him from the cover. "So that's the way you did the things you did, Dr. Gina," Mason said. "Did that get you killed?"

CHAPTER 29

Late that afternoon, Mason returned to the Cable Depot, this time to talk to David Evans about Gina Davenport's recipe for cooking the books of Emily's Fund. Earl Luke Fisher was sprawled out on his park bench across from the building entrance, his head propped on an oil-stained canvas bag, the rest of his worldly possessions crammed into a grocery cart lashed to the back of the bench with a candy-striped bungee cord. The autumnal sun, low-angled and gentle, painted him gold to match the leaves pooled beneath the bench. He called out as Mason parked his car.

"Hey, Mason!"

Mason gave him a waist-high salute as he made for the front door.

"Come here, Mason!" Earl Luke shouted, sitting up on his bench. "What's the matter? You too good for Earl Luke? Do I gotta make a damn appointment?"

Earl Luke stood, eclipsing the sun at his back, his

shadow rippling on the pavement, aiming at Mason, who looked at his watch and shrugged. It was close to dinner, and he guessed Earl Luke's meal plan was a little short.

"How you doing, Earl Luke?" Mason asked, crossing the street.

"I'm fit to spit," Earl Luke answered, closing one eye and slapping his hand over his heart, as if to prove the point.

"Something on your mind?" Mason asked.

"Always got something on my mind," Earl Luke said. "It ain't free, though."

Mason had put money into worse lost causes than Earl Luke, and didn't mind doing it again. He liked Earl Luke's approach, turning panhandling into retail at the street level. He said, "You've got to ask for the sale to make the sale."

"I'm asking, I'm asking," Earl Luke said, rubbing his hands on a denim shirt that could have been a palette for a dirt painter. "That prosecutor fella come see me again and give me a subpoena for court this Friday. Give me a check for forty bucks too."

"That's a witness fee," Mason explained. "The subpoena isn't valid without the check."

"Well, forty bucks is nothing to sneeze at, 'cept I can't cash no check seein's as how I ain't exactly got a local bank account, if you get my meaning."

"You'll have to take that up with the prosecutor," Mason said. "Maybe they'll give you cash."

"The hell with that and the hell with them!" Earl Luke said. "I'm taking up a collection to head south for the winter. Thought you might like to get me started. If I can get a stake, I'd leave today, let that prosecutor cash his own damn check. Might do your client some good if I was to be a long way from that courtroom come Friday."

Mason stepped back, not interested in Earl Luke's offer to become a tampered witness regardless of the price. "Can't help you," Mason told him. "You're under subpoena to appear in court. You better show up or the prosecutor will send the sheriff to make sure you do. Besides," Mason lied, "I'm not worried about your testimony."

"It's a goddamn conspiracy, is what it is!" Earl Luke said. "You damn lawyers are all in it together," he added, snatching up his canvas bag, spilling its contents on the ground, scrambling to shove the coarse stuffing of his vagrant life back in the bag.

Mason counted a screwdriver, a short length of thin rope, a flattened roll of duct tape, a rusty bottle opener, a butane lighter, a yellowed copy of *People* magazine, and a wadded sweatshirt among Earl Luke's inventory. Something hard tumbled out of the folds of the sweatshirt, skidding across the pavement, Earl Luke diving to recover it, Mason catching a glimpse.

"Is that a cell phone?" Mason asked. The flash of a pink faceplate had caught his eye.

"What if it is?" Earl Luke asked, crouched on the ground, hiding the phone under the sweatshirt. "I got business to tend to. Man's entitled to a telephone."

"Must be tough paying your phone bill without having a bank account," Mason said, "and I bet it's even harder to get a mailing address for a park bench."

Earl Luke spat, scooting backward to his grocery cart, dumping the bag in with the rest of his things, clutching the sweatshirt.

"Where did you get the phone, Earl Luke?"

"I didn't steal it and you can't prove I did. I found it and it's mine. Possession is the law, Mr. Lawyer!"

"I don't care if you did," Mason told him. "Like you said, a man's got to take care of business, right?"

Earl Luke cocked his head, squinting at Mason, knowing Mason was playing him, not sure for what and why. "I got my business and it's my own business, so you just stay out of it."

"You get any good tips from the psychic hotline, Earl Luke?" Mason asked.

Earl Luke stopped fumbling with the bungee cord harnessing the grocery cart to the park bench. "How'd you know 'bout somethin' like that?"

"Maybe I'm psychic," Mason said. "Too bad the phone service was cut off. I hear the more time you give the psychic, the better they do." Earl Luke's eyes dilated from slits to saucers as he listened to Mason. "Tell you what I'll do," Mason continued. "I'll buy that phone from you. You take the money, buy a phone card, and tell your psychic to give it to you straight."

"How much?" Earl Luke asked.

Mason took cash out of his wallet, letting it dangle from his fingers. "Fifty bucks," he said, watching Earl Luke wet his lips and ease his grip on the sweatshirt. "Just one other thing. Tell me how you got the phone."

Earl Luke handed Mason the phone, grabbing the cash with a pickpocket's swiftness. "Dumpster behind the Depot."

"Show me," Mason said, flashing another twenty-dollar bill.

Earl Luke snapped up the twenty and led Mason to the grassy north side of the Cable Depot, where there was less than a hundred feet from the building to the edge of the bluff overlooking the interstate highway that wrapped around the downtown. Mason could hear the pounding roar of passing traffic.

Earl Luke pointed to a Dumpster set hard against the north face of the building beneath a trash chute bolted to the brick wall. There was no sun on this side of the building. Mason craned his neck upward, catching the cool early evening breeze under his chin, tracing the trash chute to a small door on the top floor, buried in the brick, hidden even more by the advancing dusk. He followed it back down to the Dumpster, sitting on a concrete pad partially obscuring another door, this one a steel door inlaid in the concrete.

"Give me a hand," Mason said, the two of them shoving the Dumpster off the trapdoor. "That's an odd place to put a door," Mason said, kneeling and rubbing his hand across the burnished lock, fingering the passkey in his pocket, wondering if it would open the door and what he would find if it did.

"You got to be the strangest lawyer I ever did see," Earl Luke said. "You buy a phone off of me we both know don't work. You give me another sawbuck to show you a trash can you coulda found on your own. Now you got the look of a second-story man I once knowed jus' before he get caught."

Mason kept his head down, not wanting Earl Luke to see him smile. He felt like a second-story man, taunted by the mystery of what was hidden on the other side of the trapdoor, juiced by the prospect of slipping in under the radar of the straight and narrow, wondering what his life would be like if he gave sway to the part of him that got off on tempting trouble.

It was, he understood, what Dr. Gina meant by the

title of her book, *The Way You Do the Things You Do*. The impulse to step off the path, to break the rules was sometimes irresistible. It put Max Coyle and Gina Davenport in a photo album of dirty pictures. It put Robert Davenport at the naked breast of a student model, then left him dead with a dirty needle in his arm. It put Terry Nix in the black-market baby business. And it was about to put Mason on the wrong side of the line, a place he was willing to go alone but not with Earl Luke as his witness. He left the passkey in his pocket and stood up, brushing his pants clean.

"It's probably nothing," Mason said, not convincing either one of them. "Thanks," he said, adding, "I don't suppose you saw who put the phone in the Dumpster."

"Now how am I gonna see that?" Earl Luke asked. "Any fool can see that trash chute comin' out of the radio station up there. How am I gonna see who opens that little-bitty door?"

"How do you know the trash chute is in the radio station?"

"On account of I know that the radio station is up there and on account of I saw that woman what got throw'd out her window on the south side of the building. So, the radio station has to be on this side."

"You're right," Mason said, remembering the view from Arthur Hackett's window north to the downtown airport. Mason turned around, a small plane gliding in for a landing, puffs of smoke bursting from the runway as the wheels touched down. He looked back at the trash chute, finding the small door cut into the wall directly below Arthur Hackett's window.

Earl Luke watched Mason for a few more minutes, clearing his throat, shuffling his feet, baiting the air with the hope for more easy money. "Anything else you want to see?" he finally asked Mason.

Mason gazed eight stories up, not hearing Earl Luke, wondering about a father's grief and the reasons it ran so deep.

David Evans's office was locked, no light under the door, no answer to Mason's knock, Mason drawing the line at breaking into Evans's office. Outside, blue violet dusk chased the last patches of daylight, lacing the evening air with a sharp chill, making good the weatherman's forecast of an early frost. Mason sat on Earl Luke's bench watching tenants spin out of the Cable Depot's revolving door, their day finished, collars gathered around chins, cursing the unexpected cold. Earl Luke was gone, having taken his grocery cart and Mason's money out for the evening.

Mason was glad that he'd thrown a barn jacket and a ball cap in his car when he heard the forecast that morning. He was used to Kansas City's multiple-personality weather, with days that dawned bright and sunny, then descended into raw nights. He rolled his collar up and pulled his cap down, becoming invisible to those passing by, arguing with himself about the door behind the Depot, knowing the argument was more about when than if.

He tabled his internal debate when David Evans and Paula Sutton squeezed through the revolving door, setting a quick pace as they headed south, Paula trying without success to smooth the wrinkles in her clothes, Evans teasing her and the fabric with playful strokes. She gave him a shove, not resisting when he locked his arm over hers, pulling her to him as they continued on, their dance reminding Mason that a locked door with no light beneath it and no answer to his knock didn't mean that no one was home.

Remembering that Evans lived a few blocks away in Quality Hill, Mason followed them, telling himself that the door behind the Depot wasn't going anywhere. Mason liked catching a witness out of his element, away from the comfortable trappings of home turf. Evans's house was certainly his home turf, but it wasn't Paula Sutton's.

Mason gave them a good head start before following at an unobtrusive distance, lingering in doorways when they stopped at a deli, then a liquor store. Evans's townhouse was the middle unit in a row of restored, orange-brick row houses. Mason waited until the lights came on before retreating to the deli for his own dinner.

A pastrami on rye with dark mustard and darker ale gave him no great insights into the relationship between Paula Sutton and David Evans. There was nothing sinister, or even wrong, about a relationship they made no effort to hide, though Mason guessed that Paula's open resentment of Gina Davenport made for interesting pillow talk.

He called Abby, telling her he was working late, relieved when she said that she was as well, promising to call tomorrow. He wasn't ready to tell her about Emily, and he wasn't anxious to undermine their relationship by holding back. He hoped another day would bring more answers.

Realizing he had to ask questions to get answers, he retraced his route to David Evans's front door, this time drawing a response to his knocking. Evans opened the door, his shirt half-buttoned and hanging out over his pants, Sinatra playing in the background.

"Mason, what do you want?" Evans asked, glancing over his shoulder.

"Sinatra?" Mason asked in return. "I never figured you for a Sinatra guy, David. I would have guessed the Backstreet Boys."

"Who is it?" Paula asked from inside the house, appearing behind Evans wearing a man's bathrobe. "Oh, shit!" she said, answering her own question.

"Publisher's Clearing House Prize Patrol," Mason said. "If you'll just step outside for our cameras, we'll present you with the grand-prize check."

"Can it, Mason," Evans said. "You want to talk to me, make an appointment during regular business hours."

Mason shouldered past Evans before he could close the door. "We're in the service business, David. There are no regular business hours."

Evans was built lower to the ground than Mason, with a squared midsection, once solid, now soft. Mason felt Evans's muscles tense beneath the fat as he blocked Mason from getting past the entry hall.

Mason tightened in response, an involuntary primal reflex, as he realized he had pushed Evans too far. A man could do many things in defense of his home, including kill an invader, and Evans was ready to defend. Mason eased back, opening a demilitarized zone between him and Evans, keeping his hands loose at his sides, risking a glance at Paula holding the robe tightly around her.

"Get out," Evans told him, leaving no room for other choices.

"Maybe this isn't a good time after all," Mason said.

"I'll just talk to the IRS about the Form 990 reports you filed for Emily's Fund. I'm sure they'll call you for an appointment during regular business hours."

Evans didn't blink or breathe for a moment, then he found his smile. "Damn, Mason. Next time someone tells you to follow the money, run the other direction," he said, clamping his hand on Mason's arm. "Come on in if that's all you want to talk about," he added as Paula took her cue and disappeared into the bedroom.

Evans led Mason into the kitchen. The wine he'd purchased at the liquor store sat on the kitchen table unopened alongside the still-wrapped carryout from the deli. Mason had interrupted the appetizer, not the entree. The kitchen was a narrow rectangle that opened into a living room where Paula had left her shoes and skirt on the floor. She slipped out of the bedroom still wearing Evans's robe, gathered her things, and punched the off button on the stereo, cutting Sinatra off in midcroon. Firing a defiant look at Mason, she retreated again.

"Your charity reported contributions it didn't make. How come?" Mason asked.

Evans opened the refrigerator and tossed a can of beer to Mason. "You look like a beer guy to me," Evans told him. "Emily's Fund wasn't my charity, it was Gina's, and I didn't sign the reports. Gina did. I checked the books after she was killed and figured out what she had done, though I couldn't tell you why she did it."

Mason popped the lid on his beer. "I'm supposed to believe you didn't know that Emily's Fund only gave away half the money it said it did."

"I don't care what you believe," Evans said. "Don't forget, I'm the one who told you to check them out. You've seen the reports or you wouldn't be here. Gina signed them. I'll be right back." Evans retrieved his brief-case from the entry hall closet. "I signed these," he said, taking a folder out of the briefcase.

Mason leafed through the pages. "Amended reports," he said.

"That's right," Evans said. "Only these have the real numbers. I mailed the originals to the IRS yesterday. These are copies. Keep them, I've got another set at the office."

Paula returned from the bedroom wearing her own clothes. Evans handed her a beer, but Paula shook it off, lighting a cigarette instead, tapping her lighter on the kitchen counter as she drew down on the burning tobacco. Mason read through the amended reports again, searching for a reason not to feel like a fool.

"Go figure," was all Mason could muster.

He stuck his hand in the pocket of his barn jacket, his fingers closing around the cell phone he bought from Earl Luke, playing a hunch, taking it out, and putting it on the counter, watching Paula Sutton gag on her smoke when he spun the pink faceplate toward her.

Recovering quickly, she stubbed her cigarette out in the sink. "I'm going home. Call me," she said, then told Mason, "Him, not you."

"Don't leave me out," Mason said. "You can call me on my cell phone."

CHAPTER 30

Evans gave Mason the universal shrug all men use when they don't understand a woman's behavior, Mason responding with the knowing nod, meaning that he knew what Evans meant even if he didn't understand Paula's behavior any better than Evans did. Except that Mason's nod was a lie. He understood Paula's reaction to his house call and Jordan's phone.

Paula started getting an allergic reaction to Mason at the golf tournament when Mason first mentioned Abby Lieberman's name. Since then, Paula had avoided Mason, losing her libido entirely when Mason showed up at Evans's house, an effect Mason hoped was an isolated incident in his relations with women. When she saw Jordan's phone, she nearly swallowed her cigarette. Mason reached the easy and obvious conclusion that Paula had used Jordan's phone to call Abby Lieberman, putting her on a collision course with Gina Davenport.

The better questions were why Paula would go to such

trouble and how she knew to make the connection in the first place. Walking back to his car, Mason put his money on jealousy and passion. Paula's jealousy of Gina's success gave her reason to ferret out Gina's weak spots and use them to discredit Gina or just to ruin her day. The worst motive he could ascribe to Paula was the desire to stir up trouble for Gina.

Gina must have known from the beginning that Abby was Emily's birth mother, and confided the truth to Evans, relying on him to keep her secrets confidential. Evans must have been the kind of man who liked to impress a woman by sharing juicy tidbits, his knowledge evidence of his power, his power the best aphrodisiac he had to offer.

Accepting all that, Mason still couldn't make the link from Paula's phone call to the murders of Gina Davenport and Trent Hackett. The case was becoming a maddening collection of circles and false starts, none of which overcame the evidence against Jordan. By the time Mason reached his car, he was practicing his speech to Jordan about the wisdom of taking a plea that would give her a chance at a new life after most of her old life had been wasted in prison.

Forgetting the allure of the trapdoor behind the Cable Depot, Mason revved the engine of his rented Camry, banging his palm on the steering wheel, frustrated at his inability to make Jordan's case come together. Whenever he misplaced an important document in his office, he invariably found it on top of a stack of papers after he'd turned his office upside down looking for it. He usually made a bigger mess because he couldn't see what was in plain sight. As he sat in his rental car, missing his TR-6, all he saw was the mess.

* * *

Mason stopped at Blues on Broadway, taking comfort in the quiet of a slow night. Only a couple of tables were occupied. Fred, the regular bartender, waved a dish towel at Mason when he sat down at the bar. Fred was tall and thin, sometimes banging his head on the glasses hung in the rack above the bar. He had a round face like a sucker on the end of a long stick. For a bartender, he didn't say much, preferring to pour and serve.

"What'll you have, Lou?" Fred asked.

"Whatever you've got on draft," Mason answered. "You seen Blues tonight?"

"He called a while ago, didn't know if he'd make it in. You want something to eat? Connie is in the kitchen."

Blues on Broadway wasn't known for its food, the Reuben sandwich being the specialty of Connie, the short-order cook, who was married to Fred. Connie was also known for her temper, having threatened more than once to add an offending customer's fingers to the chowder she made on Fridays. Mason was hungry, but didn't want another sandwich. "Tell Connie to surprise me. Anything but a Reuben. She's got to be able to make something else."

Mason moved to a booth, nursing his beer, almost complaining when Connie shoved a Reuben under his chin, thinking better of it when he saw the hard set to her jaw. Mason looked past her to Fred, who ducked, not wanting to confess he'd told Connie what Mason had said. Connie was so short she needed a step stool to kiss her husband, but Fred valued his fingers too much to risk his wife's temper.

"Smells great, Connie. Thanks," Mason said.

"Leave a decent tip," she told him.

Mason had finished half the sandwich when Samantha Greer slid into the seat across from him. She rubbed her hands together, pressing them against her cheeks. "Boy, it's too early to be this cold already," she said.

"Frigid Canadian front," Mason said. "I heard it on the news."

"I once dated a Canadian with a frigid front," Samantha said.

Mason did a finger drum roll on the table. "Dynamite material. You should try open-mike night at a comedy club."

"Who puckered your backside?" she asked him. "Never mind, I don't want to know. I've got some news that will pick up your spirits."

"What? Patrick Ortiz resigned as prosecuting attorney to write legal thrillers and dropped the charges against my client as a going-away gift to me?"

"You know, Lou, your fantasies used to be a lot more fun."

"Yeah, but the rubber suit gave me a rash. What's up?"

"We found your car. I wanted to tell you myself. You didn't answer at home or the office or on your cell phone. I don't have what's-her-name's phone number, so I tried here. Glad I caught you," she said, not concealing the light in her eyes.

"Her name is Abby. Her number is in the book. You found my TR-6?" Mason asked, pushing the Reuben out of the way, reaching across the table for Samantha's hand, an instinctive gesture.

"Well, I didn't personally find it," she said, tentatively resting her other hand on top of Mason's, gently rubbing her finger between his. "a patrolman doing a routine check of abandoned buildings found it stashed in a vacant garage on the East Side."

"That's fantastic," Mason said. "No, it's beyond fantastic. When can I get it back?"

"Tomorrow morning," she said. "But it's a little banged up," she added.

"Banged up? How bad?"

"A little, actually more than a little, a lot. And it's not running. To tell you the truth, it's sitting. On blocks. Without wheels."

Mason slumped against the back of the booth. "Is this how you tell the widow she's a widow? I've got good news, Mrs. Smith. We found your husband, or at least most of him."

"Oh, come on, Lou. I know you love that car, but it's just a car. I had it towed to George's Body Shop. Just like you asked."

Mason let out a sigh, realizing that Samantha was still cradling his hand in hers. He drew his hand back, ignoring the slight resistance she offered. "Thanks, Sam," he said. "I appreciate you taking the trouble to come here. You didn't have to do that."

"Yeah, well," she said, pushing her hair back with one hand, hiding the other in her lap. "You know our motto: to protect and serve. This falls under customer service."

Mason wished he'd kept his hands to himself, not stumbling into another awkward, post-lover exchange with Samantha. Her not-so-subtle flirtation was a complication he didn't need.

"Good," he said, nodding like a bobble-head doll, struggling for something to say to put their conversation back on a professional track.

Samantha sat back, took a deep breath, and clapped

her hands. "Okay, I give up," she said. "A woman should never tell a man she isn't over him, especially when he's found somebody else. I'm not over you, Lou, but I guess you know that. I'm working on it, and I'd appreciate it if you'd help me out by acting like a jerk a little more often. I know you've got it in you," she said with half a laugh.

Mason smiled. "I can be a jerk," he said. "No problem. How about if I beat you up on the stand at Jordan's preliminary hearing on Friday. Then you could hate me."

"I wouldn't hate you," she said. "I'd feel sorry for you if that's the best defense you can give your client. If it is, you better make a deal."

"It's worse than that," he told her. "I don't even have anything to beat you up with."

"Tell me what you do have, Lou. I don't just want to win. I want to be right. I'll take my badge off and just be your friend. Try me," she said.

Mason considered her offer. He knew she was telling the truth when she told him she wanted to be right. He also knew she didn't want him to fail, and letting his client be sentenced to death or life imprisonment when he could have made a deal that left her some chance to live again would be a terrible failure.

"Okay," he said. "I'll tell you what I've got and you tell me what kind of deal Ortiz will make. Fair?"

"Fair," she said.

"Everything you have against Jordan is circumstantial," he began.

"I don't call fingerprints, hair and fiber samples at the scene and on the victims circumstantial," Samantha interrupted. "And I don't call an eyewitness who puts her at both scenes circumstantial, and I sure don't call her confession to Gina Davenport's murder circumstantial. The only thing we don't have is videotape of her killing them and we're damn close to having it on Dr. Gina. You know the trial judge will let that Channel 6 videotape into evidence even if Pistone wouldn't. Once the jury sees that tape, they won't hear another thing you say."

"Like I said," Mason continued. "Everything you have against Jordan is circumstantial. I have enough crap to throw on your case to raise a reasonable doubt."

"Beginning with your theory that Trent Hackett killed Gina because she was going to report him for a rape he didn't commit. And if he did commit it, Jordan has a terrific motive for killing her brother to go along with all that lousy circumstantial evidence we dug up. We only have to convict her of one murder to put her away forever."

"Fine. You don't like Trent for Gina's murder. How about Arthur Hackett? He had one of the best motives, money. He cashed in on Gina's life insurance policy, recovering the money he was going to lose when she jumped ship a year from now."

"You've seen Arthur Hackett. He's disintegrating faster than the invisible man. No one will believe he could throw Gina through a plate-glass window, then turn on his own son. Not even for five million bucks. Tell me you've got something better, Lou."

Mason emptied his beer, rolling the glass between his hands. "Maybe. Even I'll admit this next part is a little murky. Gina and Robert Davenport illegally adopted their daughter Emily. Terry Nix was the baby broker. They were all in St. Louis at the time. Nix was working at the hospital where Emily was born. He deep-sixed the medical records of the real mother. Somebody else, I don't know who, forged a birth certificate showing the Davenports as Emily's natural parents. They couldn't adopt because Robert Davenport was a drug addict and wouldn't pass the social services evaluation for a legit adoption."

"Which has what to do with the murders?" Samantha asked.

Mason pointed a finger at her. "Nix also dealt drugs to Robert Davenport back in their St. Louis salad days. Nix lands in Kansas City, hooks up with Centurion Johnson in a textbook example of vertical marketing, selling drugs and babies. They were probably supplying Robert Davenport. Somebody tipped off Emily's real mother, who, up to that point, had never tried to find her daughter. The mother is put on to Gina. Things start to come unraveled. Gina gets nervous. Nix and Centurion kill her to keep her quiet."

"Your rubber-suit fantasy has more appeal than this one. Assuming you're right, where does Trent fit in? Who kills him and why?"

"I don't know," Mason admitted. "The little shit tried to kill me. Why shouldn't someone besides Jordan try to kill him?"

"That's clear thinking," Samantha said. "Stick to soda between now and the trial. Your new—sorry, Abby—told me about her phone call to Gina Davenport. Is she Emily's birth mother? You might as well throw her into the suspect pool."

Mason hesitated, wanting to keep Abby out of their conversation, though he knew he had to put everything on the table. "There's a good chance. Abby delivered a baby at the same hospital a week after the birth date on Emily's birth certificate. The hospital can't find any record that Abby was ever a patient there."

Samantha drummed her fingers on the table, working the angle Mason had given her. "The rumor we picked up was that Abby thought she was Jordan's mother. We heard that's why she posted the bond."

Mason said, "That's what she thinks. According to the autopsy report, Gina couldn't have kids. Whoever got Abby to call Gina must have known the truth."

"Have you told Abby she put her money on the wrong baby?"

"Not yet. Not until I'm certain," Mason said. "Gina was also skimming money from the charity she set up in her daughter's memory. Maybe Nix and Centurion were in on that too. Maybe Trent was a bagman for them. I don't know. The murders should be tied together, but I can't make it work."

"I can," Samantha said. "Jordan had the motive, the opportunity, and the rage to do them both. That's what the jury is going to believe."

"Assuming you're right, what kind of deal will Ortiz make? I may not have much, but I've got enough to muddy the waters."

Samantha shook her head. "You don't have that much mud," she said. "I'd bet on pleading guilty to second-degree murder on Gina's case, taking into account Jordan's emotional history and the sympathy the jury might show her when they find out what an asshole her old man is. The jury might blame him for some of this, figuring he drove her to it. She gets fifteen years to life, maybe gets out in ten years."

"What about on Trent's murder?"

"Ortiz will want a guilty plea on that one too. He'll probably agree to the same sentence, let them run concurrently. Maybe make her serve the minimum of fifteen years. Two brutal murders a week apart is a lot to overlook."

Mason reached back across the table, patting her hand for an instant. He knew she was right. It was time to make a deal. "Thanks, Sam," he told her. "For everything. I mean it."

"Hey, listen," she said. "All in a day's work. See you in court, Counselor."

CHAPTER 31

Mason met with Jordan the next afternoon. She was anxious to see him, giving him a bear hug when the guard ushered her into the cramped, windowless room where Mason waited.

"Why haven't you been to see me?" she said, letting him go.

"I've been pretty busy working on your case," he answered. "Besides, the guards tell me you've had company."

"Yeah, Abby has been here a couple of times. I still haven't figured out how she got involved in all of this, but I'm glad she did."

"Blame it on me," Mason said, dodging the question. "Are they treating you okay in here?"

Jordan walked around the perimeter of the room, extending her arms like yardsticks, measuring the space. "You know, this room is actually smaller than my cell. I didn't think anything could be smaller than that. The guards haven't bothered me. One woman came on to me and I thought we were going to have a problem, but she backed off."

"Jordan, tell me about the baby you gave up for adoption," Mason said.

She looked at him, her arms drooping at her sides. "It happened the first time my parents put me at Sanctuary. I was pissed at them and my brother. This guy, he wasn't even cute, I just figured, what the hell, it couldn't be worse than my brother. When I missed my period, I got scared and I wanted to get an abortion. Terry talked me out of it."

"What did your parents say?"

"Don't come home until the baby was gone." Sitting down at the table in the middle of the room, she clasped her hands together, laying them out in front of her, her eyes moistening. "Lou, you've got to get me out of here. I want to find my baby."

Mason knew that people often responded to incarceration the same way they did when a doctor told them they had a terminal illness, grinding through denial, anger, and bargaining until they accepted their new reality. Jordan was twenty-one years old. Fifteen years was almost as long as she'd been alive. Mason didn't know how she could ever accept the reality he was about to give her.

"Jordan, it may be a while before you get out."

Jordan's eyes flickered, light draining from her face like a picture morphing from color to black and white. "What are you saying?"

Mason gathered himself, looking at her, not wanting to tell her, not having a choice, giving it to her straight. "I think we should consider a plea bargain, making a deal with the prosecutor."

"What kind of a deal?" she asked, her voice rising an octave, the veins in her arms beginning to bulge as she clamped her hands more tightly together. "What does that mean? That I plead guilty? I'm not guilty! You don't believe me, do you?" she accused him, jumping out of her chair, knocking it over behind her. "I'm not guilty! I can't stay here. You've got to get me out!"

Jordan planted her palms on the table, leaning over Mason, pushing him back with her demand. Mason rose, circled past her, picked up her chair, and put his arm around her. She wrestled away, Mason holding on, pulling her back.

"It's not that simple, Jordan. It should be. It should only be about guilt or innocence, but it isn't. It's about proof, theirs and ours. It's about what a jury might do. It's about the risk you are taking with your life. I need you to know all these things so you can decide. I'm not going to make you do anything."

She wouldn't bend, keeping her frame rigid, fighting his grip and his words. "If you think I'm guilty, what chance do I have?"

Mason patted her on the back. "I don't think you're guilty, Jordan, but I'm not on the jury," Mason said, dispensing the standard lawyer's bromide, not telling her that he wasn't certain of her innocence any longer, but wouldn't let his doubt stand in the way of a vigorous defense.

Mason returned to his seat, Jordan still standing, her head turned to the side, not meeting his gaze. "Your preliminary hearing on Friday will be just like the one last week. The judge will bind you over for trial for Trent's murder. You won't get bail. Your trial on Gina's murder starts in two months. Let me tell you what the jury will hear."

Mason recited the evidence in a flat, neutral monotone, letting his words fall like small hammers on Jordan, beating the resistance out of her until she fell back in her chair, her head on the table, covered by her arms.

"I didn't do it, any of it," she said, her voice muffled with sobs.

Mason said, "You've got two choices. Take your chance with the jury at both trials. If we lose the first case, we can probably make a deal on the second since you'll already be looking at a life term, maybe even the death penalty. If we win the first case, we roll the dice a second time. Your other choice is to make a deal on both cases. I talked to the prosecuting attorney. He'll accept a plea to second-degree murder on both cases with a sentence of fifteen years to life and an agreement that you'll be out in fifteen. You'll only be thirty-six years old. You can still have a life."

Jordan sat up, her face a patchwork of red blotches, her empty eyes a preview of the institutional bleakness of prison. "You really think I should do this, don't you?"

"You're risking the rest of your life and any chance of ever finding your child. The prosecutor may ask for the death penalty. He wants that hanging over your head. You need to think it over and tell me what you want to do."

"When do I have to decide?"

"Friday. The deal is on the table until the preliminary hearing. After that, we go to trial. That's the way Ortiz does business. He squeezes as hard as he can."

"I want to talk to Abby first. Will you ask her to come see me?"

"Sure," Mason said. "She'll come tomorrow. I'll see you Friday morning."

Mason called Roy Bowen in St. Louis as soon as he returned to his office. "Roy, it's Lou Mason. Did you find those records?" Mason asked without saying hello.

"Weather here isn't bad for this time of year. We understand you folks got an early frost, probably catch us tonight," Bowen said.

"Roy, I haven't got time for good manners," Mason said. "I need answers."

"You get older, Lou, you develop more patience, get used to things taking longer than you want them to. I'm navigating my way through a city bureaucracy that's dedicated to getting back to you tomorrow, only tomorrow never comes. It would be a hell of a lot easier if you had a name or two you wanted me to track down. Collecting the employment records on everyone who worked in Vital Records more than twenty years ago is a nightmare for those people. They're giving me every excuse except executive privilege and national security."

"You're right and I'm sorry, Roy," Mason said. "The prosecutor is squeezing us to make a deal by Friday or we go to trial. I've got more loose threads than a cheap suit and nothing to stitch them together with."

"Then give me some names, son, and I'll get you an answer."

Mason gave Bowen the names and Bowen promised to call him back before the preliminary hearing. Mason hung up, opened his dry-erase board, felt his eyes cross at his spaghetti graffiti, and closed it. He leaned against his window overlooking Broadway and tried to imagine making the decision he'd left for Jordan. He couldn't bring it into focus any more than he could the murders. The case had become a black hole, sucking reason and certainty into another dimension.

Blues banged on Mason's office door once, pushing it open without waiting for an invitation. He was dressed in black, a color he chose when working the streets. He once explained to Mason that he chose it because it intimidated most people and hid bloodstains from those who weren't so easily persuaded.

Mason said, "I don't care what you had to do to get it, just tell me you got something I can use."

"You're not as particular as you used to be. When we first started out, if I jaywalked, you'd turn me in. Now, you just want results, is that it?" Blues asked, filling the space between the door and Mason's desk.

"I've done a lot of things I didn't think I would ever do since I met you," Mason said. "I'm not proud of some of them, but I've learned to live with them, mostly because I didn't have a choice at the time."

"You had a choice," Blues said. "There's always a choice. You're just getting used to doing things my way."

"Are you going to tell me where you've been and what you've found out, or do I just write a check for this therapy session and call it a day?"

Blues stretched out on Mason's couch, his feet extending out over the other end. "You told me to poke around into Centurion's business, so I poked."

Mason picked up a rugby ball from the floor next to his desk and rifled it at Blues who deflected it with a flick of his wrists. "I'm not paying you for an information strip tease, Bluestone," Mason told him. "Give."

Blues sat up, grinning. "You are going to like this.

Centurion is still in the trade, cooking up meth in a little cabin in the woods, storing cocaine and heroin there till he moves all that shit to the street. Some of the inmates at Sanctuary mule for him."

"Any ties to Robert Davenport?"

"I found one of the middle men that passed the shit to Davenport. He convinced me that Centurion was his source. Didn't take much convincing. By the time we were done talking, he was begging to tell me."

Mason knew that he should feel guilty about using Blues to extract information this way, but he didn't. He would have screamed to the rafters if the police used the same tactics on a client of his. He accepted the necessity of Blues's tactics, rationalizing them in an ends-justifies-the-means framework that pushed him farther from the principles his Aunt Claire had spent her life protecting.

Each time Mason took advantage of Blues's particular skills, he felt a small piece of him die, just as he had when he'd killed a man who would have killed him, just as he had when he'd pushed a judge to compromise herself to save Blues. Just as he did as Blues made his report, the lights on Broadway illuminating the night, leaving his soul closer to darkness.

"Do you think Centurion put the cocaine in Gina Davenport's office?" Mason asked.

"My source says yes, but he doesn't know why. Tell you what else I found out. Those two boys that snatched you out of your car?"

"Yeah," Mason said.

"They were free-lancers working for Centurion."

"Centurion hired them to find out if I kept a copy of the baby ledger."

"And kill you once they knew you had it. First rule of the streets, Lou. Don't leave anything to chance. You just beat the odds."

"So why is Centurion giving me a pass now? Why hasn't he come after me?"

"Two reasons," Blues said. "First, the cops are all over him, flying helicopters over Sanctuary, following him wherever he goes. Anything happens to you, they'll be on him like stink on shit. You can thank Samantha for that."

"What's the other reason?" Mason asked.

"He's waiting to see what happens with Jordan. Word is already out that she's going to plead. If she does, Centurion figures the heat is off. He'll take you in his own time if he has to. So, is Jordan going to plead?"

"I'll find out Friday morning, along with everyone else."

"Should be a very interesting day," Blues said.

CHAPTER 32

Late September in Kansas City is a crapshoot. If it rains enough in the spring and summer, the leaves burn with fiery orange, apple red, and veins of gold. Too dry, and the leaves just burn in lifeless, brown piles raked against curbs on the days the city allows its people to strike a match. Morning might bring a warm sun hung in a pure blue sky like a child's water-paint wish, or it might belt the city with a cold, low-slung, cast-iron-cloud skillet that causes a run on antidepressants.

Friday was the last day of September and it dawned promising nothing. Mason ran in Loose Park, the shadows fighting with the sun, the clouds running interference, a raw mist spitting at him. Finished, he chose a black suit, not certain whether he would look tough like Blues in black or be mistaken for an undertaker.

He didn't know what Jordan was going to do. Abby had spent an hour with her the day before, leaving without an answer but with a message that Jordan wanted her parents to be in court Friday morning.

Mason wanted Jordan to accept the plea bargain because it would save her life, something he couldn't promise. He wanted her to turn it down because he wasn't
convinced of her guilt, a doubt he couldn't shake. He
wanted her to take the deal to protect him from Centurion, an impulse that shamed him. He wanted to fight
and win to save them both.

The courthouse steps were thick with microphones
and cameras, electronic limbs hinged to talking heads
doing the play-by-play, casting side bets on which way
the scales of justice would tip. Mason pushed through,
stopping only when Sherri Thomas held him up with
her Channel 6 mike like it was a short saber, Ted Phillips
aiming his camera at them.

"Mr. Mason, is it true that Jordan Hackett will plead
guilty this morning? Did she kill her therapist and her
brother? Is it true that she'll serve life without parole to
avoid the death penalty?"

The rest of the pack descended on Mason, surrounding him with outstretched microphones, the brass hand-
rail alongside him vibrating like a tuning fork. "I'll make
my comments in the courtroom," Mason said.

"My viewers have the right to know if a murderer is
going to be back on the streets," Sherri said.

"Your viewers have the right to the news when it happens, not when you make it up," Mason told her.

Sherri's next question was lost in the roar when another reporter spotted Arthur and Carol Hackett getting out of a car, both dressed in mourning black. The
reporters surged toward them, leaving Sherri and Mason
in their wake. Sherri signaled Phillips, who lowered his
camera, covering its flashing red light with his finger,
pretending he'd turned it off. Sherri toggled her micro-

phone switch off, lowering it to her side, Mason catching her when she switched it back on, tossing her head back and her chest forward to distract him.

"Is it easier to make a deal when you know your client is guilty?" she asked.

Mason smothered her mike with his hand, leaning in close, pressing against her breasts. "Stick this in someone else," he whispered in her ear.

Clearing courthouse security, Mason caught an elevator, its door closing, shutting out Centurion Johnson and the don't-fuck-with-me look he leveled at Mason. Mason gave Centurion credit for having the balls to show up. It was the perfect way to proclaim his innocence of any charge that might come his way. Only an innocent man would put himself under that spotlight.

The hallway outside the courtroom was clotted with people jostling for a seat in the courtroom. Mason sliced through them, ignoring offered backslaps and handshakes, relieved when he reached the privacy of the offices and witness rooms that, together with the judges' chambers, made up the inner realm of the courthouse.

There were two courtrooms at the end of the floor, facing each other across the hall. One belonged to Judge Pistone, who would conduct the preliminary hearing if no deal were reached. The other belonged to Judge Brendan Tanner, the Circuit Court Judge who would decide whether to accept the plea bargain if Jordan agreed to it, the judges' respective roles dictated by the different functions of Associate Circuit Court Judges and Circuit Court Judges. An interior hallway connected the offices of each judge and their staff out of the sight and reach of the public.

Mason met Jordan in a room reserved for lawyers

and witnesses. She was wearing the same outfit Abby had picked out for her, though it had lost the fresh snap of new clothes. She smiled weakly, her balled hands drumming against her thighs.

"It's almost time," Mason said.

"Yeah, I know. I know," Jordan answered, breathing deeply, not able to steady herself. "Okay," she said. "I'll do it. I'll take the deal."

"You're sure?" Mason asked, careful not to push.

Jordan nodded, chewing her lip. "I'm sure."

"We'll be in front of Judge Tanner. The prosecutor will announce the terms of the plea bargain. You and I will stand in front of the bench. The judge will ask you a lot of questions to make certain you understand your rights. All you have to do is answer yes to all of his questions and we'll be out of there in thirty minutes."

"Then what?" she asked.

"Then you start the rest of your life."

The spectators had split themselves roughly into thirds, one third grabbing seats in Judge Pistone's courtroom, another third betting on Judge Tanner's, and the last hedging in the hallway. No announcement was made that a plea would be entered. Instead, the news filtered out like a scent, and Judge Tanner's courtroom quickly filled, the bailiff making way for Jordan's parents, everyone else left to hustle in a herd version of musical chairs, the music stopping when the judge's bailiff said, "All rise."

Mason surveyed the room. Patrick Ortiz anchored his counsel table, flanked by an assistant nervously checking the details of the typed plea-bargain agreement Jordan had signed moments ago. Samantha Greer sat behind Ortiz in a hard, unpadded wooden chair, mouthing "smart decision" to Mason, who shrugged in reply. A courtroom deputy stood on raised toes, scanning the crowd, a Secret Service wannabe.

Arthur Hackett leaned heavily on the rail separating the public seats from the lawyers, the bailiff's well-intentioned efforts mistakenly seating the Hacketts directly behind the prosecutor. Carol Hackett, dark glasses gone, held onto Arthur's arm.

The back wall of the courtroom was standing room only, lined by Blues, Mickey, Harry, Claire, Abby, and Rachel Firestone. Mason's life in a lineup, he thought to himself, pleased they had come. Blues was playing street stare with Centurion, standing in the far corner, winning when Centurion faked a laugh and sat down, Judge Tanner taking his seat first, the bailiff instructing everyone else to be seated.

Unlike Judge Pistone, who shrank in his courtroom, Judge Tanner embraced his. A product of Kansas City's private schools and country clubs, Tanner came to the bench a conservative, evolving into a liberal, championing individual rights, now a favorite of the criminal defense bar. Mason believed that the assignment of Jordan's trials to his court helped convince Patrick Ortiz to plea-bargain. Judge Tanner was a big man with a ruddy face and silver hair whose broad shoulders spread under his black robe, his oversized presence commanding the courtroom.

"Call the next case," the judge instructed his bailiff.

"The State of Missouri versus Jordan Hackett," the bailiff replied.

"I understand that we are here for the entry of a plea. Is that correct, Mr. Ortiz?" Judge Tanner asked.

Ortiz rose, unbuttoning his suit jacket. "Yes, Your Honor. The defendant has advised us that she will plead guilty to two charges of second-degree murder in the deaths of Gina Davenport and Trent Hackett. In return, the State recommends that she be sentenced to concurrent terms of fifteen years to life imprisonment with no parole until the completion of the minimum term of fifteen years, at which time she would be released."

"Is that a correct statement of the agreement, Mr. Mason?" the judge asked.

Rising, Mason answered, "It is, Your Honor."

"Very well," the Judge continued. "The defendant will come before the court."

Mason loved the courtroom. It was the grandest stage, hosting the greatest drama, a venue where life stood still, holding its breath, waiting for a judge or jury to raise their thumbs up or down. It was a vault, guarding justice, dispensing disappointment to losers and miracles to winners. At moments like this, the audience disappeared for Mason. The prosecutor, the bailiff, the court reporter all faded as he and his client stood before the court alone in the last silent instant before unthinkable fate became real.

"Miss Hackett," Judge Tanner began. "Do you understand the charges that have been brought against you?"

"Yes," Jordan said, her eyes on the floor, her voice a subdued murmur.

"You understand that you have been charged with two counts of murder in the first degree and that, if convicted, you could be sentenced to life in prison or death by lethal injection?"

"Yes," she answered, an involuntary tremor rippling through her.

"You understand that you have the right to a trial by a jury of your peers, that you have the right to confront and cross-examine the witnesses against you?"

"Yes."

"You understand that the State has the burden to prove its case against you beyond a reasonable doubt?"

"I do."

"You understand that by asking me to accept your plea of guilty to the lesser charge of second-degree murder, you give up all those rights and that you will serve fifteen years in the state penitentiary before you can be released?"

"Yes," Jordan said, forcing her answer.

"Knowing all these rights, and knowing the evidence the State has against you and after conferring with your attorney, is it your desire that I accept your guilty plea?"

Jordan turned to Mason, eyes wet, mouth trembling. He nodded to her.

"Yes," Jordan said. "I do."

"And is that because you are, in fact, guilty of these crimes?" Judge Tanner asked.

The judge's question hit Jordan like a slap, jerking her head up as she stiffened, her face red, stung by the demand for a confession.

"Miss Hackett, are you in fact guilty of these crimes?" Judge Tanner repeated.

Mason held his breath, choking on his doubts of Jordan, who squared her back and answered, her voice filling the corners of the courtroom, echoing the rage Mason thought had expired.

"No, Your Honor. I am not."

Judge Tanner gaveled his courtroom into submission, stifling the outbursts caused by Jordan's departure from the script. Behind him, Mason heard Carol Hackett cry, "My God," Arthur shushing her, the judge exempting them from his demand for order. Jordan held steady, waiting for the judge's next question.

"Miss Hackett, perhaps you misunderstood my question," Judge Hackett began.

"I understood it, Judge."

"Miss Hackett, before coming into this courtroom today, you signed a plea agreement with the prosecutor, did you not?"

"Yes," she said.

"I have a copy of that agreement before me, Miss Hackett. In it, you state your intention to plead guilty to these charges. I cannot accept this agreement unless you tell me that you are guilty. Do you understand that?"

"I do," she said, tightening her grip on Mason's hand.

"I must warn you, Miss Hackett. If you return to this courtroom at a future date asking me to approve a plea bargain, it is unlikely that I will do so."

Patrick Ortiz interrupted. "Don't worry, Your Honor. There won't be another plea bargain in these cases. We're going to trial and we're asking for the death penalty."

Judge Tanner stared down from the bench grim-faced. "Mr. Mason, do you wish to confer with your client before this hearing is concluded?"

"No, sir. My client says she's innocent and that's good enough for me. We'll be ready for trial."

Abby wormed her way through the crowd, reaching Mason and Jordan at the same moment as Arthur and Carol Hackett. The courtroom deputy kept others away, his hand on Jordan's shoulder, a firm reminder that she was still the property of the State. Carol held to the fringes, Arthur easing inside the deputy's grasp, wrapping his arms around his daughter, their heads bowed together.

Mason couldn't hear what they were saying, but he could feel it. Abby leaned into Mason, letting her tears seep into his sleeve, then pulling herself up, straightening her clothes and her face, leaving Mason in the courtroom with his client and her parents. When at last the deputy insisted, Jordan's hand slid down her father's arm, lingered at the wrist, brushed across his fingers, tracing the lifeline across his palm, their connection interrupted but not broken.

Arthur let go, following his wife to the hallway, stopping at the door, looking back at Mason, who watched from the center of the courtroom, the last to leave. "Please, Mr. Mason," he said. Mason nodded his promise in reply.

CHAPTER 33

"I feel so stupid," Abby said to Mason. "I've made a complete and utter fool of myself, thinking Jordan could be my daughter. Especially when I saw her with her parents in court this morning."

Abby's PR firm, Fresh Air, was on the second floor of a building a block from her loft. Mason brought lunch from a deli at the corner of 21st and Baltimore, remnants of panini and Thai chicken salad littering a small round table in the corner of Abby's office, overlooking the street. Her staff busied themselves, shuttling in faxes she didn't read and phone messages she didn't return, pretending not to notice the tear-stained mascara streaks at the corners of Abby's eyes. The suite was decorated to soothe with creamy burnished wood, indirect light, and comforting music. The walls were hung with colorful photographs of people, places, and things in motion, sending the subliminal message that Abby and her people made things happen.

"Only because you look like Gene Simmons after a bad KISS concert," Mason said.

"That good, huh?" Abby answered, scrubbing her face with another tissue. "Even if Jordan is my daughter, I can't jump into the middle of her life now. The Hacketts are the only parents she's ever known. In spite of everything that's happened, Jordan wanted them to be in court this morning. That's her family. I should just butt out."

"Jordan needs friends too," Mason said. "You've connected with her. Don't let go of that."

"I know," Abby said, "but I need something else. I need to know what happened to my daughter, even if I can't be a part of her life. I need that closure."

"Closure is overrated," Mason said. "You trade one pain for another. If you found her, you'd want to meet her, be with her, make up for all those years, and she might not be interested. If you couldn't find her, you'd have a wound that never healed."

"I just want to know that she's all right, that she has a life," Abby said, gazing at the street as if her daughter would step out a door or turn a corner and wave to her.

"What if she wasn't all right?" Mason asked too carefully for his question to be academic. "What then?"

Abby looked at him, catching his meaning and her breath. "Lou, if you know something, tell me."

Mason pushed back from the table, not wanting to tell Abby what he suspected but didn't know for certain, unable to keep it from her any longer. "After we got back from St. Louis, I reread Gina Davenport's autopsy report. She had a congenital abnormality that prevented her from ever getting pregnant."

Abby wrinkled her brow. "What's that go to do with

me?" she asked, then gasped with understanding, racing to the conclusion. "Emily! That's why Gina never signed the Baby Book at the hospital and why my medical records are missing. Is that what you're telling me? That Gina Davenport took my baby!"

Mason shoved bread crumbs into a mound, smashing them with his thumb. "I don't know for certain. That's why I didn't tell you. We know that Terry Nix worked at the hospital. We know that he could have met your uncle in the alcohol treatment program, and we know that Nix dealt in black-market babies. Emily's birth certificate identifies Gina and Robert as her natural parents. They couldn't adopt legally because Robert was a drug addict. The birth certificate had to have been forged. The date of birth is a week before your baby was born, but changing the date was one more step to make it look legit. It all fits, but I can't prove it."

"Oh, my God!" Abby said, coming out of her chair, the full impact of Mason's explanation hitting her. "Emily is dead." Mason took her in his arms, Abby shuddering, dissolving, repeating again and again, "Emily is dead." Mason held her until she pulled away, walking around her office, arms crossed, finding her center of gravity.

Mason explained, "Gina must have told her lawyer, David Evans, about you. Evans let it slip to his girlfriend, Paula Sutton, who worked at KWIN and was jealous enough of Gina to hook you and Gina up. She used Jordan's cell phone to cover her tracks. All she wanted to do was cause Gina some grief. Instead, I think she put this whole thing into motion."

"Jealousy and hate," Abby said. "That's what killed Gina and Trent. What are you going to do?" Abby asked, her mouth set in a thin, fierce line.

"Terry Nix is in the middle of all of this. He was there at the beginning and at the end. He's got ties to Gina, Robert, and you. I'm going to have a come-to-Jesus meeting with him."

"You think Nix killed Gina and Trent?"

"No, especially if you're right about jealousy and hate. It's not his style. He's a let's-make-love-not-war relic, but I bet he knows a lot more than he's told me so far."

"Why would he tell you anything now?" Abby asked.

"Self-preservation. That's how guys like him survive. They use guys like Centurion for muscle. Take away the muscle, and they'll give it up. Blues and Samantha have Centurion under wraps. Nix may be ready to talk."

"I've got some questions of my own," Abby said, her jaw tightening.

"Don't even think about it," Mason said. "Write them down. I'll add them to my list."

"I'll call you," she said, returning to the window, palms against the glass, eyes on the street.

Mason wiped his dry-erase board clean, starting over with what he knew, and what made too much sense not to be true. From that, he made a list of questions, guessing at the answers. When he was done, he had a story.

Terry Nix supplied drugs to Robert Davenport when they lived in St. Louis, getting one hook into the Davenports. Nix sold Abby's baby to the Davenports, adding another hook. Years later, Nix landed at Sanctuary, using those hooks to persuade Gina Davenport to refer patients there, adding credibility to the operation, while plugging Robert Davenport into Centurion's drug supply. Gina must have feared disclosure of the truth about Emily and Robert enough to go along, even to the point of letting Emily live at Sanctuary. She lost control of her daughter, her husband, and her life. Emily's death made her more vulnerable, not less, to Nix, one more secret to be kept, the price paid by contributions from Emily's Fund.

Paula Sutton's gambit made real the rule of unintended consequences. Gina must have panicked, Mason theorized, believing that her past was going to catch up to her, and gone to Nix, perhaps to warn him, perhaps to ask his help. Mason doubted Nix killed Gina. It was more likely that Nix would slip away under cover of darkness, content to set up shop somewhere else. Centurion would have had a different solution, equally pragmatic but deadly. He had too much invested in Sanctuary to walk away. Car-jacking Mason to find out what he'd done with the baby ledger was proof enough of that.

Though he was satisfied with his analysis, Mason still couldn't make Trent part of Nix's equation. It was time to talk with Terry Nix. First, he called Blues.

"Are you and Centurion still playing Me and My Shadow?" Mason asked him.

"Gave it up. Samantha's got the cops covering him so close, every time he farts, they gotta roll down a window."

Mason said, "Centurion must know he's being watched."

"They ain't keeping it a secret," Blues replied.

"Where was Centurion when you last saw him?"

"Holed up in a big house in Sunset Hills, belongs to one of Sanctuary's sponsors. He doesn't want to give the cops any reason to go sniffing around Sanctuary."

"Perfect. I'm going to have a chat with Terry Nix."

"You need any help putting that dog in a mellow mood, you let me know."

Mason pulled into the center drive at Sanctuary just after seven o'clock. The grounds were deserted, the main house dark, except for a light over the porch, the only other illumination from October's first moon. A lone girl was climbing into a Jeep as he got out of his car.

"Where is everybody?" Mason asked.

"Sent home," she said. "I'm the last."

"What happened?"

"Something about insurance coverage. That's all I know."

"How about Terry Nix? Is he still here?"

"Yeah," the girl said. "He was packing until some woman showed up. Last I saw, they were headed downstairs."

Mason's cell phone rang as the girl drove away.

"Lou, it's Samantha. Where are you?"

"In the front yard of Sanctuary. I came out here to talk to Terry Nix. All the kids are gone. The place is shut down."

"My people followed Centurion to a house in Sunset Hills that belongs to Kelsey Bond, one of his big contributors. He made Bond smuggle him out in the back of his car and drive to Sanctuary, but Bond jumped out when they got off I-70, made it to a gas station, and called us."

Mason looked at his watch. It was 7:05. "How long since Bond jumped out of the car?"

Samantha said, "An hour, give or take."

"What kind of car?" Mason asked, walking toward the garage.

"A Lexus sedan. Lou, I'm on the way. Get out of there," Samantha said.

Mason opened the side door to the four-car garage. A Lexus, its hood still warm, was parked next to Abby's BMW. "Can't do it, Sam. Abby is inside," he said, hanging up.

Mason searched the garage for a weapon, finding a box cutter hidden under a pile of oily rags. Slipping it into the pocket of his suit jacket, he circled the grounds, looking for signs of life. He crossed a brick patio with a liquid-propane barbecue grill next to the barn, which smelled of hay and machine oil. Hoping to find a better weapon, he was disappointed when there was nothing there except for a tractor, three ATVs, an assortment of tools, and a heater already in service used to warm the barn during cold weather.

Back outside, he jogged along the perimeter of the house, the first and second floors silent and dark. Lights were on in a third-floor room on the back where, from Jordan's description, Centurion had his apartment. Mason moved on, skirting the evergreen hedge that hugged the house, coming to a break in the hedge for a pair of daylight windows cut into Terry Nix's basement office.

Though the night air was cool, Mason was sweating, his breathing accelerating when he saw Centurion, Nix, and Abby in Nix's office. Abby was strapped into a chair, duct tape holding her arms and legs in place, a small swatch over her mouth, her eyes stretched wide with fear. A syringe lay on Nix's desk next to two open gym bags partially stuffed with cash, another tall stack of currency on Nix's desk. A third bag lay open, its cargo neatly piled plastic bags of white powder.

Though he couldn't hear what they were saying, Mason could tell that Centurion and Nix were arguing. Nix's face was red and he was gesturing wildly, clutching the baby ledger, while Centurion listened, his hands planted at his sides, his head down. Judging from the body language, Nix was chewing out Centurion, an indulgence Mason expected Centurion would soon end with his fist. The argument had to be about how to divide the cash and the drugs, a dispute complicated by Abby, though Mason was worried that they were in agreement about her.

Centurion had raced back to Sanctuary to pick up the money and drugs before Nix could skip out with them. Nix was obviously on the same schedule, though Mason doubted that they were using the same travel agent. Neither one could have been happy that Abby showed up, and both were desperate enough not to leave her as a loose end.

Mason didn't like the odds of getting Abby out by tapping on the window and asking if she could come out and play any better than he liked the odds of walking in and telling Centurion and Nix that he'd dropped by to pick Abby up for dinner. Samantha was at least half an hour away, and the arrival of an army of cops would, at best, make Abby a hostage of two men with nothing to lose. More bad odds, Mason decided. He needed to get Centurion and Nix out of the office without giving them a reason to kill Abby before they left.

Mason retraced his steps, not risking being seen passing the windows, running to the patio next to the barn, almost tripping over the barbecue grill. He disconnected the twenty-pound propane tank from the grill and carried it inside the barn, setting it down about thirty feet from the heater. Pulling off the front panel of the heater, he found the pilot light, an orange and blue finger of flame barely illuminating the inside of the heater, but powerful enough for what he had in mind.

From a case he'd once handled, Mason knew propane gas escaping from a tank would pool along the ground because it was heavier than air, eventually exploding if it mixed with the right amount of oxygen and found an ignition source. Mason opened the barn door, letting cool air pour in from the outside, feeding the furnace that was designed to suck it in, warming and recirculating it. The combination, Mason hoped, would draw the propane to the pilot light, generating a rich enough mixture of propane and oxygen to turn the barn into a one-shot Roman candle. The one variable Mason couldn't account for was how long it would take before the propane ignited. When it did, he hoped Centurion and Nix would take it as a sign from God to hit the road.

Mason opened the valve on the propane tank and ran without looking back. He slipped into the garage, following the covered walkway that connected it to the house. The door into the house was unlocked and the security alarm was off. Centurion and Nix were obviously more concerned about getting out than about who might get in.

Mason walked quickly through a room lined with empty coat hooks and built-in boot baskets, then a laundry room with three washers and dryers, and a pantry stocked with food for a small army. The barn exploded as he entered the kitchen, the shock wave shattering windows, shards of glass rifling the air as he dove for cover, sliding across the hardwood floor into the dining room, its walls bathed in the incandescent glow of the fireball that poured out of the barn.

Mason flattened himself against the wall as Centurion and Nix pounded up the stairs cursing, bolted through the entry hall, past the dining room, and out the front door. Not waiting to see if they would come back, he sprinted down the stairs, stumbling on the last step, bracing himself with one hand as he regained his footing, shouting for Abby as he wheeled into Nix's office.

He pulled the tape from her mouth, covering her lips with his for an instant. "Are you okay?" he asked her as he sliced her duct tape bonds with the box cutter.

"I think so," she said. "Hurry, before they come back."

He started to say that they wouldn't be back when he saw the bags of cash and drugs strewn on the floor, mixed with broken glass from more windows shattered by the blast. Looking closer, he saw bloody fingerprints on the desk and a trail of blood out into the hallway. "What happened?"

"They were fighting over the drugs and the money when the explosion broke the windows. A piece of glass cut Centurion. Nix was already bleeding from the beating Centurion was giving him. They'll be back if they don't kill each other first."

"We're not that lucky," Mason said. "Come on. In a place this big, there's got to be another way out of here besides going back up those stairs."

Taking Abby by the hand, Mason peeked into the hallway, leading away from the stairs. A series of smaller explosions rocked the night, lacing Abby with fresh tremors.

"What did you do? Call in air strikes?" she asked, forcing humor to calm herself, stuttering the punch line.

"I blew up the barn," he said with a shrug like it was no big deal. "Those last explosions were probably the gas tanks on a tractor and some ATVs that were stored there. The fire must have caused them to blow."

The wall above Mason's head erupted in a shower of sheet rock splinters, the crack of a gunshot lost in yet another explosion in the barn. Mason spun Abby around, shoving her toward the next turn in the hall past a trophy case, glancing over his shoulder as Centurion took aim again, his next shot slamming into the trophies, raining more shrapnel on them as they ran.

They were in a corridor with doors on either side marked as locker rooms, one for each sex, and another door at the end of the hall. Crashing through that door into an exercise room, Mason tipped a rack of hand weights against the door, buying a few seconds, knowing that Centurion could power-lift him, the door, and the weights. He knocked over benches to trip Centurion, grabbed a pair of eight-pound hand weights, pointed Abby to an exit on the far side and hit the light switch, blanketing the room in darkness. Centurion collided with the door, firing three shots that knifed through its hollow interior, bullets pinging off exercise machines as Mason and Abby escaped, relieved to find a lock on the door they closed behind them, Mason jamming it down with his thumb.

"Here," he said, pressing one of the weights into Abby's hand, "hit him like you mean it."

They looked around, finding themselves in an indoor basketball court, illuminated only by the neon news on the scoreboard hanging from the ceiling that read "time expired."

"You wanted another stairway," Abby said, her breath coming in gulps. "There it is."

She pointed to a platform built high into the wall in one corner of the court, a ladder hinged on one end and folded beneath the platform. A trapdoor was built into the ceiling above the platform. Mason found a control panel on the wall with a bank of switches, cycling through them, lights turning on and off, until an electric motor engaged and the ladder began unfolding, its pace excruciatingly slow.

The ladder stopped six feet off the floor. Abby leapt for the bottom rung, Mason bracing her legs as she pulled herself up, then following her as Centurion pounded on the locked door, using bullets instead of a key. There was a power switch for the ladder on the wall above the platform. Abby punched the switch starting the ladder's labored ascent as Mason skimmed his hands across the trapdoor, finding the inlaid handle that was concealed in the dim light. Swinging the door up and in, Mason pushed Abby through the opening, taking back the hand weight he had given her as Centurion kicked the door to the basketball court off its hinges.

Crouched on one knee, Mason launched the two eight-pound weights in rapid fire succession, the first catching Centurion on the arm, the second in the neck as he turned to fire, the shot going wide. Mason scrambled through the trapdoor, flinging it shut, blinking his eyes in the pitch black of a low-ceilinged utility tunnel, barely large enough for them to crawl.

"Abby," he whispered hoarsely, "where are you?"

"Here," she answered, reaching out, finding his face with her hand.

Mason extended his arms, remembering how Jordan had measured her cell, figuring out they were at one end of the passageway. "There's only way to go," Mason said. "Take the lead."

The crawl space was made of concrete, the walls lined with pipes and electric cables. The air was dry and dusty, tasting of metal. Abby, unable to see, moved slowly, using one hand as her guide to avoid using her head as a bumper.

"Hold on," she said. "I found a shaft I can almost stand up in." She eased herself upright. "There's another trapdoor. It's propped part way open and there's light on the other side."

Mason's initial relief that they'd found their way out vanished at Abby's description. "Get back!" Mason snapped, too late as Abby screamed and a gunshot rang out, echoing in the crawl space, the bullet ricocheting as Mason covered himself. "Abby!" he shouted.

"She all right, cockroach," Centurion said. "That's what you are, Mason. A cockroach, crawling around inside the walls of my house. You go back to crawling. Your lady and I got business elsewhere."

"Lou!" Abby cried. "Help me!"

"Shut up, bitch!" Centurion told her. Mason heard the smack of Centurion's hand and Abby's muffled cry. "So long, cockroach."

The trapdoor slammed tight, the sounds of something heavy being dragged across the floor, landing with a permanent thud above his head.

CHAPTER 34

Mason crawled to the mouth of the vertical shaft, rising in a half-crouch, hands and shoulders hard against the immovable ceiling, slumping back to the bottom, knees to his chest. The passageway thinned, though he knew the sensation was more panic than real, the darkness tightening around him, the concrete scraping through his pants as he slithered back to the other end of the tunnel. Unable to see his watch, he guessed at the time, calculating the odds that Samantha would arrive before Centurion got away, measuring Abby's chances in minutes and seconds.

He scratched and pawed the trapdoor, searching for the handle, disoriented by the claustrophobic blackness, choking on the dust and his fear of being too late, finding it at last, a steel ring frozen from lack of use. Mason slipped the blade of the box cutter beneath the ring, popping it free. Pulling the door up, he poured out of the shaft onto the platform above the basketball court, pounding on the switch to lower the ladder, lean-ing over the side when nothing happened. The ladder lay on the floor, fifteen feet below, ripped from the plat-form.

Mason eased himself over the edge of the platform, dangling by his fingertips, swinging his body away from the ladder, dropping and rolling, grunting as he ab-sorbed the hardwood impact. Racing back through the weight room, he glanced in Nix's office. The money and drugs were gone. Nix wasn't.

He was sprawled on his stomach across the width of his desk facing the door, feet just off the floor, arms hanging over the sides in an embrace, blood oozing onto the desk blotter, eyes open, lips moving sound-lessly. Mason helped him onto the floor, propping him up to ease his labored breathing.

"Hang on, Terry," Mason told him. "Help is on the way."

"Too late, man," Nix whispered, fingering the gun-shot wound in his chest, Mason could hear Nix's death rattle.

"Is there another way out of here besides the main road?" Mason asked, leaning close to Nix's mouth.

"Path into the woods, behind the barn," Nix man-aged.

Mason said, "You knew Gina and Robert Davenport when you lived in St. Louis. You sold dope to Robert and a baby to Gina."

Nix nodded, wincing.

Mason asked, "What about Emily's birth certificate? How did you manage that?"

"Wasn't my part of the deal," Nix said through clench-ed teeth. "Gina said she had that covered."

"When you came to Kansas City, you picked up where you left off with Robert and blackmailed Gina about Emily. Is that how it went down?"

"Yeah," Nix said, moaning and leaning his head back, pressing his hand against his chest.

"Stay with me, Terry!" Mason said, holding Nix's head up. "Then Gina came to you when Abby called her about her baby. What was Gina going to do?"

Nix blinked his eyes, clearing the growing fog for a moment. "Just like when Emily killed herself, tell the whole fucking country," Nix said, barely able to force the words. "Said her listeners would understand and forgive her."

"Good for her, bad for you and Centurion. Did he kill her?"

"Nah," he rasped, "woulda told me to scare the piss outta me. Told me I better shut her up."

"The drugs the cops found in Gina's office. Did you do that?"

Nix smiled, a thin trickle of blood dripping from the corner of his mouth. "Get her busted, shut her up. Tipped off the cops too, 'cept they didn't bust her before she got killed. Pretty smart, huh?"

"Yeah, pretty smart," Mason said, cocking his head at the sound of sirens mixing with the rotor beat of a helicopter. "Just a few more minutes, Terry. You can make it. What about Emily? Was Abby Lieberman her mother?"

Nix struggled to answer, his words lost in his last breath.

Mason left him, emerging from the house a moment later, greeted by a SWAT team standing in the red shadow cast by the still-roaring barn fire, the helicopter hanging aloft in the near distance.

"Don't shoot him," Samantha said. "At least not yet."

* * *

"Centurion took Abby," Mason began. "If you didn't see him on your way in, there's another way out through the woods."

"We didn't pass anyone," Samantha said, radioing instructions to the helicopter pilot, the chopper tilting toward the woods, cutting the night with a broad-beamed searchlight. "What about Nix?" she asked, motioning the SWAT team into the house.

"Office in the basement. Dead. Centurion shot him."

"What about you?" she asked, losing her cop's edge.

"I'm good," Mason said. "Ruined another suit, but none of the blood is mine."

"Give me the details," she instructed him.

Mason told her what had happened, ignoring her raised eyebrows when he described setting the fire in the barn, explaining why the law of necessity trumped the law against arson. She took it down, shaking her head.

"All clear in the house," a member of the SWAT team radioed to her. "One dead in the basement. No sign of anyone else."

"Give me your car keys," she told Mason.

"Why?"

"Because I'm not letting you run loose until I have a better idea where Centurion is."

"You can't do that," he told her.

"Really?" she asked, folding her arms across her chest. "I can arrest you for arson and handcuff you to a tree if I want to. I'm not going to waste manpower having someone drive you home and I'm not going to let you play Junior G-man and race off into the woods after Centurion and your girlfriend. I know you, Lou, and it's not happening. We'll find them and we'll get Abby back, so save the I'm-going-with-you speech because you're not. You're staying here until we're all ready to go home."

Mason hesitated, hands in his pocket, fingering his car keys.

"Sergeant!" Samantha snapped over her shoulder at a cop who materialized at her side.

"Okay, okay," Mason said, raising his hands in surrender, and giving Samantha his keys. "I'll behave."

"Sergeant, station a man at the door of the house. Make sure Mr. Mason stays inside until I get back."

Mason looked at Samantha, taking comfort in the hard set of her face as she issued commands, directing search teams into the woods, setting up roadblocks on the highway, studying a map one of her men held up while another shined a flashlight on it. He walked slowly toward the house.

"Lou," she called to him, turning him toward her. "I'll get her back."

Mason wandered around the first floor of the house, his failure to protect Abby gnawing at him, his love for her turning his frustration and fear to a simmering rage. They had not talked about their feelings for one another, expressing themselves instead with touches, looks, and embraces. Their reticence was mutual, springing from past disappointments, an intuitive superstition that speaking of love too soon was bad luck. Threatened with losing her, Mason regretted his reluctance, and resolved to cast it aside if Samantha made good on her promise.

Touring the house was a small distraction. In addition to the standard rooms for eating, dining, and sitting, there was a well-stocked library, a media room with a big screen and video games, a sunroom, a study, and a music room, each room sponsored by people and companies trying to do the right thing.

Whether by intent or accident, Centurion and Nix had done a few right things, Mason conceded. For many of the kids who lived there, Sanctuary was exactly that. Nix, for all Mason knew, may have been a decent counselor, handing out good advice even while he was working the angles. Centurion proved that a successful partnership between business and social services was possible, even if he corrupted the model. The trouble was no one would remember any of that. Instead, they would only remember the deceit, making the right thing that much harder to do the next time.

Mason sat down in an easy chair in the study, examining the frayed patches of wool that covered his knees, rubbing his hands over the fabric of his suit, able to sit still for a full minute before launching himself into another tour of the house. He stopped at a phone on a counter in the kitchen, pacing in short circles as he checked his voice messages at the office, stopping cold when he heard the last message.

"Mason, it's Roy Bowen. Next time you ask me to thread the bureaucratic needle, it's going to cost you. I don't speak their language or trade in their currency, but I got what you're looking for, I think."

Mason listened to the rest of Bowen's message, replaying it twice to make certain he heard it correctly, calling Mickey when he was sure.

"Drop whatever you're doing," Mason told him.

"No problem. I'm not doing anything," Mickey said.

"I get what I pay for," Mason said. "Find Blues and

Harry. Tell them to sit on Arthur and Carol Hackett round the clock until I catch up to them."

"That's it?" Mickey asked. "You tell me to make a phone call and you complain that I'm getting paid to do nothing? I make a pretty damn fine phone call."

"The best in the business," Mason told him. "Don't forget to dial the area code first. I left the passkey to the Cable Depot in the center drawer of my desk. Get over there and see if you can get into Trent Hackett's office."

"What am I looking for?" Mickey asked.

"Trent's the wild card in all of this. I can't connect him to Centurion and Nix. I need someone to take a fresh look, find what I'm missing."

"Didn't the cops go through everything after Trent was killed?"

"Sure they did, and once they charged Jordan with killing her brother, they forgot about it."

"What are you up to?" Mickey asked.

Mason told him, extracting Mickey's promise not to round up Harry and Blues for a posse. He made his way to Sanctuary's second floor, trying to make sense of Bowen's discovery. Mason found the explanation in the image of the trash chute that ran from Arthur Hackett's office to the Dumpster behind the Cable Depot, and in Paula Sutton's reaction when he showed her Jordan's cell phone. He understood it more fully when he thought about Carol Hackett's maternal detachment.

The second floor was a dormitory, eight bedrooms, two to a room, three large bathrooms for the sixteen full-time residents. Mason poked his head in each room, the stripped beds, empty drawers, and torn corners of posters left on the walls reminiscent of college dorms everywhere, giving no hint that they were a grand illusion intended to conceal the black market run by Centurion and Nix.

The center stairwell went from the basement to the second floor. Mason went downstairs, looking for access to Centurion's third-floor apartment, finding it behind a pair of French doors that concealed an elevator. Stepping in, he picked up a queasy chill, an involuntary reminder of the last ride he took on a private elevator. SWAT team boot prints were still visible on the carpeted floor of the elevator, comforting Mason with the knowledge that the elevator worked and that Centurion's apartment was empty.

The elevator opened onto a space that no corporate donor could have underwritten unless Centurion was sleeping with the CEO. The floor was polished parquet wood, the rugs Persian, the walls papered with gold-fleck fabric. The ceilings were high, the art was modern, the furniture oversized and plush. The place was also a wreck, with chairs and sofas pushed out of position, tables overturned, and paintings hanging at cockeyed angles. Mason couldn't tell whether the disarray was the result of Centurion's hurried departure or the SWAT team's search.

The burnt smell of the fire drifted throughout the apartment carried on a cold breeze through the open sliding door in the master bedroom that led onto the widow's walk. He had noticed the widow's walk the first time he came to Sanctuary, a narrow passage around the outside of the third floor. At the time, it had seemed like an architectural indulgence, a feature without a purpose. He stepped outside. It was five feet wide with a waist-high rail, affording an expansive view in every direction. He could see the helicopter's searchlight stabbing into the woods. He could make out the red taillights of the SWAT team vehicles bouncing down the rough path behind the barn. Beyond the woods, he could see the emergency flashing lights of roadblocks set up on the highway and the fire trucks racing to put out the fire he had started.

Three stories below, the outer walls of the barn had collapsed, bringing down the remains of the roof, the fire subsiding for lack of fuel, though still hot and dangerous. Gray smoke rose from the pile, accented by eerily glowing debris and sporadic bursts of flame. Mason gripped the wrought-iron rail with one hand, pounded it with the other, tormented by what he saw, tortured by what he heard.

"Jump," Centurion said from behind him.

Mason wheeled around, his back to the night. Centurion stood just inside the bedroom, framed by the sliding door, his left arm wrapped around Abby's neck, his right hand holding a pistol to her temple. Compared to Centurion's bulk, Abby was a rag doll, wedged against his chest, her head jerked up against the barrel of the gun. Her face was flushed, her eyes frantic, darting from Mason to Centurion.

"I said jump," Centurion repeated.

"Is that the same offer you made to Gina Davenport?"

"Mason, you are hardly worth killing, though I'm going to enjoy doing it. I didn't kill that radio bitch. Now get that out of your head. If you woulda just left well enough alone and let Jordan plead guilty, none of this woulda happened, man. You wouldna gone sniffin' around my business, and I woulda lived happily ever after and you woulda just lived. Now you gonna die."

"I can get you out of here," Mason said. "Let Abby

go. There's only one cop outside. I'll distract him, you take the Lexus in the garage. You want a hostage, take me."

"Mason, I am not stupid. You're about the most worthless hostage there is. Who gives a shit what happens to a smart-mouth lawyer? Now this little girl," he said, yanking on Abby's neck, "she be worth something."

"You're running out of time," Mason said. "The fire department will be here in a few minutes, the cops will give up on the woods and come back. You'll be trapped no matter how many hostages you have."

"Uh-uh," Centurion said. "I'm not trapped. I'm hiding. I got me one of them panic rooms built behind my closet. Got all the conveniences and enough supplies for a week. I just come out to see what was going on. I can wait a couple of days if I have to. No one is going to find me."

"Then you can't kill me," Mason said, "or the cops will know you're still here and they'll take this place apart a brick at a time to find you."

"That's why you're gonna jump, cockroach. Ain't nobody gonna blame that on me."

Mason looked over his shoulder. The cop Samantha had left behind was on the other side of the house. Mason put his hands in his suit jacket, grasping the handle of the box cutter in his right side pocket.

"No, thanks," Mason said. "You better shoot me."

Centurion grinned, a demon smile. "I'll shoot your girlfriend first, Mason. You want to save her, kill your own damn self."

Mason and Abby looked at each other, seeing nothing else for an instant, pledging themselves to one another with a slight nod. Mason turned his right side toward the rail so Centurion wouldn't see him draw the box cutter, palming it as he gathered himself. Mason gazed over the rail, then looked back at Centurion, flashing his own delusional grin.

Abby screamed, a piercing shriek distracting Centurion as she plunged her hand into his groin, squeezing his testicles with a fury. Enraged, Centurion flung her off of him, aiming his gun at her as Mason launched himself through the open door, adding his own primal yell. Centurion swung his gun toward Mason, firing and missing as Mason, wielding the box cutter, opened bloody gashes on Centurion's arms. Another swipe on the wrist severed Centurion's grip on his gun. Centurion smashed Mason in the face, the blow knocking him out the sliding door, onto the widow's walk, and halfway into next week, the box cutter skittering over the edge into the gutter.

With no room to maneuver, Mason ducked Centurion's next swing, stepping inside, punching the bigger man in the chin and kneeing him in the gut, getting caught in a suffocating bear hug, Centurion dangling him over the rail like a bag of dirty laundry. Mason squirmed, kicking his legs, hitting air, pounding Centurion's ears with his fists, catching Centurion's sweat in his eyes, not believing the gunshot that loosened Centurion's grip. Mason held on to Centurion as he swayed unsteadily, his eyes fixed, his mouth wide, his body crumbling and falling over the rail. Mason grabbed the wrought-iron bars as Centurion tumbled past him.

Mason's hands slid down the bars, his grip holding at their base, his feet scraping the side of the house. Abby shouted for him, reaching through the bars, her hand clasping his wrist.

"I've got you," she said, pulling him up enough that he could throw his leg onto the ledge, then helping him back over the rail.

"I killed him," Abby said.

"Don't apologize," Mason told her.

CHAPTER 35

"You deserve each other," Samantha told Mason and Abby. "I pity the fool that tries to come between the two of you."

The fire was out, the crime-scene technicians were finished, Centurion's and Nix's bodies were on their way to the morgue. Even the press had gone home, its insatiable appetite slaked for another news cycle. Dawn was close. Mason and Abby leaned against his car, arms interlocked, neither letting the other go.

"Thanks for your help," Mason told Samantha.

"What help?" she said. "I took your bait about Centurion escaping through the woods so you could put on your cape and save the day," she teased.

"Works every time," Mason said. "Have you talked to Ortiz?"

"Yeah. He'll wait until he gets my report to make a final decision, but he agrees that it's an easy call. Centurion was justifiable homicide. No charges. He says you'll have enough trouble with Sanctuary's insurance company that he's not going to bother with an arson investigation."

"What did he say about Jordan?"

Samantha shook her head, not hiding her exasperation. "The same thing I've been telling you. Jordan's case led to the investigation of Centurion and Nix. That happens all the time, one crime exposes another. It doesn't mean the two are related or that Jordan is innocent."

"So you're not going to reopen the investigation, even after what I told you about St. Louis?"

"Ortiz said he'd look at it next week, but he wants you to know he's getting ready for trial."

"Swell," Mason answered. "Can you have someone drive Abby's car back to her place?"

Abby interrupted, "I don't need anyone to drive my car."

"I just thought," Mason began.

"Then don't. I saved you, remember," she said, kissing his forehead.

"Like I said," Samantha replied. "You two deserve each other."

They chose Mason's house, Abby scrubbing the blood from Mason's body, Mason washing her with gentle strokes, knowing the stain of killing someone never comes out, no matter how justified the act. Their lovemaking was desperate with the fresh memory of nearly losing each other.

"I love you," he told afterward, tangled in her arms.

"I know," she said. "I couldn't live with all of this if you didn't."

He propped himself on one elbow. "What about you? Do you love me?"

She lay on her back, stroking his face. "You know I do. Do you need me to say it?"

"Yeah, it has a nice ring to it," he answered.

"I love you, Lou. Now, forever, and always."

They slept until late morning, Tuffy climbing into bed between them, whimpering, thumping their legs with her tail.

"What's she saying?" Abby mumbled, covering her morning breath with the sheet.

"I think she's trying to tell us that dogs don't do brunch," Mason answered. "Come on, dog," he said, rubbing Tuffy's nose. "Chow time."

Abby joined him in the kitchen wearing a pair of Mason's sweats, cinched tight at the waist, and one of his rugby shirts that fit her like a tent. He was standing at the sink wearing boxer shorts and a hooded sweatshirt that zipped in the front, watching Tuffy chase scents in the backyard, an early frost melting into a thin ground fog speckled with sunlight as the day warmed. Abby hugged him from behind, slipping her hands under his sweatshirt, pulling him close.

"What do we do now?" she asked, her wistful tone casting the question in capital letters.

He covered her hands with his, raising them to his heart, pressing her hands down to feel it beating. "Live," he answered.

"It's not that simple," she said. "I killed a man. I know I did it to save you, and I'd do it again, but how do I live with that?"

"Living is the first choice you have to make. Getting up every day, going to work, doing your job, coming home. Loving me. Do that every day, and it gets easier."

"But I won't forget," she said.

"You're not supposed to," he told her. "But each day you live your life, you understand even more why you did it. That's how you live with it."

"Is that what you did?" she asked. "I mean after, you know, you . . ."

"Killed a man," he said, finishing her sentence. "It doesn't get easier to say the words, believe me. It's not like introducing yourself at a twelve-step meeting. Hi, my name is Lou and I'm a killer. And it's not one of those catchy pat-yourself-on-the-back slogans. Hi, my name is Lou. I'm my kid's dad, and I also kill people."

Mason turned around, keeping Abby's hands locked behind him, wiping a tear off her cheek. "Hi, my name is Abby. I love Lou Mason and I'll kill anyone that tries to hurt him," she said.

"That's another approach," Mason said. "You're better protection than taking my vitamins. I'm canceling my life insurance."

"How much life insurance do you have?" she asked with a sly smile.

"A lot," Mason said.

"Don't cancel it. I'm a reliable lover, but I wouldn't count on the killer thing."

"I'll sleep better knowing that. All the same, we need to talk about last night," he told her.

The police had questioned Mason and Abby separately, testing one version of the events against the other. When they finally got to Mason's house, the last thing they wanted to do was debrief one another.

"You told me not to go out there," Abby said. "I should have listened."

"You can't un-ring that bell. Tell me what happened."

Abby sighed, rolling away from Mason, leaning against the kitchen counter. "Coffee," she said. "I need coffee."

"Tea," he said. "I don't drink coffee."

"I'll start a list," she said. "At least make the tea strong."

"I'll brew, you talk."

"Okay," she said, rubbing her palms against her sleeves. "The kids were packing up when I got there and Nix was running around, yelling at them to hurry up. He acted like he didn't know who I was, but he hustled me down to his office before I could even tell him why I was there."

"He didn't want any of the kids to hear what you had to say," Mason said.

"He played dumb at first, which made me act dumber. I kept telling him what we knew, thinking that would make him talk. Instead, he got real jumpy. Then Centurion showed up carrying the bags with the drugs and the money and they started to argue like I wasn't even there. When I tried to slip out, Centurion slapped me and made Nix duct-tape me to the chair while he cooked up some crack and loaded the syringe. They were going to kill me," she said, the words catching in her throat.

Mason handed her a steaming cup of tea, Abby held it to her neck, fighting the chill from telling her story. "I know they were arguing about the dope and the cash," Mason said. "What did they say?"

"Centurion yelled at Nix for not telling me to leave earlier. He said they had to kill me since I'd seen the drugs and the money and that you would come after him, but that they had no choice."

"What about Nix?"

Abby shook her head. "You were wrong about Nix. You said he was a make-love-not-war type. He laid into Centurion, telling him that the whole scam was his own idea, bragging about using pregnant girls to run drugs and as a source for babies. The bastard called the girls renewable resources. He was willing to split everything with Centurion, but Centurion wasn't going to give him anything. Centurion came there to kill Nix."

"Did they say anything about the Davenports?"

"Centurion said it was a good thing Gina and Robert were dead, so they couldn't testify. He called it the best luck they've had. Nix called Centurion an idiot. He said that Gina Davenport gave them credibility and that Robert bought drugs and peddled them to his students. He blamed Centurion for ruining everything."

"If Centurion didn't kill Gina and if Robert OD'd on his own, how did Centurion ruin anything?" Mason asked.

"Nix said he shouldn't have come after you, that he should have left you out of it and the cops would have left them alone."

"What did Centurion say?"

"That's the part I didn't understand," Abby said. "Centurion said he would have done it even if you hadn't caused him so much trouble. He said it was payback for someone else."

"Payback for someone else?" Mason asked.

Abby sipped her tea slowly. "Centurion said he was doing it for someone else that owed you big-time. Nix said that Centurion wasn't paid enough to risk their entire operation. Centurion said he didn't have a choice. Then you blew up the barn."

Mason tugged at the stubble on his chin, finally understanding why the car-jackers showed no interest when he told them about the baby ledger. They were just supposed to kill him. He searched his memory for someone who not only wanted him dead, but also had the money and means to convince Centurion to do it. Before he could match anyone to those exclusive criteria, Tuffy shimmied through the dog door, rubbing herself against Abby, shoving her nose into Mason's thigh, feinting toward the back door with a grab-the-leash-and-let's-hit-the-road stutter step.

"You're lucky the dog lets you live here," Abby said.

"We have an understanding," Mason said. "I provide the food and she makes sure I get enough exercise."

"You better let her take you on a walk. I've got to go home and clean up. Showering with you is too distracting."

"I've got to catch up with Mickey, Harry, and Blues. I'll call you later. Stay busy. It's harder when you're alone with nothing to do."

Abby kissed him. "I can do alone," she said, patting him on the chest. "But it's nice not to have to."

Mason took Tuffy for a spin in Loose Park, tracking down Blues with his cell phone.

"What have the Hacketts been up to?" Mason asked Blues.

"Harry and I met down the block from the Hacketts' house last night after Mickey called us. We watched the house for a couple of hours. They had a steady stream of visitors until about ten o'clock. People dropping by like somebody died."

"Two somebodies died," Mason said. "Centurion and Nix."

"Heard it on the news while I was sitting in my car, peeing into a bottle with your name on it," Blues said. "Somebody in the Hacketts' house turned on a television. Big screen. I could see it from the street. They were watching the live reports from Sanctuary. Did you start that fire?"

"Got into the habit playing with matches when I was a kid. What happened after the news was over?"

"Company left. Then things got interesting. Arthur Hackett went for a drive. Harry and I flipped a coin and Harry got the old man. A few minutes later, Carol Hackett left, and I followed her. Arthur paid a visit to Paula Sutton and Carol got some late night legal advice from David Evans."

Mason stopped in his tracks, forcing Tuffy onto her haunches, straining to reach a squirrel. "Anybody have a sleep-over?"

"Nope. It didn't look like that kind of a visit to me. Harry said the same thing."

"Do you think Arthur knew that Carol went out too?"

"Hard to say. She got home before he did. If she didn't tell him, he wouldn't have known she was gone. Any idea what's going on?"

"It's coming together," Mason said, telling Blues what Roy Bowen had found out.

"You still have a pretty big hole in your story, you know that," Blues said.

"Yeah, the son. Trent doesn't fit into any of this. Neither does this," Mason added. "Centurion didn't set me up to be car-jacked and whacked because I was shining the light on his operation. Somebody paid him to do it."

"Who hates you that much?" Blues asked. "All the rich people you pissed off are in jail."

"Hard to imagine, isn't it," Mason answered. "Jimmie Camaya is the only person I can come up with who kills people to get even. Last time I saw him, we were buddies."

"Jimmie wanted you dead, he'd do it himself and make sure you knew it was him. So, it isn't him. Besides, Jimmie is a businessman and he's got no business with you since your old law firm ate itself alive."

"Then I'm back where I started. Which is no place."

"I'll tell you one thing," Blues said.

"Is this where you make me feel better?" Mason asked.

"Since you aren't dead and Centurion is, you better keep your head up and your eyes open or go home and lock your doors. What's it going to be?"

"House calls, but not at my house," Mason said, giving Blues his itinerary.

"I get overtime on weekends, you know that," Blues said.

"I've got to stay alive for you to get paid, you know that, don't you?"

"That's what makes me so good at what I do. You owe me too much money for me to let you get killed."

"Good," Mason said. "I'd rather owe you than cheat you out of it."

CHAPTER 36

Things don't always work out. Mason knew that, had been raised on it, and had made a living because of it. People plan, pray, and connive and, still, things don't always work out. The brutal truth, Claire told him when he was ten and came home from the roller rink with a bloody nose, is that things generally don't work out, at least not the way people intend. Life is more ad-libbed than scripted, people more reactive than proactive, trouble more easily found than avoided.

That's the daily dynamic. People manage. The chaos takes on its own unpredictable charm. At the end of the line, most people shrug and say their lives could have been better, could have been worse, that they have no complaints that count and who would listen anyway.

That's most people. Mason knew that killers were different, whether they were thoughtful, vengeful, or impulsive, jealous, psychotic, or greedy. They demanded order, accountability, and control they imposed through the death of others. They did what they had to do or couldn't keep from doing. Just ask them. But tighten the circle around a killer and learn the meaning of nothing left to lose.

Mason had not come to this moment in his life by design, proving again that his aunt was right. He had migrated from a small plaintiff's personal injury law firm to a big corporate firm, then to solo practice, always looking for an elusive something he was certain he would find at the next stop. Claire had warned him each time that he wouldn't find what he was looking for in a place. He'd find it in himself.

What he found was completely unexpected. He could kill a man and cloak it in pop-psychology bromides. He could risk his life without worrying whether he was responding to a heroic imperative or whether he was just too stupid to live. It wasn't only about the law, or justice, or taking the bad guys down. It was about the jolt, the rush of diving into dark water and coming out on the other side alive.

Sitting in his car outside Paula Sutton's apartment late on Saturday afternoon, the battle at Sanctuary still fresh in his mind, he wondered when taking the dive had become the reason for taking the dive. A gathering chill crept into the car, the sky a slag heap of scrap-metal gray, its broken edges rusted by the failing sun, giving him a different jolt, one that drained the courage he lived on. He was sliding fast toward the hazy ground where rationalization made anything possible and everything right, where strong arms blurred with strong wills, where men killed because they could. It was a world Blues navigated without losing his soul, a dead reckoning Mason wasn't certain he possessed.

Looking at his image in the rearview mirror, he promised himself that this day, this case would be the last of it, knowing that his promise was more for Abby than for him. She had killed a man, though he didn't mourn Centurion. He felt responsible, not for Centurion's death, but for putting her in that moment when she had to kill one man to save another. He wouldn't let her follow his path. He needed her to retreat from his.

It was this new calculus, factoring love against loss, that scared him, that could cause a fatal hesitation, fulfilling the prophecy. Swallowing against the dryness in his throat, he stepped out of his car, glancing around for Blues, not finding him or expecting to, knowing that Blues worked best from the shadows.

Mason liked working from the bottom up, building a strong foundation for a case, each piece snug against the next, each layer supporting the weight of the accusations or defenses above it. This case was the opposite. It reminded him of a child's game made of small cubes stacked one on top of another. Each player pulled out one cube at a time, the loser being the player who caused the stack to collapse by pulling out the last cube holding everything in place.

Samantha, Mason conceded, was right. Gina Davenport's murder had led to the exposure of Centurion's operation at Sanctuary, a deadly example of the rule of unintended consequences. Centurion's admission that the car-jacking was payback for someone else turned his other assumptions about the case on their head.

He had been looking for a link between Gina Davenport and Trent Hackett that would exonerate Jordan and convict a single killer. Now Mason wondered if he should look for something that tied *him* to both victims or someone who had reason to kill all three of them.

Samantha was convinced that Trent Hackett had orchestrated the elevator attack on Mason, closing her investigation when Trent was murdered. Trent may have been innocent of the act but known of the attempt, the latter enough to get him killed. Mason hoped Mickey found the common thread in Trent's office. He shook his head to clear the internal fog that permeated this case, stamping his feet on the pavement.

Paula Sutton lived in an apartment complex north of the Missouri River off I-29 and 64th Street. Kansas City was divided by a lot of things, including race, the state line between Missouri and Kansas, and the fight over who made the best barbecue sauce. The river, with distinct worlds north and south of its banks, also divided it. Those who lived south of the river rarely went north, except to go the airport. Those who lived north rarely went south. The reasons lay in the perception that each had it better than the other, neither side able to make the case, both sides comfortable in their parochialism.

The apartments were new, banners dipped in primary colors fluttering from the arched entrance, shrubs freshly planted around each building, neatly manicured roads winding throughout, a jogging trail threaded like a ribbon across abundant green space, the emphasis on community, not on complex. Each building was named after an island, a salute to bad marketing, Paula's building the Tahitian. Mason checked out the surrounding buildings, disappointed none were named Staten or Rhode.

Paula lived on the first floor. Mason knocked, peering through a gap in the curtains covering the front window, hearing footsteps, a shadow blotting the peephole, the door not opening. Mason knocking harder, the footsteps retreating, Mason catching a glimpse of Paula through the window, a sleek Doberman on a taut leash at her heel.

"Paula, it's Lou Mason. We need to talk."

Paula didn't, but the dog did, Mason hearing its bark from the backside of the building. Paula was running, the dog her escort. He raced around the building, picking up the jogging trail as Paula disappeared around a turn a hundred yards away.

Mason chose a solid pace, figuring to close the gap without sprinting into the Doberman's jaws, guessing that Paula would be wheezing when he caught up to her, gasping for air and a cigarette. He found her leaning against a tree, holding her side, the dog coiled, its ears flat.

"Paula, I'm not going to hurt you," Mason said. "I just want to talk."

"Go away," she said, still heaving. "Or I'll turn the dog loose." She eased her grip on the leash enough for the dog to lurch at Mason, teeth barred, a guttural growl and demon eyes giving the threat its heft.

Mason backed up a step, keeping his hands at his sides, palms out, his body language lying to the dog that Mason was a friend. The dog didn't buy it, ratcheting its growl to a sharp bark.

"I'm not going anywhere until we talk," Mason said. "If you run, I'll find you. Besides, you can't bring the dog to the courtroom."

"No," Paula said, the pain in her side subsiding, her breathing still ragged. "You can't make me."

A real jogger, a lycra body stocking stretched tightly over his lean, well-muscled frame, interrupted their standoff. Mason guessed he was in his late twenties and, from his quick stop and concerned look at Paula, ready to jump to the obvious but wrong conclusion.

"Miss," he said to Paula, "is everything all right? Do you need help getting home?"

"No," Mason said. "This isn't what you think."

"Yes," Paula said. "He followed me onto the trail."

The runner turned to Mason, measuring himself, counting the dog as an ally, not certain it would be enough. "Look, man," he said. "Just back away and let me take the lady home." He reached for a cell phone at his waist. "I can call the cops," he added.

"Do that," Blues said, stepping onto the path, a gun at his side. "Ask for Homicide Detective Samantha Greer. Tell her that Lou Mason and Wilson Bluestone are holding a material witness in a homicide investigation and ask her to send a car for the witness, an ambulance for you, and a canine officer to pick up a dead dog."

"Hey, man!" the runner said, his hands up in the air. "Don't get radical. The lady looked like she was in trouble."

"She is," Mason said. "Make the call." The runner opened his phone, his hands shaking, his fingers hesitating above the keypad. "It's 9-1-1," Mason added.

"Right, right," the runner said, nodding, eyes darting between Blues and the snarling dog, wishing he'd kept on running.

"No!" Paula said, "it's okay. I'm fine," she added, stroking the back of the dog's head. "Really, I'm fine," she insisted.

The runner drew a deep breath. "Good. I mean, great. That's really great. Glad to hear it, sorry I bothered you," he said over his shoulder as he sprinted away.

Blues holstered his gun inside his jacket and walked slowly toward the dog, the dog throttling back its growl, Blues taking the leash from Paula, clicking commands at the dog, letting the dog sniff his hand.

"You two have a nice chat," Blues said. "Rover and I are going for a walk."

Mason watched Blues and the dog until they were out of view, Paula fishing in her jeans pocket for a cigarette, lighting it, the shakes making her match dance around the tobacco, sucking the smoke like a hungry newborn.

"Your friend is a freak," she said. "He was going to shoot my dog."

"You maybe, but definitely not the dog," Mason said. "Blues is very strong on animal rights."

"Fuck you," Paula said.

"Sorry, I'm spoken for," Mason said. "Why did you run?"

"I didn't run. I was taking my dog for a walk. You chased me. Make that assaulted me. I'm going to sue your ass."

"Fucking me and suing my ass, is that a package deal?" Mason asked.

Paula threw her cigarette at Mason's feet, grinding it with her heel, blowing smoke in his face. "I'm out of here," she said.

Mason took her by the arm, pressing his thumb into the notch of her elbow, ignoring her pained yelp. "I know about Jordan's cell phone. I know you called Abby Lieberman and tipped her off about her baby and Gina Davenport."

Paula yanked free from Mason's grasp, rubbing her forearm and hand. "Good for you. So what?"

"So your phone prank triggered this whole mess. You're right up there with Mrs. O'Leary and her cow and Typhoid Mary."

"It's not my fault!"

"You wanted to stir up trouble for Gina because you were jealous of her. You didn't count on Gina deciding to go public about Emily."

"I should have," Paula said. "Gina would do anything for ratings."

"Problem was," Mason said, "Gina's story threatened to expose what was going on at Sanctuary."

"I didn't know any of that until it was all over the news last night! How could I? Besides, that detective said Sanctuary had nothing to do with Gina's murder. She said that Jordan killed Gina."

"Don't count on it," Mason said, though Paula was, her defiance gaining momentum as she lit another cigarette, holding the smoke deep in her lungs. "If there's no connection, why did Arthur Hackett come to see you last night after the news broke on Sanctuary?"

Paula dropped her hands to her sides, smoke leaking from her mouth, Mason having knocked her back on her heels. "Your friend the dog lover?" she asked.

"Doesn't matter," Mason answered. "I'm giving you first chance to explain. Don't waste the opportunity."

Paula squashed her cigarette into the rough crevasses of a tree trunk, stuck her hands into her back pockets, and dug the toe of her shoe into the dry dirt at its base, scattering the soil, studying it for wisdom. Finding none, she answered without looking up.

"The phone call was Arthur's idea," she said, folding

one arm across her chest, hand tucked under her arm, raising her other hand to her mouth, forgetting her cigarette was gone. "Gina wanted out of her contract. Arthur was looking for some way to pressure her. He figured she would give up to avoid letting the truth about Emily come out."

Mason said, "You knew about the contract negotiations so you told Arthur about Abby and volunteered for the job. If it worked, Arthur owed you. If it didn't, Arthur still owed you."

Paula shook her head. "No. It wasn't like that. Arthur told me about Abby. I didn't know anything about her or Emily."

It was Mason's turn to be surprised. "David Evans didn't tell you?"

"Not David. The man is a vault. He doesn't talk about business. He never mentioned Emily. Not once. He wouldn't even talk about Max Coyle's case when I brought it up. You're the only one he talked about."

"Me? What did he have to say? I don't suppose I'm on his Christmas list."

"He says you're tough, that you beat him, but the world is round."

"That's what the losing lawyer always says about the winning lawyer," Mason explained. "There's a lot of wait-until-next-time in the practice of law."

"Not for David," Paula said. "He hates you, says you ruined him. He told me that the bad publicity from Max's case chased away the rest of his clients except for Gina and Sanctuary."

Mason took a deep breath. "So David wanted to get even with me. Did he tell you how?"

"No. He just kept saying the world is round like it was his mantra," Paula said.

Mason had an idea what Evans may have meant, but doubted that a man who was a vault would confess attempted murder to his girlfriend. He chose another tack. "Gina was David's client. Did you tell him what you were doing?"

"Not a chance. He would have exploded."

Mason asked, "Has a bad temper, does he?"

"Trust me," Paula said, punctuating the air with a dying ember of tobacco. "He's one man I wouldn't want mad at me."

"I'll keep that in mind," Mason said. "What did Arthur Hackett want last night?"

"He was in a panic. He was afraid you'd find out about Jordan's cell phone. I told him that you already knew; that you showed up at David's house with the phone. Arthur said that wasn't possible since he had thrown it down the trash chute in his office."

"If the only thing he's guilty of is unethical negotiating tactics, why the panic? Unless he killed Gina and is willing to let his daughter take the blame?" Mason asked.

Paula ran her fingers through her hair, pulling more than combing. "All I know is that he offered me a three-year contract extension with a hundred-thousand-dollar signing bonus to keep my mouth shut."

"I guess he didn't offer you enough," Mason said.

"It was enough last night," she said. "But not when I saw you standing outside my door. The only thing I could think to do was run. I'm not going to do that for the rest of my life."

Blues reappeared, the dog's stubby tail pointed skyward, its tongue dangling over its teeth in a half smile.

Crouching next to the animal's ear, Blues whispered something, patted the dog on the rump, and handed Paula the leash.

"Nice dog," Blues told her.

CHAPTER 37

"I'm a no-show for dinner," Mason told Abby, calling from his car. "I probably won't make it until late tonight."

"It's okay," Abby said, her hollow cheerfulness telling him that it wasn't. "I don't feel like going out anyway. Looks like the weather is turning nasty. It's a good night for curling up."

"I'll call you," he promised.

"Just come," she said, her request slicing Mason with its quiet urgency.

Rain began spitting against Mason's windshield, moisture and dropping temperature painting the glass with fog. Mason turned on the defroster, the blast of dry warm air clearing his view, if not his thinking.

Arthur Hackett was acting like a man guilty of more than hardball negotiating, Mason wasn't willing to believe he would risk his daughter's life just to avoid his own embarrassment. Killing Gina could have been Hackett's final negotiating position. As for Trent, the father was the son's alibi for the evening Gina was murdered. More accurately, the three Hacketts—Arthur, Carol, and Trent—were each other's alibis.

A father who would sacrifice his daughter to hide one murder wouldn't hesitate to sacrifice the son who could betray him. If he was right, Carol Hackett was Arthur's last loose end. Maybe, Mason thought, she had gone to David Evans for protection. Mason flashed back to the image of Arthur Hackett silently pleading with him as he left the courtroom, Mason believing the plea was for Jordan, wondering now if Hackett was pleading for himself.

Mason called Harry Ryman. "Are you still on Carol Hackett?" he asked, wanting only one answer.

"The way you ask that, makes me nervous," Harry said. "Yeah, I'm on her. Been on her all day and I'm ready to get off her."

"Where is she?" Mason asked.

"At home," Harry snapped. "She went shopping on the Plaza this afternoon. I kept my distance. The house was quiet when she got back, but I figured people would start showing up, same as last night. So I picked up Chinese and I'm having a feast in the front seat of my car."

"Do they have company yet?"

"Nope," Harry answered. "Still quiet. Just a couple of lights on."

Mason looked at his watch. It was past eight o'clock. If people were going to visit the Hacketts on a Saturday night, they would have been there by now.

"Go knock on the door, find out if Carol is home," Mason said, explaining why he was worried about her.

"You really think it's Arthur Hackett?" Harry asked.

"He's on my short list. Call me back. I'm on my cell."

Mason couldn't plug the hole in the Arthur Hackett scenario left by the attempts on his life. Mason had never met Arthur Hackett before Gina Davenport was murdered. The only debt Hackett owed Mason was for legal fees Mason had refused to let him pay. Nonetheless, he felt better sending Harry to check on her. While it was possible that there was more than one killer—one for Gina, one for Trent, and yet a third trying to kill *him*—his gut told him there was only one. He liked the single-killer theory because it was simpler than the alternative, though he had yet to see a simple murder.

David Evans was his other choice because Evans was the only one carrying Mason as a big payable on his books. Paula described Evans's temper as explosive, his intent to get even with Mason a near obsession. Mason wouldn't allow himself the luxury of questioning whether Evans was the kind of man who could kill two people and try to kill a third, having learned long ago that such surface appraisals often miss the capacity for violence that percolates inside. No one would look at Mason or Abby and guess they were capable of killing, though Mason knew there was a gulf between self-defense and premeditation even if the outcome was the same.

While Evans was the leading candidate in the who-wants-to-kill-Mason sweepstakes, Mason couldn't put the tag on him for killing Gina. If, as Paula said, Mason had driven away all of Evans's clients except for Gina and Sanctuary, Evans would guard Gina with his life, since he was finished without her. Unless, Mason realized with a start, Gina was finished with Evans. If that were true, Evans would lose more than Gina. He would lose his connection with Sanctuary, the last of his clients, putting him in the deadly zone of nothing left to lose.

Mason recognized another flaw in the David Evans theory. Whoever tried to kill him by tampering with Gina's private elevator had to have access to the room that housed the elevator controls. Evans didn't. Arthur Hackett did. That same person also had to have a special relationship with Centurion, the kind of bond that made Centurion set Mason up for the car-jacking and crack-house tour.

Both Evans and Hackett knew Centurion through Sanctuary. Evans was, for all practical purposes, Centurion's lawyer, while Hackett was his investment advisor. Either or both could have known that Centurion was running drugs and illegal adoptions through Sanctuary. For an instant, Mason tried to remember whether he'd ever seen Evans and Hackett together, his best explanation now being that they were one and the same person. Like Superman and Clark Kent, only both of them bad guys.

In every scenario, Mason decided, Trent was probably a victim of circumstance or complicity. Given his winning personality, Trent was a problem that found a permanent solution.

Mason, apologizing to his arteries, picked up a hamburger and fries at a fast-food drive-through, eating in his car, kept company by rain that had kicked up from spitting to steady, spilling the fries when his cell phone rang.

"Boss, where are you?" Mickey asked.

"In a parking lot near 33rd and Main plucking French fries out of my lap. Why the hell haven't I heard from you? What did you find in Trent's office?"

"Whoa, Boss! No need to get cranky on me here. I'm putting in my billable hours."

Mickey was right. He was taking out his frustration on Harry and Mickey and they weren't trying to kill him. He took a breath. "Sorry, Mickey. The days are running into each other and I'm running out of days. What do you got for me?"

"Bupkis from Trent's office," Mickey said.

"Mickey," Mason said gently. "Irish kids don't do Yiddish. It's like me saying top of the morning, governor."

"Thanks for the reminder, Boss. I didn't find squat in Trent's office. How's that?"

"It sucks, but it sounds better," Mason said, swallowing his disappointment. "What else have you been doing since last night?"

"Staying on task, like my teachers used to say. You told me to follow the money and that's what I've been doing."

Mason stuffed the last chunk of hamburger into a paper bag and sat up, catching the excitement in Mickey's voice. "Okay, Mickey. Give it to me."

"I started with the IRS forms for both Emily's Fund and Sanctuary. I broke down the compensation paid to employees, directors, consultants, the works. Guess who the big winners are."

"Centurion Johnson, for one," Mason answered. "I'd guess Nix came in at number two."

"Half right, Boss. Centurion was number two. David Evans was number one. He was knocking down legal fees and investment consulting fees. Between both gigs, he was taking out almost half a million a year."

"Real money for real people," Mason said.

"That's the good news. The bad news, for Evans anyway, is that he was canned the day before Gina was killed."

"How did you find that out?"

"I went down the list of Sanctuary's board members until I found someone that wanted to talk. A guy named Ransom Stoddard."

Mason said, "Why do I know his name?"

"He used to run a string of suburban newspapers, sold it to a national chain, and made a pile of dough."

"Why was he willing to talk to you?"

"I caught him at a good time. He was half in the bag and shitting his pants about the directors getting sued after what happened last night at Sanctuary."

"Did you get him down on tape?" Mason asked.

"No, but I did get him down to the bar. The guy has a taste for scotch."

"Did he say why Evans was canned?" Mason asked.

"He said it was Gina Davenport's idea. She accused Evans of skimming from Emily's Fund, then falsifying the IRS reports to cover it up. She said he was probably stealing from Sanctuary too."

"Evans blamed Gina for the phony IRS reports," Mason said. "At least that's what he told me. An easy shot to take since Gina was in no position to argue. Evans showed me the amended reports he claimed to have filed. The guy is slick. I wonder why word of this hasn't come out."

"Evans was putting on a full-court press to be reinstated and was blaming Gina for the skim. He flashed the amended IRS reports and told the board only a stupid crook or an innocent man would turn himself in to the IRS. Stoddard says that the board was afraid Evans would sue, so they were trying to make a deal with him. Guess who the board picked to negotiate with Evans."

Mason asked, "Who?"

"The chairman of Sanctuary's investment committee, Arthur Hackett." Mason whistled. "Don't do that, Boss. It's like chalk on the blackboard. Irish guys whistle. Jewish guys say holy shit."

"I'll remember that," Mason said. "Evans says he borrowed the money to settle Max Coyle's case from Gina Davenport. Samantha said the promissory note was legit. He probably forged Gina's signature on the note."

"Wouldn't surprise me," Mickey said. "If half of what Stoddard said is true, there's no way Gina would have loaned Evans a dime."

"If Evans paid Max with stolen money, Max will have to give it back. Which means we lose our fee. This case is getting too expensive."

"Don't ask me for my share. I spent it already," Mickey said.

"You still have that passkey to the Cable Depot?" Mason asked.

"Burning a hole in my pocket."

"Don't lose it. Meet me there."

Mason's cell phone rang again.

"Nobody's home," Harry said.

"It's a big house. Maybe they're in the basement or upstairs and didn't hear you knock."

"I knocked. I rang. I called. Nobody's home. I'm getting too old for this. I knew better. I should have stayed put," Harry said, not sparing himself.

"Forget it," Mason said. "Did you check the garage?"

"Yeah. Carol drives a new Lexus. It's in the garage. Arthur drives the Mercedes. It's gone."

"They probably went out to eat. They'll be back," Mason said.

"If you believed that crap, you wouldn't have sent me looking for Carol. I'm going to call Samantha."

"And tell her what?" Mason asked. "That the Hacketts aren't home and I think Arthur may have taken Carol out to kill her? Samantha will quit taking your calls."

"You got a better idea, I'm listening."

"Last night, they split up, Carol went to see Evans, Arthur went to see Paula Sutton. Maybe they went back tonight, this time together. Take a run up north and check on Paula. She was not in a good mood when I left her a little while ago, but Blues made friends with her dog."

"What kind of dog?" Harry asked.

"Doberman."

"Figures. I hate Dobermans. Blues had a thing for them. We busted this meth dealer one time, had a Doberman. Guy turns the dog on us, figuring it was going to tear us a new asshole. Blues did that clicking thing with his tongue like he was talking in code and the dog practically humped his leg on the spot."

"Mention Blues's name to the dog, maybe it'll remember."

"Where are you going?"

"Cable Depot. Mickey is meeting me there. I'm going to take another tour."

"What about Blues?"

"He's around doing his guardian-angel thing. I'll tell him to drop by Evans's place. It's only a few blocks from the Cable Depot. Stay in touch."

"Right," Harry said, still beating himself up with a heavy tone.

"Harry," Mason told him. "Shake it off. We'll find them."

The rain was steady, like a marathoner hitting his stride in the middle miles, vapor halos orbiting the street lamps along 6th in front of the Cable Depot. Earl Luke Fisher was dodging the weather under a tarp perched over his bench, his grocery cart anchored to the bench with a bungee cord. Mason parked in front of Earl Luke's bench, tapping his impatience against the steering wheel, waiting for Mickey, keeping his eye on the building as if the killer was about to walk out holding up a sign that said "Guilty."

Mason jumped, nearly banging his head on the ceiling of the car, when Earl Luke rapped on his window. Mason rolled the window down.

"Hey, second-story man," Earl Luke said. "You're blocking my view. It ain't like I got a goddamn big screen TV to look at."

"Sorry," Mason told him, backing up. Earl Luke crawled under his tarp as Mickey pulled in behind Mason.

"Nice night if it don't rain," Mickey said as he and Mason crossed the street, caps low on their brows, collars up.

"Give me the key," Mason told him, Mickey handing it off, Mason jiggling it in the lock, first gently, then hard, the lock not giving. Mason removed the key, tried it again, repeating the process, banging on the glass door when the third time wasn't the charm.

"What's up with that?" Mickey asked. "The key worked last night."

"Hackett changed the locks," Mason said. "Why would he do that?"

"To keep us out, Boss," Mickey said.

"It would be easier to ask me to give the key back, assuming he even knows that I still have it. He wants to keep someone else out. Who else has a passkey?"

"Wait a minute," Mickey answered. "Last night, I'm going through the stuff in Trent's desk. There's a copy of a bill he sent to David Evans for a new lock when Evans moved into his office. Maybe Trent loaned him a passkey until the new lock was installed."

"And maybe Evans didn't return the passkey," Mason said.

"Been known to happen," Mickey said.

Mason said, "Which means that Evans had access to the elevator control room for Gina's private elevator."

"Which also means he could have sent you for your thrill ride. Holy shit," Mickey said.

Mason looked at him. "You converting?"

"Nah," Mickey answered. "It's tough to whistle in the rain. What now?"

"Let's talk to the doorman," Mason said, motioning to Earl Luke.

CHAPTER 38

Mason peeled back Earl Luke's tarp, swinging Earl Luke's feet off the bench, forcing him upright, Mason and Mickey sitting down on either side of him, each supporting one end of the tarp in a rough lean-to, breathing through their mouths.

"Can't break into the Depot, you gotta break into my house, is that the way it is, second-story man?" Earl Luke said.

"Something like that, Earl Luke. Nice place you got here," Mason said. "When were the locks changed?"

"This morning, early. Woke me up, in fact. People are damn inconsiderate, you ask me, course nobody does. I'm just a goddamn street bum, piece of trash, people can ignore, move in on in the rain like they goddamn please!"

"Don't worry. We aren't spending the night," Mason said. "You remember Labor Day, the night Gina Davenport was killed?"

"Course I do. I was on TV with that good-looking reporter and that shrink come flying out the window like a bird with no wings. Scared the piss out of me, I'll tell you what, and I seen lots of dead people, believe you me, I have."

"Earlier that night, were you here, on the bench, watching the building?" Mason asked him.

"You know I was, so why you ask me?"

"I imagine you know all the tenants in the Cable Depot," Mason said.

"Listen, second-story man," Earl Luke said. "I been all over this with the cops. Just 'cause I'm a bum don't mean I'm stupid. You wantta ask me somethin', ask it and get outa my house. Leave me be!"

Mason shook the tarp, bouncing a pocket of water off the back. "Who'd you see that night coming and going from the building?"

"I done told the cops all that. Give 'em all the names. Saw that big ox what they call Mad Max. Saw that skinny gal what does the morning show. Saw that girl what kilt the shrink, your client, what's her name?"

"Jordan Hackett," Mason said.

"That's her," Earl Luke said.

"What about her parents? Did you see Arthur or Carol Hackett?"

"Never see them. They always park in the garage under the building. Garage door is on the east side. I watch the front door."

"How about David Evans? Did he use the front door that night?"

Earl Luke flashed his yellow, gap-toothed grin at Mason. "Now there's a right interesting question. No, sir, Mr. Evans did not use the front door that night."

Mason looked at Earl Luke, whose washed-out eyes were lively, flickering with a mischief Mason hadn't previously noticed. Earl Luke was right. Just because he was a street bum didn't mean he was stupid. No doubt he'd been questioned, rousted, and harassed by cops enough times to learn the toughest lesson for any witness. Only answer the question he was asked. Earl Luke was waiting to be asked the right question.

"Did you see David Evans that night?"

"That I did."

"When?" Mason asked.

"A little while before that TV lady showed up."

"Was that before or after you saw Jordan go in the front door of the Cable Depot?"

Earl Luke nodded, holding his grin. "Before."

"Where were you when you saw Evans?" Mason asked.

"Comin' up the bluff behind the Depot."

Mickey interrupted. "That bluff leads down to the interstate highway. What were you doing there?"

Earl Luke cast a closed-mouth glance at Mickey, resenting the intrusion. "It's okay," Mason said. "He's young and doesn't know any better, but it's a good question. Why were you on the slope?"

"People dump stuff there, cans, bottles, sometimes more valuable stuff they don't know they throw'd away. I was lookin'."

Mason said, "I don't imagine Evans was on the bluff too. Where was he?"

Earl Luke laughed, a quick burst of bum breath that stiffened Mason's spine. "You lawyers are all alike," Earl Luke said. "Every one of you a second-story man. Mr. Evans, he was opening that old cable works door you was fancyin' the other night."

"Holy shit," Mason said as Mickey whistled.

"Did you tell the cops about Evans?" Mason asked.

"They didn't ask. All they was interested in was who went in and out the front door and that's all by God I tole 'em."

Mason patted Earl Luke on the back. "Thanks, Earl. Appreciate you inviting us in," he said, surrendering the cover of the tarp, glad to be back in the rain, Mickey joining him.

"You know, for such a smart fella, you ain't too bright," Earl Luke said, gathering the tarp around him like a gown, the rain beating against his face.

"That so?" Mason asked. "I make the same mistake as the cops and not ask you the right question?"

Earl Luke answered with a silent, smug smile, pulling his head inside the tarp like a turtle. Mason and Mickey looked at one another, debating whether to climb back under the tarp.

"I've got it!" Mickey said. "The lock on the cable works door. I'll bet Hackett forgot to have it changed."

Earl Luke stretched out on the bench, wrapped in the tarp, and rolled onto his side, his back to them, a disgusted snort his only response. "I don't think so, Mickey," Mason said. "I mean, you could be right about the lock. Earl Luke probably figures we're smart enough to check it out, but I don't think that's the question he wants us to ask."

"What is it, then?" Mickey asked.

Mason shoved Earl Luke in the butt with the toe of his shoe. "Earl! Wake up! Something I want to ask you."

Earl Luke rose slowly, still covered in the tarp, a poor man's mummy come to life, parting the folds of the tarp enough to peek at them. "What's your question, second-story man?"

"Hackett may not have had the lock on the cable works door changed. But if he did, we'll need to find another way inside the Depot. Care to lend a hand?"

Earl Luke licked his lips, rinsing his gums with rainwater, spitting onto the sidewalk. "Expect you might could use some help," he said, stuffing the tarp onto the bottom rack of the grocery cart, tightening the rope belt around his worn pants, zipping his Army fatigue jacket, all but snapping a salute. "Nice to be asked," he added.

"You ever been inside?" Mason asked him. "In the basement or wherever the cable works used to be."

"Practically grew up in that building," Earl Luke said. "My daddy, he worked there when the cable cars still ran. Chief mechanic, he was. Place was my playground and my school until I was ten years old. Then the city shut down the cable cars. Times was hard and my daddy started drifting. Like to say them times was my real education. Growing up, I figured I'd end up like my daddy, a mechanic and all. Guess I did end up like him, drifted right back here. Ain't been inside in a long time. Kinda like to see it."

The backside of the Depot faced north, an eight-story shadow in the sun, an unlit, black curtain at night, the ground sloping away toward the bluff, the pale glow of headlights filtering up from the interstate like a planetary ring. The distant lights of the River Market blurred in the rain, the Missouri River flashing for an instant under the blinking lights of a private plane landing at the downtown airport. His back to the wall, Mason, trailed by Mickey, followed Earl Luke to the Dumpster that sat on top of the concrete pad housing the entrance to the cable works. The three of them shoved the Dumpster onto the grass.

Mason looked up, shielding his eyes from the rain with one hand, tapping Mickey with his other, pointing to the lights on in Arthur Hackett's office. A woman appeared in the window, too far away for Mason to identify her, though he had no doubt it was Carol Hackett. A man impossible to recognize at that distance materialized at her side, grabbing her arm, the woman pulling away, the man giving her the back of his hand, the woman collapsing against him, the light going out.

"Son of a bitch!" Mason said, grabbing the door handle, a six-inch L-shaped lever hinged to swing up, allowing the door to open skyward. It was locked tight. Mason slid the master key into the lock, his heart picking up a beat as he struggled with the key before the tumblers clicked into place, the key rotating clockwise, the bolt sliding open with a sharp clack. The lever handle offered no resistance this time, but the door held fast, Mason yanking so hard he lost his footing.

"What's up with that?" Mickey said, helping Mason to his feet, both of them looking at Earl Luke for an explanation.

The old man scratched his chin stubble, not answering. "Come on," Earl Luke said, walking toward the edge of the bluff.

"What is it?" Mason asked. "Why won't the door open?"

"There's another bolt on the inside. Locks both ways," Earl Luke said over his shoulder, not looking back.

"Where are you going?" Mason shouted.

"You ask too many questions," Earl Luke said, disappearing in the darkness like he was walking out to sea.

"Mickey, stay here," Mason said.

"Like hell I will, Boss!"

"You've got to watch the garage and the front door. Blues went to check out Evans's house. He'll be here in a few minutes. Call Harry and see if he found anything at Paula Sutton's." Mickey started to argue, Mason holding up his hand. "You know I'm right, so just do it. If I don't open the front door in ten minutes, find a brick and open it yourself."

Mason scrambled to catch up with Earl Luke, standing at the edge of the bluff, peering down into the dark tangle of weeds grown into rough hedges. He gauged the distance to the highway as the length of a football field, barely making out a zigzagged goat track worn across the face of the bluff.

"Earl Luke!" Mason shouted, the roar of eighteen-wheelers swallowing his words. He saw Earl Luke's head bob between a pair of stunted trees halfway down the bluff, their height exaggerated by the sharp descent. Mason followed, picking his way, fighting for footing on the slick surface.

"You ain't much for the outdoors, is you?" Earl Luke asked him when Mason found him sitting on a shallow ledge cut into the bluff.

"I'll show you my merit badges if you'll tell me what the hell we're doing down here," Mason told him.

Earl Luke leaned over, clearing a layer of wet brush around his feet, stamping his boot, the loud thwack of shoe leather smacking against wood. Mason squatted down, sweeping away the rest of the brush, running his hands over a weather-beaten square of wood, his fingers finding the hinges of a small door.

"What is it?" Mason asked.

"Cable cars used to run up and down this slope, all the way down to the River Market. That was before they cut the bluff down so they could build the streets south from the river. In those days, the bluff ran all the way down to Third Street."

Earl Luke stopped, staring into the night, remembering the past or forgetting the present, Mason couldn't tell. "Earl Luke," Mason said, "the door. Tell me about this door."

"Cable car company cut a shaft straight through the bluff to run the power lines for the cars. A short man couldn't hardly stand up in it, but it was great for a kid like me. Better than digging a hole to China. My old man used to tan my hide when he caught me playing in that shaft. This here door was like a manhole cover for a sewer so's you could get to this part of the shaft without going all the way down from the top. They was put in every fifty feet or so. Guess the city forgot about it when they tore up the tracks. Long time ago, it was."

Mason felt around the edges of the door, prying at the corners, searching for a handle. "Will it open?"

Earl Luke got down on his hands and knees, popping up one of the wooden slats, exposing a steel ring, grunting as he raised the wooden door. "Say the magic word."

They hovered over the black opening, the rain beating against their backs, Earl Luke lost again in his memories, Mason dreading another dark, claustrophobic passage. He'd crawled through enough tunnels and shafts to be a charter member of the Mole People, and every time the light at the end of the tunnel had turned out to be a train coming straight at him.

"Old times," Earl Luke said, as if making a toast, and dropped into the opening.

Mason took a deep breath and followed him, Earl Luke's street scent a better guide than any flashlight. Mason paused for a moment, using his hands to measure the shaft, finding he could scurry in a tight crouch, saving his knees from an uphill crawl, keeping one hand outstretched against low-hanging obstacles. The angle of the shaft was not as severe as the surface of the bluff, though Mason had to brace one hand against the side of the shaft to keep his balance. The air in the shaft was cool and fresh, encouraging Mason that there was a way out at the top. He slipped twice when Earl Luke disturbed rats that ran squealing past him.

The climb took only a few minutes, though it felt longer, the darkness distorting the passage of time, Earl Luke kicking out a wire mesh grate at the mouth of the shaft cut low on a wall, the two of them sliding out onto a smooth cement floor. Feeling his way along the wall, Mason found a light switch, his eyes happily adjusting to a wide room dominated by a round wooden platform in the center of the floor, a large gleaming black gear marking a bull's eye in the circle.

"Where are we?" Mason asked.

"Turnaround room," Earl Luke said. "The cars came in through there before they bricked it up," he added, pointing to a section of the wall against the bluff that was covered in brick, unlike the cement that formed the rest of the wall. "The big gearbox turned a giant wheel, like a wagon wheel turned on its side, and kept the cables moving. My daddy kept the gearbox greased and humming, checked them cars over, fixed 'em if they needed it, and sent 'em back out. I wonder why they kept all this old equipment down here."

"The Depot is registered as an historical landmark. The preservation people probably required it. We must be in the basement. Where's the parking garage from here?"

"Gotta be through that door over there," Earl Luke said, pointing to the far side of the room. "You go on. I'm gonna have me a look around here."

Mason stood at the door, listening and hearing nothing before he eased it open, stepping into the garage, seeing Arthur Hackett's Mercedes parked nose-first against one wall. A short, steep driveway led up to a garage door that opened onto Washington, the street bordering the east side of the Depot.

The remains of Gina's private elevator shaft were to his right, slabs of plywood nailed to what had been the elevator door. The elevator control room was next to it, its heavy steel door resembling a bank vault knocked off its hinges when the elevator crashed.

Mason turned on the light in the control room, looked at the switches that had been used as a deadly weapon. The switch labeled "Emergency Brake Release" still had traces of the powder the forensic cops had used in their search for fingerprints. A ten-inch black-and-white monitor was mounted on the wall above the control panel. Mason turned it on, watching the snow-filled screen for a moment, turning it off when he heard another door open and Carol Hackett scream.

CHAPTER 39

Mason turned the light off, stepping back in the shadows, keeping a thin view of Hackett's Mercedes. He resisted the impulse to race to Carol Hackett's rescue since, without a weapon, he was likely to die stupidly, though nobly, without saving her, an end he thought would make a poor epithet.

David Evans dragged Arthur Hackett across the garage floor to the Mercedes, a blood-splattered gun in one hand, the collar of Hackett's jacket tight in the grip of the other. Hackett, bleeding from a wound on the side of his head matching the blunt shape of the gun, raised an arm in semiconscious protest. Evans had hit Hackett hard enough to put him down but not kill him. Carol was screaming as Evans, indifferent, propped Hackett up against a rear tire.

Mason looked at his watch. It had been twelve minutes since he left Mickey, thirty since Blues had gone to Evans's house, sixty since he'd talked to Harry. By now, all three would be at the Depot, Mickey taking a brick to the front door, Blues and Harry holding Mickey back while they conducted a systematic search, Mickey telling them about the scene in Hackett's office, sending them to check that out first. Not knowing whether or how Mason could have gotten into the basement, they would leave that search for the last.

Evans opened the trunk to the Mercedes, stuffing the gun in his belt and shouldering Arthur, his back to Mason, giving Mason the opening he needed. Running hard, Mason bolted toward Evans, Carol screaming again, Evans whirling as he dumped Arthur in the trunk, reaching for his gun as Mason hit him in the gut, the impact folding Evans in half, Evans whipping his legs up, falling backward into the trunk on top of Hackett.

Evans's reflex kick caught Mason in the chin. Mason tumbled backward, skidding on the floor as Evans struggled to get out of the trunk, waving his gun. Mason got to his feet, launching himself at Evans as Evans fired, the bullet grazing Mason's shoulder, Mason slamming the trunk lid closed.

Mason felt the narrow trace of the bullet across his shoulder, more singed than shot. Carol Hackett was puddled on the floor, knees to her chest, whimpering.

Evans bellowed from inside the trunk. "Open it, Mason, or I'll kill Hackett!"

"Sorry," Mason said. "No key. I'll call a locksmith and we'll have you out of there in no time. Try not to talk. You'll conserve oxygen."

"Damn you, Mason! One more doesn't matter to me. Open the trunk!"

Mason said to Carol, "You choose. Do I let him out?"

She raised her head. "Why would you ask me a thing

like that? My husband is in there. He may be dead already."

"Then it should be an easy choice for you. I let Evans out and he kills me. What does he do with you, Carol?"

"I don't know what you mean," she said.

Mason took her by the arm, pulling her to her feet, a red welt rising beneath her right eye, the imprint of the slap he'd witnessed from outside the Depot. "Don't play me, Carol," Mason said.

Carol jerked her head back like she'd been struck again, breaking away from Mason, her back to him. "You don't know anything!"

Mason said. "I know a lot, but not all of it. I know that you and Arthur were living in St. Louis at the same time as the Davenports and David Evans. I know that Arthur was selling ads for a radio station and you were working for the city in the Vital Records department. I know Gina Davenport couldn't get pregnant and couldn't adopt because her husband was an addict."

Carol turned around, her mouth open. "We were young. We had a child. We needed the extra money," she said, giving the long-rehearsed answer to the question Mason had yet to ask.

"Nothing wrong with that," Mason said. "Selling advertising was tough, I'll bet, and the city couldn't have paid much. Is that why you did it? For the money?"

"Did what?" she asked, arms folded over her chest. "I didn't do anything."

"If you don't count forging Emily Davenport's birth certificate," Mason said, Carol going pale. "You wouldn't have done it on your own. Evans must have put you up to it. How did he get to you? Was it money or sex or both?"

"Please, Mr. Mason. My husband!" she said.

"Evans isn't going to kill your husband. If he does, he knows the cops will open the trunk before I do. Besides, crocodile tears aren't your strong suit. Arthur must have hit you pretty hard tonight," Mason added, taking a guess.

Carol covered her cheek with her hand. "How could you . . ."

"How could I know?" Mason asked. "What matters is that I do know, and I know that you went to see Evans last night. You're starting to look like an accomplice to the murders of Gina Davenport and your son."

"No!" Carol said. "It was Arthur!"

"Try again. If your husband were the killer, you and Evans would have turned him in so the two of you could have lived happily ever after. Instead, Evans cold-cocked Arthur until he could get rid of him someplace else. You probably screamed because he got blood on your clothes."

"He's my husband," she hissed.

"And Trent was your son and Jordan is your daughter," Mason said.

Carol deflated, staggering backward against a pillar supporting the ceiling, Mason's words hitting harder than her husband had. "I never wanted children," she said softly. "It's terrible to say, but I didn't want them. I thought I was done after Trent was born, but Arthur insisted we adopt Jordan."

"All you wanted was David Evans. How did you hook up with him?"

Carol nodded her head, shaking with the confession. "He was the lawyer that took care of Jordan's adoption."

"He take his fee in favors?" Mason asked.

"It wasn't like that," she answered.

"It never is."

Carol said, "He told me Abby Lieberman was the baby's mother, but she didn't want the baby, that the Davenports did but couldn't adopt because of some technicalities. He made it seem like the birth certificate was a small thing, that it was an easy way to get everyone what they wanted."

"Jumping your lawyer's bones while your husband was home with the kids seem like a small thing too?"

"It must be nice to always have such a finely tuned moral center, Mr. Mason. I wasn't so fortunate. I got over David and did my job as a wife and mother," she said, squaring her shoulders and straightening her clothes, ironing out her guilt with a sharp crease.

"Don't tempt me," Mason said. "You did your job so well that when Trent raped Jordan, you and your husband swept it under the psychiatric rug."

Carol squeezed a bitter glare from narrow eyes. "What would you do, Mr. Mason? You make it sound so simple. One child accuses, the other denies. It happens a dozen times a day with children, a hundred times a week, a thousand times a year. Which one would you pick? What would you do?"

"I would have had her examined by a doctor. I would have asked the hard questions. I would have tried to find out the truth. Did you do that?" he asked, Carol not answering, Mason boring in. "No, you called Jordan a liar and let her brother call her a slut until she went crazy. Then you called Gina Davenport."

"That was Arthur's idea."

"You couldn't tell Arthur he'd picked a therapist who committed a felony to get her own baby because he would find out what you had done. Is that why he hit you tonight? Did you finally tell him?"

"He knew about the birth certificate from the start, except I told him someone else in the office had done it and that I wasn't supposed to know about it. That's why he picked Gina. He was worried Jordan would tell her therapist about the rape and that the therapist would have to report it to the social services people. He said we could use the information about Gina's baby to keep her quiet, but we didn't have to because Jordan didn't tell Gina about Trent."

"Not until just before Gina was killed," Mason said. "By then, Arthur was using the information to pressure Gina on her contract. Did Arthur know about you and David?"

"Not until tonight," she answered, fingering the welt on her face.

"It must have made for interesting dinner conversation when Arthur hired Gina to do the radio show. What a small world it is, he must have told you. I hired Jordan's shrink. Her lawyer is David Evans. Remember him, honey? He's the lawyer that helped us with Jordan's adoption. After all those years, you still had a thing for Evans and you hooked up with him again."

Carol looked away, another silent admission. Mason said, "Things really got complicated when Arthur used the information about Emily to pressure Gina on her contract. Evans couldn't have liked that."

Carol shook her head. "No, he didn't. He told me to get Arthur to back off or he'd tell Arthur about us and about what I had done."

"Some boyfriend," Mason said. "Didn't you know he was screwing Paula Sutton too?"

"I'm not proud of myself," Carol said.

"That's a relief," Mason answered.

"We were afraid Jordan was guilty. Then she confessed and we thought it would be over soon. When Trent was killed, we couldn't imagine who else could have done it."

"Innocence can be inconvenient," Mason said.

"Arthur knew you suspected him and was afraid you would find out about the phone call to Abby Lieberman."

"And you were afraid I would find out about you," Mason said.

Carol said, "After we saw the news last night about Sanctuary and the police said it had nothing to do with Jordan, Arthur knew you would keep pushing until you found out what he'd done."

"So Arthur went to see Paula Sutton to make sure she stayed quiet."

Carol looked at the Mercedes, covering her hand with her heart as the car shook from the struggle inside the trunk. Mason ignored the muffled sounds, keeping the pressure on her. "Why did you go see Evans last night?"

"Gina accused David of stealing from her and from Sanctuary. She fired him and convinced Sanctuary to fire him too. David told me Gina had embezzled the money and he was going to sue Sanctuary if the board didn't reinstate him. Arthur was trying to work it out."

"You told Evans what Arthur had done so Evans could use that against Arthur, level the blackmail playing field," Mason said. "Did Evans tell you to set up the meeting tonight at the radio station so the two of them could make a deal?"

"Yes," Carol said, fresh tears icing her makeup. "The

studio is automated on Saturday night. The programming is all syndicated. No one else would be there."

"The negotiations must not have gone well."

"They started screaming at each other. David threatened Arthur and told him about us. Arthur hit me and accused David of killing Gina to cover up his theft. David had a gun. Then all of this happened," she said, waving her hand.

The Mercedes roared to life, its tires squealing and burning against the polished cement floor as Evans gunned the car into reverse aiming at them. Mason dove out of the car's path as it fishtailed, the rear bumper catapulting Carol against the wall, the Mercedes careening up the drive, the garage door slowly rising, the roof of the car clipping the bottom of the door as Evans swerved into the night.

Carol lay crumpled against the wall, her arms and legs askew like a rag doll, eyes open, lips barely moving, mouthing Mason's name. He leaned over, his ear to her mouth.

"Trent," she managed. "David blamed you. He said he would get even," she added, the soft puff of her last breath dying against Mason's cheek.

Earl Luke called to Mason. "Is it safe to come out now?"

"Not hardly," Mason said.

CHAPTER 40

Mason sat on the floor, his back against the wall, staring at the spot where Carol Hackett died, Blues, Harry, and Mickey standing in front of him, a protective wedge. Carol's mangled body was gone, but Mason could still see her lying there, another deadly image hung on permanent display in his mental gallery, her last words a blot against his soul. Evans had pushed down the backseat of the Mercedes, climbing over Arthur Hackett, slipping into the front seat. Mason hadn't killed Carol and couldn't have saved her, but that didn't end it. The books didn't balance.

David Evans had killed Gina to get even with her for exposing his theft, and tried to kill Mason to get even with him for Max Coyle's lawsuit, using the passkey Trent Hackett had given him to get into the elevator control room. Trent, Mason realized, must have figured that out and put the screws to Evans. Evans killed Trent, rationalizing that murder as another debt owed to Mason.

* * *

Soon after Samantha Greer and her forensic crew arrived, Mason called Abby, telling her what had happened, promising to come over as soon as Samantha let him go. Abby, her voice brittle and sad, said okay, Mason feeling her slipping away, the violence that surrounded him and stained her too much to absorb.

It was nearly one in the morning, cold air pouring down the basement drive from the open door forcing Mason to his feet, the flashing red glare from a squad car parked at the entrance washing the walls. Samantha, combing her hair with her fingers, her eyes hollow with fatigue, her jaw set, was running the show, listening to the latest reports from her people, saving him for the last.

"We missed him at the airport," she said to Mason.

"Evans?"

"No, the tooth fairy," she said. "He dumped the Mercedes at one of those private parking lots a couple of miles from the terminal. Security guard was monitoring the police band, heard the APB, and called it in."

"What about Arthur Hackett?" Mason asked.

"Dead," Samantha said. "Evans took a shuttle to Terminal A. A sales clerk ID'd him, said he bought a travel bag and some clothes."

Mason said, "He'd have a better chance of getting through airport security if he had luggage, but I'm still surprised he'd try. He'd be arrested the minute he got off the plane."

"He didn't try," Samantha said. "He took another shuttle to Terminal B and bought a ticket for Oakland, but he never got on the plane. Instead, he rented a car. It was a pretty sloppy effort to cover his trail, but it bought him some time. The rental car has one of those GPS systems, lets us track him by satellite. He just crossed into Iowa, probably heading for Canada. Highway patrol should have him in custody soon."

"What about Jordan?" Mason asked.

"Ortiz says she'll be ready to go by nine o'clock tomorrow morning. Check that," Samantha said, looking at her watch. "Make that nine o'clock this morning."

"Thanks," Mason said.

Samantha shook her head. "Don't thank me, Lou. Just do me a favor. Hang up your spurs. Let somebody else play cowboy. This isn't for you. You're not good enough or lucky enough to keep this up."

Mason breathed deeply, Samantha giving voice to his own fears. "I'm thinking about taking some time off," Mason said.

"Take it with your new. What's her name? Abby?" Mason nodded, knowing that Samantha knew her name. "Yeah, take it with her. Get him out of here," she said to Harry.

Time off with Abby. It was a simple antidote, Mason thought, driving to her loft, windows down, the chill air a brisk reminder he was alive. He'd dived into the dark water again, scraping the bottom before coming out on the other side, weary, not exhilarated. Samantha was right. He had been more lucky than good and luck was too thin a hedge against death, particularly when he had more to lose than ever before.

Mason had used the law not just to save Jordan and the other desperate clients who had come before her.

He had used it as an excuse to dive into the dark water, playing blindman's bluff with demons. He resolved to stay out of the water, unless it came with a beach, a cold drink in a tall glass with a floating umbrella, and Abby. It was time for time off.

He practiced the closing argument he would make for Abby, beginning with his love for her, of which he was certain. He would tell her that a couple of weeks on the beach wouldn't erase the memories of the last month, but it would give them time for a proper beginning. He would promise to change his law practice, give up criminal defense work—embrace the ambulance chase, he would add with a smirk she wouldn't be able to resist.

He hadn't called to say he was on the way, hoping she was asleep, not wanting to wake her. Now he wanted her awake, as wide-eyed with his vision of their future as was he. Taking the stairs two at a time, he raced to the fourth floor, fumbling with the key she had given him, calling her name.

"Abby! Start packing!" he boomed, swinging her door open. David Evans was waiting for him, twisting Abby's arm behind her back, a knife to her throat, the dark water swallowing him again.

Mason saw Evans, saw the knife, blocked them out, focusing only on Abby, his eyes promising her everything would be okay, hers not believing him, Evans slicing Abby's neck with the tip of the knife, drawing a trickle of blood, breaking Mason's silent promise.

"Paybacks are hell," Evans said.

"I'll kill you," Mason said.

"Sure you will," Evans answered. "She'll be just as dead. You'll have to live with that. I won't have to spend ten years on death row waiting to get the needle. We're even."

"All because of Max's lawsuit?" Mason asked.

"You don't get all the credit, Lou, but you did put me on the road to ruin. I could settle cheap with the other clients who complained. Especially since I was taking the money out of Emily's Fund and Sanctuary."

"I don't settle cheap," Mason said.

"You pushed too hard, cost too much money. Plus the bad publicity was a killer. The money to settle Max's case was too much to get past Gina. She caught me. I killed her. I didn't think I could do it, but I did."

"Trent figured you for the elevator since you had a passkey. Instead of telling the cops, he tried to cash in and you killed him." Mason knew he was right, and didn't care whether Evans confessed. He was buying time, blood running down Abby's neck like sand running out of an hourglass.

"That's one kid no one was going to miss. He was like you in a way. He just kept pushing until I couldn't take it anymore."

"You cut Centurion in on the skim from Sanctuary," Mason said. "That's why he agreed to kill me."

"With Trent gone, I needed someone else to take the blame. Centurion owed me."

"Carol with the car and Arthur with the gun. Back on your own."

"Necessity," Evans said.

"Why aren't you in Iowa?"

Evans laughed, pressing his knife against Abby's throat. "Why the hell would I be in Iowa? There's nobody there I have to kill." Mason didn't answer, but Evans caught on. "Oh, I get it! The rental car. I was counting on the GPS to keep the cops busy. I picked up a hitch-hiker near the airport. Gave him the car and he dropped me off at a hotel and I caught their courtesy shuttle downtown."

Abby's phone rang, all three of them jumping at the noise, Mason glad to see that Evans wasn't as cool as he pretended. The phone was on a small table ten feet from Mason, three from Evans and Abby.

"If she doesn't answer, whoever is calling will get suspicious."

"I don't care if they get religious," Evans said. "She doesn't answer the phone."

Mason couldn't remember how many times Abby's phone would ring before the answering machine picked up the call. "You're having too much fun now," Mason told him. "You can't screw it up by not letting her answer. You don't want to die. You want to get away so you can gloat over my dead body."

Evans licked his lips, his eyes flashing from the phone to Mason. "Okay. There's a speaker button. Use that," he told Mason, then to Abby, "Play it cool or you die after hello."

Mason crossed to the phone, punching the speaker button, Abby answering, her voice dry. "Yes," she said, Mason loving her more for her greeting. Abby always answered by saying "It's Abby," even when he'd called her earlier that evening. She was sending a message that something was different, a little thing that could make a difference if the caller knew her well enough.

"Miss Lieberman? It's Detective Samantha Greer. I'm sorry to bother you so late and I hope I'm not being presumptuous, but I'm looking for Lou Mason. Is he there?"

Evans shook his head, Abby answering, "No, Detective. He left a while ago. I'm afraid we had a fight."

"I'm sorry to hear that," Samantha said. "And I'm sorry I bothered you."

"You should be," Abby said, summoning a low-grade outrage, continuing before Evans could cut her off. "We fought about you. He said he was still in love with you and I threw him out. I thought he'd be with you by now."

Samantha didn't answer at first, Evans edging toward the phone, pushing Abby in front of him. Samantha finally went on. "Then I'm doubly sorry. I didn't mean for that to happen. I'll leave you alone now."

Evans kept his knife on Abby, reaching around her to disconnect the call. Mason took his chance, pivoting inside on Evans, grabbing Evans's knife hand, jamming his shoulder into Evans's chin, taking both of them to the floor, knocking Abby free. Mason rolled, Evans plunging the knife, catching Mason's bicep, then his chest, Mason grunting, scrambling away. Then Evans was on him, Mason blocking the knife with his forearm, blood spurting from his wounds.

Abby screamed, leaping onto Evans's back, hanging on, clawing Evans's eyes. Evans bucking Abby off him, Abby hitting her head on a brick pillar, her body limp. Evans raised his knife over her, Mason crawling toward Abby, slipping in his blood, his reach too short, Evans kicking him, the blow unfelt, the bellow of a gun spinning Evans around, the bullet taking him down.

Mason looked up, his vision clouded. Samantha was standing over him, Blues checking Evans's body, Harry picking up Abby.

"No pulse," Blues said.

"She's good," Harry said.

"He's a mess," Samantha said, Mason smiling as he passed out.

CHAPTER 41

Mason kicked his legs, extending his arms in long strokes, pulling the water past him, kicking again, bubbles erupting from his nose and mouth as the surface beckoned, a gleaming light fracturing the water, voices breaking through his anesthesia-induced dream.

"He's coming out of it," Claire said.

Mason blinked, opening his eyes, the room shifting, his mouth a desert, his limbs deadweights, sensation returning in slow motion. His arm itched, an IV drip taped over his wrist, his chest tingling from electrodes tracking his heartbeat. Turning his head, seeing the equipment surrounding his bed, he broke out into a loopy grin.

"Not dead," Mason said, his tongue getting in the way.

"Not yet," Claire said, sitting on the edge of the bed, her hands cupping his, Blues, Harry, and Mickey hovering behind her.

"Abby," Mason said.

"She's fine. Rest easy. We'll be back," Claire told him. Mason was too weak to argue, drifting again, Samantha watching him from the foot of his bed the next time he woke, ignorant of the day or passage of time.

"I'm tired of watching you wake up in the hospital," Samantha said, "but you look great."

"You're a lousy liar," he told her.

"You can't stand the truth," she said.

"Thank you, Jack Nicholson. What happened at Abby's?"

Samantha breathed deeply, the memory still raw. "Iowa Highway Patrol stopped the car Evans had rented, only Evans wasn't driving."

"Hitchhiker," Mason said.

"That's right. Based on what Carol Hackett told you, we figured Evans was still in town looking for you and we assumed you were at Abby's."

"You got there pretty quick."

"Blues and Harry figured it the same way and were out the door as soon as I got word from Iowa. I had to catch up to them. We didn't want to barge in without knowing what was going on, so I called Abby from the first floor of her building. She told me what I needed to know."

Mason laughed, his chest begging him to stop. "You didn't mind being the other woman?"

"At least I'm in the equation, even if it's on the wrong side," she said.

"Was it you?" Mason asked her.

"Yeah," Samantha said softly. "It was me. Ortiz called it a justifiable shooting all the way. I'm back on duty to-morrow."

"Your first time?"

"Yeah," she said again. "First time. Can't say that anymore."

"I'm sorry, but thanks," Mason told her, Samantha waving him off.

"Lou," she said.

"I know," he interrupted. "Time off."

After Samantha left, Mason found the controls for his hospital bed, raised himself up far enough to see the television, turning it on with the remote control just to find out what day it was. CNN convinced him that it was Monday morning. He'd been in the hospital since early Sunday morning, with no memory of the surgery to repair the damage Evans had inflicted.

He'd seen doctors, nurses, orderlies, friends, and relatives, but not Abby. He'd been poked, prodded, and palpated, but had not felt Abby's touch. The only information he had about her was Claire's promise that she was fine, and he wasn't certain whether he'd heard that in one of his dreams.

Mason reached for the call button, hoping the nurse would know or find out what had happened to her, his gut twisting as he speculated why she hadn't been to see him and why no one had told him more about her condition. The moment he pushed the button, the door to his room swung open, a nurse pushing Abby in a wheelchair, her dark hair pulled back from her bandaged neck, her skin as gray as her hospital gown, the nurse parking her next to his bed, leaving them alone.

Abby took his hand, Mason covering hers with both of his. "Hey," she said.

"Hey yourself," Mason answered, neither one letting go, Mason biting back tears, Abby's leaping off her cheeks.

"I don't remember the last time I made a turkey," Claire said, as she sat down at the new dining room table Mason had bought in time for Thanksgiving.

"I was sixteen," Mason said. "I brought a girl home for dinner you didn't like and you roasted the turkey until it tasted like leather. My girlfriend thought you were sending her a message and dumped me."

"This turkey tastes great," Abby said, passing the large serving plate to Jordan Hackett.

Abby never told Jordan that she had thought she might be her mother, deciding that Jordan needed a friend, not someone else with an uncertain title. She helped Jordan find a new doctor, and Jordan was going back to school, working part-time for Abby, putting her life together a day at a time before she tried to find her baby.

Mason delivered his closing argument to Abby as they walked around Loose Park two weeks after they were released from the hospital, the last apple and gold leaves clinging to the trees, the sun battling the first hard frost to a draw. He told her about the dark water, promising he wouldn't go back, telling her he couldn't take the chance of losing her.

"Don't make a promise you can't keep. It's who you are," she told him. "You can't be anyone else."

"I can be anyone I have to be for you," he answered.

"No you can't," Abby said, "because I can only love the one you are."

Their wounds healed faster than their souls, Abby

trading her loft for an apartment, grieving privately for a child she never knew, Mason not pushing her, understanding the nightmares that shattered her sleep. Work provided an anchor, normal gradually feeling normal again, Mason turning down criminal cases, Mickey starting a pool betting on when he'd relent, Blues winning the pool a week before Thanksgiving, Mason telling Abby, Abby nodding.

"Be careful. Make the case about the client, not about you," she said, Mason trying to figure out how.

Mason bought the dining room table and the living room furniture after Abby explained that she could never be with a man that used his dining room as a dock for a rowing machine and his living room as a kennel for his dog. Mason moved the rowing machine to the basement and Tuffy's pillow to the master bedroom.

Mason looked around his new table, covered with a Thanksgiving spread. Mickey spun trash to the amusement of Rachel Firestone and her partner, Mickey's girlfriend sticking her finger in her mouth, pretending to be sick. Claire read Harry an article Rachel had written, Harry struggling with the small print, listening close, learning to accept Claire's eyes as his own. Blues came without a date, saying this was family time, talking jazz with Jordan. Tuffy roamed the room in table-scrap heaven. Mason's picture of his great grandparents hung on the wall, Mason sure they were smiling.

Each conversation rose from the table, punctuated by laughter and the clink and clang of crystal, china, and silver, verbal notes mixing, a beautiful noise. Mason reached for Abby's hand. She covered his with hers.

For a sneak preview of *Deadlocked,*
Joel Goldman's next
Lou Mason thriller,
coming next year from Pinnacle Books,
just turn the page. . . .

Ryan Kowalczyk knew something few people ever knew: the exact time he would die. He had spent the last fifteen years watching each month melt away until only one month, July, remained. He lingered through July, indifferent to the merciless heat that claimed a dozen lives across Missouri, waking early on Sunday, July 14th, his last day. His gut twisted, the hard floor cool to his bare feet as he sat on the side of his bed, head in his hands, wondering for the millionth time how it would feel when the drugs hit his veins at midnight.

Two kinds of people knew what he knew: suicides and death row inmates. He couldn't kill himself. Not because he clung to the fantasy that some court more supreme than the one that had condemned him would grant him a new trial, though his mother promised him that each time she visited. Not because the governor might commute his sentence, the last chance his lawyer was still pursuing in the last hours of his life. And not because he lacked the courage. He had thought of plenty of ways to kill himself, beating the guards who were sworn to keep him alive until the prison's execution team could poison him.

Ryan Kowalczyk wouldn't kill himself because he was innocent. That's what he told the police when they came for him. That's what he told his mother when she clung to his bony shoulders, the jury's verdict a knife in both their hearts. That's what he told Father Steve, the priest who sat with him now in the death-watch cell, counting down the final sixty minutes of Ryan's life.

"Ryan," the priest said. "Don't waste these last precious moments, boy. Confess your sins and go to God with grace."

Ryan ignored the priest, as he ignored his last meal, a thick steak swimming in bloody juice. What's the point? Ryan thought, rising from his bed, pressing his face against the small window cut in the door of his cell, the glass cool against his lips, a guard sitting on the other side, staring back at him. The guard checked his watch, impatiently tapping the crystal face with his finger. Ryan was already dead, numb to fear or regret, consumed by one question. How will it feel?

"What's it like?" Ryan asked Father Steve, not turning around, his breath fogging the glass.

"Heaven?" the priest asked, placing his hand on the condemned man's shoulder. "It's God's glorious kingdom, but it's reserved for those who accept God and come to Him with a clean heart. That's why you have to confess, Ryan. Before it's too late."

"Not heaven, Father. Dying. I don't believe in heaven

or God or any of that bullshit. If all that were true, I wouldn't be here and you and me know that."

Ryan pivoted, facing the priest, his face inches from Father Steve, Ryan tasting the sour scent of stale tobacco soaked into the priest's black clothes. Father Steve's lips twitched; he needed a smoke. Ryan was lanky and a head taller than Father Steve, who was thick, his fat neck stuffed inside his collar, a trickle of sweat staining the white.

The death-watch cell was close, crammed with a cot, toilet, basin and chair all made of steel. The floor was tile, the ceiling cast in concrete. Weak fluorescent light bathed the priest's face with a pale purple hue, reminding Ryan of faded vestments.

Ryan held the priest's eyes, catching a flicker of doubt that confirmed Ryan's certain disbelief in the deity.

"Your mother believes in heaven and a merciful God," the priest said, covering his own lapse. "She wants that for you."

Father Steve had known Ryan's family since Ryan was a small boy. His mother, Mary, was a regular at Mass. Ryan's earliest memories of the church were the sweet fragrance of incense and Father Steve patting his head as Ryan clutched his mother's hand, a small boy in a strange place.

Growing up, Ryan never gave much thought to heaven or hell, putting more faith in his ability to hit a three-point shot from the top of the key with time running out, the memory of his last game-winner still sharp. The ball spinning perfectly, dropping through the net as the gun sounded, his best friend Whitney King and the rest of his high school teammates mobbing him. He was seventeen then. That was fifteen years ago. The last good thing he ever did.

"She wants it for her," Ryan said. "I'll be dead and buried."

"Then why not give it to her, boy?" the priest asked. "Is it such a hard thing for you to leave to your mother?"

Ryan looked at the priest, then through the narrow window to the long hall outside the death-watch cell. Two guards rounded the corner pushing a gurney toward him. Wrist and ankle restraints hung off the sides, leather slapping against metal, rough wheels clacking. The time-keeping guard stood and removed a pair of clear IV tubes from a cabinet marked Medical Supplies. Silver needles gleamed like mini-bayonets.

"No, I guess not, Father."

"Kneel with me then, boy."

Father Steve placed his hands on Ryan's shoulders. Ryan bowed his head, dredged his rote confession from childhood memory, admitted to sins against God and man, and begged forgiveness. His prayer was generic, silent about murder.

Ryan stumbled at first, his heart racing ahead, slamming against his chest, his words catching up, becoming a torrent as the door to the death-watch cell swung open. The guards cleared their throats. Harsh white light from the hall washed into the crowded space, sharpened by a rush of cool air. The priest lowered his head and raised one hand against the advancing guards holding them back. One guard scraped mud from the sole of his shoe against the frame of the gurney. Another softly thumped the IV lines against the mattress.

Father Steve rose first, drawing Ryan to his feet. Ryan blinked, not against the light, but against the involuntary steps he took as he was passed from the hands of his priest to the hands of his executioners. He looked at Father Steve over his shoulder with wild eyes, his throat tight, last words frozen in his heart.

"It's time," one of the guards told him.

"Go with God, boy," the priest said.

"How much longer?" Harry Ryman asked Lou Mason, drumming his fingers on the center console dividing the front seat of his Chevy Suburban.

It was Harry's car, but he was sitting on the passenger side, letting Mason drive, Harry's concession to his fading eyesight. A retired Kansas City homicide detective, Harry was used to running his own show, not being chauffeured. Harry had loved Mason's Aunt Claire for the better part of Mason's life, the two of them filling in for Mason's parents who had been killed in a car accident when Mason was three. His long relationship with Mason was the only thing that made Harry's transition from driver to passenger a little easier.

"Fifteen minutes less than the last time you asked me," Mason told him. "Relax, Harry. It's just after ten o'clock. We'll be there in plenty of time to see Kowalczyk executed."

"I don't want to be late, that's all," Harry said, shifting his weight from side to side. Harry liked the Suburban because it fit his bulky frame, unlike a sedan that made him feel like he'd been shoehorned into the middle seat on a discount airline. "This damn thing with my eyes drives me crazy."

Harry shook his head, squinting against the night, trying to capture the stars. He sighed quietly with the knowledge that they now eluded him, taking little solace in the moon, which had become a smudge against the sky. They had turned off I-70 a while ago, speeding down a succession of two-lane state highways lit only by the headlights of an occasional pickup going in the opposite direction. Harry felt more than saw the undulating, curving road, wondering if it was true that the loss of one sense heightened the others.

Patrick Ortiz, the prosecuting attorney, had invited Harry and his former partner, Wilson Bluestone, Jr., to witness the execution since they were the arresting officers in Graham and Elizabeth Byrnes's murders for which Kowalczyk was to be put to death.

Bluestone, whose friends called him Blues, was another ex-homicide cop. Only Blues hadn't retired. He played jazz piano at Blues on Broadway, a bar he owned in midtown Kansas City. It was a long, strange trip for a full-blooded member of the Shawnee Indian tribe that included dispensing rough justice for Mason's clients and attitude adjustments for those who stood in the way.

Blues declined Ortiz's invitation, telling Ortiz he didn't believe in the death penalty because he didn't trust the system to always get it right. Some rule, Ortiz had said, telling Blues he should apply it to himself, Blues answering that he trusted himself just fine.

The system got it right this time, Harry thought, the big Chevy swinging wide on a curve, Mason overcorrecting, making the chassis shimmy. Ryan Kowalczyk was a stone-cold killer, beating that couple to death with a tire iron like he was taking batting practice. It was a goddamn miracle he didn't know their baby was in the backseat of the car or there would have been three bodies. Nobody ever deserved the death penalty more than that kid.

Trouble was, Harry conceded, the system got it wrong about Whitney King, Kowalczyk's buddy and co-defendant. Harry rubbed his temples with his finger-tips and ran his knuckles across his eyes, trying to clear his memory and his vision.

Graham Byrnes had been twenty-seven years old, his wife, Elizabeth, only twenty-five. Harry silently recited their names as he'd written them in his report of their murders fifteen years ago. Their baby, Nick, had been three and couldn't fall asleep. They had taken him for a drive because that always helped quiet him down. Worked too. The kid was sleeping in the backseat under a quilt. Slept through the whole thing. Imagine that. Harry couldn't.

It was near midnight. They were in a new subdivision. Roads were in but no houses or streetlights. The Byrneses had just bought a lot to build their first home. Nick had given them an excuse to go take a look. Kowalcyzk and King were out in Kowalcyzk's car. Saw the Byrneses. Tried to rob them. Graham Byrnes fought back. Kowalcyzk and King killed them.

Harry tried focusing on the snaking road, headlights reflecting off the highway sign, cursing under his breath when he couldn't read the sign. June bugs splattered against the windshield like airborne lemmings.

"How far?" Harry asked Mason.

"Sign said ten miles to Potosi. The prison is just out-side town."

Harry grunted, holding his watch to within an inch of his eye to check the time again, remembering how he and Blues had caught the killers. Usual brilliant police work, Harry had explained to his lieutenant. The killers were stupid, and they caught a break with a witness who saw the suspects sideswipe a street lamp about a mile away, the lamp shining right on the license tag, the witness writing it down. They traced the car and found the bloody clothes belonging to both boys in Kowalcyzk's basement.

The boys told the same story, down to the punctuation. They played basketball on the same team and had won a big game that night. Partied afterward and were out driving around. Said they took a wrong turn, ended up lost in the subdivision. Saw the Byrneses and stopped to ask them for directions. Said the Byrnes was having car trouble, each kid saying he went looking for an all-night service station, couldn't find one, came back and found the Byrneses murdered. Claimed the kid that did the killing made the other one help hide the bodies. That's how they both ended up with blood on their clothes. Harry could still see Blues shaking his head when they walked out of the courtroom, King acquitted, Kowalcyzk convicted.

Harry cracked his window, the hot night air too humid to cool even at highway speed. Mason slowed down turned onto a county road, following the signs to the state penitentiary, easing the big Chevy into a visitor parking spot. A handful of cars were in the lot, only couple of them from the press. Executions had become too common to make it off the back page.

Mason cut the ignition, pocketing the keys. "An chance the jury got it wrong? That Ryan Kowalczyk is innocent?"

"Not a chance," Harry said.

More Nail-Biting Suspense From Your Favorite Thriller Authors